THE COCAINE SALESMAN

THE COCAINE SALESMAN

CONNY BRAAM

translated by Jonathan Reeder

This edition has been generously supported by the Foundation for the Production and Translation of Dutch Literature

© Conny Braam 2009, first published in The Netherlands by Uitgeverij Nieuw Amsterdam, The Netherlands. Original title: *De Handersreiziger van de Nederlandsche Cocaïne Fabriek*

Copyright of the English translation © Jonathan Reeder 2011

First published in Great Britain in 2011 by
Haus Publishing
70 Cadogan Place, London SW1X 9AH
www.hauspublishing.com

The moral right of the author has been asserted

A CIP catalogue for this book is available from the British Library

ISBN 978-1-907822-05-6

Designed and typeset in Garamond by MacGuru Ltd
info@macguru.org.uk

Printed and bound by CPI Group (UK) Ltd, Croydon, CR0 4YY

1

The morning of Dad's birthday

Early on the morning of Tuesday 31st July 1917 – it must have been about a quarter to four – Robin clipped his bayonet onto his rifle. As he did so, the thought struck him that, all along the front line dozens, hundreds, maybe thousands of other soldiers were doing exactly the same thing. And as he braced his booted foot against the muddy face of the trench, he guessed they'd be doing just that, too. There could well be ten thousand or a hundred thousand of them, or maybe even more, along the entire front … Only the commanders knew precisely how many. And they were all waiting for the signal. The officer had his whistle clamped between his teeth, his gaze fixed on his wristwatch. All the officers of the nine divisions of the British Fifth Army, whistle in mouth, stared at their synchronized watches. Ladders were propped up, ready, in the network of trenches that ran for miles on end.

His first battle. His war would begin today, and he, Robin Ryder, twenty-six years old, a schoolteacher from Great Yarmouth, would give it his all.

The British artillery had pounded away for more than a fortnight, raining millions of shells down on the German position called the *Wilhelmstellung*, almost four miles away, until it was

| 1 |

completely destroyed. Wiped right off the face of the earth! At least, that's what the officers had told them. Day and night, the relentless bombardment had strained Robin's nerves to breaking point. He saw it as his final test. The ultimate trial of endurance, which he had passed with flying colours. So much so that now, after a couple of hours of dead calm, he longed for a renewed outburst of gunfire. Today, the huge offensive that had been going on for weeks would achieve a decisive break-through. Today of all days. Wasn't it a marvellous coincidence? The 31st of July, Dad's birthday. Fifty-three today. Mum would surely have baked a cake. Or were apples too hard to come by nowadays? Robin tightened his grip on his rifle and tried to steal a glance at his wristwatch, a gift from his parents the day before he shipped out with the BEF. The face was spattered by the driving rain. But he knew anyway. It could happen at any minute. At home they were still sleeping. Who'd be at the birthday party later on? One thing was certain, Dad would keep on reminding the guests of his brave son, who was in Flanders defending his homeland: 'Go on, go on, have another one, my boy's out there fighting for your freedom!' Of course, he wouldn't forget to refill his own glass at the same time. Robin smiled. Cheers, Dad, cheers! Many happy returns! Your son won't let you down, not today…

The shrill blast of the whistle came as a surprise all the same, as though he hadn't been anticipating this moment for weeks, and it penetrated all the way to his bones. Oh my God, it was really happening, finally, finally… His comrades were already clambering over the parapet. Caught up in the surge of eager soldiers, he jostled his way towards the ladder, grasped its wooden rungs and in three strides was over the top, up on level ground. After all that time in the cramped trench, the vast, open terrain had a liberating effect. As far as the eye could see, soldiers were emerging, one after the other, out of the ground and forming long lines. Each line created a human shield for the next, as wave after wave of troops surged out of the trenches. How many lines were there? Only the generals knew for sure. As the offensive gathered momentum, the British Fifth Army rolled forward like a well-oiled machine. And he was part of it.

The long lines advanced at a snail's pace, those were the orders. A few yards forward, then flat out on the ground, and on the officer's signal back up on their feet again, pushing ever further on. Even with the German positions shattered, there might still be a few desperate snipers around. Otherwise, it was child's play. That afternoon, the officers had promised, they'd be drinking tea amid the ruins of the *Wilhelmstellung*.

The first red glow appeared on the horizon, and in front of him Robin saw the churned-up mud illuminated in a soft pink. It had rained non-stop for three days and the ground was sodden. With no sniper fire in evidence, they no longer had to keep dropping into the mud, but now moved cautiously, hunched over, across the harsh landscape. Now and then falling flares lit up the immense no-man's-land, covered in craters filled to the rim. Then they were enveloped once again in semi-darkness. What time was it? How long had they been on the move? He looked down the row. Two men further on was James Foyler. James was also from Great Yarmouth. A baker, and father of four children. His eldest son was in his class, quite a good pupil. Decent fellow, Foyler. He'd keep an eye on him.

Suddenly a violent torrent broke loose. In a shrieking wave of sound, countless projectiles flew over them, followed by a deluge of airbursts. Robin stared up, his mouth agape. The sky exploded above his head. Where had this sudden barrage come from? From behind? Was it friendly fire? Field guns thundered on all sides. It took his breath away, his knees seemed to give way underneath him. Someone yelled, 'Hold the line!' followed by a massive explosion some way off. The ground quaked beneath his feet. Alongside him, soldiers ducked low. Nearby, a sergeant screamed furiously, but his orders were lost in the deafening noise. Forward! Forward! he gestured. Robin felt his legs start to move. Of course, forward. Don't stand still. Never stand still. Don't stop for anything, it saps your stamina. The rattle of machine guns came rushing at him. It was coming from the German camp... Impossible, it couldn't be, the *Wilhelmstellung* had been completely destroyed, there was nothing to fear, nothing but the desperate fire of a few lone snipers. Forward, don't stand still, don't stop for anything. His boots got sucked into the mud. He tugged his left boot loose, then the right. Not far from him a grenade exploded. The ground quivered like thick soup and the shock throbbed through his body. His skull felt like it would be crushed by the unbearable pressure. He reeled, regained his footing and felt the bitter taste of cordite on his tongue. Through the rain he could just make out, some twenty yards further on, a couple of men slumped over. They lay there motionless in strange contortions. Before he could pull his mud-caked boots from the sludge to help them, there was a demonic screech. Another hit. The ground creaked and shuddered... Where was the line? Where was his division? Where were the officers, the sergeants? A few shadows appeared and then vanished back into the mist. Searching for cover, they reappeared only to melt away once more. Where was he, should he go to the left or to the right?

How far had they advanced, how many more miles did they have to go? Where was Foyler?

Bullets whizzed past his head, hot splinters of steel grazed his temples. Off to his right, two soldiers clutched at one another. Weren't these the inseparable brothers from his trench? No, no, he would have recognized them at once, he'd never seen these men before, although… everyone looked alike now. In an intense embrace, the two sank in deathly slow motion into the fresh mire of a shell-hole. He cut across towards them. He had to try to save them. But just then the earth opened up, as a shell landed right in the shell-hole he was making for. The shockwave threw him backwards and in a swirling spiral of smoke he saw an arm fly by. He wondered whose arm it might be. He had to keep moving, don't stop, never stop… Why was it raining so hard? The raindrops clattered deafeningly on his helmet. He slogged on, constantly having to brace one leg in order to drag the other one free of the mud… Keep going, he had to keep going… Where had his rifle got to? Had it been wrenched out of his hand? He'd forgotten it entirely. He had to find his weapon. A soldier without a weapon is useless, his only function is to take aim and pull the trigger. He turned, staggered back, fell to his knees and groped around in the claggy crater. His arm was buried up to the elbow when his fingers suddenly touched something hard. Thank God, his rifle. But the mud wasn't about to give up its prize that easily. Making one final superhuman effort, he managed to pull out his arm without losing his grip on the rifle. He could see his wrist, with the wristwatch from his parents, and with one last tug he freed his hand. But what his fingers held was not a rifle, it looked more like piece of a human ribcage. There was a shred of uniform attached to it: grey, *Feldgrau*. A German uniform?… He carefully unclenched his fingers. Gasping for breath, he reeled backwards away from the crater, stood up and stumbled on. Away, get away from here. He had to find the others, report to the sergeant that he had found a dead German and had lost his rifle. But there was nothing but thick mist, rain and a constant stream of deadly shrapnel. Could he be the only one still here?

All of a sudden, a group of soldiers appeared out of nowhere, nearly knocking him over. Their bloodshot eyes stared straight through him. He wanted to tell them about his rifle and the German corpse, but then he thought he'd better latch onto these men, then at least he'd no longer be alone. Dazed, the group staggered every which way, swung to the left, then made a U-turn, searching through the smoke for the right direction, but there was no right direction anymore, only wrong ones, and soon enough the roving band broke up. Robin did not know who to follow and screamed, with his mouth wide-open, but no sound came out. He had to warn them, they were surrounded, most of them were heading straight into the line of fire. He tried to catch up with a pair of soldiers, but hesitated when he saw a roll of barbed wire in front of him, blown to smithereens but still impassable. Bodies hung in it; some still twitching. That one there, with the brown hair, wasn't that James Foyler? It was! James was just hanging there, left to his fate. Robin's lower lip trembled and a wave of compassion and warmth swept over him. He called out to Foyler and kept on calling… James had to know that help was on its way. Another grenade exploded nearby. It no longer bothered him, he crawled towards the barbed wire. Where had James gone? He stood up, his legs trembling, and peered about exhaustedly.

A searing blow struck Robin's arm. He spun around and

sank to his knees. The rain continued to clatter against his helmet. His head slumped slowly forward. Strangely, the cool mud felt really pleasant against his cheek, all he wanted was to crawl deep into it and sleep, he was tired, so tired… Robin smiled. The birthday guests sat around the table in the front room. Mum served everyone a slice of apple pie on a plate with a little fork. He could hear his uncle's voice. But he was out on the street, of course, playing football with his father. They'd put their jackets down as goalposts. Dad dribbled back and forth in front of him, the ball dancing on his feet, arms outstretched. He laughed loudly, let him score a goal, lifted him up in the air and swung him round and round…

2

A superior and dependable product

It had been raining for days, and the Houtplein was covered in puddles when an automobile came careening around the corner. From behind the window of the Café-restaurant Brinkman, Lucien Hirschland recognized the car at once. He craned his neck to get a better look. You didn't often see such a beauty in Haarlem: a Mercedes 37 Tourer with a radiator grille angled like the bow of a ship, chrome-plated headlamps, detached mudguards and, of course, a powerful engine with a four-speed gearbox. A sporty automobile, and a pricey one too: it must have cost someone a pretty penny. The tires squealed over the wet paving stones. The driver wouldn't be able to see much in the pouring rain. And sure enough... He just managed to swerve clear of a milk float, but was too late to avoid a cyclist who, appearing out of nowhere, hit the front of the car with a resounding smack. The Mercedes skidded and dragged the bike with it, pinned between the front wheels. Lucien leapt out of his chair. The cyclist lay in a filthy puddle against the kerb in front of the vacant terrace. He wasn't moving.

A few concerned passers-by stooped over the victim. The Mercedes had come to a stop a metre or two further on and the door was flung open. Lucien would have liked to catch a glimpse of the luxurious interior, with its leather upholstery and fine wooden steering wheel. The driver strode round to the front of the car and tugged irately at the bicycle, but it didn't budge. A young woman crouched alongside the injured man, supporting his head with her hand. Two other women and a fellow in work clothes were talking excitedly and gesticulating at the Mercedes. By now the driver had put on his mackintosh, pulled his hat down over his forehead, and marched over to them with hunched shoulders. He shouted something in a loud, authoritative voice. Even from inside, Lucien could make out what he was saying. The man was furious. Damn it all! That idiot is a menace! His new automobile was damaged, it was going to cost him a packet! He's going to pay for this! The women – working-class Haarlem fishwives, judging from their appearance – joined the labourer in forming a protective wall around the victim. The stoutest of them stood with her fists on her hips. 'Not a chance! Dirty scoundrel!' she screeched, 'just look at that poor wretch!' She gestured dramatically at the cyclist, who still lay motionless on the pavement. 'You and your fancy bloody motorcar! Who's to pay for the ruined bicycle?! And his torn trousers! And the hospital!' She took a few steps forward with the posture of a boxer, as though she might attack him at any moment. The labourer had to restrain her, while bawling children clung to her legs. 'Don't fight, mother!' cried a small girl.

The driver shrugged his shoulders and made a move to turn back to the Mercedes, whose door still stood wide open. He clearly yearned to return to the safety of his automobile. But the woman wasn't done with him yet. 'He might die, mightn't he!' she yelled, 'and then you'll be paying for the funeral as well!' The man hesitated. Rain streamed off the brim of his hat. 'Call the police!' shouted a boy, adding to the general consternation. 'Yeah, let's get the police!' the others chimed in. Lucien leant further over the table. He'd wager the man wasn't keen on getting the police involved. And indeed, the driver had already reached into his inside pocket, pulled out a wad of bills, counted out a few and pressed them into the woman's outstretched hand. She'd clearly appointed herself to look after the matter of damages. The man strode angrily back to his car and climbed in. In the meantime the labourer had, without much difficulty, wrenched the bicycle free. As far as Lucien could see, only the glass of the car's headlamp was damaged. The driver fired up the engine and the Mercedes bolted off across the square.

By now, the cyclist was back on his feet, and trying to brush the mud and muck of the street from his trousers. The boy who'd wanted to call the police handed him his cap, and the group formed a little circle. Lucien's guess was that the takings were being counted and divvied up. He smiled to himself: that war profiteer in the car had been well and truly fleeced.

He glanced at his watch. Brian Kirkpatrick had been upstairs in his hotel room for more than half an hour. He'd be having a good wash, no doubt. Not that the poor fellow need have any illusions – you don't get rid of that kind of stench so easily, it seeps all the way into your clothes. An unpleasant task awaited the family's maid back home in London.

That morning he had watched Kirkpatrick, ashen and shaky, disembark from a British steam trawler, dishevelled and stinking of fish. Judging from the bags under his eyes he hadn't slept a wink. A humiliating entrance for a gentleman like Kirkpatrick, who prided himself on his dapper appearance. They shook hands without exchanging a word. Lucien, ignoring his guest's appalling condition, ushered him into the company car with his usual courtesy and immediately set off from the bleak wharf towards Haarlem.

Hoping to set a positive tone and forestall any complaints about the journey, he mentioned the improving weather forecast – it was, after all, the first day of August, the height of summer, and it couldn't go on raining forever. He predicted a sunny afternoon. But the crossing was still too fresh in Kirkpatrick's memory to be banished with idle chit-chat. 'It was damned unpleasant,' he began, less formal than usual. 'Good God, through a war zone in total darkness and rough seas... At full steam ahead so as not to alarm the German submarines! As though the roar of such a powerful engine doesn't resonate far below the surface. I wasn't born yesterday, you know!' he scoffed. 'At first I set myself up in the cargo hold with the fish. I felt relatively safe there, until the captain ordered all the passengers on deck. And to really put us all at ease they passed out lifejackets. In case of emergency we were to jump overboard. I'm sure he thought long and hard about that one: in case of emergency, simply hurl yourself in the direction of an enemy submarine... And tomorrow evening I've got to go back. Looking forward to it immensely, as you can imagine.' He had to catch his breath after this outburst.

'Put it out of your head for now,' advised Lucien, 'and in a week you'll look back on it as an adventure, an exhilarating anecdote to share with your friends at the next cocktail party.' He gave him a sideways glance. Kirkpatrick stared sullenly out of the window. This wasn't at all the type of man to boast to his friends about a perilous sea journey. Quite the opposite, in fact. The Englishman was modest and diffident, devoid of any ostentation whatsoever. Lucien noticed it from their first encounter, almost three years earlier. He'd felt somewhat intimidated by a visit from Kirkpatrick, buyer for the influential pharmaceutical firm Burroughs Wellcome & Co. in London. At first the lanky Englishman, whom he guessed was around forty, met all his preconceptions to a 'T'. His entire being radiated British correctness and decorum, whether it was his perfectly trimmed moustache, the refined cut of his Savile Row suit, his unruffled way of speaking or the circumspect look in his eye. It didn't take long for Lucien to realize there was much to be learned from him in the area of gentlemanly business dealings. Back then he saw himself as a greenhorn, a novice who still had to get the knack of the trade, and he had involuntarily emulated Kirkpatrick's manners, which were utterly at variance with his own rather impulsive character. But he soon learned that what Kirkpatrick valued above proper manners was reliability. And rightly so: reliability was essential in their field. Once he had convinced Kirkpatrick that he was 100 percent bona fide and always delivered a superior and dependable product, their contact became casual and even what you might call friendly – as far as was possible, in any event, given that Kirkpatrick remained a typically stiff English stuffed shirt.

Lucien had even invited him to his home, introducing the Englishman to his younger sister. Swanny was excited: she and her best friend had been taking English lessons for the past year, and the visit provided a golden opportunity to put her studies into practice. She certainly wasted no time. Kirkpatrick had hardly sat down with his cup of tea before she subjected him to a barrage of embarrassingly crude English, inquiring as to the state of affairs within the British Empire, whether his family had recently been plagued by ill health, and if her tea satisfactorily complied with the strict English rules in respect to the brewing of the leaves. Kirkpatrick was delighted by her charming and candid questions. Within half an hour he had informed them of the current situation throughout Britain's overseas territories, from Canada to New Zealand and from South Africa to Hong Kong, they learned that he was blessed with a beloved wife and five school-aged children, lived in a pleasant house in North London near his dear brother and his three sons, all of whom were serving on the front, that there were regular family get-togethers and that they were all in excellent health. This was more than Lucien had learned in all the years he had known him. The Englishman also made a point of complimenting Swanny on the quality of her tea.

After the meal Kirkpatrick was persuaded to light up a cigar, and, liqueur in hand, proceeded to give a detailed reply to Swanny's interest in his firm, which she had heard nothing but good reports about. Where she got all this from, Lucien couldn't imagine – he had never mentioned Burroughs Wellcome at home. But Kirkpatrick was once again pleasantly surprised. 'Indeed, Miss Hirschland, my firm owes its reputation partly to the fact that our laboratories have devised a way to compress our product into tablets, so that medicines no longer have to be distributed as powders or in an elixir.' Swanny understood at once that medicine in tablet form not only had a longer shelf-life but was more hygienic.

'That's why they're so in demand at the front, given the conditions there. No doubt about it, we're talking about a revolution in the world of pharmaceuticals.' For years, Kirkpatrick had been one of the many travelling salesmen who crisscrossed the nation promoting new products in tablet form. 'It took some getting used to…' he confessed with the hint of a smile.

'It's a typically American sales method to approach doctors and pharmacists directly and give them free samples of medicines. In England we weren't used to what the Americans call "creating a demand".' Lucien had to translate the expression for Swanny, whose instant response was that illness was something that just happened, wasn't it, you couldn't 'create' it, let alone create the need for a medicine when a person wasn't even sick? Kirkpatrick, taken aback for a moment, emptied his glass in a single swig. 'No, certainly not, you're quite right. But our objective is prevention: in addition to hospitals, we visit prisons and poorhouses, where one is often completely ignorant of what illnesses the inmates are exposed to. My firm sees it as our duty to provide advice and information to future patients concerning proper medication.'

'Ah, so that's "creating a demand",' Swanny replied. Lucien felt sure that she'd be trying out this new addition to her English vocabulary on everyone by and by.

'This new method is the brainchild of our director, Mr. Wellcome, a true American pioneer,' continued Kirkpatrick enthusiastically. 'He believes in modern sales techniques and is a genius where promotion and publicity are concerned. For instance, he encourages scientists to give lectures at medical institutions and endorse our products. He's also ensured greater exposure for the tablets, which are marketed under the brand-name *Tabloid*, by offering them at a discount to missionaries, adventurers and athletes, and by running advertisements for them in the better medical journals. But what's really brought our products worldwide attention are the medical kits Burroughs Wellcome has put together for explorers like Henry Stanley. You'll doubtless know of him from his expedition to Africa and his historic meeting with Dr. Livingstone.

And let's not forget Captain Scott, who led a British expedition to Antarctica in 1912 – alas, a month behind his Norwegian rival Amundsen, who by the way also uses our *Tabloid* medicines. But when the well-being of explorers is at stake, we can't afford to favour one over the other, however competitive they are.' Concluding his disquisition, he sighed contentedly: 'You know, there's scarcely an attempt at a trans-Atlantic flight, hardly an expedition or balloon voyage, athletic feat or even a war that doesn't involve our tablets.'

The visit had been a great success. 'So informative and interesting!' Swanny enthused. 'At last, a caller with something worthwhile to say.' Thereafter, she'd often ask him when Kirkpatrick might pay them another visit, and if she could invite her friends next time. But in the past year Kirkpatrick had preferred to communicate by telegraph, and had even telephoned once or twice. All the more surprising, then, that he was here in person on this occasion, given the dangers he'd had to face. It must be something important.

Lucien was roused from his reverie by the sight of a motorbike racing across the square. He was craning his neck to catch the make and model when Brian Kirkpatrick suddenly appeared at the table. He had, as anticipated, done his best to freshen up. His wet hair was plastered to his head and he'd put on a clean, starched shirt. His face, though, was still ashen. He stood there motionless. 'Would you mind if we went upstairs to my room?' he murmured discreetly. 'I'm feeling rather under the weather, you see. My guts are still churning.'

'Of course,' Lucien replied with an understanding nod and stood up. Kirkpatrick obviously preferred to be within easy reach of the toilet next to his room. As they weaved across the busy café-restaurant, Lucien asked a waiter to bring some coffee up to Kirkpatrick's room, reminding him of the number. He followed his client up the stairs to his room, which was furnished with a bed, a chest of drawers a table and two chairs. He noticed immediately that it reeked of fish, but kept it to himself. No need to make the situation more embarrassing than it already was. 'Bit of an unpleasant smell in here,' Kirkpatrick apologized. Lucien shrugged and said it didn't matter. Shooting a glance at a perfectly dreadful landscape hanging above the chest of drawers, he changed the subject by asking after Kirkpatrick's family in London. He hoped for a lengthy answer, which would divert their attention from Kirkpatrick's bowels and lighten the atmosphere.

'Fine, thanks,' was all Kirkpatrick said. Then, clutching his stomach with both hands, he suddenly excused himself and dashed out of the room. In his absence the waiter arrived with a tray carrying two cups of coffee. 'Couldn't you have brought us a whole pot?' asked Lucien, disgruntled. The waiter raised an eyebrow. Lucien leant over and smelt the brew. Ersatz. Even Brinkman couldn't get their hands on the real thing anymore. 'Maybe tomorrow, sir,' the waiter promised, and when Lucien asked him to bring them tea instead he got the same grimace in response. Then we'll just have to make do with this vile coffee substitute, he thought. Ironic that a buyer for a pharmaceutical company didn't even have a remedy for diarrhoea with him. He'd have to improvise something. Lucien was dying to find out what had brought him over with such urgency.

Kirkpatrick returned, visibly relieved, apologized again and answered Lucien's question as though nothing had happened: 'My family was rather upset when I left. A nephew of my wife is on leave from the front and the day before yesterday he paid us a visit. What he had to tell us was absolutely ghastly. But that wasn't the half of it: the poor lad was unrecognizable, half-crazed from what he's been through. Really at the end of his tether. The horrors he'd witnessed, so much carnage and suffering. We had to send the children out of the room.' He lowered his eyes. 'The only thing three years of war has brought is ruination. May God put an end to this butchery.'

Lucien steepled his hands pensively against the tip of his nose and said nothing. Perhaps a decent lunch might help: a nice thick pork chop would surely sort out Kirkpatrick's insides. But before he could even suggest it, Kirkpatrick continued sombrely: 'We're still waiting for the Americans. They've declared war on the Central Powers, but their troops haven't landed yet. I just don't understand why they're making us wait so long.'

'You're right, it's baffling,' agreed Lucien. He hadn't had the slightest idea that the United States had declared war. Damn it, he'd better get onto the American drug company Parke-Davis straight away; they might be supplying the US Army. Or had the wily Mr. Wellcome already beaten him to it? That might be the reason for Kirkpatrick's visit: Burroughs Wellcome must have instructed him to place an extra-large order – and of course wring a generous discount out of Lucien in the process – to supply both the British and the American troops. Well, depending on the quantity he might be amenable. A hefty order was just what he'd been hoping for, after all. The extra commission would come in handy – he had his eye on a Harley Davidson that he'd finally be able to afford. 'Shall I order some lunch first?' he offered. 'A good glass of wine will see you right.'

Kirkpatrick winced: 'No, thanks, just the thought of food and alcohol...' Again he placed his hands gingerly on his stomach. 'Let me explain why I've come.' Lucien held his breath and gestured to Kirkpatrick to continue. He made a conscious effort to appear nonchalant, and not to seem too eager; there might be a considerable sum at stake here.

'As you know, there's been heavy fighting in Flanders over the last few weeks. The Allies have launched a major offensive around Ypres.' Lucien nodded, even though he hadn't followed the war news at all closely for some time. 'The aim is to take Passchendaele and then advance on the ports of Ostend and Zeebrugge, where the German submarines are based. They're a serious threat to our ships – and to yours too, I don't have to tell you that.'

Lucien crossed his legs and nodded again. It seemed most unlikely to him that Dutch ships were in danger; if so, he'd surely have heard about it at the factory, and besides, arrangements had been made with the Germans.

'Well, the long and short of it is that this offensive isn't going too well at all. Disastrous might be a better word. The Germans are putting up really stiff resistance. Our losses are, I'm afraid, very heavy. Every day there's a shocking number of casualties.'

That was the nub of the issue, then: a shocking number of casualties.

'On the German side too, I understand,' Kirkpatrick went on, 'maybe even worse than us.'

Lucien listened, his face an expressionless mask. So the Germans were in the same boat. Even allowing for Kirkpatrick exaggerating enemy casualties, there'd be a grain of truth in it. All of which meant injuries on a grand scale, and then some.

'If this goes on much longer, we'll soon be overrun by the Germans. It doesn't bear thinking about... defeat would be catastrophic for the world, for mankind… we absolutely have to force a breakthrough on the Flemish front.' Kirkpatrick hesitated and wrung his hands. Lucien was surprised: he'd never heard him speak so frankly before about the vulnerability of the British Army, and certainly never so emotionally. It genuinely appeared to affect him deeply. 'Apparently no one anticipated a setback on this scale, and the medical services are struggling. That's why we need to beef up our supplies.'

'Of course, of course, naturally…' said Lucien, with as much composure as he could muster. Aha, so they probably *were* supplying the Americans.

'But just as importantly, we're in a tremendous hurry. That's why I've come in person. Ideally I'd like to take the entire shipment back with me tomorrow. Is that possible?'

'That depends on the quantity, of course,' Lucien answered a bit too hastily. To avoid giving the wrong impression, he added: 'What I mean is that we do sometimes make an exception for such large orders. Pity I didn't know beforehand that it was so urgent.'

Kirkpatrick sighed and leaned confidentially toward him. 'My dear Lucien, the telegraph and telephone simply aren't safe any longer. The Netherlands is riddled with spies, and we don't want the Germans to know any more than they already do.'

'I understand completely,' said Lucien. Heavens above, spies! Wire and phone no longer safe! The war had clearly begun to take its toll on Kirkpatrick's common sense. Strange, he'd always taken him for an intelligent and rational man. It was probably down to that nephew of his and his horror stories. Lucien took his fountain pen from his breast pocket and unscrewed the cap. Time to do business. Now Kirkpatrick had to get to the point and place the order.

'So you reckon it won't be a problem to deliver at short notice?' Kirkpatrick reached for his attaché case, which was leaning against the table leg. 'Of course, I don't know if you people have enough in stock. Or if there are other orders pending.'

He appeared to be fishing for information. Was he trying to figure out, Lucien wondered, who else the company was supplying? That was none of his business. He had strict orders never to discuss one client with another. His answer was businesslike. 'As soon as I know how much you need I'll confer with my director and let you know straight away how soon we can deliver.' Kirkpatrick opened his case and took out a notepad. This was the signal Lucien had been waiting for. He too reached for his briefcase and, in an effort to conceal his excitement, dug around in it longer than he needed to.

'A thousand kilos,' said Kirkpatrick.

That was a good three hundred kilos more than the previous order. But Lucien was careful not to react. He took his time, and stared at the hideous painting as if wrestling with a weighty issue. 'Do you really think a thousand kilos is enough?' he asked seriously. 'Wouldn't it be wiser to boost the stock a bit, so the medics don't come up short again? Not to mention your soldiers.'

'Well…' It was obvious that Kirkpatrick had his nephew on his mind again.

'No one knows how long the offensive will last. You said yourself it's a make-or-break situation.'

'Perhaps you're right.'

'I'm trying to put myself in your position, especially considering your dangerous crossing… and tomorrow you're putting your life at risk again. Who knows, in a fortnight they might send you back to sea.'

That did the trick. Kirkpatrick went pale around the gills and the spasm in his belly caused him to bolt half upright. He winced, but then sank back into his chair. 'Let's say I'll place another order in three weeks' time. Then I'll only need to send a telegram.'

Lucien eyed him apprehensively. 'A telegram specifying the quantity? Is that advisable, with all those German spies about? We could agree on it now. Then all you have to do is send me some innocuous wire, saying that your auntie is doing well or some such, and I'll see to it that the order is dispatched immediately.'

To his surprise, Kirkpatrick seemed to take his proposal seriously. He must really be dreading the crossing to fall for such a cheap sales trick. 'Okay then, but what about tomorrow?'

'I'll check on that immediately.' Lucien figured that a little tension over whether the order could be fulfilled might bump the price up in his favour. He leapt to his feet, intending to ring the factory from the downstairs call box to notify them of the impending order.

'Preferably not by telephone…'

Taken aback, Lucien raised his hands apologetically. 'Of course, how stupid of me.' Damn it all, now he'd have to telephone from home and then return to the hotel to report back to his client. As if he didn't have plenty of other things to worry about. 'Let's work on the assumption there's plenty in stock,' he said, pulling out two contracts.

'In that case make it fifteen hundred kilos now and the same in three weeks, once you've got the wire about my aunt.'

'Fine. If I draw up both contracts now there won't be any additional charge. But the transport costs have unfortunately gone up, because of the German attacks on Dutch cargo ships.'

'How's that? This time I'll be picking up the shipment myself, so you don't have to charge any transport costs.'

True enough. Lucien had overstepped the mark again. 'Tell you what, I won't charge for delivery from Amsterdam to IJmuiden. We all have to do our bit to alleviate the suffering on the front,' he said in a show of humanitarianism.

Kirkpatrick shot him an unexpectedly piercing look. 'By supplying the Germans as well?' He swallowed hard and brushed his hand over his stomach. 'Sorry. It just slipped out. None of my business.'

'No matter…' Lucien let him off the hook. 'The Netherlands is neutral, you know. As a manufacturer of pharmaceuticals we do what we can. Everyone has free access to our help. Every wounded soldier has the right to the best anaesthetics. The Dutch government takes the view that we can't assist one warring party to the detriment of another. See us as the Red Cross.'

'The Red Cross…' Kirkpatrick sighed with a forlorn smile. 'You're right, of course, your neutrality is vital. No one dares imagine a German occupation of this country; your ports would be turned into submarine bases in no time.'

'Exactly. You can't choose your business partners or your friends in wartime.' He was determined not to let the mood go sour – the orders were too substantial to let things slip now.

'Tell me who your friends are, and I'll tell you who you are,' Kirkpatrick remarked as Lucien filled out the two contracts. Lucien didn't take the bait. He knew the Englishman had a low opinion of Dutch business practices, but he didn't feel like arguing about it today. He slid the contracts over to Kirkpatrick, who signed them with a sad little scrawl. Lucien, wanting to add some flair to this fantastic deal, signed his own name in elaborately stylized capital letters. He promised to go to the factory in person to get everything in place for tomorrow. 'Even if we have to plunder our entire stock…' he reassured Kirkpatrick cheerfully. No sooner had he said it than the Englishman was caught short again. He bolted from the room doubled-up, with a pained expression on his face. Lucien leaned back in his chair, took out a cigar and made some mental calculations. Fifteen hundred kilos of cocaine at eight hundred and seventy-five guilders per kilo, times two… that would make his commission… The final amount exploded in front of him like a fireworks display against a jet-black sky, and in his mind's eye arose the tantalizing phantom of a gleaming Harley Davidson.

3

The scar

While here and there a lone grenade hissed its way toward a new victim, a stretcher-bearer pulled Robin, after many hours of blissful semi-consciousness, up out of his mud-hole. He had lost all sense of time and space. The first thing he wanted to know was what time it was – something the stretcher-bearer evidently didn't give a sod about. Robin then asked exactly where they were. 'Piccadilly Circus, y'fruitcake,' was the answer he got. He imagined the man was trying to cheer him up. But the fellow's good humour had its limits, for when Robin inquired whether they'd won, the orderly simply took him roughly by his loosely bandaged arm and shoved him in among a group of soldiers, all with bloodstained dressings. They stood around like naughty boys who'd been caught at some mischief, meekly waiting for someone to bark them back into action.

At a shout from the stretcher-bearer, they pulled their boots out of the mud and let themselves be prodded forward around the smoking and flooded craters. The rain ticked serenely on the calm surface of the puddles. Robin couldn't shake himself out of his daze; he still had no idea where he was or what time it was, he couldn't find his watch anywhere. No one he asked seemed the least bit concerned about the time. Meanwhile he slogged through an extraordinary landscape. Everywhere, foreign objects jutted out of the churned-up earth: swollen cadavers of half-horses, a body minus its head, a head without its face, a face without eyes, a torso without arms, an abdomen out of which crawled a rat. And then suddenly he saw, right next to his boot, a hand, just a loose hand, that had simply been thrown away or lost.

Lost… Something had been nagging at him ever since he'd regained consciousness. But his brain was too knackered to focus on exactly what. From time to time the group of wounded soldiers was overtaken by remnants of divisions and units, who, judging from their exhausted expressions, were obviously in retreat. So they hadn't won after all… Lost, the battle had been lost. A little further on, a tank had tipped forward, its nose sunk in a shell-hole, the gigantic iron rump sticking helplessly up in the air, and then… he could have shouted for joy: protruding out of the mud was a rifle with a glistening bayonet. Now he remembered what had been worrying him. He'd lost his weapon! Lost, while he… Found at last, at last! He was no longer an unarmed soldier, there was no need to be ashamed any more. With a sigh of relief he wandered off from the group in the direction of the rifle. 'Hey, hey, you there, stay in line, damn it!' the stretcher-bearer shouted.

Robin froze and opened his mouth. He wanted to explain that he…

'God dammit, do what you're told!'

Of course, of course, the man was right, completely right. Stay in line… Keep the line straight, damn it! Don't stop, never stop… He mustn't let himself get distracted, just follow the medic's orders, don't talk back and be grateful they didn't abandon him in this hell-hole. But hadn't someone else been left behind? Who was it now?

Robin was still racking his brains when they reached a first-aid post somewhere along the second or third trench line, and were instructed to join a long procession of wounded soldiers in ragged uniforms. Their dog-tired faces were encrusted with grime. Next to him stood a young soldier; he asked him the time, but the boy didn't seem to hear him. He stood stock-still, and once in a while his body convulsed in a shudder, or his limbs shot out wildly in all directions. His eyebrows were raised and his mouth hung open, his face was one big astonished question mark. Now Robin remembered who had been left behind. James! Where was James Foyler? He looked around, took a step sideways so as to peer down the line, but couldn't see him anywhere. In fact, he didn't see anyone from his outfit. Good God, James was still hanging in the barbed wire, a sitting duck for the German machine guns... He'd abandoned him! Somebody had to be warned. Foyler had to be fetched without delay. No, he would go and get him himself, it was his sacred duty to bring a fellow townsman to safety. He broke out in a sweat, his hands trembled and a nauseating fear paralyzed his legs. No, no, not again, not back into that hell... Besides, you weren't allowed to break rank, you mustn't fall out of line, even if you wanted to save a wounded comrade, someone who lived just two streets away. He fingered the temporary bandage on his arm. It was drenched in blood. He wasn't just a coward, but a common coward. He had failed on Dad's birthday... What a disgrace, what an unbearable disgrace. Tears burned the back of this throat. Hit in the arm... he had let himself be put out of action: not only had he lost his rifle, now he couldn't even hold one!

From the field hospital, which was no more than a tent, came shouts followed by piercing screams that slashed through his eardrum as though someone had twisted a shard of broken glass into it. Maybe they were amputating someone's arm without anaesthetics. Field hospitals were nothing but abattoirs, he'd overheard the veteran Tommies say in the trenches. The wounded simply had their uselsss limbs sliced off before being sent unceremoniously back to the front line. Even with no arms, you got a boot under your arse back to the front, one bloke had joked. It made them laugh, just picture it... and then they laughed some more. How long ago was that now?

The line of soldiers listened in silence to the screams, until suddenly a ruckus broke out at the back, where by now more than sixty, perhaps as many as eighty new wounded had joined the queue. A few men, cursing and shouting, had tried to cut in. They were bandaged to the hilt but it didn't stop them from challenging those in front. At first it was only a bit of push-and-shove, but soon enough it turned into punching and kicking. They attacked one another, their faces twisted in rage. Altercations exploded along the entire queue. The highly-strung boy next to Robin burst into a monotonous fit of wailing and flailed his arms uncontrollably. No one paid him any attention; everyone was preoccupied with the brawl. The onlookers even egged on those who were fighting. Robin tried to calm the boy down, but someone kicked him hard in the calf from behind. He wheeled around angrily at the tangle of men, which by now was only a few yards away. 'Stop it!' he shouted. 'Do stop this fighting!'

His appeal was met with derisive laughter. 'Oh sure,' someone jeered, aping his words: '"Do stop fighting!"' A soldier with a deep scar across his cheek eyed him insolently. Robin hadn't seen the man before – he must have taken the opportunity to cut in from the back of the queue. Not wanting to appear impolite, Robin groped for an explanation. 'I just don't like fighting, see. In fact, I can't bear it.' It came out before he had the chance to realize what an odd thing this was for a soldier to say.

'Now mate, you're in the right place!' laughed the scar. 'Pacifist, are you?'

'But why fight with each other?' implored Robin, genuinely indignant.

'Because it doesn't make a bloody bit of difference who we bash up, as long as somebody gets bashed up.'

Satisfied with this line of reasoning, Robin gave an understanding nod. Despite being mangled, the soldier had a friendly face. It was nice to conduct a normal conversation with someone… Right away he thought of James. But before he could ask about him, two officers appeared from behind the field hospital. They strutted across the open ground in front of the entrance, chins in the air and one hand behind their backs. With their free hands they whipped their boots rhythmically with their riding crops. As the brawling horde caught sight of them, the fighters delivered a few last well-placed kicks and simmered down, falling back into line. 'Watch your step,' whispered the scar. 'I know those clowns…' Robin nodded in assent: there was indeed something ludicrous about the officers, like two comic figures conjured up by a theatre director either for comic relief or to underline the gravity of the other characters' actions.

Grinning menacingly, the two officers strode towards the rear of the line, which had settled into an edgy calm. They stopped in front of the worst of the scrappers, swayed back slightly, as though their noses had caught a whiff of something unpleasant, and with a tight-lipped sneer surveyed the bedraggled crew. 'Can't wait until the next heroic battle, eh?' the taller of the two shouted.

'Certainly not! Not after today's stunning victory!' replied the other.

'Ever seen such a pathetic bunch?' asked the tall one.

'Never! This is without a doubt the sorriest pack of good-for-nothings in the history of the British Army!' roared the other, rocking to-and-fro on the heels of his boots. 'Getting themselves wounded without permission and leaving the battlefield against orders! Subordination of the most grievous kind!' There was a cowed silence. Despite their unconventional manners, the officers seemed to Robin to be well-informed of the situation. Perhaps they were trying to round up any fit troops to strengthen the depleted regiments. They strutted past the pathetic rabble as though they were inspecting the royal guard. When they reached Robin, he did his best to salute with his injured arm, called out his name and rank and asked, 'Could you tell me if soldier James Foyler has been found yet?'

The officers looked at each other. The shorter one stretched his neck and inclined his cheek in Robin's direction as though he was hard of hearing. Robin repeated the question, although he could feel the fellow with the scar prodding him in the back. 'And who, for Christ's sake, might soldier James Foyler be?' the shorter one demanded. Robin swallowed and stammered: 'James, James Foyler from Great Yarmouth, his son is in my class.' He was aware of the sniggering around him, and suddenly the strength drained from his legs. The corner of his eyes dampened. He sunk to his knees and began to cry. 'I just left him there…' he sniffed, 'I failed, I wanted to give it my all, for England, for Dad, especially for Dad... I've let everyone down...' He heard the stifled laughter but nothing could stop him now. 'I haven't fired a single shot, I've lost my rifle and what's more I'm wounded and James, oh God, James...' His hand went to his mouth and his shoulders shook uncontrollably.

He was aware of a pair of strong hands lifting him up. The scar had a firm grip on him, and politely informed the officers that his friend was a little confused, in fact he had just fought with admirable courage on the battlefield.

'Put a sock in it! Keep out of this, you bastard!' screamed the tall one. 'He's nothing but a weakling, just look at 'im, typical shirker, a skiver! And the same goes for you!' They were both hauled out of the line and segregated. The two officers, slapping their crops in the palm of their hands, carried on in their pursuit of skivers like a pair of hunting dogs.

Robin was still sobbing, he couldn't stop, now out of shame as well as grief. He couldn't control himself; he'd humiliated himself by bawling like a child. This was worse than getting yourself injured.

'Hey mate, quit your blubbering,' whispered the scar. 'Those are two dangerous customers. They'd like nothing better that to drag nice blokes like us in front of a court-martial. They're barking mad. They're out to find a couple of suckers for the firing squad, it's their calling, their life's work.' The scar nudged him a few steps back, just out of sight of the officers, who by now had lost interest in them. They were busy chewing out a soldier who had lost his jacket and shirt, and who, bare-chested, was trying to defend himself.

'Let's get back in line,' the scar suggested, and only now did Robin notice that his companion had a bandaged knee and dragged his leg. They shuffled backward as unobtrusively as possible until Robin's heels bumped into a stretcher. A man lay there with a severe abdominal wound, entirely without assistance. No one seemed to take any notice of him. 'Forgotten,' gasped Robin, shocked. 'They've forgotten him!'

'Nah, he'll be dead in a couple of hours,' the scar replied quietly. 'The walking wounded have got priority.' Again Robin tried not to lose control, he had to buck up, he couldn't let him down, this friendly soldier with the scar, not him too, not after everything that had happened, not after James… But his emotions refused to obey commands, no longer responded to instructions from his brain. He doubled over and the tears welled up again in full force. The scar cursed, looked around and spotted, amid the chaos, a medic standing in the entrance to a first-aid tent. They seemed to know each other, because after a moment of confidential whispering the medic, an older man, came over to him. His eyes scanned Robin's face. 'Don't cry, son,' he said in a fatherly voice. 'You'd better stop, otherwise you'll have those idiots on your back again. Come on, I'll help you.' Saying this, he led Robin along the throng into the first-aid station.

Inside, the tent stank of sweat, puke and rot – not even the sharp odour of disinfectant could cover it up. It was dark and clammy. The only light came from an acetylene lamp above the operating table. Behind it stood a doctor, his deathly pale face streaked with dark lines of exhaustion. A severed leg stuck out of a bucket on the floor next to his feet. Flies swarmed around the toes. Two men were holding someone down on the table. 'We're low on morphine!' the doctor shouted over his shoulder. 'Whad'ya want me to do about it!' the medic yelled back. He unrolled Robin's temporary bandage, helped him out of his uniform and inspected the wound. 'Oh, this isn't bad at all, it'll mend quickly,' he reassured him, and reached for a wad of cotton wool that smelled of antiseptic.

'What'll happen to me now?' asked Robin anxiously.

Without looking at him, the medic said: 'Everyone who can stand on his two feet has to go back to the trenches. That's our orders.'

Robin swallowed.

'They need all the manpower they can get. Too many casualties today.'

Robin summoned up all the energy he could muster and squeezed his eyes tightly shut, but a loud sob still escaped from his throat. 'It's not your fault, mate.' The medic nodded to a young man with unkempt hair and a cigarette in the corner of his mouth. At one point his jacket had been white and his hands clean, but he tied on a new bandage quickly and routinely, and was already finished when the older medic returned with a syringe. He prodded Robin's arm for a vein and stuck in the needle. It smarted like the devil. 'There, that'll do you for now,' he said as he led him towards the opening in the tent. He lifted Robin's chin with his index finger and looked deep into his eyes. When he saw what he was looking for he gave a satisfied nod. 'All right, Charlie, come and collect your new friend,' he said with a smile, and Robin felt the scar, who it seemed had also slipped into the tent and was standing waiting with a fresh bandage on his knee, grasp his arm.

They walked to a high embankment where, huddled close together, they sought refuge from the rain. Dozens of men were hanging around, all of them freshly bandaged and awaiting further orders. Hundreds of wounded soldiers were still queuing for the first-aid station, the long, snaking line disappearing into the drizzling mist. Robin was startled to see the two officers reappear, talking loudly. They were pushing someone along in front of them. Wasn't it the boy with the convulsions, the one who had stood next to him? But Robin became distracted. He felt dizzy and his face tingled. His heart began to pump faster and faster. Blood raced to his head. He shivered and pressed his hands to his temples in an attempt to fend off the rising storm in his head. He wanted to say something to the scar, but now his entire body was trembling, like a kettle being brought to boiling point. He sucked in a lungful of air and his neck muscles tightened. As the two officers passed by, the taller one shot him a glance and seemed about to recall something, but then took a long drag on his cigarette and gave their captive shirker a violent kick in the backside. Robin licked his dry lips. He arched his back, poised to attack the two monsters, but the scar held him, unobtrusively but firmly, by the sleeve, and Robin's anger subsided at once. He burst out laughing, leant back against the embankment and closed his eyes. Behind his eyelids it was pleasantly dark with red, yellow and blue flashes, like his own personal fireworks display. His head was suffused with a flush of agreeable warmth he hadn't felt in ages. The fatigue and agonizing grief dissipated, and he opened his eyes with renewed vigour. The scar smiled at him. 'Feeling better now, eh?' Robin nodded, his nostrils flared and eyes twinkling. The scar held out his hand: 'Charlie Durban.'

Robin hugged him. He didn't know where to begin, he wanted to tell Charlie everything, everything... that he came from Great Yarmouth, was a schoolteacher and that it was Dad's birthday... But Charlie gave him a friendly thump. 'There you go again with your song and dance!' Robin noticed that all the soldiers around them were chatting animatedly.

They didn't even stop when the two officers reappeared on the scene. They strode past the group of soldiers, shrewdly eyeing them, one by one. 'Well, well, well… Looks like our boys have regained the fighting spirit!' announced the short one in the tone of a vaudeville comedian. 'I'd say so…' replied the other. 'I do believe they're fit enough to die for king and country!' Someone laughed out loud, and even after the officers left, there was no end of jokes and wisecracks, until a lieutenant got up and called for their attention. He began shouting out a list of numbers and regiments, but the men had already slung their packs over their shoulders and made ready to depart. Robin's new mood of optimism evaporated for a moment; he had totally forgotten which regiment he belonged to. Not that he really gave a damn, but he didn't much fancy staying behind at the field hospital with that pathetic bunch of milksops.

Charlie approached the sergeant and after exchanging a few words, returned and said: 'We can join this bunch of layabouts!' To Robin's utter delight, a new rifle was thrust into his hands. He was overjoyed. Charlie the fixer, Charlie his best friend, his very best friend, Charlie who he'd follow everywhere, wherever, straight to hell if necessary. He chuckled. Of course, to hell, to damnation, to the dogs, where else would you go here! He wanted to hug Charlie again, this time because he had finally found a friend. He was no longer alone, he didn't have to feel so lonely on the front. 'Whad'ya mean, lonely?' Charlie retorted, 'soon there'll be a million of us face to face!' He was dead right, as well: it was all about to kick off again… Suddenly he was overcome by a feverish haste. He wanted to run, he had to run, as fast as he could. The other soldiers were in a hurry too, they had no time to lose and jostled each other like hungry animals on their way to the trough.

From that moment on, it was plain sailing. The rain cleared, the sun peeked through the clouds. Robin floated through the labyrinth of trenches as though he had wings. He had lost his bearings long ago, but what did it matter? The others seemed to know exactly which way to go. They marched on and on, triumphantly – as though victory was already theirs – through a brown, churning sea of mud that glistened in the sunshine. They marched over miles of duckboards, through inundated trenches infested with mosquitoes, overflowing with corpses and swarming with rats, sometimes so close you could see their sticky whiskers. Behind him, Charlie was talking non-stop. Robin had taken a liking to his deep, sonorous voice. Presently he realized Charlie was speaking about a woman. 'I'm telling you mate, she's a one-of-a-kind totty, a fantastic Flemish bird with jet-black hair and eyes like glowing coals.' Charlie clapped Robin on the back and thrust a photograph over his shoulder, a photo of a woman with wild hair and a radiant gaze. Robin was deeply impressed by his friend's fiancée, but he quickly passed it back, for he was in a hurry, a big hurry. An agitated voice in his head told him they were nearly there. The irresistible draw of the front coursed through his whole body.

4

The travelling cocaine salesman

The *Nederlandsche Cocaïne Fabriek N.V.*, conveniently situated on an industrial estate on the south side of the Weespervaart, was in Lucien Hirschland's opinion the epitome of modernity. The sleek, contemporary design of the complex, a row of six pointed gables surmounting the factory building like a proud cockscomb, exuded efficiency and functionality. Although the plant had recently been equipped for thermo and electric power, the column of smoke belching from the towering chimney indicated that the steam engine was still fully operational. For Lucien, this billowing cloud of steam was the outward sign of the firm's dynamism and success. Characteristics he himself hoped to embody.

Taking his foot off the car's accelerator, he coasted slowly over the bridge in order to get a good look at the recently completed extension. Full marks to the management for their foresight, he thought: nine years ago, they'd decided to shift the plant from the Schinkelsekade to this newly-developed industrial zone along the Amstel River just outside the city limits. Their former location in town had become just too cramped for the rapidly growing company, and the storage of combustible materials there had become a real headache. But even before construction began on the new plant there had been an outcry in the local community – or so he had heard from Thomas Olyrook, head of the laboratory, for that was before Lucien's time. A modern chemical plant was guaranteed to stir up all sorts of irrational fears, just like when the first railway trains came in, which people had seen as steam-belching monsters, dreamt up by the devil himself. This time it was a band of illiterate farmers behind the kerfuffle, afraid that chemical effluent would be dumped into the irrigation channels in the fields where their livestock grazed. Mr. Cremers, the company's technical director, had assured the farmers during a hearing at city hall that at most, small laboratory vials would be rinsed in the Weespervaart. Whereupon some market gardeners complained that if hazardous materials ended up in the canal where they washed their vegetables, it would be catastrophic for the health of the people of Amsterdam. Mr. Cremers delicately suggested that they'd better take that up with the livestock farmers, whose manure was far more polluting. The owner of a nearby mill, Olyrook recalled, had been even more strident in his opposition. During the hearing, the miller melodramatically highlighted the danger of explosions: 'I've worked here for years in complete safety. And now my very existence is threatened by a factory filled to the brim with volatile materials!' He went on to paint an apocalyptic picture of buildings exploding left and right. 'We'll be blown to kingdom come!' he wailed. 'Lives are being put at risk!' But Cremers informed the mayor, who chaired the hearing, that the factory would be constructed entirely of stone and that inflammable materials would be stored in a separate facility with an underground bunker. Having assured those present that safety precautions included a huge stockpile of sand in the event of fire, and the guarantee that harmful waste would only be discharged at a reasonable distance from crop-growing areas, the mayor issued a building and operating license.

The situation had been resolved to everyone's satisfaction when, shortly thereafter, a large number of new businesses relocated to the Ouder-Amstel industrial estate, expanding the site and causing the arable and livestock farmers to move their orchards and herds further out into the countryside, away from the dreaded chemicals. This was a golden opportunity for the company: even though the plant was equipped with the most up-to-date apparatus – processing kettles, boiling cauldrons, stirring and cooling vats, steam and air pumps – since the outbreak of the war, production had increased to the point that by 1915 a further expansion was necessary. The factory nearly doubled in size. Another storey was added to the original building, which for the sake of efficiency was connected to the storage facility – itself expanded appreciably – by a footbridge. By now the personnel had grown to the point that in addition to a canteen, washrooms and changing rooms, they even needed to install a bicycle shed. But even this expansion wasn't enough. Just a few months ago builders had finished construction of a new, spacious area where coca leaves could be inspected and weighed, as well as two new laboratories that would step up the already impressive rate of production.

Lucien was wholly justified in regarding the factory as a shining example of a modern pharmaceutical company, where science was in the service of manufacturing. It was no empty boast when he told his clientele that his firm's products were admired worldwide for their superior quality. Who else supplied such pure cocaine? What other product contained such a high concentration of alkaloids? Who else still exclusively used the high-quality coca leaves grown on Java? It was, indeed, no surprise that the company was the world's leading cocaine producer.

But, Lucien reminded himself as he approached the entrance gate, no matter how modern the factory and how superior the goods, the most important thing was to sell the product. And who was the one who brought it so successfully to market? None other than him, Lucien Hirschland, the company's travelling cocaine salesman! Though he said so himself, he'd wager that the company had never had such an outstanding sales rep. he was still under thirty, but his youthfulness was more than compensated for by certain admirable qualities: he was reliable, well-mannered and articulate, and, last but not least, he was fluent in several languages. Since the company owed its prosperity in large part to exports – and hence to foreign clients – Lucien's command of English, French and German was invaluable. And although he didn't need it these days, he even spoke a bit of Javanese, not enough for an in-depth conversation, at best well enough to order a whiskey or to complain of too much *Lombok rawit* in his food.

He turned into the factory grounds. A lighter was moored at the dock across from the main building, and from it four workers were carrying bales of coca leaves, brought over from Het Nederlandsche Veem, the warehouses on the other side of Amsterdam, to the storage facility. He was relieved to see that the bales were packed in moisture-resistant bags, to prevent any loss in alkaloid content. In the past they'd had problems in this regard, and with such large orders on the horizon they couldn't afford any mistakes. He parked in the courtyard and as he got out of the car he was hit by the heavy, bitter odour coming from the nearby cocoa factory. He detested that smell, and latterly he'd even found himself repelled by the chocolate milk that Swanny drank. The same went for the stench of soap that wafted over from the aromatics factory further along. But soap was something he wasn't about to give up.

Mr. Cremers' Peugeot was not parked behind the office. Strange that the director was absent, now such a large order had to be filled. He usually kept a close eye on business dealings. Pity, Lucien had wanted to speak to him personally about Kirkpatrick's request to take the entire shipment back to England with him this evening. Lucien hoped for, even expected, some commendation from Cremers – although he was a stand-offish type never very forthcoming with compliments – for having closed this impressive deal. Well, W.H.J. Cremers, B.Sc., might be a cold fish who underestimated the value of an encouraging word to his staff, especially his sales rep, but the company undeniably owed much to its energetic director.

'You can rely on Cremers,' Thomas Olyrook had told Lucien when he joined the company. 'He'll go out on a limb for the company.' As a case in point he cited Cremers' decisive actions just after the war broke out, when the Dutch Cocaine Factory, along with numerous other firms, received a panicked directive from the government banning the import and export of a long list of goods, including medicines and hence also cocaine. 'Those government cowards handed the business bigwigs The Hague on a silver platter,' Olyrook said conspiratorially. 'Leading bankers, commissioners, businessmen, brokers – they basically took over. After all, why should our economy suffer on account of a war that wasn't of our making? Cremer is a clever businessman, he knows who his friends are and went straight to them with his request for an exemption.' Only after that did he go to the Ministry of Agriculture, Industry and Trade. Assured of twofold support, he presented his case to the War Ministry, pointing out existing sales contracts and the large stocks of perishable coca leaves. Domestic use was negligible, so the argument that the domestic market had priority over export was irrelevant. Now more than ever, the export market was wide open. The minister was receptive to Cremers' reasoning: *cocainea hydrochloras* could be exported immediately and the firm was free to continue production. 'In fact, the war gave us the perfect opportunity to choke off the competition in neighbouring countries, because with the export ban on coca leaves from Java in place, pharmaceutical companies in Germany and elsewhere were cut off from their raw materials. So as a result,' Olyrook concluded with a laugh, 'we cornered the market in cocaine.'

'Holland's neutrality is a godsend. Our geographical position in relation to the fronts, where the demand is highest, means we can deliver large quantities in short order. Business is booming, Hirschland, the sky's the limit! There's no sign this war is going to end anytime soon – it could go on for months.' Those were Olyrook's words back in September 1914, a few weeks after Lucien had been taken on as sales rep, and now – almost three years later – his words rang truer than ever. There was still no sign the war would be over anytime soon.

Lucien went straight to the administrative offices at the front of the factory. The previous evening he had 'phoned Jannes Jongejan, the bookkeeper, from Haarlem. He had to be absolutely sure that there was enough stock to fulfil Kirkpatrick's order the next day. As expected, Jongejan's answer consisted of huffing and puffing into the receiver, followed by a series of grunts and groans. He first wanted to confer with Mr. Cremers, who was out of the office. Other clients were in a hurry too, if you please. As if Lucien didn't know that – hadn't he secured those orders in the first place? Fifteen minutes later he got a call back confirming the availability. That's how it always went: he arranged big orders and Jongejan conjured up a problem that turned out to be non-existent. What did that sodding book-keeper take him for? Of course he knew they had thousands of kilos of coca leaves in stock, but he could never pin down how much processed cocaine they had at any given moment. That was top-secret information to which only Cremers, Jonge-jan and the laboratory chief, Olyrook, were party. One day, he hoped to get that trio into a real bind by pulling down a massive order. But not this time, not with so much at stake.

As usual, Jongejan was at his desk, glasses perched on the tip of his nose, his lacklustre eyes squinting out from under the eaves of his heavy eyebrows. Lucien had never known the office otherwise: Jongejan was simply always there, he never even took a day off for a wedding or a funeral. He wondered if the chap was even human, or if he had been manufactured at some workshop that turned out consummate, self-sacrific-ing bookkeepers. Next to his desk was a large safe and Lucien made a play of nonchalantly propping himself against it, which always elicited a grumble of disapproval, as though the thing might sag and break under his weight. The secretaries, behind typewriters and telephones, were seated in the corner near the window. The two youngest ones could always look forward to extra attention from Lucien, mainly with the aim of irritating Jongejan even more.

But now was not the time for games. Lucien took out the Burroughs Wellcome contracts and lay them, one by one, on top of a pile of other papers right under Jongejan's nose. Straight away he reached for his adding machine and Lucien watched carefully for a reaction. But when Jongejan remained tight-lipped, even after pulling the handle for the last time and ringing up the sales commission. Lucien prompted him: 'Fifteen hundred kilos times two. Adds up to a tidy sum, right? You see, I do everything I can to please you! Soon we can close this year's books with a whopping profit, thanks to yours truly!' He put on a saccharine smile and gave a chivalrous bow.

The secretaries tittered.

'We'll see about that,' Jongejan answered coolly.

Lucien smelt a rat. 'What do you mean, 'we'll see'?'

'Hirschland, you might occasionally take the trouble to keep abreast of the latest war developments and their consequences for the firm.' He cast Lucien a disparaging look. 'The management, Mr. Cremers included, is in an emergency meeting at the head office on the Herengracht. A few days ago a Dutch ship was torpedoed off the Belgian coast. We lost a major shipment of leaves. The Germans are now attacking anyone and everyone, even ships from neutral countries. Cargo worth millions has already been sent to the bottom of the sea. If this goes on, soon not a single ship from Java will get through.'

Lucien slowly sank into the chair facing the desk.

Jongejan picked up one of his pencils and inspected the tip. 'To make matters worse, the Javanese planters have started supplying the Americans and Japanese, which of course is simply not on, but on Java apparently money is the only thing that matters. You know as well as I do that without a steady supply of leaves, we're done for. Fortunately our stocks are in order at present, but we don't know if it will last us for the next few months.'

Peering over his glasses, Jongejan tried to gauge whether this bad news had deflated Lucien's triumphant mood. 'I sometimes wonder if you have any idea of the bind we're in.' He was clearly laying it on thick. 'Our ships can't refuel in Port Said anymore, not even in Cape Town – the Brits have seen to that. So now they have to go through the Panama Canal, and when they finally reach the English Channel they have to run the gauntlet of those damned German U-boats. The only ones who are profiting are the cargo companies, they're absolutely raking it in. They're driving up the cost of shipping to absurd levels.' His indignation seemed genuine now, and he irritably whittled a new point on the pencil. 'Their shareholders are being paid out dividends of fifty to a hundred percent! And of course we have to pass the shipping costs on to our customers, but when they start coming to fetch their orders in person – like your Mr. Kirkpatrick – it eats directly into our profit!'

'How come I didn't hear anything about this?' Lucien asked.

'Even a happy-go-lucky *bon vivant* like you, Hirschland, could pick up a newspaper once in a while. I know you were hired for your flair for securing contracts, your persuasiveness, your knack for languages, your great familiarity with the product and your astounding insight into the markets,' said Jongejan with barely concealed sarcasm, while he laid the pencil back in the pen tray, 'but there is a war going on in Europe, which not only puts money in the bank but also brings all sorts of complications with it.'

Lucien stared angrily at the ceiling. He'd given this snippy pen-pusher the perfect opportunity to humiliate him in front of the secretaries. He asked matter-of-factly: 'What's management going to do about the submarines?'

'It's an awkward business. We had a deal with the Germans

to let our ships pass unhindered. Apparently they've now chosen to flout that agreement, so the Dutch government has to put pressure on the German war ministry, make it clear that if they keep this up they'll be cutting off their noses to spite their faces.'

'Well, then, problem solved! No reason to be so melodramatic about it!' Lucien snapped, absentmindedly taking the pencil out of the tray. He didn't know what vexed him more: that rat of a bookkeeper who did his best to rile him, or Kirkpatrick, who had slithered out of having to pay higher transport costs. But the thought of the Englishman reminded him of something: 'I have it on good authority that the English have launched a large-scale offensive in Flanders aimed at taking the submarine bases at Ostend and Zeebrugge. So the problem might be settled sooner than you think!' He doodled a shining sun on one of Jongejan's papers.

'Then I can tell you that the Allies have got hopelessly bogged down around Ypres. Also on "good authority", by the way: the morning papers.' The corner of Jongejan's mouth curled up slightly into what resembled a smirk.

That was precisely what Kirkpatrick had said. Lucien decided to cut his losses; it was more important to know where they stood. 'How long do you expect the battle to last?'

'Don't ask me, I'm no bloody general.' Clearly Jongejan had had enough of this discussion.

'Oh, I thought Master Jongejan not only reads newspapers but in matters of unforeseen difficulties also regularly consults a fortune teller.'

The secretaries sniggered.

Lucien decided it was time to concentrate on the business aspect of the offensive. 'So who's involved, then?'

'I don't know exactly. But in any event the English, Canadians, Australians, French and of course the Germans – no Germans, no war.' Lucian wondered if Jongejan was having fun at his expense. Without looking up, the bookkeeper handed him a duplicate of the first contract, with Lucien's commission filled in at the bottom.

Trudie, the senior secretary, seemed to have been waiting for this moment to catch his attention. 'Mr. Biedermann phoned this morning from Darmstadt. Asked if you'd call him back.'

'Aha!' Lucien couldn't help remarking, 'you people just be sure to keep those stockrooms filled! It's not my job to negotiate with the German war ministry about our supplying them!' Jongejan shook his head, as though he was dealing with an exasperating apprentice, and his fingers resumed their dance over the keys of the adding machine. Lucien smacked the pencil against the edge of the desk. The freshly sharpened tip broke off. 'Oh, I *do* apologize.' He laid the pencil with feigned meticulousness back in the pen tray and sauntered over to Gerda, the attractive stenotypist who also manned the modest telephone switchboard. She always gave him coy glances with her big doe-eyes, and he suspected that shapeless dress concealed a delectable body. He'd meant to ask her for a date today, but that would have to wait. With a wink as a down payment on future advances, he sidled up to her desk and asked if she'd be so kind as to get Franz Biedermann on the line for him.

After a brief conversation he sat listlessly, wondering how and when Kirkpatrick's crates would be sent out to IJmuiden. 'Albert Ketting will take the shipment to IJmuiden at the end of the day,' said Jongejan unbidden.

'Let's hope he's on time for a change!' Lucien replied, irritated. It was an entirely unjustified remark. Ketting was never late. But Lucien was feeling stroppy, and even the call to Biedermann, promising as it was, didn't help his mood any. He slammed the door behind him and folded up the invoice. Annoying though he was, there was no denying Jongejan was good with numbers, although the total would have come out higher if transportation costs had been included... Still, it was more than enough for what he had in mind. He would call at the cashier straight away and then hurry back to Haarlem, as he wanted to drop in somewhere else before fetching Kirkpatrick at his hotel.

Above the entrance to the run-down building near the Koningstraat hung a freshly painted sign: 'Deumers – Automotive Garage and Motorcycle Repairs'. The two front doors stood wide open, allowing the sunshine to show off the Harley Davidson 11-F to its best effect. Lucien circled the machine, caressed the long, curved handlebars and the low-rise saddle that formed a single horizontal line with the petrol tank and luggage rack. He crouched down to inspect the air-cooled four-stroke engine with V-twin cylinders and three speed transmission. Everything was in top-notch condition. This model, introduced in America in 1915, was the most stylish and powerful motorbike on the market. But the supply was limited. 'How did you get your hands on this gem?' he asked Deumers, who was busy shining up the headlamp. 'I guess it was meant to go to the US Army in Flanders,' answered the mechanic. 'But well, they're fickle ones, these Harleys. Once off the ship he seems to have gone his own way. Bet 'e didn't much fancy the war...' He checked the pressure in the rear tyre. Now Lucien understood why this was going to cost him an arm and a leg: black market goods. But on the other hand, the fact that the Harley had been intended for an American officer made it even more attractive. That afternoon he'd buy a full-length leather coat, driving cap, goggles and lace-up calf-length boots. The deal was sealed with a handshake. 'I'll collect it tomorrow at 6 a.m. sharp,' he told Deumers. 'Lube it up good and fill the tank, I've got a long trip ahead of me.'

Lucien dashed into café-restaurant Brinkman just after five o'clock. He took the stairs two at a time, drummed his fingers on Kirkpatrick's door and went straight in without waiting. Kirkpatrick sat on the bed, his hands folded in his lap. He cut a despondent figure. Lucien put on a serious face to mask his own ebullient mood, and removing a small box containing a vial from his bag he inquired after his guest's condition. Kirkpatrick clearly hadn't slept a wink. 'Fine, fine,' he answered dully and gathered up his things, which he'd laid out on the nightstand.

'Look, there's no need to worry,' said Lucien. 'The shipment's on its way to IJmuiden. We spent the whole night getting it ready.' Kirkpatrick, unimpressed, sat down at the table. 'Swanny asked me to send you her compliments,' Lucien went on. He was anxious to lighten the tone, more in keeping with his own mood. 'I explained that you'd a bout of tummy trouble. She sends you all her best and hopes you'll come and dine with us on your next visit.' Kirkpatrick went pale. He obviously didn't want to think about a 'next visit'. 'That's awfully kind of her. Please give her my kind regards, too. I'd be happy to join you for dinner.' Lucien regretted not having told Swanny that Kirkpatrick was in town. It might be some time before they saw him again; the Englishman was unlikely to want to brave the North Sea again before the war was over.

He had placed a small glass plate on the table and sprinkled a bit of white powder onto it. Kirkpatrick uncorked a vial of his own and tipped a few drops of violet liquid onto the powder, which immediately turned red. He nodded his approval and packed everything back into his travel bag. Lucien carefully slid the plate with the powder into a paper bag to give to Olyrook, who was always curious as to what kind of litmus test was being used to check his cocaine.

After one last trip to the toilet, Kirkpatrick grabbed his hat and they left the hotel. Once in the car it became instantly apparent once more how badly the Englishman's overcoat stank. This was part of the reason he hadn't set foot outside the hotel since his arrival. Lucien fervently hoped this visit would never be mentioned in Swanny's presence. She'd be furious if she found out that the poor man had spent an evening alone in his hotel room, stinking to high heaven, when she could have easily washed his clothes. The stench reminded Lucien to pick up some fish for her in IJmuiden.

They rode in silence along the Rijksstraatweg. Lucien irritably recalled his meeting with Jongejan, who had taken him down a peg in front of the secretaries. He also suddenly found himself annoyed by the company car, a Peugeot Bébé, not so much because of its puny top speed, but because it was a car without any status whatsoever. Honestly, that such a successful firm could allow its sales representative – its calling-card, so to speak – to drive around in such a heap was simply appalling. By now, they were already south of Santpoort, where the spacious dune landscape opened up, but Kirkpatrick was lost in thought. Lucien, not fond of silences, said, 'You'll be home before you know it. And I inquired about the German submarines: they're really only after warships, certainly not a fishing trawler.'

Kirkpatrick gave a little cough into his fist. 'I won't be on the trawler for long. As soon as we're offshore, I'll be transferred, cargo and all, to one of our torpedo boats.' Lucien wished he'd kept his mouth shut. 'Oh, right! A torpedo boat, now that's something! I dare say a cannon's better protection than a life vest. And it shows your company is looking out for your safety, and that of the cargo, of course. They'll be delighted to have you back.'

'I'm not so sure my company is best pleased with me,' Kirkpatrick said hesitantly.

'Why not? What nonsense!' exclaimed Lucien, 'there's no doubt you're one of their best buyers, if not *the* best.'

Kirkpatrick fell silent, like he was mulling things over. 'There was an unpleasant incident recently,' he began. 'It led to a quarrel…' Lucien waited for more, but Kirkpatrick seemed to want to leave it at that. 'Come on, what happened?' he prodded. 'We've known each other for so long now, you can confide in me.'

Kirkpatrick rummaged in his bag, pulled out a small bottle and held it over the steering wheel. 'Ever seen this?' Lucien recognized the famous Burroughs Wellcome label with the word *Tabloid* underneath. 'What is it exactly?' Kirkpatrick withdrew his arm, evidently preferring that Lucien kept his eyes on the road. 'It's called *Forced March*, one of our products, excellent quality and…' They had to brake suddenly for a farm cart. The horse had decided for no apparent reason to stand bang in the middle of the road. Lucien took advantage of the interruption to inspect the bottle. The label said: 'Allays hunger and prolongs the power of endurance. One tablet to be dissolved in the mouth every hour when undergoing continued mental strain or physical exertion.' At the bottom it gave the active ingredients as kola nuts and coca leaves. Meanwhile, the farmer had managed, with a few choice words, to get his horse under control and waved them through.

'What's the matter with it?' asked Lucien.

'In principle, nothing. But now large London department stores like Harrods and Savoy & Moore are selling it over the counter.' His voice had a note of disapproval. 'They're even advertising it in *The Times*: "A useful gift for friends on the front." I wonder how many people realize that this is pure caffeine mixed with cocaine.'

Lucien shot him a sideways glance. 'So?'

'I'm not in favour of marketing this type of product openly. It's a substance that should only be prescribed by qualified professionals like doctors and pharmacists, not freely available to every Tom, Dick and Harry. You have to be careful with it. Damn it all, it's not candy!'

'But your company manufactures it?'

'Yes, and that's exactly what upsets me. Profits over precautions. It reminds me of the days when quacks brought all kinds of rubbish onto the market without any regulation. I thought we'd put that kind of thing behind us. And I told my directors as much.'

'Ah, I get your drift – employers don't tend to react well to criticism.' Lucien wondered how Kirkpatrick, ever the diplomat, could have done something so stupid.

'Newspapers have already published articles strongly criticizing the open sale of this type of product. It's negative publicity for our firm.' He put the bottle back into his bag. 'And that's just the beginning. All the palaver has alarmed the Home Office, the Army Council is angry, no one wants cocaine to be delivered willy-nilly to the front. The dispensing of medicine has to be kept in responsible hands – in this case, the army top brass and their medical services. Certain restrictions have already been put in place: cocaine is only available with a doctor's prescription, and the Home Office is now supervising the cocaine trade. Importing it is now officially prohibited.'

Lucien fell silent for a moment. 'Cocaine imports prohibited?'

'It doesn't apply to us, naturally. Burroughs Wellcome has been given an exemption, but of course I don't know how things stand with the other pharmaceutical companies.' He glanced out of the window. 'But you'd know, wouldn't you? You can't only be supplying us.'

Lucien drummed his fingers on the steering wheel. Kirkpatrick had already irked him yesterday with his prying; now he was angling for inside information about other English clients. Could that nervous Home Office have instructed him to find out who was buying cocaine, now that the trade was under government control? He leant over towards Kirkpatrick and said amiably: 'It's none of your business, actually, but just to put your mind at ease, Burroughs Wellcome is an excellent customer – truly one of a kind.' Of course he supplied other British companies, including their main competitor, Boots, but it was none of Kirkpatrick's damned business and Lucien reckoned there was little chance he'd ever find out. Pharmaceutical companies didn't go around advertising their production methods and supply channels, but they were desperate to know all about the competition. He had to stay out of it. Let the English drug companies fight it out among themselves.

'And your sales in Holland?' asked Kirkpatrick.

'Oh, there's not much demand here. Only dentists and ophthalmologists use it for minor operations,' answered Lucien, relieved that Kirkpatrick didn't press him further about his English customers.

'Yes, quite,' said Kirkpatrick, 'although to tell you the truth, I much prefer morphine as an anaesthetic.'

Lucien snorted. So that's what it was all about. The British could produce morphine, thanks to the opium imported from their colonies in the East, but not cocaine. Kirkpatrick was frustrated by their dependence on the Dutch. Morphine a better anaesthetic! Brian Kirkpatrick hadn't shown his know-all side before. No wonder he was having trouble on the home front.

They drove into IJmuiden and Lucien parked at the fishing wharf, amid heaps of nets and heavy chains. The British trawler was already under steam and ready for departure. The deck was loaded with crates and barrels, and Lucien guessed that Kirkpatrick would have to take refuge, even if only for a short time, down in the stinking hold again. He spotted the company lorry parked a little way further on, in front of the ice factory. Albert Ketting stood by its rear doors, smoking a roll-up *sjekkie*; with him were the two workmen he'd brought with him to unload the goods.

Kirkpatrick got out and went straight over to the lorry. Ketting opened the doors so he could climb in and count the crates. Before Lucien could join him, Kirkpatrick turned around and signalled that everything was in order. 'Now, there's fifteen hundred kilos they won't have to buy at Harrods,' Lucien said jovially. He was keen to restore normal, friendly relations before he left. Kirkpatrick, who was of the same mind, replied: 'Our soldiers will be ever so grateful.'

'Shall I arrange a parcel of fish for your wife?' offered Lucien.

'There's no fish to be had, Mr. Hirschland,' Ketting chipped in, 'I've already inquired. Almost everything goes directly by train to Germany.'

Kirkpatrick shook his head; Lucien could read his thoughts. 'Well, then your wife will just have to make do with the smell,' he quipped. He immediately regretted saying it. As they approached the trawler the colour drained out of Kirkpatrick's face and his eyes were filled with dread. Lucien shook his hand and in a sudden fit of camaraderie threw an arm around his shoulders. He slapped him on the back and wished him a safe voyage.

'Hope to God I get myself and this cargo to the other side unscathed,' Kirkpatrick muttered as he walked up the gangplank.

5

The Oriental prince

No matter how discreetly Lucien turned his latchkey in the lock, no matter how softly he closed the front door behind him, that damnable cockatoo, like some enemy spy, always raucously announced his arrival. The wretched beast sat there on his perch all day long, waiting in silent anticipation. Lucien peeked round the corner of the salon. The parrot was hopping back and forth, bobbing its head; it let out a high-pitched screech followed by a series of disapproving guttural noises that always made Lucien feel as though he was guilty of something. 'Shut your trap! Bloody traitor!' he hissed, and wished from the bottom of his heart he had never given his sister the bird in the first place. He tiptoed along the passage to the kitchen with the surprise under his arm. The door was closed to stop cooking smells pervading the rest of the house, but he managed to open it noiselessly; Swanny stood at the cooker with her back to him, stirring a steaming pan. With her free hand she gave her apron a little tug and then brushed away a wisp of hair with the back of her hand. 'I heard you, you rascal!' she laughed, without turning around. 'No one can sneak in unnoticed, Karel's an ideal watchdog!' Except after dark, thought Lucien. Then even the watchdog slept too deeply to react to his drunken stumbling around the entrance hall after a night out on the town.

'Why don't you ever let me know whether you'll be eating at home?' Swanny asked, glancing over her shoulder with the stern look of a kindergarten teacher. But her eyes betrayed the sparkle that Lucien was so fond of. She turned back to her pot. 'A hard-working man like me never knows what each day will bring,' he replied, squeezing her neck, but gently so as not to hurt her. She let out a yelp, and with a graceful flourish he suddenly whisked the parcel round under her nose. She snatched it from him and unwrapped it. 'Fish!' she cried, delighted, and laid four glistening cod on the table. 'Oh, Lucien, fish is *so* difficult to get. People would kill for this!'

'You've no idea of the drastic measures I had to take to get hold of it,' he said with mock gravity, and poured himself a glass of port.

'Well then, I'd better put them away before you get arrested.' She thought a moment. 'I'll give two to Pleun.'

'That's right, make the old woman an accessory.' Lucien reached for the *Haarlemsche Courant* that Swanny always laid out on the table for him. Usually he only skimmed over the advertisements; he could barely summon up the interest or patience to read the latest news on this tedious war, but now he really had to make an effort. He bent over the table, his arms spread wide, and scanned the front page. Under the headline *Armageddon* he read that a ferocious offensive had been launched in Flanders. London reported that on Tuesday morning, the 31st of July, at 3:50 a.m. British forces, supported by the French, had attacked along a broad front north of the Lys. They'd been engaged in a fierce artillery battle for days. So Jongejan was right: the French were also involved. He'd send a telegram to the French buyer first thing tomorrow, since this meant there would surely be wounded soldiers on their side as well.

Swanny stuck her head under his arm, scanning the page with her index finger for a news item she wanted to bring to his attention. She read aloud: 'The entire British army has advanced approximately a hundred metres, a negligible territorial gain, a meagre result indeed. And yet the English newspapers insist that their troops are certain of victory. The facts, however, underscore the superiority of the German military leadership.' She turned towards him. 'The nerve of this paper being so pro-German. We're supposed to be neutral! And look here: "These developments do not bode well for the English and the French. The Germans have apparently also scored a major success at the Chemin des Dames…" Who do they think they are, talking about success when referring to the Germans?'

Lucien grinned. 'And all along I thought you were neutral!'

'Heavens above, Lucien, of course I'm against the Germans, *they* started it…' She slipped back out from under his arm and returned to the stove. An article on the next page caught his eye: *The escalating submarine conflict.* 'The German and Dutch governments are conferring about the unfortunate incident in which a German U-boat sank a Dutch freighter in a blockaded zone. The German admiralty had pledged to allow Dutch cargo ships free passage. As a friendly neighbour, Germany sincerely regrets the incident.'

Lucien sat down. This was today's newspaper, which meant that the Dutch government was already dealing with the matter. Once again Jongejan had sown panic unnecessarily, just to taunt him. He folded the paper and put it in his inside breast pocket – he'd face down that miserable bean counter this time. Besides, it was useful information to have for tomorrow's meeting with Franz Biedermann.

Swanny brought the plates and serving dishes to table, undid her apron and sat down.

'And how was your day, Sis?' he asked, spooning out onto his plate something that resembled corned-beef hash, but without the meat.

'Oh, we took some food around to the old folks. It's so sad… More and more essentials are being rationed: bread, milk, margarine, clothes. It's nigh on impossible to get meat, unless you're prepared to use the black market. But the worst of it is you can't even get potatoes. Everything's exported to England or Germany in exchange for fuel.'

'Which we need badly, Swan – it's what keeps the factories going. Surely you don't want our entire economy to collapse.'

'All well and good, but some people are starving while others are raking it in. Little wonder that poor folks are losing their respect for the law.'

'You know what I saw yesterday?' Lucien suddenly recalled. 'While I was sitting at Brinkman waiting for… ah, someone… some idiot on a bike deliberately hurled himself in front of a Mercedes. His sidekicks managed to con the driver out of a wad of money by threatening to call the police.' He chuckled.

Swanny failed to see the humour in it. 'You see? People are even prepared to risk their lives for a few cents. By the way, I heard that a bicycle was stolen a couple of doors up the road.'

'Same one, I expect.' Lucien wondered where he could safely store the Harley. Maybe in the shed at the back of the garden. He'd better own up to the new purchase now, even though it could cost him a tongue-lashing. But there was no way out of it; the shed was stacked to the rafters with old junk and Pleun would have to get it cleared out before tomorrow evening. He put down his fork and rubbed his stomach contentedly. 'Swan, you've done it again, your cooking tops any restaurant.' She beamed with satisfaction. 'You should write a cookery book.' Now she cocked her head to one side, her sign that he was exaggerating again. 'By the way, something else I meant to mention…' he continued offhandedly, 'I bought a motorbike today.' He patted his mouth with a serviette and watched as her eyes grew in amazement. 'A secondhand Harley-Davidson, a once-in-a-lifetime opportunity.' Hopefully she'll have never heard the name before and not realize how much he'd splashed out.

She clapped her hands to her cheeks. 'Oh Lucien, how wonderful for you. A Harley-Davidson! Finally, your dream come true!' Now it was his turn to be amazed. But of course, he'd forgotten how often he pined openly for a Harley. Then a brief scowl passed over her face: 'Aren't they terribly expensive?'

'I got a great deal. Who knows, it might come in really handy.'

As she cleared the table she stood, lost in thought, with the empty plates in her hand. 'Now that you mention it… You could help with our food deliveries; it can be quite a trek to get to those old people. The distribution centre only has that rickety cart, and we just can't do it all by bicycle anymore.'

Lucien leant back, relieved. 'You see? I knew it would be practical. Tell you what, I'll order a sidecar as soon as possible, we'll be needing one.' Swanny planted a kiss on his head. 'What a brilliant idea. I'll tell them first thing tomorrow.'

Lucien took a cigar out of its tube, turned it between his fingers and sniffed it. 'Why don't you wait until I'm sure about the sidecar. We wouldn't want them to get their hopes up.'

Suddenly he felt tired and got up from the table. 'I'm going to call it a night, I've got an early start tomorrow. It's going to be a long day – I'm taking the Harley to Arnhem.' He was already at the door when she stopped him. 'I hope you haven't forgotten about my little soiree this Saturday.' In fact, it had slipped his mind. 'I've invited a few guests especially for you, one in particular as a surprise. Lisette will play the violin, of course, and Dineke has finished a few new poems.'

Lucien smiled. 'Of course I haven't forgotten. I'm so looking forward to it.'

He loosened his necktie on his way up to his bedroom. *I'm so looking forward to it* – what a damned hypocrite he was! Swanny's monthly soirees – now reduced to the status of 'little' since the war broke out – weren't just stultifyingly boring, they were out-and-out torture sessions conducted by a standing committee of tormentors. Her girlfriends were the worst: not satisfied with polite small talk, they demanded his full attention on topics that didn't interest him in the slightest. How they all managed to be so tiresome and unattractive, he couldn't imagine. The violinist took the biscuit: after launching into an exhaustive introduction – enough to make any sane person cut and run – she obliged the company to sit silently for a good hour while she sawed away. Then there was the poetess, what's-her-name, whose latest offerings all concerned the sufferings of war. And Casper, of course, the next-door neighbour and successful portraitist, with the voice of a half-deaf town crier. Lucien had once suggested to Swanny that she try an evening without Casper, but no, apparently he was indispensable: alongside the musician, poet and sundry skilful conversationalists, a painter was essential in giving the soiree its proper artistic and intellectual balance. Thank God for Swanny's best friend, Tosca Tilanus. At least her sense of humour kept him from bursting into fits of hysterical laughter. The cockatoo, incidentally, wasn't so forebearing, accompanying the violin sonatas and doggerel with a volley of catcalls. It was invariably banished to the hallway.

Lucien undressed, fingered through his collection of kimonos in the wardrobe and chose one that suited his mood: the blue one with a dragon embroidered on the back. He stretched out on the bed and sank into the Chinese silk pillows. Glancing at the *klamboe*, he recalled the protests of Pleun, the Hirschland's long-serving housekeeper, when he tried to teach her how to fasten the mosquito net to the bedposts, like they do on Java. 'But we ain't *in* Indië, sir,' he imitated her whining drawl. 'It was bad enough you were out there when…' He shushed her at once and thought wistfully of the docile obedience of his Javanese servants.

But she'd touched on a raw nerve, all the same. It was three years ago already that he'd been forced to return to Haarlem. His bereaved sister was alone in the villa on the Oranjekade; he was all she had now. Aged just twenty-two, she was already an orphan and a divorcée, although the latter status was actually a blessing, seeing as her husband had turned out to be a no-good swindler who'd brought the family nothing but misery. Lucien was spared a face-to-face meeting with him, as the marriage had been celebrated and dissolved in his absence. He'd have been happy never to have mentioned any of it again – not the disastrous marriage, nor the demise of the family business, and especially not the death of their father – and would have been happy to get back to business as usual. But Swanny's melancholy silence became too much for him, and so he'd turned to Pleun for all the details. After much sniffling and two glasses of jenever she gave him her version of the events. 'Oh, mercy above, it was dreadful… your father give 'im the entire publisher's on a silver platter. And the villain made a right mess of it, he did! Debt collectors at the door and all manner of nasty folk that come wanting money from 'im, such a disgrace for the family! Your father done everything to save the business, but it was either sell or go bankrupt. The scoundrel vanished into thin air, and Swanny just sit there cryin' and cryin', poor child, beside herself she was.'

That was when his father's urgent telegrams began to arrive, imploring him to return to Holland without delay. Nothing doing! From the other side of the world he had no inkling as to the seriousness of the situation. How could he know that the forced sale of the publishing company would be such a blow to his father? With hindsight, of course, he should have been more understanding, but at the time his mind was preoccupied with other things. His father sat bitterly in his armchair by the salon window for the next six months, Swanny told him once the worst of her grief had subsided. One morning she found him dead in his chair. His heart had just given up. Not difficult to imagine what went through the old man's mind. The publishing house, pride of the family for a hundred years, was led to ruination by a stranger in the blink of an eye, while his own son refused to come home to help salvage the business. Lucien, his crown prince and name-bearer, on whom he had pinned all his hopes. Against his better judgement, mind you, because Lucien had never shown a shred of interest in the publishing business: in his eyes it was a relic that stubbornly churned out stuffy schoolbooks and atlases. As a boy he had only one desire: to get out of Haarlem as soon as possible and travel the world. His father didn't object in the least when he left for Java. He had managed to wangle a job there, trading on his father's reputation, the family name, and the entirely unfounded notion that they were moneyed. His father's only parting words were that he hoped to see Lucien return before long as a grown man. 'Use your time wisely, my boy.' Shrewdly, he sent him off without a penny, expecting that financial troubles would hasten his return home so that he could follow in his father's footsteps after all. His son's refusal to even come to his aid when the business teetered on the edge of ruin must have cut him to the quick.

Once Lucien had decided to remain in Haarlem, at least for the time being, Swanny offered him their father's bedroom, the choicest room in the house with a splendid view over the Leidsevaart. At first he refused, not wanting to be visited by the old man's reproachful, droopy-eyed ghost every night. Nothing but superstition, he told himself, picked up in the East. The alternative, after all, was his dreary boyhood room at the back of the house. He slept in the guest room until the movers' crates arrived. Then he had his father's bed, cupboards, rugs and Dutch landscapes, with their typical threatening skies – Hirschland Sr. was an admirer of a local Haarlem painter – moved up to the attic. The room was refitted with teak furniture he had purchased in Batavia's Arab quarter, his collection of Chinese vases and plates, the extravagant four-poster bed with the carved Buddha, the Persian rugs and the rest of his souvenirs. After some months the room settled into an exotic ambience in which he could wallow in nostalgia for Indië.

Swanny had followed the transformation with misgivings. She thought it heartless of him to erase their father's memory just like that, and in protest she hung the gloomy Dutch landscape paintings in the salon. But eventually her resistance waned, and she even came to enjoy visiting him in his Oriental paradise. 'Just one flight up and it's like I've travelled to another continent,' she exclaimed the first time. Occasionally she played the foreign gentlewoman paying a call on a distinguished Oriental prince. He would then put on his fanciest kimono and twist a swath of silk into a turban. Swanny wore the sarong and batiste *kebaya* he had brought back for her, and once she even came carrying his other gift on her arm: the cockatoo, which, she insisted, longed for the tropics. Overjoyed, the bird flapped excitedly among the leaves of the potted palm, swooping dangerously close to Lucien's costly porcelain. Ever since then, Karel – named after a deceased cousin – had had to stay behind in the salon. Swanny installed herself with a glass of port on the chaise longue amid the Atjeh lamps and coconut palms he had acquired from a botanical garden in Amsterdam.

By the light of flickering candles and the scent of incense, they set sail together for the Dutch East Indies. He took her across the oceans, shared with her the first sun-drenched glimpse of the East Indian archipelago, mooring that evening by moonlight in the enchanting bay of Padang on West Sumatra. They strolled arm in arm along the Emmahaven, eating *dukus* and mangosteens, and continued their journey along thousands of palm-lined islands, finally steaming into Tanjung Priok harbour. There he immersed her in the colourful, wild Javanese nature and the exotic gardens of Buitenzorg. Seated on a bench under ancient trees and with orchids at her feet, she admired the vista of his glorious career.

Lucien had started in a relatively lowly position, but his impeccable behaviour soon made a favourable impression on his superiors. Presently a highly-placed civil servant, a man he drank afternoon tea with on the veranda, recognized his talents and got him a job as assistant to an adjutant of the governor. It was a great honour. Admittedly, the family name and his father's reputation played no small part in the appointment, a fact that pleased Swanny no end. His new status allowed him to take an active part in the social life of the Dutch colony, attending official receptions and elegant parties, where the ladies and the gentlemen dressed in white linen and conversed in jovial but civilized tones. And they danced: waltzes and German polkas… Swanny recoiled with a cry of 'how terribly old-fashioned!' But he wasn't much of a dancer anyway; he much preferred discussing the latest books, music and culture with friends. That was what he liked best… The same went for the custom of joining the other gentlemen at around half past five in the afternoon, dressed in a suit of Nanking silk, for a whisky and soda and a fine cigar on the front veranda among whitewashed flower pots overflowing with roses and chrysanthemums, looking out over a lawn ringed with agaves and shrubs, before retiring indoors to join the ladies who were waiting for them seated on rattan furniture.

Swanny relished his stories, although the tilt of her head suggested that she knew half of them were outright lies and the rest a pot-pourri of Lucien's fantasies. But hang it all, he couldn't tell her about the drinking binges and raucous sprees with his friends, could he? About the wild nights that usually ended up in some dive or another in the *kampongs*, or about the women, his many conquests… In just a short space of time he had managed to seduce a fair number of civil servants' daughters, picking out the least homely and frumpish for a brief fling with plenty of necking and petting and fumbling under corsets, and once the novelty had worn off, setting his sights on fresh prey. Like a hunter, his desire expanded to take in big game: the wives of higher functionaries, especially those who looked down their nose at him. These dalliances became a pricey pastime. Floral arrangements, gifts, outings in hired cars. His salary wasn't remotely equal to it, and he was forced to approach Chinese moneylenders. Never mind, it was worth every penny.

Lucien ran his hand over a silk pillow and recalled how Martha had made sheep's eyes at him. He didn't find her particularly attractive, but the fact that she was married to the highest adjutant to the governor-general made her a very desirable object indeed. First prize, a real trophy. They had met at the club during a propaganda evening given by the 'Defence of the Indies' organization. He was bored out of his mind, first during the pastor's lecture on the education of the Malay races, then by a women's choir that specialized in Dutch songs. He noticed her immediately, stifling yawns with her hand. After considerable effort on his part, they made eye contact, first conveying their mutual boredom with the choir and then, much more clandestinely, their interest in furthering the acquaintance. Not that Martha was much bothered about discretion: one evening she brazenly came to fetch him at his house, for all the world to see, in an open carriage with a native driver. She got a thrill from taking risks, and managed to find a great variety of venues, preferable in the wild, for their passionate trysts. He'd come to work covered in insect bites and red blotches and so had to wear a long-sleeve jacket despite the unbearable heat, and flee from time to time to the toilet in order to scratch himself with a letter-opener. Martha didn't mind in the slightest, she seemed used to it – which made him suspicious that he wasn't her first adulterous liaison. Nevertheless, he insisted on discretion; gossip was the deadliest poison in the East. He didn't want to have to up sticks in a hurry, and besides, he had his career to consider.

And suddenly it all started to unravel. Friends warned him that people in the governor's circle were starting to talk, and it wouldn't be long before it reached the ears of the adjutant. But before the scandal had time to erupt in earnest, he received the news of his father's death and the urgent appeal to return home at once. The tragedy gave him an excuse to leave without losing face – not, however, before a passionate farewell rendezvous with Martha, who pulled out all the stops one last time – and just a step ahead of the Chinese loan sharks and their henchmen, champions in martial arts to a man.

The trip back home on the cargo ship laden with colonial goods was a complete nightmare. He'd hoped to keep the tropical heat, which he'd so often cursed but now craved, safely contained in his cabin. But during a heavy storm in the Indian Ocean, the spice-infused warmth escaped through wide-flung doors and clattering portholes. Spray swept over the deck, the engines throbbed, everything lurched and shuddered, everyone fell and cursed. He lay in his own vomit in the gangway. In the Red Sea they suffered biblical plagues of sand and locusts, and in Port Said he was overcome by deep melancholy at the sight of the featureless desert. He no longer showed his face on deck, either playing whist with the captain and a couple of fellow passengers or getting drunk alone in his cabin. After that he spoke to no one. His only company was the cockatoo, which sat quietly on his perch, its head tucked into its feathers. Lucien often wondered if Swanny's present would make it home alive.

Beyond the Bay of Biscay he peered through the porthole and saw a few grey warships pass in the distance. It was his cue to take off his tropical white linen suit, and change into the dark clothing he had not worn since leaving Holland. He recalled that for the past five weeks, Europe had been at war.

6

Biedermann

The next morning it was bucketing down when Lucien took the Harley-Davidson 11-F Tourer out for its first trial run. While the summer of 1917 could, in business terms, be deemed successful and even cheerful, he mused irritably, you certainly couldn't say the same about the weather. The last few weeks had been the wettest and gloomiest in recent memory, and today was no exception. He had a rough and unpleasant journey ahead of him.

An hour later he made out, through gaps in the drizzle, a blue glow on the horizon. His mood changed at once. This was a good sign. It seemed the weather was clearer in the East, where he was heading on business. The strip of bright sky beckoned. He looked up at the black mass, pregnant with cloudbursts, that had been pursuing him all the way from Haarlem. He had to shake off this storm. Shifting to a higher gear, he hunched further forward over the U-shaped handlebars. This was going to be a speed trial between the thunderclouds, driven onward by westerly winds, and his 11–horsepower motorbike. The forces of nature versus technical ingenuity. A race he was determined to win. He was tempted to push the machine to its advertised top speed of 95 kilometres per hour, but restrained himself to avoid overheating the engine. They first had to get to know and respect one another before he could call himself the boss – in that sense it wasn't much different from a horse.

After about fifty kilometres the rainclouds finally gave up the struggle. Lucien glanced back over his shoulder, shook his fist triumphantly and welcomed the blue skies as a trusted ally. At last he could sit back in the saddle and listen to hear whether the machine lived up to its nickname: *Silent Gray Fellow*. His upbeat mood had returned and he looked forward to meeting Franz Biedermann in Arnhem. He had high hopes: after all, the Germans, like the English, had suffered grievous losses in Flanders, so Franz might well be about to place a sizable order.

On the other side of Utrecht the traffic picked up, calling for quite some adeptness on his part. He raced along paved trunk roads and cobbled lanes, zigzagging between cyclists and lorries, startling carthorses and forcing cursing market women onto the berm. He was overtaken only once. The driver of a six-cylinder Napier shot past and tooted derisively a couple of times. Lucien immediately took up the challenge, opened the throttle, shifted into the highest gear and pushed the motorbike to its limits. He gradually gained on the Napier and would have easily had the measure of it if the driver had not taken a cowardly turn into a side road.

He reached Arnhem's city limits exactly on schedule, having calculated an average of 40 kilometres per hour and taking into account congestion caused by road users, topping up with petrol and a brief stop at a village café. The trip had taken him five hours. Riding into the busy city centre, he was forced not only to shift to a lower gear but also to put the brakes on his adrenaline as well. He drove down the high street towards the Oranje-Nassau Hotel, across from the station. Franz

Biedermann lodged there whenever he needed to travel from Darmstadt to conduct business in person – a frequent occurrence, even if it was just because he enjoyed being pampered.

Lucien pulled in behind the hotel, hitched the motorbike up onto its stand, and looked for the kitchen boy who always kept an eye on the company car. It was a while before the lad came running up. He gaped at the Harley, wiped his fingers on his apron and asked if he could touch it. 'Sure,' said Lucien, 'but take care, the engine's scalding hot.' The boy extended his hands carefully towards the engine, as if to warm himself at a lighted stove, and shook his head in disbelief. 'If you look after it properly you can start it up later, and maybe we'll even take a spin.' Lucien was certain that the boy wouldn't let the Harley out of his sight for even a second.

Once in the hotel lobby, he removed his leather cap and ran his fingers roughly through his hair. He let the goggles dangle under his chin. Even though it was far too warm inside for a leather motorcycle jacket, he decided to leave it on for the time being. He immediately attracted the attention of two ladies on their way out, who furtively admired his athletic turnout and whispered to one another. He thought he picked up something about a pilot. Cheerfully greeting the cloakroom girl, his attention was drawn to a poster that hung in an adjacent glass case. *The Secret of Delft*. The film had been showing for some time but had apparently only just reached Arnhem. Of course he'd seen it already, twice in fact, first on his own and the second time with Pola. Afterwards he sang the praises of her acting abilities and her sense of drama, the subtlety of her interpretation, the naturalness of her style… simply breathtaking. When she refused to believe him he swore blind that not a word of it was exaggerated. It was patently obvious to every cinema-goer that she stood head and shoulders above her rival, that second-rate vaudeville entertainer, the dread Annie Bos, who once again had managed to snatch the leading role. Naturally, he knew that the tramp had thrown herself at the director Mauritz Binger, grabbing not only the top billing but the accolade of 'Holland's Most Famous Film Star' as well. Pola Pauwlova's name appeared in smaller letters just under Annie's. Poor Pola, for years she'd had to make do with supporting roles – no wonder she had such headaches. His beautiful, passionate Pola. He was obsessed with her, totally addicted to her luscious body… He decided to buy a piece of jewellery for her later that day, an attractive necklace with a few precious stones – just how precious depended on his commission from Biedermann's order.

In the lounge, the German was nowhere to be seen. Strange, Franz was always there to meet him usually. Maybe he'd lain down for a nap after the long train journey and had over-slept. Although, Lucien noticed on checking his watch, he was on the early side. Pity, now Biedermann would miss his entrance in full motorbike regalia. He weaved through the tables, picked up a menu and a local newspaper in passing, and positioned himself in a corner of the lounge in full view of the other guests. He glanced at the menu. Nothing particu-larly piqued his appetite, but no matter, he had another idea. During his last visit Biedermann had made no bones about being unimpressed by the hotel's kitchen. Lucien's plan was to eat elsewhere, in a pleasant establishment reasonably close to the hotel, but too far to walk, so he could suggest that they take his motorbike. He looked forward to Franz's wounded German vanity, for even Biedermann would have to admit that the American Harley-Davidson left German motorcycles standing. Strange, actually, that he always felt such a need to impress Biedermann. The German in no way elicited the kind of respect that he felt for Kirkpatrick. They were each other's opposites, first and foremost physically.

Biedermann was a stocky man with a red-veined snub nose and a pouting mouth that was almost entirely hidden by an enormous moustache of indeterminate colour. His head was shaven except for a little crown of straw-coloured hair with a sharp parting. Lucien thought him a bit shabby for a representative of Germany's most prestigious pharmaceutical company. His store-bought suits and stained neckties gave him more the air of a door-to-door broom salesman. But he must have been presentable once, for before going to work for Merck he'd been employed at Universum Film AG in Berlin. Franz had told him about his career as a producer after hearing about Lucien's relationship with Pola Pauwlova.

After closing a deal, they were wont to repair to a local gentleman's club for drinks, where they could chew the fat over such personal matters . Of course, any real confidences always came from him; Biedermann never offered so much as a glimpse into his private life. He did, however, enjoy listening to Lucien's embellished tales of his adventures in the Far East, particularly his affairs with women. He'd even managed to coax Lucien into divulging some intimate details of his open-air trysts with Martha. Biedermann lapped it up – he could never get enough of the racy stories, despite already being over fifty. As a result, Lucien thought him a bit of a dirty old man at first and even rather credulous; he seemed to believe absolutely everything he was told. But he'd underestimated him: Franz Biedermann turned out to be far from naïve. Lucien knew from experience that it was a mistake to take him for granted.

But the main contrast between Kirkpatrick and the German was in their way of doing business. Lucien and Franz both enjoyed the game immensely. Their banter always followed the same formula: Biedermann began by casting doubt on the quality of the product, tested the powder extensively – nobody knew the difference between Peruvian and Javanese coca better than he – and then brazenly declared that the stuff had been 'messed with', as he put it, that Dutch cocaine didn't deserve its high reputation. He'd come within an ace of accusing Lucien of being a common swindler, and then conclude by sighing that he regretted having made the long journey. This was followed by protracted haggling over the price, which Biedermann spun out until he'd secured a special discount – precisely the amount that Lucien had had in mind in the first place. Biedermann was fully aware of this, because when it came to cutting a deal, no one could hold a candle to this canny fellow. Once the contract was signed they both sat back contentedly like horse traders who'd just cheated one another. The one thing Lucien did have a real problem with was Biedermann's frugality, or better put, his downright stinginess. It wasn't about the money, but the gesture: Franz had never, in all these years, ever stumped up for anything himself, not even a cup of coffee…

Lucien opened a newspaper, but before he had time to scan the advertisements, he noticed Franz Biedermann standing in the doorway. He couldn't have been there long, not more than a few seconds, just long enough to spot him in his motorcycle gear, jacket draped nonchalantly over his shoulders, cap and goggles on the table. Lucien put down the newspaper, stood up and held out his hand in greeting.

'Have a good trip on your Harley-Davidson?' asked Biedermann.

Lucien looked at him, startled.

'I saw you from my room,' he said, smiling, and twitching his moustache.

'Have you ever ridden a Harley?' asked Lucien, slightly disappointed.

Biedermann sneered. 'Don't really go for those things; I'm not much of speed freak.'

'Well, you'll just have to grin and bear it. I know you don't think much of the food here, so I'm taking you to an excellent restaurant in Sonsbeek Park.' Without waiting for an answer Lucien put on his jacket and picked up the cap and goggles. 'And you're riding pillion.'

Biedermann seemed less than delighted at the prospect; even so, he said nothing and followed Lucien into the lobby. Pausing by the film poster in the display case, he asked: 'Good film?'

'Very,' answered Lucien. Biedermann always inquired after Pola's latest film, not surprisingly, considering his background. He'd suggested once that they meet, and Lucien, his eye on a potential order, pretended to agree, although there was no way on Earth he was going to introduce Pola to Biedermann. A former film producer, even a slob like Biedermann, would excite her no end, and straight away visions of a film career in Germany would dance before her eyes.

Biedermann tapped on Pola's name through the glass. 'I'm surprised your girlfriend doesn't have a more prominent role,' he remarked.

Lucien did not feel like discussing Pola, but Biedermann stood pensively in front of the display case with his hand on his chin. 'Oh, that doesn't mean much…' Lucien said in the hope of closing the subject. 'That Annie Bos gets offered her leading roles on the casting couch.'

'Of course, that's how it works,' sighed Biedermann. 'I couldn't keep the women off me either.'

Lucien briefly flirted with the distasteful image of the fat little German pressing his filthy moustache against the lips of a young actress. 'Fortunately Pola doesn't need to go that route,' he said quickly, 'and besides, it's a major supporting role. She's got some excellent reviews.'

'Has she got a new role now?' Biedermann asked.

'There have been a lot of offers. For the time being she's considering her next move.' Lucien had no idea if there was a new film on the horizon, the last time he'd seen her they didn't exactly conduct what you'd call a conversation.

'A few days ago I ran into an ex-colleague from Universum Film,' Franz went on. 'He's just started work on a new film and is still looking for a suitable leading lady. I could introduce her to him.'

Alarm bells rang in Lucien's head. Franz was trying to get his hands on his beautiful Pola, using a film role as bait. 'I know for a fact that she's got no time this coming year,' he quickly responded, making a move towards the door.

But Biedermann didn't budge. 'It's a golden opportunity, a splendid role in a romantic movie, and she won't have to go to bed with the director.'

'But with the producer, I'll bet...' Lucien gave him a tug on his elbow. 'Come on, Franz, we're not here to talk about showbiz.'

The ride out to Sonsbeek Park was short, but still long enough for Lucien to open up the throttle and tear around a sharp curve, forcing Franz, perched uncomfortably behind, to grab tightly onto him. Inside the park Lucien brought the motorcycle to an abrupt halt, skidding along the gravel path in front of the tea house terrace. If Biedermann was terrified he didn't let it show. He swung his leg over the luggage rack and hobbled up the steps to the terrace, where the diners were following this spectacular entrance with keen interest.

Lucien chose a table with a view of the pond, which was surrounded by the impressive copper beeches that gave the park its name. He hailed the waiter and, to make amends for the wild ride, ordered half a dozen fresh oysters – Biedermann's favourite appetizer – and a bottle of excellent Moselle. Biedermann did his best to plaster down his little tuft of hair; Lucien was pleased to note that he looked a little peaky.

'To return to the subject of Pola Pauwlova…' Franz began, once he had recovered, 'my friend is thinking about asking Asta Nielsen, but I've already brought your girlfriend to his attention. It's a terrific role, it would fit her like a glove. She'd top the bill and be famous overnight.'

Damnation, there he was prattling on about Pola again. He had to muzzle the old goat. 'I don't think she's interested in an international career,' he said bluntly and studied the main courses on the menu. 'Let's order straight away. We've got business to discuss and I'll need to be getting back to Haarlem soon.'

'Perhaps she should be the one to decide,' Biedermann persisted, 'it's an opportunity she won't get in Holland any time soon. The German film industry is simply producing the best films these days.'

Now Lucien was annoyed. 'Don't be so modest, Franz,' he said without looking up. 'Not only films… Your people also produce excellent submarines.'

Biedermann lifted his wine glass to his nose, sniffed noisily and glugged down a small mouthful.

'I don't understand you Germans,' continued Lucien on his impulsive tack. 'By attacking our ships you're only hurting yourselves. That's in no one's interest, especially your own.'

'Come now, Lucien,' interrupted Franz, smiling, 'you know as well as I do that that mistake has long been rectified. We apologized to your government, the shipping company and the factory, and offered handsome compensation for the damages.'

Lucien studied his hands. So they did pay damages, and large sums at that… Why hadn't that damned Jongejan say anything about it? But despite realizing that he'd chosen the wrong weapon, he kept up the attack: 'And so you should. Fact is, an entire shipment of coca leaves is now lying at the bottom of the sea. Your submarines blow anything that floats to kingdom come, and I bet this won't be their last "mistake"… I wonder where you'll get your cocaine then.' Lucien realized he had committed a capital offense. He had broken one of Cremers' cardinal rules: never allude to the company's monopoly, never let on that you have clout, least of all to a German client. 'My dear Franz,' he said, trying to smooth it over, 'you do understand that if our supply of coca leaves is disrupted we can't maintain production.' And to emphasize their shared interest in the situation, he continued in a confidential tone: 'The plantation owners on Java aren't stupid; they're already looking for new and safer markets.' The moment he said it, he knew this last remark was better left unsaid; it had slipped out and now he'd fed Biedermann inside information. This was worse than his first faux pas, and the reason for his clumsiness was that he'd been thrown off balance by all that talk of Pola's film career.

The oysters arrived and Biedermann tucked in. After slurping the first one he grunted appreciatively and asked casually:

'I presume that the loss of just one shipment won't endanger your entire stock?'

'Of course not… Our warehouses are full. But that's not the point,' Lucien reassured him. It struck him that he'd just inadvertently ruined his chance of driving up the price by playing the 'depleted stock' card.

'That's fortunate,' Biedermann said as he slid a second oyster under his moustache. 'Otherwise we'd have to find a way to import coca leaves directly from Java.'

Lucien cursed under his breath. That would be a disaster. Would Merck really try to buy directly from the plantations, despite the international blockade that included the Dutch East Indies? Merck's current cocaine production may have been stymied by the Dutch government's ban on exporting leaves to Germany, but before the war there was no question they'd been a major producer. Indeed, their laboratories were the first to extract alkaloids from coca leaves; they had the equipment and the know-how… Lucien had made a whopper of a blunder. Or had he?

Biedermann dabbed his moustache with a napkin, covered a burp with his hand and grinned at him. 'Lucien, we really don't want to go buying coca directly from the Indies, even leaving aside whether that would be feasible. Too circuitous… And as far as that little accident with the U-boat goes, the captain was for some reason poorly informed about the agreement to leave your ships alone. It really was no more than a bothersome misunderstanding. As soon as I heard about it I asked Merck's management to complain to the Ministry of War. That's why they immediately paid those huge damages.'

Lucien heaved a sigh of relief. Biedermann had been bluffing all along. The Germans were still dependent on Dutch cocaine, and to save face he'd played up his influence at Merck.

The appetizers were cleared away, and Biedermann gave his full attention to the wild duck that appeared at their table. No sooner had the waiter wished them *bon appétit* than Franz jabbed his fork and knife into the breast and served himself a generous portion. Having sated his immediate appetite, he balanced his cutlery on the edge of the plate and said: 'Just to be clear, I must explain something to you. Recent policy dictates that supervision and distribution of cocaine intended for the army fall directly under the responsibility of the Ministry of War. So since my company now takes its orders directly from the ministry, things will be a bit different this time around. The army high command wants the consignment in Flanders as soon as possible, as it's needed on the Western front. So we prefer to avoid a detour via Germany.' To give Lucien time to digest this request, he sank his teeth into a duck wing.

'You want us to deliver the shipment directly to Flanders?' Biedermann nodded and eyed him over the piece of meat between his fingers. So Lucien had been correct in assuming that the Germans, like the English, were in a hurry to replenish their stocks. Perhaps both sides were preparing to intensify the offensive. But he was still surprised that the Germans were so hard up. 'Listen, Franz, this is going to involve a lot of extra paperwork. We're neutral: getting authorization to export directly to the front in Flanders is a tricky business. There's going to be an awful lot of red tape.' Of course, it wasn't a problem at all – Cremers could arrange export papers from The Hague in a trice – but since he'd squandered his chance to jack up the price by pleading a low supply, he had to come up with other specious obstacles like complicated clerical procedures.

'I'll have to discuss this with the management,' he concluded formally.

'Hirschland, we're talking about a big order here. Besides, the city where the shipment is to be delivered is just a few kilometres behind the front.' Biedermann pulled a bone out of his mouth and gazed into his empty wine glass.

'How much do you need?' asked Lucien, waving the empty bottle at the waiter.

'A thousand kilos.'

Lucien watched as a pair of stately swans crossed the small lake. Perhaps the request for such a large order provided him with a new opening. He'd milk it for all it was worth. 'In that case the price per kilo will be higher than normal, because we're talking about a special transaction with a lot of extra paperwork, and of course the transportation costs will be higher too, seeing as we're having to deliver to a dangerous war zone.' As Franz didn't reply immediately he couldn't help adding: 'I can see our driver being shot at because one of your soldiers was "poorly informed" about the agreement not to attack our delivery lorries…' He prepared himself for a sarcastic retort, followed by the customary haggling over the price, but Biedermann's attention was elsewhere. Franz had his eye on an attractive woman who was descending the staircase to the terrace. She walked past them; her face was partially concealed by a wide-brimmed hat with feathers, but they could see she had dark eyes. Like most of the women there, she was wearing an unflatteringly straight-cut dress, but still with an old-fashioned tapered waist, which gave her hips an alluring curve. She was clearly alone.

Franz turned back to Lucien. 'Certainly, no problem at all, I understand completely.'

Lucien was astonished: since when did Biedermann give up without a wrangle? Before he had the chance to reconsider, Lucien whipped out his attaché case, extracted a contract in duplicate and said nonchalantly: 'I'll submit the order, but I can't fill in the amount yet, I still have to confer with the director. I'll ring you as soon as I have an answer.'

Biedermann nodded, signed the contracts and slid them next to Lucien's plate. He scribbled the delivery address on a loose sheet of paper along with some brief directions.

Lucien read the name of a street in Thielt, West Flanders. He'd never heard of it – Albert Ketting would just have to figure it out himself. 'When do you need it?' He tried to work out how far they could crank up the usual price.

Biedermann squinted at the sun, which was just about to disappear behind a dense cloud. 'As soon as possible. Can you arrange to dispatch it from Amsterdam first thing tomorrow morning, so that we have it by the end of the day?'

Lucien stared at Franz in amazement, as though he'd suddenly been transformed into Kaiser Wilhelm himself. 'Are you mad? It'll be evening before I'm home. I can only get to the factory tomorrow morning, and then the export papers have to be arranged… No, forget it, it'll take a couple of days at the very least.'

'*Mein Gott*, Hirschland! You can phone them from here! I'm in a hurry, man, I have to let them know immediately that everything's in order. You said yourself there's enough in stock. What kind of operation are you people running? Surely you can fulfil an order like this in an evening. And as far as all that penpushing is concerned: my experience with you Dutchmen is that bureaucracy suddenly vanishes when there's a decent profit to be made.' He glowered at Lucien. 'I'm not going to let the Ministry down simply because you can't be bothered to make prompt arrangements!'

Biedermann had never used this tone of voice with him before. What an arrogant bastard! Lucien took a few moments to suppress his anger and leave Biedermann on tenterhooks. 'I'll ring from the post office,' he said as he got up.

Biedermann refilled his glass, stretched his arms back over the chair and grinned at him.

Not wanting to be a spoilsport, Lucien laughed: 'You certainly know how to turn on the charm to get your own way!' As he reached for his case, his caught sight again of the woman in the broad-brimmed hat; she noticed his gaze and lowered her eyes. 'What a beauty,' he sighed, pulling on his jacket. Franz nodded in agreement. Lucien leaned toward him and asked in the confidential tone reminiscent of their intimate tête-à-têtes at the gentlemen's club: 'Shall I invite her to keep you company in my absence?'

The surprise with which Biedermann raised his eyebrows could not conceal his eagerness. Lucien went over and had a brief word with the woman. Duly persuaded of the charisma of his German guest, she picked up her handbag and followed Lucien to their table. Franz was already on his feet, kissed her hand and gestured to the empty chair, which she accepted with an obliging smile. Biedermann snapped his fingers at the waiter and asked for an extra glass. Lucien nodded at him: what difference would another bottle make?

When he returned half an hour later, the atmosphere at the table was extremely convivial. Lucien assured his client that all the arrangements had been made. 'It's no problem, we can deliver tomorrow evening, or failing that early the next morning.' In fact, Jongejan had given him an earful over the telephone, ordering him to report to Cremers that very evening. He needed to get back to Amsterdam at the double. That suited him fine, he didn't want to risk Biedermann changing his mind and starting to haggle over the price after all. He apologized for his hasty departure and out of politeness thanked Biedermann for being so understanding. Franz raised no objections and turned his attention back to the lady, who'd confessed to speaking practically no German at all. It hardly appeared to trouble him.

Lucien kick-started the Harley and drove off satisfied. Biedermann would get his order of a thousand kilos of cocaine at an inflated price; let him explain that to the *Kriegsministerium*. Plus, his dalliance with this undoubtedly expensive prostitute would take his mind off any meeting with Pola for the next few hours. Lucien had warned the woman not to bring up the question money until after. His German friend was an incurable romantic.

7

A courageous soldier

It must have been past midnight. Robin was getting worried. How many hours to go… two, three? Then they'd give the signal for a fresh attack, and Charlie wasn't back yet. Two days ago a lieutenant had taken him away; there was a special assignment and Charlie Durban was just the man for the job. Robin hadn't even had the chance to say goodbye properly – why should he, they promised he'd be seeing his mate again soon. The hours ticked by, unnoticed at first, but presently every hour became an endless succession of minutes and seconds. The days dragged on interminably. And still no Charlie. He was refused permission to go look for him. Was he out of his mind? As though there wasn't enough work to be done! He looked out for him while lugging support beams, filling sandbags and repairing collapsed trench walls, and especially when he was sent out to fetch food half a kilometre away. He searched high and low, asked everyone. But no one knew anything, no one had seen him. That night, too, he kept himself awake, not daring to close his eyes, afraid that Charlie wouldn't be able to find him in the dark.

It went without saying that they became bunkmates in the new trench. As soon as dusk fell they huddled together under a tarpaulin, and in their cocoon, the thunder of the guns at a safe distance, Charlie the fixer would bring out the day's booty: biscuits and chocolate, sometimes rum and cigarettes – there seemed no end to his supply. But the main purpose of his daily forays was to do some bartering with a certain medic. Robin wasn't sure what Charlie had to offer, but what he got in return, Robin looked forward to more and more. It got to the point where he couldn't care less about the chocolate or even the rum – it was all about the moment that Charlie, having waved his fist teasingly under his nose, finally opened his hand. And there they were: two pills, sometimes four, once in a while even six. Every evening was a winner. These were their most precious hours, but they had to be careful not to get too boisterous in their conversations.

Even so, things sometimes did get a bit heated, especially when Charlie vented his feelings about the war and the army. He fulminated about the millions of hare-brained imbeciles prepared to die for a freedom they didn't even have a part in. Idiots! Who in his right mind would let himself be blown to smithereens for a bunch of upper-class crooks? Unbelievable! This war served only the interests of the bloody powers-that-be, exploiters – the rest of us were no more than dirt to them! Robin asked him why he'd enlisted in the first place. Apparently it wasn't entirely voluntary, as in Robin's case. Although the more he talked to Charlie about it, the more he wondered about what 'voluntary' really meant. Two years earlier, he'd taken up a challenging teaching post. He'd genuinely set out to cram something of use into the heads of the working-class children from the local slums. It wasn't easy; they were difficult and restless. 'I wanted to understand them, see,' he explained to Charlie, 'so I went round to the homes of the worst troublemakers. But the things I saw there… poverty, drinking, ignorance, you get my drift…' Charlie not only got his drift, it infuriated him. 'I adapted the lessons to try and spark their interest. So that at least a couple of them might have a better future. But it led to terrible rows with the head-master, you know the sort, an old-school authoritarian.'

'I know just what you mean.' Charlie snorted contemptu-ously. 'Typical bloody boarding-school prick.'

'Exactly. For him, a bit of writing and arithmetic was more than enough. You mustn't weigh them down with too much knowledge, otherwise they'll lose their respect for authority. Forget their place.'

'Up against the wall with that bastard!' Charlie kicked the tarpaulin so hard that it made Robin quite nervous. To lighten the tone somewhat he told him about Mary Maclean, a young teacher who also taught at the school. He found he could share his views about a decent education with her, and sometimes his frustration with the headmaster. He confessed to Charlie that he was in love with her. 'Women either go for he-men or ponces, nothing in between…' was Charlie's response. Robin wondered which category he fell into, but Charlie asked if he'd ever taken her down a back alley to discuss his theories in more depth. In truth, it had never got that far, with the exception of a couple of walks and pleasant conversation. This approach won Charlie's approval: 'Clever strategy: soften 'er up first, then get down to the real business.'

But it never got as far as the 'real business', Robin confessed. A year ago the headmaster started making remarks, especially in front of Mary and the other teachers, about the young men serving their country on the front and the others who were taking the easy way out. Weaklings who shirked their duty.

Robin had defended himself: giving youngsters a proper education was a great service to the country. With so many casualties, the younger postwar generation would be vital to the nation, not only in factories but in offices as well. Mary thought he was an idealist, but the headmaster accused him of harbouring suspect socialist ideas that had no place at his school. Not even Mary, who had always stood up for him, could defend him against that. Of course, he understood: she had her own future to think about.

'Well, she was a bit of a let-down,' was Charlie's conclusion. But Robin didn't want him to think ill of her. It was the other teachers, and particularly the headmaster, who were guilty of poisoning the atmosphere and questioning his integrity. Their conversations in the staff room kept harping on about the young men who were ducking their responsibility by not enlisting. They were nothing but conchies, cowards who deserved to be locked up... When Mary tried to help by suggesting they split his class between herself and their colleagues for the duration of the war, the die was cast. He enlisted the following day.

'And then the misery started...' said Charlie.

'My mother was against it. She was furious. But my father brought out the beer. Told me even he'd started to wonder if I was a coward.'

This was the conversation they'd had the night before Charlie disappeared. He suddenly remembered having met James Foyler in the queue for the medical exam. James ran a small bakery two blocks away from his parents' house. While waiting their turn, he told Charlie, he'd tried to convince James to let his young son, a pupil in Robin's class and an excellent student, stay on after primary school instead of putting him straight to work at the bakery. He was a bright lad and might have a promising future. Foyler was open to the idea, he'd give it some thought. 'Nice bloke, James… Where d'you suppose he is now?' he asked Charlie, concerned. 'Surely not tangled up dead in that barbed wire?' Charlie assured him that his baker friend was probably sitting somewhere in a trench, just like them, with a fag in his mouth, shooting the breeze and waiting for the next attack… Of course, Charlie was right, not to worry, when the war was over James would go back to the bakery and he'd go back to his class…

How he missed Charlie. Ever since he left Robin was lonely, afraid and confused. Every muscle in his body ached and the wound in his arm was acting up more than usual. The pain increased by the hour; the wound was infected and if he left it much longer it might turn nasty. And so he went in search of Charlie's friend, the medic, that afternoon. Maybe he knew where his mate had got to? And, by the by, had he by any chance got some of those pills to ease the pain? But the medic had no idea where Charlie-boy was hanging out, and the pills, sorry to say, weren't available at the moment.

What time was it? The balloon was going to go up before dawn. Their regiment was part of the advance guard, which was why they'd been transferred to the forward trench that afternoon. He'd said he couldn't go with them, that he had to wait for his friend Charlie Durban, otherwise they'd never find each other, but the sergeant dismissed him as though he was mad. So here he was now without Charlie, the bombardment getting fiercer by the hour. The ground shook beneath him. How long had Charlie been wandering around looking for him? Robin didn't even know himself where he was in this labyrinth of trenches. Perhaps no one had told Charlie about the new offensive. In that case he was lost, he'd have to face no-man's-land on his own. He couldn't do it without Charlie. He didn't dare. Oh Christ, just a few more hours to go now.

His tongue rasped against the roof of his parched mouth. There was nothing to drink and he was hungry – the watery broth they were given did little to satisfy the appetite. But above all he was tired, dog tired, exhausted from waiting. He had to try to sleep, even for just half an hour. But how could he sleep with all that groaning and wailing going on? He'd been trying to shut it out for hours now. First by putting his fingers in his ears, but he couldn't keep that up. Then with a blanket wrapped around his head, which didn't help at all. The terrible, pitiful groaning penetrated through everything. And someone calling out… At first he wasn't sure, but now there was no denying it, he knew that voice, he'd recognize it out of thousands. It was James Foyler, hanging there, just outside the trench, stuck on the barbed wire. He first heard him, softly and far away, shortly after Charlie disappeared. The keening grew gradually more piercing, and since he'd come back from the medic empty-handed, it had become intolerable. Shouldn't he go and release James from his terrible misery? But it was strictly forbidden to stick your head above the parapet, you'd be a sitting duck for the German sharpshooters. He'd discussed it with Sgt. Farwell, a kind and understanding man. He listened attentively to Robin's story but claimed not to hear James's cries. 'It's your nerves, Ryder, you're hearing voices!' But Robin didn't give up. 'I'll go off my head with all that wailing!' he shouted, so Farwell gave him a mug of rum. That kept James quiet for a bit. But now he'd started up again. The cries went right through him. He even heard Foyler calling his name: 'Robin! Robin Ryder!' Bloody hell, didn't Foyler understand that he couldn't leave the trench! He wanted to, but it wasn't allowed!

Robin began to cry. Next to him a group of soldiers, huddled up in their coats trying to get some sleep, shot him angry looks. 'Shut your mug!' someone yelled. Immediately James fell silent. Robin fought back the tears. Once he was up and out of the trench, he reassured himself, he'd find James easily enough. He saw him clear as day, dangling from the barbed wire in that boggy no-man's-land, the endless, empty Flemish farmland, drenched in terrified sweat, blood and half-decomposed cadavers... How many of them would die this time? According to Charlie more than seven thousand had been left behind on the battlefield last time around. Robin recognized no one from his regiment. They were probably all dead. This was his second battle; he'd survived the first one with no more than a wounded arm. Suddenly it dawned on him that his chances were nil. Simple logic: you had a fifty-fifty chance, and now it was his turn. He wouldn't make it this time...

James was screaming piteously again. Were rats gnawing at his insides? What was the time? Where the hell was that watch he'd got from Dad? Why had he lost all track of time? Suddenly it became clear to him: he was as good as dead! Here he was, a half-dead man who didn't yet realize he no longer belonged to the living. That's why Sgt. Farwell didn't catch on, he simply couldn't understand what he was saying, no one could hear him, he was a zombie. Farwell hadn't heard James either. Of course he couldn't hear him. He was calling from the dead! James... they'd enlisted together, they were dispatched together and they gave their lives together. That's why he was so tired, it explained his desperate urge to sleep. But as soon as he closed his eyes he'd be dragged into Hades. Oh God, he mustn't fall asleep! Away, away, get away from here! He had to flee somewhere out of James's reach. Once out of earshot he wouldn't have to listen to his pleas to join him. But how could he run, his legs were paralyzed, his body showed all the signs of rigor mortis. He screamed. 'I'm dead, I'm already dead!' His shouts dissolved into piercing wails. All at once he fell silent. Was that him? Was that his voice? A couple of soldiers passed by, giving him dirty looks.

Then he remembered. He had to run, death was hot on his heels. 'I have to get out of here! I must go now!' he shouted. He snatched up his gun before the men could grab him. They backed off. No one was going to stop him. He shuffled backwards step by step, his rifle aimed at them, until someone behind seized him by the legs. There was a scuffle. He was fighting for his life. Strong hands restrained him and wrenched the rifle from his grasp. 'Must get out of here...' he sobbed.

'Shut your gob!' hissed Farwell, shoving him to the ground. 'Don't tell me you're one of those weaklings who's going to shit himself at the last minute?'

There are always weaklings who shirk their duty, he heard the headmaster say.

'Jesus Christ man, if an officer hears you, you'll be court-marshalled! You want to be executed? Come on, buck up!' Farwell slapped him twice in the face.

'I'm so proud of you,' said Mary, smiling, on the platform of Great Yarmouth railway station.

Robin shuddered. Someone lit a petroleum lamp. Terrifying faces loomed over him in the flickering light. An older man with a pockmarked face shook his head pityingly. 'It's always the greenhorns who go weak at the knees.'

'By God, if I were a few years younger...' his father said as he opened another bottle of beer.

'What's up with that bastard?' demanded a lieutenant in response to the commotion.

'Just an anxiety attack, lieutenant,' said Farwell without releasing his grip.

'Where's the medic?' The lieutenant looked around. A medical officer was already making his way towards them; he ordered everyone to bugger off and bent over Robin. He reached into his first-aid kit, took out a small bottle, removed the cap and shook it into his hand. 'Open wide!' Robin eyed him with trepidation. He didn't trust him. This wasn't Charlie's friend. This was a stranger. But the medic prised open his jaws, pushed in a tablet and gave him a swig of rum. He watched Robin intently. 'Give "im another one!' insisted Farwell, and a second pill was forced into his mouth. They grabbed him by the armpits, hauled him upright and leant him against the mud wall.

The trembling stopped, his heart pounded and life crept back into his body, radiating up from his ice-cold feet. Robin smiled. Charlie was back. The others crawled back under their blankets. Only Sgt. Farwell stayed with him: 'Take it easy, lad, you'll be feeling better in a jiffy.' What a fine fellow that Farwell was. 'It's good stuff, you'll see, you won't be shitting your pants any longer,' he reassured him.

'I know. May I have some more rum?' Drink made the pills work even better in his experience.

Farwell reached for the yellow flask and raised it to Robin's lips. There wasn't much left. The medic came to check on him. 'Does he have his own bottle?' he asked.

'I don't think so, give him one, otherwise our friend will be without his pills, and we wouldn't want that, would we, Ryder? We want brave soldiers, not sissies.'

Yes, of course, brave soldiers, not sissies… Robin gave Farwell a grateful look. He raised his hand to the others under their blankets. They smiled back. His fatigue, his infinite fatigue rolled back like the tide from a beach. He was back in the trench, his sense of belonging returned, he was at one with his comrades, together in victory! He wanted to tell that to Farwell but he'd already returned to his spot with his long army greatcoat pulled over him. 'Just try to relax, Ryder,' he said.

Relax? How could he relax? Behind his closed eyelids he was being treated to a spectacular fireworks display, coloured sparks spattered every which way, the explosions joining with the thunder of the bombardment to give him a feeling of ecstasy. He opened his eyes. He wasn't at all tired. How much longer now? How long did he have to wait for the whistle? Why all this waiting, damn it, the ladders were ready! He'd prepare his rifle, then polish the bayonet until it gleamed, check his ammo…

At last, at last they were getting ready to move out. The troops, lined up shoulder to shoulder, were being briefed by an officer. He looked impressive in the green glow of a falling flare. His face looked like that of a general in an oil painting, heroic, invincible… Just like this regiment. He mentioned Field Marshal Haig, who he said was certain of victory. Today would be their big breakthrough – hurrah! – the German positions on the Western front would be wiped off the map once and for all – hurrah! – Passchendaele would be taken! – hurrah! – Robin's heart pounded furiously from pure exhilaration and he let himself get carried away by the officer's eloquence. He invoked King, Country and especially God, because God hated the enemy as much as we did, which was why He was on our side. Praise the Lord!, Robin almost cried out loud in his enthusiasm. But he didn't want to interrupt the officer, who by now was extolling the virtues of the British Empire, its sacred mission against the barbarians, against the Krauts, against the Hun! – hurrah! – The officer praised their valour. Who dared doubt that they'd prevail? 'Do your duty, prove that England can be proud of its brave sons, for our soldiers know no fear, only courage!'

Robin was euphoric. He pulled out his bottle and quickly swallowed another tablet. He saw the others do the same. God damn it, enough of this bloody rambling! Why wait any longer! The line bristled with impatience. They could hardly restrain themselves; they were itching to go over the top. Robin was impressed by the single-mindedness of his comrades. They'd crush the enemy like an unstoppable steamroller.

'Men, forward to battle!' roared the officer, his eyes bulging and his face suffused with the glow of victory. His whistle and the cheers were drowned out by the thunder of artillery fire. The soldiers crowded to the ladders, growling and jostling like mad dogs finally unleashed. Their bodies quivered with anticipation. Robin panted heavily, he had to get out, get up the ladder. That was where redemption lay. Out of the trenches! Forward, towards the light! He was convinced he was a model soldier. As soon as he stuck his head above the parapet into the deafening roar and saw the wide vista before him, he was overcome with fury. The enemy! Those dirty German bastards! The enemy emplacements in the distance gave off a red glow. In front of him, the others were running straight through a barrage of explosions. 'We'll skin them alive!' Robin yelled. The soldier next to him wore the expression of a devil, a dark, crazed look in his eyes. They bared their teeth at one another in a shared grimace. Devils, they were! Murderous devils!

Robin hesitated for a second. Who was that fellow next to him? Suddenly, there was a huge blast, and his unknown comrade vanished! No time to stop; Robin ran on blindly, Robin Ryder, the fearless soldier. Was someone calling him? Yes, no doubt about it, someone was calling out his name... Sod off, James! Not now, no time, he had to lay into those German bastards. Look how far he'd got already, my God it was going well! Victory was at hand! An obstacle... he saw how the courageous soldier Ryder clamber over a couple of corpses and wade onward through the red-stained mud. Red as the cheeks of his dear, sweet Mary when she and his entire class had come to wave him off. Now look at him! A proud volunteer admired by all and sundry. A handsome chap too, never turned down on the dance floor, because he could dance, God could he dance! He saw his body duck and weave through the barrage of German grenades, tripping over a wounded soldier. Pillock! He looked at the fellow in astonishment, he hadn't any feet and begged to be put out of his misery. Robin shouted: 'Sorry mate, saving my bullets for the enemy. I've got victory to think about!' He ran further. What idiot loses his feet, anyway? If there's one thing you need in a war, it's your feet. No, he wouldn't be that daft. He was invincible, impervious to bullets! An unquenchable fire burned in his head, his body was an inferno, his heartbeat raced in time with the machine guns.

Suddenly someone grabbed his ankle, a wounded soldier. Robin looked at him, annoyed, and tried to shake his leg free. He was in a hurry, he had to move on, he couldn't afford any delays. Who was this bloke, anyway? He was caked in mud. Why wouldn't he let go? Was he even one of theirs? Or was it the enemy? He certainly looked German. The boy gazed at him with big blue eyes and opened his mouth, but all that came out was a groan. 'Quit moaning!' shouted Robin, 'you're here to die, you fool!' And he stuck his bayonet deep into the boy's belly. With some difficulty he pulled his weapon out and saw the big, surprised eyes glaze over. Poof! Out went the light… Idiot! His leg was finally free. He'd been held up, now he had to make up for lost time. Run faster, run, run, euphoric at having dealt a blow to the enemy! He wanted to scream: finally he was in the thick of battle!

Then someone struck his head with an enormous hammer. All at once, he was somersaulting, clutching vainly at thin air and watching his legs and boots whirl over his head. He floated in mid-air and settled slowly to earth like a single seed head blown from a dandelion in Dad's garden in the spring.

He landed in a soft patch of mud. Winded, he lay there motionless for a few seconds, while above him the clouds parted, revealing a clear blue sky. Sweetly chirping birds flew by carrying long coloured streamers in their beaks. He smiled and saw his pupils. They were still sitting in the classroom, but were looking at him full of anticipation. The morning session was over: class dismissed, it was breaktime.

8

Even Sigmund Freud...

Lucien rubbed the life back into his cheeks. Shivering, he got off the Harley. He'd battled against a bitter wind and drizzle, hunched over the handlebars, all the way back from Arnhem. And he was hungry too – the lunch with Biedermann had been his only meal that day. As he pushed the fogged-up goggles over his cap, he noticed that despite the late hour – it was nearly nine in the evening – the factory was all lit up, with bright electric light streaming out of both the laboratory and the main hall. So, everyone already knew that Hirschland had pulled in another big order. Behind the window of the administrative offices he could see the concentrated beam of a desk lamp, but he preferred to avoid Jongejan for the time being.

As instructed, Lucien went directly to Cremers' office, located in a detached house some distance from the factory and even further removed from the chemical storerooms: in the event of an explosion, only the windows would succumb and not the director himself, who – despite differing opinions on the subject – was irreplaceable. The front door stood ajar, and in the vestibule Lucien removed his wet leather jacket, patted down his damp trousers and tried in vain to stamp the mud off his boots. Never mind: Cremers should see the trouble his commercial traveller went to, that no hardship was too great, no weather too inclement, to promote the interests of the firm.

Lucien knocked on the door, paused for a moment for courtesy's sake and entered. Director Cremers was on the telephone. He was in black evening dress with a starched white collar. Mrs. Cremers, he knew, was an aficionado of music and theatre, and always insisted on having her husband at her side, whether it was convenient or not. So it was not uncommon to see him at the factory in his dinner jacket, sometimes complete with top hat. His staff respectfully refrained from sniggering until the boss and his wife had departed.

His back to the door, Cremers was saying something about an extraordinary situation, and in response to some muffled comments at the other end of the line he promised to do his best to be there after the interval. Lucien retreated discreetly into the doorway. He thanked his lucky stars that Cremers would have to keep their meeting brief. His good lady wife was not known for being an especially understanding woman.

'Come in, Hirschland,' Cremers said impatiently, straightening a penholder and inkwell on his desk. 'So, the Germans have placed a big order and want it delivered tomorrow,' he announced, more succinctly than was his wont. He looked Lucien up and down, with a scowl of disapproval. Lucien handed him the contract, pointing out the precise quantity and the price, which he had filled in on the way back. 'I've charged Biedermann extra to make up for the shipment one of their U-boats sank.' Cremers did not correct him; he'd have assumed news of the hefty damages paid by the Germans had not leaked out yet. 'I hope this meets with your approval.'

Cremers nodded almost imperceptibly. Quite right, quite right, Hirschland. Two large orders in such a short space, excellent, my compliments. But as far as the transportation is concerned… Look here, allowing Kirkpatrick to take his consignment with him, all right, there was nothing to be done about that. But this is a different kettle of fish. I'd have preferred to send the shipment via Germany, as usual.' He tugged on his too-snug bow tie. 'It worries me that the Germans suddenly want their orders delivered directly to Flanders.'

'I only went along with it, sir, to justify the extra delivery charge,' Lucien replied. 'It'll make up for Kirkpatrick. Of course, I also factored in the high fuel prices and the exorbitant shipping costs from Java, which we have to recoup somehow.'

'Quite so. Those bloody freight companies are really sticking it to us. Good that you thought of that, Hirschland.' His index finger hovered above the steep transport fee. 'I'm surprised Biedermann went along with this.'

In fact, Biedermann hadn't gone along with anything: not with Lucien's surcharges, and certainly not with the expensive prostitute's fee. 'He took some persuading,' Lucien said modestly, and paused a moment. 'I trust there's not a problem?'

'That remains to be seen. I gather from Jongejan that the goods are to be delivered close to the German front. He's got his doubts about that, and I'm not so keen on it either. Other Dutch companies do it, but it's something I'd rather avoid. The war could go either way, and whoever wins is going to take a very close look at our neutrality. We've got to think of the future.'

'Nobody has to know who we deliver to, or where.'

'Impossible to keep it a secret. The Allies have an extensive espionage network. They – and the English in particular – won't appreciate our carting the Germans' orders all the way to the front.'

Lucien studied the portrait of Queen Wilhelmina behind the desk. Next to it hung a photograph of a man with a black beard. His name escaped him momentarily. 'With the offensive at Ypres underway, a little extra effort on behalf of the Germans seemed acceptable,' he said in his defence. 'If the English asked us to supply them in Belgium, we'd do that too.'

Cremers shot him a sceptical glance. 'To do that, we'd first have to breach the German lines, which run unbroken from the North Sea to the Swiss border. If that were possible, Hirschland, I do believe we could also win the war.' He went over to a large wall map of the war zone, on which the fronts appeared in wavy blue lines.

'Or isn't there enough time to arrange export authorization?' Lucien asked quickly in an attempt to cover up his witless remark. Joining Cremers in front of the map, he caught a glimpse of a duplicate of the application lying on the desk: *I hereby kindly request permission on behalf of the Netherlands Cocaine Factory N.V. for the export of 50 crates, containing a total of 1000 kg cocaine, to Belgium.'*

'No, Ketting's already on his way back from The Hague,' Cremers responded. 'That's not it...' Lucien waited for him to invoke the name of Mr. W.L. Peereboom, president-director of the Koloniale Bank, the company's de facto owner. Whenever Cremers wanted to convince him of the importance of anything, he'd always mention Peereboom: the factory's godfather, the brains behind the first coca plantations on Java; the man who, with unfailing intuition, had foreseen the unprecedented potential of cocaine. A great man with uncommon foresight, who would not be best pleased with... whatever was at issue at that moment. And if he didn't invoke Peereboom, then it would be the shareholders – Lucien couldn't name a single one, although Cremers had once admiringly referred to a certain major investor who lived in Switzerland but followed the factory's activities closely. 'Heart-warming, the interest she shows,' Cremers sighed. 'She regards the factory almost as her own baby.' Lucien thought that was a strange way to put it.

'The thing is, Hirschland, the Dutch-Belgian border region has become a sort of Wild West. It's crawling with dangerous smuggling operations. We're responsible for the cargo until it's delivered to its destination, you understand. And as far as Flanders goes: that's a war zone, and I'm not fond of war zones. They tend to be highly unpredictable.' As he studied the map he asked over his shoulder: 'Where exactly does it have to go?'

'Thielt, some town or other south of Ghent. A fair distance from the front, as far as I know.'

'Well, well, Thielt.' Cremers's finger slid down from Amsterdam and pinpointed the city just below Ghent. Lucien said, 'You see, sir? Kilometres from the German trenches. Nothing more than a Flemish *dorp*, a safe way-station.'

Cremers wheeled around. 'Thielt, Hirschland! Thielt is the headquarters of the German Fourth Army, their key unit in the region! The high command, Sixt von Armin, is stationed there. It's the base for military operations in the whole of West Flanders!'

Lucien cursed under his breath. Biedermann might be rollicking in bed with a pricey whore, but he was definitely the one who'd been screwed.

'I believe it's a *Sperrgebiet*...' continued Cremers.

'Restricted area, fine, but no fighting there, surely?'

'No, true enough. But once things flare up there, it's curtains for the Germans.'

Lucien felt another wave of embarrassment wash over him.

Being a brilliant salesman was one thing, but his knowledge of the current military situation left a lot to be desired. Irritated with himself, and in an attempt to extricate himself from this awkward situation, he said impetuously: 'Maybe I should accompany this delivery personally; then you'd have the guarantee that it'd get there safely.'

Cremers furrowed his brow. But Lucien persisted: 'I lived in the Indies for years; I've been in tighter spots than this before. I often had to deal with sticky situations in the kampongs, and let me tell you, sir, those aren't the safest places on earth.'

The telephone rang. Cremers closed his eyes for a moment and answered. 'Certainly, dear, of course, yes, I'm almost finished. Everything will be fine.'

Lucien turned to the portrait of the bearded man next to the queen. *Alles sal reg kom.* Of course: Paul Kruger, former president of the Orange Free State, who, thanks to Queen Wilhelmina, was able to rally support for the Boer Republic in South Africa. Thank goodness, he wasn't so ignorant of current events after all.

Cremers covered the receiver with his hand and turning to Lucien, said tersely: 'That's settled then. You'll go along. Make arrangements with Ketting and go and see Olyrook.' He dismissed him with a wave, but the conversation with Mrs. Cremers was already over before Lucien shut the door behind him. The last he heard was, 'I've got my coat on already, dear.'

Lucien strode angrily across the courtyard, kicking an empty chemical drum as he went. It reacted like a startled skunk, emitting a gust of ammonia. How could he have been so stupid as to make such an offer! Yes Mr. Cremers, of course Mr. Cremers, I'll go there myself Mr. Cremers! Remember my vast experience in the kampongs and how cleverly I resolved things there. Getting into drunken fistfights with a bunch of natives who beat the daylights out of me and left me to lie in the mud half the night. Bugger! Instead of having a quiet dinner at home and crawling into bed with a whisky and a cigar after what had already been a long day, he was facing another long slog.

He knocked at the porter's lodge near the dock, where Albert Ketting and his wife lived, and was welcomed in at once. A tempting smell of food filled the house. 'You're hungry, I can tell,' said Mrs. Ketting. Her friendliness melted his ill humour. Without waiting for an answer she led him to the table and dished up a plate of steaming *stamppot*.

The meal warmed him. As he ate, Mrs. Ketting cleaned and buffed his boots, and put his jacket to dry in front of the wood-burning stove, where a kettle of water was boiling. He thanked her from the bottom of his heart and told Ketting how lucky he was to have such a caring wife.

'We leave tomorrow morning at four o'clock sharp,' he growled. 'Don't be late.'

Lucien sighed as he closed the door behind him. The idea of being cooped up with the surly Ketting for the next two days… He took a short cut through the factory on his way to the lab. Work there was still in full swing; the steam engine was going like the clappers. He stuck his head round the corner of the storeroom, where coca leaves, chemicals and tools were kept. A rinsing-boy quickly stubbed out his cigarette and swatted frantically at the smoke. Lucien gave him an angry look. 'You might want to wait for New Year's Eve for the fire-works display, idiot.' He considered reporting the boy to the foreman, but the hot meal had made him too sluggish to cause a fuss. He went through to the extraction room. All twenty kettles were in use; it stank of kerosene and hydrochloric acid. Personnel in brown overalls bustled to and fro, checking pressure gauges. During his first tour of the factory, Olyrook had explained the production process: the liquid extracted from the coca leaves was pumped into sealed stirring drums, where the precious raw alkaloid was treated in an acid aqueous solution. All he remembered from the subsequent stages was that the brew was boiled, shaken, stirred, neutralized, filtered and distilled, poured into separating funnels and soaked in alcohol, dissolved in ether and re-filtered. One last distillation released the final product: crystallized cocaine hydrochloride. It was an extremely thorough and exacting process, and Lucien was so impressed with it that he'd dubbed Olyrook 'the black magician of the white powder'. But the laboratory chief liked to compare himself with the sixteenth-century alchemist Paracelsus, who saw alchemy not as a means of creating gold, but medicine. 'And *voilà…*' Olyrook laughed, 'in the process of creating medicine, we struck gold!'

Lucien found Olyrook in the main laboratory. He was standng at a scales built into a glass cabinet to prevent even a single grain of the precious powder being lost. Although not yet fifty, Thomas Olyrook already had the stoop of an old man and terrible eyesight. He virtually had to press his thick horn-rimmed spectacles against the glass in order to weigh the powder with precision. His view was further impeded by a thick head of hair that tumbled over his eyebrows.

Lucien made his way between the work surfaces laden with mixing containers, funnels, measuring beakers, bellows and flasks. 'Keep your mitts off the equipment!' Olyrook called out without looking up.

'And you just take care you don't botch it!' Lucien retorted.

'I'm supposed to deliver this shipment to Flanders tomorrow in person, and I don't want the Krauts accusing me of diddling them.'

Olyrook looked up, surprised. 'So you're going yourself. Very brave. Up for anything, aren't you?'

'Yes, I quite fancy the idea,' Lucien said. He was suddenly looking forward to the trip. 'Straight through the *Sperrgebiet* to Thielt, headquarters of the German Fourth Army you know, it's where all the bigwigs are.' He couldn't quite remember the name of that general.

'You've got a personal audience with *Herr General* Sixt von Armin, then?'

'Not really, I've got to make the drop at a convent somewhere.'

'Cocaine for the Carmelites?'

'Ha ha... No, there's a medical stockroom somewhere behind the church.'

Olyrook closed the glass cabinet and took off his white coat.

'Is everything ready for tomorrow?' asked Lucien.

'The shipment's being packed now, so you can move out first thing. This here is for a French client. What time do you leave?'

Lucien lingered for a moment, picked up a flask with blue liquid in it and held it up to the light. Olyrook plucked it out of his hands. 'Tomorrow at 4 a.m.!' As he said it he realized there was no point going back to Haarlem now. 'I'll have to kip here,' he said peevishly, 'and I've nothing with me.'

'You can use my dressing room. Shall I bring you some shaving things from home?' Olyrook offered, 'and maybe a change of clothes? You're not going on a business trip in that motorcycle outfit.'

'Thanks, Thomas, much appreciated.'

'You can eat well around Ghent, if you know where to go. I'll give you a few addresses. I might even know of a good hotel in Thielt.' Lucien was about to ask if he'd ever been there, but he suddenly thought of Swanny. He'd have to ring her up to say he wouldn't be coming home that night, and probably not the next one either.

While Lucien was sitting at Olyrook's desk fibbing to his sister that he had to go to Maastricht and promising – cross his heart! – to be back in time for her soirée, Olyrook gestured to a mattress and some blankets behind a chair, put on his coat and left the room.

After he'd hung up, Lucien sat down on the edge of the makeshift bed, unlaced his boots, flung them into a corner and stretched out on a blanket that smelled of chemicals. Odd that Thomas kept a mattress and bedding in his dressing room. Maybe he took the occasional catnap, or perhaps even stayed overnight – strange, though, considering that he lived in that magnificent townhouse with the beautiful gable on the Weesperzijde, just a short walk from the factory. Was it still chock-full of antiques, he wondered. And did he still have that reclusive lodger? When had Thomas last invited him around? Of course, it was shortly after they'd met at Het Nederlandse Veem, where cargo ships from the colonies were unloaded. His first stop back in the Netherlands, a fresh repatriate with the fragrant scent of the East Indies still in his pores. He remembered feeling somewhat bereft as he watched the stevedores lugging crates and bales down the gangplank to the quayside. As he stood there with the swell of the sea still in his legs, he pondered what life had to offer him now.

Looking back on it, the man with the stooped shoulders had read his mind exactly. He cast him only the briefest of glances before turning his attention back to his consignment, opening one bag at a time to check their contents before they were taken to the warehouse. He fingered the leaf-dust, took a pinch with his fingers, smelt and tasted it. Having nothing better to do, Lucien struck up a conversation, asking the man if this was a new kind of tea. 'No, it's far better than tea,' came the answer. They fell to chatting: about the Indies, his return trip, the death of his father, a whole range of subjects. And then Thomas Olyrook had inquired after his future plans. Lucien admitted to being without work and handed Thomas his card, in case he heard of anything. Maybe a job in this 'better than tea' business would suit him. Olyrook recognized the surname immediately from his father's publishing company. Olyrook might be aware of the bankruptcy, so he made up a story of having been sent to the Dutch East Indies because his father didn't want him meddling in the business – a pity, perhaps the company wouldn't have gone bust if he'd been allowed to stay and meddle.

Two days later they met again. They had a drink at a club and Thomas asked whether he'd found work yet. 'I'm taking care of my father's estate and then... who knows, what with the mobilization and all. I'm afraid of being called up for border patrol. That's the last thing I want to do. I haven't got the makings of a soldier, I'd sooner point my gun at an animal than a person. On Java, you know, we often went hunting.' He spun a particularly exciting yarn that ended with a single well-placed bullet and a dead tiger. Once the tiger had ended up as a rug in the home of the governor-general, Olyrook got down to business: 'Would you be interested in coming to work for us? I assume you speak some foreign languages?'

'Of course. English, French, German and Malay.'

Olyrook nodded approvingly. 'Just what we need. What's more, you've got looks, manners and a vivid imagination.'

Olyrook had wasted no time in preparing the ground and Cremers, the technical director, was already persuaded by the time Lucien showed up for his interview. All he needed now was a crash course in cocaine. After a tour of the factory and lab, Olyrook invited him to his home, where he was initiated in the secrets of the product before embarking on his new career as a sales rep.

At Olyrook's townhouse on the Weesperzijde, dinner was prepared by one Jan Palacky, a young Czech who cooked and cleaned for Olyrook in return for board and lodging. The stockpile of antiques must have made housekeeping quite a chore, and judging by the sour face of the otherwise handsome Czech, he was of similar mind. Lucien suspected that the young lodger took his revenge by preparing some quite inedible dishes and presenting them in his thick accent as traditional Czech cuisine. The glare he shot Olyrook as he plonked the dishes down on the table was so spiteful that Lucien could imagine the day when he'd lace Thomas's food with arsenic. Jan Palacky would see that as poetic justice for a crafty chemist.

After the meal the two of them settled into comfortable armchairs with large snifters of cognac. Jan was constantly called back to refill their glasses, but as the evening went on he pointedly sloshed so much over the side that Olyrook finally invited him, with a sigh, to join them. Meanwhile Olyrook expounded on the history of coca plant, which for centuries had been used for ceremonial purposes by South American Indians, who had nothing better to do all day than sit around chewing on the leaves. Only in the last century had a German chemist discovered, after much experimenting, that alkaloid could be extracted from the leaves. Whereupon an enterprising businessman shipped a few plants from Peru to Java, where they were propagated in the botanical gardens at Buitenzorg. 'It was in a Dutch laboratory that the leaves revealed their truly magical qualities. The Indians regarded the plant as sacred, but we raised its status to divine,' Thomas announced – and Lucien suspected that Olyrook himself had tasted its heavenly virtues. Then he got down to business: 'Most clients are well aware of the efficacy of the product. Your job is to push the quantity. People think they can make do with a small amount, a gram or two at a time. You have to make it clear that you can only achieve the desired effects with regular and long-term use, especially when the aim is to get a patient back on his feet. You can always suggest to a hesitant client that he try it for himself – nothing works as convincingly as a sample.' Thomas had neatly, with obvious enjoyment, and with much unsolicited help from Jan Palacky, provided Lucien with an array of arguments he could use to coax clients into ordering more than they intended. It had been a convivial evening, and thereafter he always felt comfortable with Thomas, although he'd never been invited to his house since.

Olyrook returned to the dressing room holding a small valise under one arm and, draped over the other, a suit that looked several sizes too small for him. With his free hand he carried a covered dish, which he introduced briefly as 'plum pie, one of Jan's culinary exploits. Traditional Czech cuisine, he tells me. Well, it'll fill you up, anyway.' Lucien resolved not to touch it.

Olyrook opened the valise and placed three bottles of jenever on the table. 'Might be useful along the way, you never know who you'll have to make friends with. In fact, let's christen one right now.' He opened one of the bottles and took two glasses down from a cabinet. Thomas was obviously in no hurry, because from the same cabinet he produced a box of cigars. He pulled up a chair and soon the room was filled with bluish smoke. Reassuringly industrious sounds wafted in from the factory.

'Do you remember that evening three years ago, when you taught me how to promote our product? Lucien asked, knocking back a mouthful of jenever. It burned pleasantly in his throat.

Olyrook laughed. 'You were pretty green as a salesman.'

'Remember the tips you gave me?'

Olyrook shook his head.

Lucien made himself comfortable. Holding his glass casually in one hand, he took a pull on his cigar and blew two perfect smoke rings. 'Should you ever encounter someone who still harbours doubts concerning our product…' he began, mimicking his mentor's speech, 'then you must parry their scepticism with certain well-known names who have sung the praises of cocaine as the wonder drug of the age. Sigmund Freud always works well with German clients… You should simply mention that the esteemed client, while undoubtedly acquainted with the world-famous psychiatrist and founder of psychoanalysis, is perhaps unaware that *Herr Doktor* Freud, having experimented extensively with cocaine on himself, his friends and patients, wrote a glowing report of his agreeable effects: *Über Coca*, a classic treatise, highly recommended. With your English clients you should mention Robert Louis Stevenson. Weakened and exhausted from a bout of TB, he wrote the masterpiece *The strange case of Dr. Jekyll and Mr. Hyde* in just six days, aided by the white powder so carefully administered by his loving wife. And never forget to bring up the famous detective Sherlock Holmes, praised far and wide for his intelligence and insight: another habitual cocaine user. The fellow might be purely fictional, but your clients won't care. That's the beauty of our product: no need for boring sales pitches like for agricultural equipment…'

'All it takes is a little imagination,' continued Olyrook himself, smiling as he refilled their glasses.

'You were right,' said Lucien. 'Still, I've never needed to call on Freud, Stevenson or Holmes. Buyers are only interested in quality, price and prompt delivery.'

'You can thank the war for that. These days buyers hardly need to be talked into ordering the stuff.'

'That's what I keep telling my sister. Like me, she's extremely wary of medicines. I always tell her: first and foremost, it's a really effective painkiller, indispensable on the front. Without our product, wounded soldiers would suffer unnecessarily and hospital personnel wouldn't know where to turn. It's my chief selling point.'

'You don't say!' Olyrook laughed out loud. 'That's rich! Little sisters always believe what big brother tells them!'

Lucien was taken aback. Was Olyrook pulling his leg? His older colleague stood up, picked up the bottle and thumped him on the shoulder. 'You're a decent chap, Lucien. Without a doubt the best salesman we've ever had, there's no better advocate for our product.' He split the remainder of the bottle between their glasses. 'But of course you're completely right, our product is indispensable on the front. It's by far the best painkiller there is.' He raised his glass. 'To the soldiers in the trenches!'

9

Grand Hôtel de la Gare

A firm hand roused him from his slumber. Lucien groggily swung an arm in the direction of the disturbance, rolled over and pulled the blanket up under his chin. Again he felt himself being shaken by the shoulder and when he managed to pry open his eyes Albert Ketting was standing over him, scowling. Where on earth… In the glow of Ketting's lantern he saw two white lab coats hanging on a coat rack. Ah, Olyrook's dressing room. As he pulled himself upright he rubbed his neck and forehead, which felt stiff and aching. He felt like his brain was about to implode. 'What time is it?' he croaked.

'Four o'clock, sir, like we said.' Disapproval oozed from Ketting's every word.

Lucien couldn't decide what he regretted more: last night's drinking binge with Olyrook, who was nowhere to be seen, or his offer to accompany Ketting to Flanders. How could he have been such a fool? Now he had to drag himself out of bed in the dead of night to embark on a road trip with a throbbing hangover. And to a *Sperrgebiet* at that: the word alone made him shiver. For a brief moment he considered crying off, claiming he was too ill to travel, but the empty jenever bottle and full ashtray on the table would not have escaped Ketting's notice, and Mr. Cremers would surely take a dim view of him wriggling out of the deal with a lame excuse.

Half an hour later, dressed comfortably in Jan Palacky's suit, he slid into the passenger seat of the lorry. Ketting was fresh, alert and thoroughly prepared for the journey. A map lay across his lap and judging from the smell of petrol that permeated the cab from the cargo space, he'd had the foresight to bring spare cans of fuel. A bottle of water and lunch box was propped behind his seat: the ever-considerate Mrs. Ketting had apparently seen to the provisions. But food was the last thing on Lucien's mind, only water. His mouth was bone dry and his tongue felt like a flap of old leather. He took the bottle and emptied it in a single gulp.

'Well, that'll want refilling,' Ketting remarked coolly.

'Sorry about that, I had a long meeting with Olyrook…'

Ketting sniffed and placed his hands high up on the steering wheel.

The lorry was heavily laden and slow-moving, and Lucien reckoned it would be several hours before they reached the border. It was still dark, and there was nothing to see outside, so he decided to take forty winks, even if just to avoid having to converse with Ketting, who kept his eyes fixed on the road, his jaw clenched. Once they'd crossed the border and his stomach had settled, he'd get a decent breakfast, although he wondered if Albert would be allowed into a good restaurant in his work clothes.

Ketting gave him a shove on the leg. 'Wake up, we've already passed Roosendaal.'

Lucien was slumped against the window. He smacked his dry lips several times, hauled himself up into a less awkward position, looked outside and then sat bolt upright. Not a moment too soon: the Dutch border post was already in sight.

Ketting pulled over and Lucien climbed out, smoothing down his jacket and trousers as best he could, running his fingers through his tousled hair and clamping his attaché case under his arm. A group of uniformed men stood in front of the customs office; three of them, two constables and one border patrol guard, made their way toward him. To their questioning, he responded, 'I'm on my way to Ghent with commercial goods,' in a businesslike but courteous tone. He decided against mentioning the German headquarters. Now that he was committed to the journey it seemed more exciting, even a bit adventurous, to keep their destination a secret.

One of the constables accompanied him to the customs office, where border guards and customs agents were loitering around. Behind the desk marked *Special Customs Officer for Direct Taxation, Import and Excise Duties* sat a man who did his utmost to live up to his job title. On seeing Lucien, whom he pegged at once as a salesman from the city, he puffed up his chest and placed his hands fingertip to fingertip. Lucien wished him a respectful good morning and slid the export papers across the desk. The man studied them intently, read them through twice and even put on his pince-nez for a third perusal.

Lucien looked around the office, his thumbs stuck loosely behind the lapel of his jacket. In the furthest corner stood a respectable-looking couple. Apparently they also wished to cross the border but had run up against a problem – quite likely a problem that was sitting behind a desk. The woman's arm rested demonstratively in the man's elbow. They stood at attention, determined not to surrender their pride, even if it meant being dragged off to the lock-up.

The customs officer had removed his spectacles and had just

opened his mouth to speak when a tumult erupted outside. The border guards left the room at once to see what all the fuss was about. Lucien peered through the window to see if his vehicle might be the cause of the disturbance. But Ketting had planted himself squarely in front of the lorry's rear doors, arms crossed and legs slightly apart. 'What's going on?' Lucien asked the clerk, who answered with an irritated shrug of the shoulders. 'We've had a hell of a lot of trouble with smugglers. Bloody nuisance, and it's only getting worse. Now these blokes even come armed with clubs and hunting rifles. Since the siege started we fortunately have a mobile unit, and they manage to intercept a lot of it. They hit the jackpot again yesterday…'

The ruckus outside grew louder. There was a volley of shouting and cursing, and several young men made threatening gestures, their caps pulled down low over their eyes.

The customs officer got up from his desk and stood next to Lucien. 'Our people shot a smuggler from the next village last night. Damned unpleasant business. This morning our officers brought the bloke's body to his parents' house. So now the locals are hopping mad. Hardly surprising, of course.'

'What kind of things are they smuggling?' asked Lucien.

'Oh, you name it, anything and everything… food, mostly.'

'There's nothing left to eat in Belgium,' chimed in the respectably-dressed man in the corner, 'and these so-called smugglers are just trying to earn a few extra cents. Their families are hungry too.' The clerk ignored him. Lucien glanced over his shoulder and thought: Looks like we're here for the long term. 'The law's the law,' the clerk said to Lucien. 'Smugglers have to be dealt with rigorously.'

'By gunning them down?' The man wouldn't give up.

'Isn't there enough bloodshed these days?' his wife added,

indignantly. The clerk exchanged a glance with a border guard who had remained behind, and the couple was hustled unceremoniously into an adjacent room.

'Socialists, I'll bet.' He went back to the window. The situation outside the office had escalated. Soldiers were aiming their rifles at the screaming mob. Ketting had already climbed back behind the wheel and drove right up to the border gate, away from the hubbub. Another soldier had positioned himself protectively alongside the lorry. 'We're in rather a hurry,' said Lucien, 'is this going to take long?' The clerk kept watching the commotion outside. 'As long as it takes,' he replied evenly. The crowd of young men inched defiantly towards the soldiers. Lucien experienced a frisson of excitement: from the safety of the office. It was as though he were watching a scene from an action film. He wondered if they would come to blows, and who would come out on top – although the locals, despite outnumbering the soldiers, were unarmed and so at a clear disadvantage.

It appeared that the mob came to the same conclusion, for it backed off, cursing. The clerk returned to his desk with a sigh and read aloud from the export papers: 'Pharmaceutical articles…' He reached for a thick book, thumbed through it, and since he did not appear to find what he was looking for, Lucien volunteered: 'Cocaine.'

The clerk nodded.

'Not suitable for military use,' Lucien added.

The man stamped the papers. 'In order. You can drive through.'

'Are we far from the German border control?' Lucien asked as he buckled up his attaché case.

'A bit further on, but they won't detain you. They know the cargo is for them and not for the Belgians. Safe trip.'

Before stepping outside, Lucien peered around to see if the rabble was still hanging around. Ketting had already spotted him and waved to him that the coast was clear. 'That was a close call,' he said. 'I really thought they were going to lay into those soldiers.'

'Nah, just a gang of pumped-up lads. Seems a smuggler was shot dead last night.'

'I heard,' answered Ketting pensively. 'A boy of seventeen.'

As they drove through the barrier it occurred to Lucien that the palaver had cost them a good three-quarters of an hour. Hopefully it'll go more quickly this time, he thought as they approached the German border post. A pair of older-looking soldiers – unfit for active service, to judge by their bandaged arms and heads – sauntered up to the lorry. Lucien threw open the door, bounded off the running board onto the ground, and announced in flawless German that he had a delivery for the *Oberkommando* in Thielt, on the orders of the *Kriegsministerium*. The elder of the two leafed through the papers and Lucien instructed Ketting to let them to examine the cargo. But the soldiers were less interested in the cargo than in the bottle of jenever he had strategically placed in front of the crates. 'You only drink beer, I suppose?' Lucien proffered with a smile. They didn't even take the trouble to answer. 'You don't mean to say you like Dutch jenever!' he asked with feigned amazement. The two exchanged tired glances and without a word took the bottle and handed Lucien back his papers.

'Damn, what a waste of good jenever!' Lucien exclaimed once they had entered Belgian territory. 'Olyrook and his advice! Totally pointless!'

'Glad to be rid of the stuff. One hangover's enough for this trip, if you ask me.'

'Do you belong to the temperance movement or something?' Lucien snapped. He didn't appreciate being reprimanded by someone like Ketting. 'How long till we're in Ghent?' He was in need of breakfast and plenty of black coffee.

'Not more than two, three hours.'

Lucien managed to sleep until then. He awoke revitalized, but his empty stomach made him slightly dizzy. He thought ruefully of the Czech plum cake he'd thrown away, and cast a furtive glance at the lunchbox behind the driver's seat. Albert nodded.

While Lucien helped himself to the sandwiches and water – Ketting had refilled it along the way – he studied the passing Flemish countryside. He'd never seen it before. It more or less resembled a Dutch landscape, except for the badly damaged farmhouses and the fallow farmland in between. The villages were nearly deserted, aside from the odd shabbily-dressed figure here and there. There was an all-pervading atmosphere of gloom: entire buildings and even churches were battered and dilapidated, and many of the houses were in ruins. And not a restaurant in sight.

The traffic gradually increased as they approached Thielt. At first they were overtaken by army vehicles carrying soldiers and equipment, and before long military police waved them off the road. Ketting concentrated on manoeuvring the heavy lorry so that at least two wheels remained on the gravel; you never knew how much weight the muddy verge could take. In the end, though, a furious soldier forced them to pull completely onto the shoulder.

Lucien watched as a long column of soldiers with heavy packs marched past. There was something impressive about the uniformity of their appearance and kit, the co-ordination of their movements, the rhythmical stomping of boots. An army that had overrun half of Europe, the invincible Teutonic military machine he only knew from magazines and cinema newsreels, was marching past the cab window. He pictured himself in military garb, not the drab Dutch or German kind, but the trim-cut white regalia worn in the tropics. He'd only want to serve in an army where the officers wore elegant uniforms with gold galloon draped over the chest and shoulders, ostrich plumes protruding from a bicorne, and a long sabre that slapped against your calves as you walked. He studied the passing German soldiers more closely. Most of them, he noted with surprise, were young, much younger than himself – big children, in fact. Pale faces under heavy helmets, glazed expressions and mechanical movements. They looked chin-strapped and vulnerable.

After an hour he had lost all interest in the interminable ranks of troops and columns of transport vehicles, and sat slumped in his seat, yawning, when Ketting suddenly gunned the engine. The lorry jerked off the shoulder and back onto the road. They proceeded slowly so as not to catch up to the convoy. Their first glimpse of Thielt were enormous rolls of barbed-wire barricades as far as the eye could see. Heavily-armed soldiers checked the papers of a long queue of civilians at an opening in the barrier just short of the city. Two young men had been taken aside and were being held at gunpoint. As they waited, Lucien heard the purr of aeroplanes overhead as they banked and descended towards the outskirts of the town. Fokker triplanes, Albatrosses and Halberstadts. He'd have loved to see them up close. After motorbikes, aircraft were his passion.

When they finally reached the checkpoint Lucien presented

the papers while Albert opened the cargo bay for inspection. They were ordered to open a crate and remove one of the vials from the wood-wool packing. Lucien struggled to convince the officer in charge that this was a pharmaceutical product intended for their medical services and that the contents of the vials mustn't be exposed to the open air.

They were stopped and searched three more times before they reached the town centre. Lucien was beginning to lose his patience; when they were ordered to open yet another crate, Ketting reminded him to keep calm: 'This isn't just any city, sir, it's a military base staffed by their top brass.'

They drove over bumpy cobblestone streets; the thick bundles of telephone cables stretched along the front of the houses all appeared to lead to a single point. Lucien imagined Sixt von Armin sitting calmly at the centre of this enormous web, awaiting news of victory from his generals. Thunder rumbled in the distance, a few kilometres away. Lucien looked up at the threatening sky and hoped the storm would only break once they had reached their destination.

'We'll have to ask for directions,' Ketting said, reducing his speed. They pulled up alongside a high-ranking officer with an umbrella under his arm. Lucien opened his door, greeted him deferentially and told him the address, specifying that they needed to be at the Paterskerk behind the Franciscan monastery. He added that they were delivering medical supplies from Holland. The officer called to a soldier who, after being given brief instructions, squirmed uninvited into the cab next to Lucien. They soon reached the church, and alongside it, the monastery. Not a single monk in sight, but plenty of German officers. After one last sharp turn the soldier instructed Ketting to stop in front of a building with large wooden doors. He leapt out of the lorry, shouted something, and as though they'd been expected all along, the doors immediately swung open and the soldier waved them inside.

They were approached by a smiling military man, his uniform jacket casually unbuttoned. He shook Lucien's hand and introduced himself as Peter Wammeier, a medical pharmacist and staff officer from the medicine reserve depot. Albert had already opened the rear doors and a couple of soldiers clambered in. Lucien apologized for their lateness, explaining that the roads were terribly busy, but as Wammeier's attention was distracted by the unloading operation, Lucien added: 'Of course, that's to be expected in a *Sperrgebiet*.'

'*Sperrgebiet*?' Wammeier beckoned a soldier to bring him one of crates. 'Oh no, the entire region has been declared an *Operationsgebiet* for several weeks now.' He dismissed the soldiers and instructed Albert to open the crate.

'So that would explain the constant checkpoints,' Lucien said blithely.

'Danger of espionage, you know. Everyone has to be checked, friends included,' Wammeier laughed as he watched Ketting remove a vial from the wood wool and hand it to Lucien. He broke the seal and removed the glass stopper. Producing a little spatula, he scooped out a small amount of powder and carefully passed the spatula to the staff officer. Wammeier pressed a wet finger into the powder and touched it to the tip of his tongue. He stood for a moment with his head bent forward and then nodded, satisfied. 'You Dutch deliver good stuff.' He clapped Lucien jovially on the shoulder. The vial was returned to the crate and Ketting resealed it. Wammeier signed the receipt and Lucien, relieved, asked about the situation at the front.

'It's rough going,' answered Wammeier, 'but it won't be long now… we'll be forcing a breakthrough soon. By the way, did you have any trouble finding us?'

'No, Herr Biedermann provided excellent instructions.'

'Good old Franz…' Wammeier laughed loudly. 'You can certainly count on him.'

Lucien recoiled a bit, astonished. 'You know each other?'

'Of course, we worked together for many years. Franz is the best chemist around.' Wammeier guffawed again for no apparent reason.

'Chemist?'

'You bet, and a fine one too! The very best! He was the head of the laboratory when I first went to work at Merck as a junior lab assistant. The man's a genius!'

'Good Lord, I had no idea,' said Lucien. He wondered why such a brilliant chemist, a laboratory chief at that, would be working as a commercial buyer.

'You've just missed him, by the way,' Wammeier said nonchalantly. 'He was at HQ but I believe he left for Berlin a few hours ago.'

How on earth…? Did Biedermann go directly to Thielt from Arnhem? Why didn't he say anything? Left a few hours ago… He knew the shipment would be delivered today. Why hadn't he waited for it? Then he could have taken delivery of the cocaine and tested it himself; he was always so keen on that…

'I only know Franz Biedermann as a buyer for Merck,' Lucien said cautiously.

'Naturally! You don't think Franz would leave that to anyone else, do you?' Again Wammeier gave his strident laugh. 'So where are you two lodging?' he asked.

'In Ghent, I suppose,' answered Lucien, remembering

Olyrook's list of good restaurants, though right now his urge to get out of Thielt outweighed his appetite. He couldn't put his finger on it, but this place gave him the creeps. He was unnerved by the presence of all these Germans, and the city was suddenly overshadowed by the obscure figure of Franz Biedermann.

'You'll never make it. The roads are jammed in the evening, and besides, there's an obligatory blackout from 9 to 6 as well as a night-time curfew. That goes for you too, my dear friends. Why not stay here? I can arrange something for you in the monastery, it gets quite jolly here in the evening!'

'No thanks, that won't be necessary,' said Lucien hastily, 'we'll find a hotel.'

'There aren't many hotels in business anymore. Most have had to shut down. Dirty Belgian whores and the like... our boys kept coming back with the clap.' Wammeier's laugh thundered through the space again, and Lucien's only thought was to get away as quickly as possible. 'But you could try the hotel across from the station. Lots of officers stay there and the food is good.'

Good food, that was something at least. Lucien nodded to Ketting, and as he climbed into the passenger's seat Wammeier promised to let Franz know the shipment had arrived in good order, and said he'd pass on Lucien's greetings.

They turned into the alley alongside the monastery, following Wammeier's instructions. Lucien glanced over at Albert, who hadn't said a word since they'd stopped to ask for directions earlier. 'Decent fellow. That's some laugh he's got,' he said, trying to break the ice. But Ketting remained silent.

They drove parallel to the railway tracks, where a locomotive pulling a long line of freight wagons stood stationary.

Thundering from the opposite direction – the east, most likely Germany – were freight trains laden with tree trunks and sawn planks, followed by flat-bed rolling stock carrying heavy artillery. 'Cannons for the Yser front,' Ketting said so unexpectedly that it made Lucien jump. Presently they got caught up in a chaotic hubbub in front of a nondescript-looking train station. It must have been a transport hub of some significance, as it appeared to lie on a major railway line serving the German Fourth Army. The teeming mass of soldiers made it impossible for them to get across the square.

Determined to sound out the situation, Lucien got out and pushed his way through the crowd. Behind the waiting soldiers, a stream of horse-drawn carts and ambulances was bringing in the wounded. Medical personnel unloaded one stretcher after the other, depositing them in front of the terminal. The walking wounded, their eyes covered with bandages, shuffled forward, hand to shoulder, in cautious single file.

Lucien felt like he was drowning in the pandemonium: the clatter of the passing trains, the howl of the steam locomotives, orders being screamed, medics running to and fro trying to calm the wounded, and the heavy rumble of a storm in the distance. Through all this came the piercing cries and groans of the serious casualties. He'd never heard so many people crying out in agony all at once. A hellish cacophony, almost unbearable. Nor had he ever seen so many maimed men, with stumps of arms or legs sticking out of bloody dressings and covered in scabs and pus. Never had he smelt such a vile stench. He shoved his way through a group of soldiers, only to be brought up short by an impassable line of stretcher cases. Meanwhile, the crowd had closed in behind him. In front of him lay a man with no legs and whose head was wrapped up like a mummy.

All of a sudden, in the place where the mouth should be, the bandage opened and let out a piercing shriek. Lucien was paralyzed. The shriek descended into a drawn-out wail of inhuman suffering. Lucien panicked; he wheeled around and fought through the crowd with all his might. His whole body was shaking.

Suddenly someone caught him by the arm. 'Come with me, Mr. Hirschland,' Ketting said calmly. 'I've found the hotel.'

Lucien allowed himself to be led to the lorry, which Albert had manoeuvred so they could pass behind the soldiers. They parked in a side street. Lucien remained seated with his head bent forward; he did not want Ketting to see him in this state. Ketting pulled Lucien's small suitcase and his own satchel from behind the seats, close the driver's door behind him, walked around to the side of the vehicle and waited discreetly, his back to the cab. Once Lucien had got a grip on his emotions he stepped down and they walked together to the Grand Hôtel de la Gare.

They were met at the reception by a stocky Belgian with an unhealthy, suffused complexion and a blank expression. His mouth curled bitterly. Lucien asked him for a double room.

The hotelier gave him the once-over before answering. 'Hollanders?' he asked with an undertone that betrayed a certain wariness. Lucien nodded. 'What's your business in Thielt?' he inquired brusquely.

Lucien was immediately on his guard. It seemed 'Hollanders' couldn't automatically count on the man's sympathy. 'We've lost our way and want to find a place to stay before dark.' It seemed to him the safest response.

The man glanced at Albert' s work clothes as he weighed his response. 'Been dropping off goods, then?'

'Yes, food aid for Belgium.'

'Food aid for Belgium,' the hotelier repeated pensively. 'Well, in that case I happen to have one room free.' He led them without further ado up the stairs, thumbed through a bunch of keys and unlocked a door. He walked across the room to the window and quickly drew the net curtains.

'Lot of action out there,' Lucien said offhandedly, hoping not to rile the man any further.

'It's a strategically vital station. There are two tracks, one leading to Diksmuide and the other to Ypres by way of Kortrijk. There's no end to the trains coming and going.'

'The place is crawling with Krauts,' said Ketting suddenly.

The hotelier's mouth twitched ever so slightly out of its dourness. 'You can say that again. There must be a couple of hundred thousand of them stationed here... And they keep coming. Just like the cannons – they're bringing them in by the hundreds, I've heard. The Germans are nervous, it's not going well for them... The churches are full of soldiers; can't imagine what they're praying for.'

Lucien sank onto one of the beds. He desperately wished he was back home.

Now the hotelier addressed Ketting. 'Sometimes I feel sorry for them. They're just boys. They're not allowed in here, this hotel is exclusively for officers, who only come to stuff themselves and get blotto.'

Ketting shook his head disdainfully.

'You should see it, they behave like animals.'

'And you're stuck with them.'

'Hopefully not for too much longer.' He lowered his voice. 'Our veterinarian has just come back from Germany; he was being held prisoner there. According to him, they've hardly any young soldiers left, all dead… Now there's just the elderly, the arthritic and the crippled. And a nun who escaped from Passchendaele also told me they're on their last legs. I didn't believe it at first but last night a German pilot, in a drunken stupor, said that if they didn't get new reserves fast, the English would break through from all sides.'

'That's encouraging,' Ketting said.

The hotel manager sighed and made a move to leave.

'Thank you for letting us have this room,' Lucien said. He got up and reached for his suitcase.

'You were lucky. I'm not allowed to give this room to Germans for the time being, instructions from higher up. Bad for morale. Day before yesterday a German officer hung himself here. Guess he couldn't face it anymore.'

After dinner they went straight back up to their room. Lucien was exhausted, but mostly he was angry at Ketting, who had given him the silent treatment throughout the meal. 'Damn it, Albert, what was I supposed to say? That we were bringing medicine for the Germans?'

Ketting ignored him, closed the curtains tightly to comply with the blackout and lit a petroleum lamp. He stripped down to his underclothes and climbed into bed. Lucien was preparing to undress when someone knocked at the door.

The hotelier hurried inside and lingered self-consciously with a flickering lantern in his hand. 'What I, er, wanted to ask you was…' he stammered, '…are you heading back tomorrow?' Lucien nodded. The man took a deep breath. 'Would it be possible for my son to get a lift with you? We're not allowed to leave the city without permission. Thielt's a prison. He wants to go to Holland and then further afield… surely you can understand…' Lucien waited for the rest. 'You're travelling with that large lorry around the corner, well, maybe you could hide him in there.'

Lucien thought about it, but then recalled all the check-points. He saw those two young men again, who had been plucked out of the group and taken away at gunpoint. 'They check you ten times before you've even left the city,' he answered hesitantly, 'and search everything thoroughly…'. He raised his hands apologetically. 'I'm sorry, I don't think it's going to work.'

'I thought not.' The hotelier reached for the doorknob. 'Please don't tell anyone about this. They'll execute you for a whole lot less.' He closed the door noiselessly behind him.

Lucien glanced at the hump under the blankets. Only a tuft of hair was visible. He thought better of asking Ketting's opinion, he could guess what it would be. He lay down on the bed fully clothed and his eye was drawn involuntarily to the ceiling, where the hook for a lamp must have been. Now there was just a gaping hole with frayed edges in the plaster. Outside the thunder grew louder. The windowpanes shuddered and through the curtains he could see the occasional flash of light-ning. He got up, put out the lamp, went over to the window and gingerly tweaked the curtain aside. It was pitch-black out on the street, but searchlights were crisscrossing over the roof-tops. Further on, beyond the station, the sky looked as though it was on fire. The wind blew the sound of artillery fire in all directions, now off in the distance, now close by. Underneath his window, countless boots tramped over the cobblestones.

Lucien was suddenly overcome by a fear he had not expe-rienced before. The Germans are on their last legs, the hotel manager had said, the English will break through from all sides, and then the French, the Canadians… Had the American reinforcements arrived yet? Had they all come together in the trenches to force a breakthrough? How far had the Allies advanced by now? Was it his imagination, or was the artillery barrage coming closer and closer? Would the Germans – the elderly, the arthritic and the crippled – already be beating a retreat, or had Sixt von Armin ordered one last-ditch offensive? My God, soon these armies would be descending on Thielt, tonight of all nights, for one final, decisive battle. And he was stuck in the middle of it. No way out… What did he have to do with this bloody war! He wasn't even sure which side was good and which was evil. Who was fighting a just war here? Which side had 'right' on its side? The English, the French, the Americans? Or the Germans and Austrians? Or was it simply a matter of 'might makes right'? Is that what this war was about? About who was right? And what about those who hadn't taken sides? Would the victors assume that whoever was neutral – like himself – was automatically on their side? Was that the great advantage of neutrality? In that case he could rest easy: whoever came out on top, he'd be on the safe side…

10

The vast emptiness

The train, slowing its pace, glided to a halt and the locomotive emitted a few last puffs of damp steam. Robin was annoyed that the jolting and chugging had stopped. He tried to wriggle back under the lavender-scented down quilt and get back to the perfect body that awaited him there. But before he could retreat into the warmth and safety of his bed, his reverie was disrupted yet again by pair of medics lifting his stretcher. Although they were out of sight he could hear them panting and talking. 'Hurry up! Hundreds more are on their way, all of them from Ypres!' They carried him off the train and set his stretcher down on a paved floor. A railway platform. He recognized the sound of train doors slamming, the voices of passengers in transit, hurried footsteps on their way to somewhere. He was able to open one eye. No blue sky, but the underside of a sooty roof: a city railway station.

Why didn't anyone come and tell him where he was? Was he being transferred to a different hospital? Yet another abattoir where they'd sooner amputate than patch you up? He'd heard men screaming and begging, who always got the same impatient reply: 'Sorry, mate, no time, soon as we're done with you there's a few hundred more who can kiss their limbs goodbye.'

They never bothered to ask a soldier if he'd appreciate keeping his arms or legs intact. Or whether he might be needing them once the war was over. What had they done with him, he'd like to know. What had they amputated without his permission? He had to find out.

He felt no pain now; he only remembered feeling it. At least he still had his right eye, and his arms and hands too, even his fingers – he'd made a point of moving and counting them. But what about his legs? He couldn't feel his legs or feet, it was as though they were detached and had been left behind, miles away. It was that damned morphine, they'd half knocked him out with it… 'Now at least he'll keep his trap shut,' he'd overheard a medic say. He still had his ears, that much was certain. But his mouth – had they taken that away too, because even the morphine couldn't keep him quiet? His head was completely bandaged, with just a slit for his one eye. Maybe they'd amputated his whole head. Was there a fancy new technique that meant the surgeons could connect his ears and right eye with the muscles and blood vessels in his neck? Was all that bandaging just a ruse, to give the illusion of having a head, while all that was there was an empty shell?

He felt his stretcher being lifted again; he was being carried into another railway carriage. Was it the same train, or a different one? Why didn't they tell him anything? The carriage was already filled with stretchers, judging from the muffled sounds around him; he must have been the last one they brought in. He reckoned they'd deliberately left his hearing intact, to keep him from blocking out the disgusting hawking and rattling of the dying. Was this his punishment? Did he have this coming to him? As if he'd been responsible for that bloodbath out there in no-man's-land! Had he started this war? Why had they dumped him in this madhouse? He'd expressly told them he wanted to be alone! These morons just lay there groaning. Keep it down, will you! Now he knew why he no longer had a mouth, they'd taken it from him, otherwise he'd have shouted: 'I hate you all, you sorry bunch of losers!'

He thrashed his legs around furiously. Good God, he still had his legs! Finally some positive news: with legs you could run, and running away was just what he planned to do. He kicked again, harder, harder, he grasped the blanket with his toes and, with a huge effort, pulled it down off him. The pink face of a nurse appeared above him. Now where had she come from? She held a needle in her hand and was poised to give him an injection. No! No, not more morphine! He wanted to run, make a dash for it, not lie there helplessly while they amputated something else. The nurse smiled and pulled away the needle. It was only a threat, she was only teasing him, naughty girl!

As a punishment he took her into his bed, where Mary was still waiting patiently. She was naked. Her white, unblemished skin was like polished marble. He longed desperately for her untainted beauty. He would take her like a passionate lover. He didn't even need to exert himself, the rocking of the moving train was enough to set his loins in motion. My God, there was nothing more delicious than this…

Suddenly he could no longer feel her. Mary had wriggled free. Didn't she want to share him with the nurse? What! She'd lost interest? Rejected him because he didn't have a head? How dare she, the dirty little bitch! If she wouldn't give it out of love, then he'd take it by force, penetrate her with his bayonet, stick it deeper and deeper into her body… Oh yes, look at me with those big scared eyes, go ahead and cry! Stupid cow! You were so keen on me enlisting, remember? Now I'm a soldier, a brave soldier who selflessly serves God, King and Country…

The train came to a halt. They'd been travelling for a long time. Robin got a glimpse of the clear blue sky. This must be an English station. Home at last. He tried to shake off the flush of the morphine; he had to get to Great Yarmouth. Dad had been standing at the window, gazing down the street, for so long now. When would his son finally come home? Mum had baked an apple pie. Welcome home, dear! Of course, he wanted to go home, but where was his bottle? One little tablet would give him the energy to get up on his own. But his stretcher was being carried away again, and he nodded off.

Then he clearly heard someone speaking French. French? How was that possible? He managed to open his one eye. They were carefully removing the bandages from his head. Now they'd see what had been done to him! The doctor's face came closer; his nostrils were large, with little black hairs sticking out.

'*Grand Dieu*…' exclaimed the doctor. 'What a mess they've made of this,' he said indignantly in French-accented English. Other voices whispered insistently. The patient was conscious! '*Excuse-moi*…' said the French doctor, and although Robin desperately wanted to hear what he was saying, his attention wandered and the voices dissolved into an unintelligible murmur. But Mary was back. He'd entirely forgotten that he'd tied her to the bed with barbed wire so she couldn't get away. She was all wrapped up, encased in swathes of bandages, his beautiful Nefertiti… He reached out to release her, but first he demanded she give him back his bottle – surely she understood that every soldier had the right to his personal belongings. His fingers hovered above the bandages, and suddenly he knew there was nothing inside. There was nothing except a vast emptiness…

'Don't you worry, my boy, everything will turn out fine,' said the voice with the French accent. He saw the nostrils again, and then an index finger coming closer and closer, touching his… his skin. The Frenchman gave him a big, toothy smile. 'We're sending you to Sidcup. You'll make a fine job for Dr. Gillies. Harold will patch you up.'

Robin didn't understand, and wanted to ask the Frenchman what he meant, but in his place stood the nurse, the same one who had threatened him with the morphine needle. She had managed to escape from the barbed wire. He'd had to tie her up, just like Mary, but apparently she didn't hold it against him. On the contrary. She said affably: 'You're a lucky fellow, Robin Ryder. Soon you'll be aboard a hospital ship to England, to Queen Mary's Hospital, a brand-new hospital where one of England's best surgeons is going to try to restore your face.'

Now he had to know. He first formulated the words in his head, then stammered, 'So I still have a head?'

She let out a chirp of laughter. 'Of course, silly! What did you think? Your body's unscathed and you still have the sight in one eye. Be grateful for that!'

11

The soirée

Lucien spent the entire night sitting at the hotel room window. He tried to estimate, from the flashes darting across the sky, how far they were from the fighting. Surely it was possible to tell whether the danger was approaching or receding? You could measure the speed of light. What was it he'd learned at school about electromagnetic waves? Light travels faster than sound. Now what was it about its relation to the speed of sound, so he could try and work out the distance to the artillery fire? Try as he might, he couldn't remember a thing. His head was empty. And even if he could remember, what good would it do? After all, he knew absolutely nothing about military strategy or tactics, or what was going on in the heads of the Allied generals who, somewhere behind the front, were hunched over their maps plotting the day's fighting? And how could he have any idea of what decisions Sixt von Armin and his staff were taking just a few hundred meters away? Was the plan to battle it out right here and now in Thielt?

He'd got fully dressed a few hours earlier, just to be on the safe side. Jacket on, hat on, suitcase within arm's reach: prepared to flee should the city be stormed. He'd even taken Albert's clothes from the cupboard and laid them out. He glanced over his shoulder from time to time, but Ketting seemed to sleeping through it all, or at least pretending to. Every time he looked back into the room, his eyes were drawn to that hole in the ceiling, where the German officer had hanged himself just two days before.

Lucien felt his sinister presence, imagined him pacing up and down. His final moments. Was he still agonizing, or had he made up his mind? Was he weighing doubt against resolve? Had he really hit rock bottom, justifying taking his own life? Was it the fear of being maimed on the battlefield and a slow, painful death? Or was it the shame of a humiliating defeat for the German army? Perhaps it was another reason entirely: maybe a woman had broken his heart and now life wasn't worth living anymore. Once he'd reached his final decision, had he climbed up on a chair and carefully unhooked the lamp and set it on the floor, to avoid causing unnecessary damage? How did that hole get there? Either it had torn loose under his own weight, or the German military police, furious at the cowardliness of a fellow officer, had yanked him down hook and all.

Daylight had already begun to creep in, and the clatter of cart wheels on the cobblestones and the revving of engines began to push the sound of the barrage into the background, when Ketting nudged him out of his restless slumber. They left without breakfast, despite the hotelier's protestations. At the door Ketting gave him one last imploring look, but Lucien was in too much of a hurry to pick up on the question implicit in his eyes. Only later, on their way back, did Ketting's meaning dawn on him: was he really such a selfish sod as to refuse to smuggle the hotelier's son back to Holland, too spineless to take a bit of a risk? Lucien's perfect German, their Dutch papers and the remaining bottle of jenever would probably have been enough to sweet-talk their way through. Even if they'd been rumbled, he could also have feigned shocked surprise at the discovery of a stowaway. Looking back on it, they could have taken the boy with them. But now they were already past Roosendaal.

Neither of them brought it up. Ketting kept his mouth shut the whole way. Nor was Lucien in any mood for small talk, not now and certainly not that evening, when he had hoped to return the borrowed clothes to Olyrook's dressing room unnoticed, jump on the Harley and head home. How could he know that Thomas would be there waiting for him, nestled in an armchair with a cigar and a cognac? He was obviously looking forward to a full report. But Lucien begged him to desist. 'I'm bushed, man, shattered... not up to it now, maybe tomorrow...'

By the time Lucien opened the front door of his house on the Oranjekade, at almost eight o'clock in the evening, he wasn't just physically shattered, but emotionally drained as well. He noticed that the coat rack was full of unfamiliar jackets, and the copper bin alongside it crammed with umbrellas and walking sticks. The sounds of a party wafted out from the salon. The cheerful voices, high-spirited laughter and Karel's chirping jogged his memory: Swanny's soirée. He fought against the urge to slip back out of the house and ride directly to Pola's, where he could at least get some sleep in a warm embrace. But he couldn't do it to Swanny. She had been reminding him about this evening for weeks; it was to be a really big do, and some guests had been invited especially for him. She'd feel betrayed if he stood her up.

Swanny came out into the hallway to greet him, looking

beautiful with her hair up and the wide-cut dress that just revealed her lace-up boots. The Javanese shawl with the silver stitching was draped elegantly over her shoulders, a way of signalling that he was tonight's guest of honour. 'I'm so glad you made it,' she exclaimed, beaming. She spread her arms; between her fingers she held a long cigarette holder. The flush on her cheeks betrayed a few liqueurs. But instantly her face fell. 'Why Lucien, you look perfectly awful... You're as white as a ghost! Was it such a gruelling trip to Maastricht?'

He rubbed his forehead and thought about keeping up the pretence, but he didn't have the energy. 'It wasn't Maastricht. I've been in Flanders.'

'Flanders!' she cried. 'But that's... You haven't been at the front, have you? Good heavens, it's dangerous there!'

He hesitated. The front. The dangerous front. The images it evoked more or less tallied with what he'd seen in Thielt. 'The front, yes,' he said quietly. 'It was awful, absolutely awful.' He figured that this would excuse him from having to discuss the trip any further. She threw her arms around his neck. 'You should've told me,' she said, dismayed. 'I'd... I'd have gone with you!'

He smiled and stroked her blushing cheek. 'I've come back in one piece, as you can see.' He was suddenly aware of his motorcycle gear. 'I'll go up and change.'

Swanny squinted at him and emphatically shook her head. 'Nothing doing. Let them see that you've risked your life to deliver medicine to soldiers at the front!'

'Swanny, please. Don't go mentioning it...'

'Why not? They've all got such big mouths about the war, but what do they actually do about it? Nothing!'

He decided not to fight it. So, he'd just risked his life for a noble cause: what better excuse to bow out early? Swanny propelled him into the salon with an air of pathos, as though she was introducing a soldier who'd been given up for dead. The room went suddenly silent and all the guests turned to him in surprise. The cockatoo seized the chance to let out a shrill shriek that sent a chill down Lucien's spine. 'Hold your tongue, you odious little bird!' Swanny scolded. She grasped her brother firmly by the arm – he suddenly wondered what had become of that couple in the customs office – and announced: 'You'll have to excuse Lucien's lateness. He's had a dreadful journey. He's just come from the front in Flanders!' An anxious buzz filled the room. He gestured tiredly and, after a brief silence which indicated to them that there was to be no public account of the journey and subsequent discussion, as one might expect at this kind of intellectual soirée, the conversations resumed.

Lucien was relieved when Tosca Tilanus sidled up and kissed his cheek. 'You look like a swashbuckling adventurer,' she whispered in his ear. He smiled and made a mental note to stay close to her. Tosca would have enough sense not to press him to talk about his foray into a war zone. The same could not be said for that tedious ninny Lisette Adriaans – she could easily have been ignored but for the fact that she'd inevitably impose her so-called musical talent on the other guests – nor for Dineke Bergmans, who would no doubt try to build his recent tribulations into one of her interminable antiwar poems.

But Swanny prevented Lisette and Dineke from latching onto him by announcing him as a 'guest of honour' – somewhat beside the point, since this was his own house – and taking him on a circuit of hand-shaking. Casper Bartholomeus squeezed his hand almost to a pulp and boomed in his deep bass voice: 'So, old bean, been to the front, eh! Must hear about that! Bully!' Most of the guests, newcomers to Swanny's soirée, were only vaguely familiar to him, but they all appeared to know him from the club or some other social venue, before his spell in the Dutch East Indies.

Meanwhile, Swanny told him who she'd managed to invite as the evening's 'mystery guest': Marnix Christiaans. She'd bumped into him in town; he'd recently moved to Haarlem, although he worked in The Hague. 'Some important post at the Ministry of Foreign Affairs.' But the real reason she invited him was that he'd also spent some time on Java. Lucien remembered Marnix from high school; he'd been a few years ahead of him. A brilliant student. Later, he'd run into him occasionally at the rowing club, where Marnix had been on the winning team. Naturally.

He'd already caught sight of the new guest, half-hidden behind a large potted palm near the window, when Swanny grasped his hand and led him over. 'You two haven't seen each other for ages, I'll bet!' she bubbled. Funnily enough, Lucien recalled exactly when they'd last seen one another: about two weeks before his departure from Java. Marnix was at the club with a few friends. They had exchanged polite nods, but hadn't struck up a conversation. Now Marnix greeted him like an old pal and immediately brought up their meeting in Batavia. 'I wanted to offer you a drink,' he said. Lucien doubted it. It was at the height of the flurry of gossip regarding his affair with Martha. Marnix must have known about that, and maybe he'd even got wind of Lucien's debts. 'What say we have that drink now, then?' Lucien laughed. He assumed Marnix would have the discretion not to mention those embarrassing events to Swanny.

'Hey, Lucien, what about your war adventures!' shouted

Casper from across the room. His lanky frame was propped against the piano and he was pretty drunk. As usual, he was oblivious to the civilized tone of the conversation around him. 'Dodge some bullets over there?' he bellowed. Again the room went quiet in anticipation.

Lucien stared at his knees. His trousers were splattered with dried mud, a legacy of his trip to Arnhem to meet Biedermann... The brilliant chemist, the genius. 'Not much to see, actually,' he said, in an attempt to deflect the question.

'Come on, man!' Casper persevered. 'The papers are full of horror stories, and you say you didn't notice a thing?'

'Maybe he doesn't feel like talking about it,' protested Swanny as she went round the room with a box of cigarettes.

Lucien shot her a grateful glance and sat down next to Marnix on the couch. 'Been back long?' He closed his eyes for a moment, realizing he'd stupidly reopened a tricky subject.

'Not long after your... unexpected departure,' answered Marnix, casually crossing his legs.

'Of course, my unexpected departure...' Lucien stared into his glass.

'Don't worry, my lips are sealed.'

Lucien nodded, and managed to cast Tosca a pleading glance in the hope that she'd join them and forestall any more talk of Java. She picked up on it straight away, crossed the room swinging her hips and wriggled in between them on the sofa. She hoped, of course, that the other guests would be scandalized. 'Swan tells me you bought a Harley-Davidson,' she said, filling all three of their glasses from a bottle of whisky she'd picked up on her way.

'A Harley-Davidson, eh?' remarked Casper, who had abandoned the piano and was now lounging against the mantlepiece, perilously close to the expensive Chinese Yué vase. Fortunately he was also dangerously near to Karel. 'Those things cost a fortune! But of course you'll be making a packet at the cocaine factory.'

'Not as much as you with your doodles.' Lucien drained his glass and reached for the bottle Tosca had set at her feet. He turned demonstratively towards her. So as to include Marnix in the conversation, he mentioned that Tosca and Swanny were taking English lessons and that they often practised on him.

Casper had sauntered over to the palm, much to Karel's displeasure, who lunged at him with his beak, missing his ear by a fraction of an inch. 'Tell me, old chap, d'you ever help yourself to the stuff?'

Lucien gave him an uncomprehending look.

'That divine cocaine…'

'Give over, will you! Of course not, why should I?'

'Well, why not? Out in the Indies you surely smoked the odd opium pipe?'

'You've obviously never seen an opium smoker!' snapped Lucien. 'It's evil stuff, that.'

'I've heard cocaine is toxic as well,' Lisette Adriaans cut in out of the blue.

How come all the unbearable guests managed to gravitate to him like a magnet? 'Let's be grateful that there's such an effective medicine for wounded soldiers,' Lucien said coolly. His listeners nodded: evidently someone just back from the front could speak of the soldiers' suffering with some authority.

'Well, I've read that novocaine is a perfectly good substitute,' continued Lisette. She worked at a pharmacist's. 'Cocaine affects the central nervous system. Even a small dose can be dangerous.'

Marnix took a breath, but before he could get a word in, Lisette went on: 'Researchers have done tests: dogs injected with cocaine quickly showed symptoms of poisoning. They experienced increased respiration and extreme mental agitation, followed by spinal cramps, paralysis of the respiratory system – and, in many cases, death'. The other guests, confounded by such detailed knowledge, looked at each other in surprise.

Stupid cow, thought Lucien, she's just regurgitating information from some obscure medical journal.

'Nonsense, Lisette!' said Tosca. 'Lots of important scientists have published glowing articles about cocaine. Sigmund Freud, for instance, is wholeheartedly in favour of it. He calls it a miracle drug, a blessing for mankind! It's got so many applications. Why, in America even singers use it to give themselves clearer voices.'

'My, how interesting,' said Swanny, 'I didn't know that.'

'Yes, but there's also a strong lobby in the United States against the use of…'

'In America everyone drinks Coca-Cola,' interrupted Tosca again. 'It contains caffeine as well as cocaine. The perfect remedy for migraine and melancholy!'

'Oh, what would you know about it!' Lisette glared at Tosca indignantly. 'I'm not talking about Coca-Cola, I'm talking about pure cocaine, the kind the Negroes snort. Did you know that the incidence of rape against white women by coke-crazed niggers has shot up? It turns even decent Negroes into dangerous criminals. Police reports show that cocaine makes them incredibly strong; they can even survive regular pistol shots!'

Tosca let out a contemptuous howl. She was a dyed-in-the-wool socialist and sensitive to discriminatory remarks about

Negroes. Sometimes Lucien found her principles tiresome, but now he applauded them.

'They've also proved it can make you homosexual!' Lisette continued.

'Strange that those Negroes go out and rape white women, then,' said Casper, who was doing his best to follow the conversation. 'You'd think...'

Marnix Christiaans burst out laughing so hard that the sofa shook. 'You mustn't read so much nonsense, Miss,' he said in a condescending voice. 'Cocaine's a first-rate product. It invigorates the body and the spirit, and is a wonderful anaesthetic. Doctors couldn't do without it, most of all at the front. Of course, improper use can cause complications, as with any medicine. Morphine, for instance, is no different... There are bound to be those who abuse certain kinds of medicine, purely out of ignorance... usually lowbrow types.' Lucien presumed he refrained from saying 'labourers' or 'Negroes' so as not to rile Tosca. 'The same is true for opium, an excellent pharmaceutical product. But in Asia it's a problem because the Chinese and other natives use it to excess. Lucien's absolutely right: opium smoking's the really dangerous habit, and should be vigorously opposed.'

That's not what I said at all, thought Lucien, but he had to hand it to him: Marnix had managed to muzzle Casper and Lisette in one fell swoop.

'And what about this stuff?' said Tosca, raising her glass. 'We all drink alcohol, some of us *to excess!*' She flopped back on the sofa and gave Casper a swift kick in the shin. They all laughed, and Swanny seized the opportunity to move to the middle of the room and, wringing her hands, announced that in about ten minutes Lisette would be performing a violin sonata, with a short introduction, followed by two new poems by Dineke.

As Lucien turned to Marnix to thank him for intervening, he noticed him eyeing Swanny. He hadn't come to his rescue, but hers! Leaning over towards Marnix, he said quietly: 'I've got to get going. Business, you understand… Let's get together soon.'

Marnix turned to him, startled. 'Capital idea. Perhaps I can invite you and Swanny to dinner sometime, what do you say?'

Lucien nodded, patted Tosca's knee and winked at her. He nonchalantly crossed the room and pulled Swanny with him into the hall. He apologized for not being able to stay any longer, but there was an urgent meeting he had to attend in connection with his trip.

'Oh, Lucien, I do apologize for that horrible Lisette with her idiotic comments. I only invite her because she plays the violin so beautifully.' He thought it best to bite his tongue. 'Next time I'll invite some different people, maybe some ex-colonials,' she promised.

'Good idea of yours to invite Marnix,' he said as he pulled on his jacket. 'Pleasant fellow.' On his way to the door, he added over his shoulder: 'And I believe he fancies you.'

A quarter of an hour later he rang Pola's doorbell. The stroll in the fresh evening air had done him good. He was invigorated by the thought of this evening's rendezvous. It was a good thing he had left the Harley safely at home. He'd have loved to have shown it off, but the narrow street where Pola lived housed several cafés and he was reluctant to leave his fancy motorbike outside unattended. He rang again and checked his watch: two hours too late. But then again, he did have a damned good excuse.

Pola opened the door as he was reaching for the bell a third

time. Without a word, she turned her back on him and teetered back down the narrow corridor. The game had begun.
Lucien followed the carefully-planted trail of saffron and san-
dalwood, scents from the Far East that did the trick every time.
And she knew it. Her thick black hair, casually tied back with
a ribbon, hung halfway down her back over the floor-length,
flaming red caftan. Lucien couldn't tell if she was wearing anything underneath. Nor did he want to know just yet. She went
straight through to the bedroom. It was lit only by two small
table lamps. She slid gracefully onto the bed, settled into the
brocade pillows and chastely averted her gaze. Her eyes were
made up extra dark so they'd look bigger and more sultry. Her
lips were pursed into an innocent pout.

Lucien slowly removed his motorcycle jacket, sat down at
the end of the bed and grasped her ankles before she could
pull them back. He caressed her calves, pulled off the floral-
patterned slippers, peeled back the thin stockings and kissed
her toes one at a time. She draped her fingers, the nails painted
green, over her forehead, turned her head away and sighed
deeply. Lucien smiled: what an actress! The disillusioned lover,
the mistress who suffered the torments of waiting, a woman
who did not deserve this base treatment. Two hours too late
– this could not go unpunished. Nothing aroused his desire
more than that. With a firm grip on her ankles he pulled her
toward him over the silk sheet, causing her robe to shift up and
reveal her well-formed legs. He stopped just short of finding
out whether or not she was wearing a slip. He wanted her in
this pose; he glanced at the exciting spot and his lips glided
upwards over the creamy skin of her legs.

Just as he was about to make his discovery, she grabbed him
by the shoulders, halting his advance. 'I've got a migraine...'

she groaned with a pleading look. He tried to free himself from her nails, which had dug straight through his shirt into his flesh. But she had too good a grip on him. He knew this moment well, it only heightened the excitement. 'You've made me suffer so. How can I ever forgive you?' she sulked, releasing her nails, as though she'd simply run out of strength.

He bent forward and kissed her on the lips. Then he stood up, reached for his jacket and fished out a small paper wrapper from the inside pocket. In a reassuring tone he said: 'Dr. Hirschland is here to take care of your headache...' Pola swung her legs over the edge of the bed, opened the drawer of the nightstand and took out a small silver spoon. Lucien set the paper wrapper down in front of her. She carefully scooped up the glistening white powder, held the spoon under one nostril and sniffed it up.

Meanwhile Lucien slowly removed his boots without taking his eyes off her. She licked the remains from the paper, closed her eyes and sank back onto the pillows. Her long eyelashes fluttered open as he unbuttoned his trousers. The migraine never took long to dispel. He undressed, draping his clothes, one by one, over a chair. It always worked to his advantage, he knew from experience, to take his time. Her eyes filled with desire, she propped herself up and yanked the robe over her head. Indeed, she wasn't wearing any underclothes. She reached out to him, her fingers grabbing impatiently at the air. He knelt at the foot of the bed so he could begin his delectable journey up her parted legs.

Pola was always an energetic lover, and Lucien had to concentrate to avoid the disappointment of a premature climax. But this time his fatigue was stronger than his willpower, and Pola pounded her fists angrily on his back. She scratched his skin until it bled. He yelled and fell onto her; he needed all his weight to restrain her. When she had calmed down, he rolled off to one side and at once was overcome by sleep. Weird visions played out behind his eyelids. Pola tugged on his shoulders. 'Bastard!' she shouted. 'Why did you keep me waiting for two hours? You know I need my medicine! Don't you have any more on you?'

He preferred to save the second wrapper for next time, when he had more energy. 'It's difficult to get without a doctor's prescription,' he said as he reached for the whisky bottle on the nightstand. He wondered, as he took a swig, why Olyrook charged him so much lately for just a few grams.

'Come on, you can get it easily enough.'

'Not as easily as you think.' Lucien didn't feel like yet another debate about his product. 'Be careful with it, will you, they say the stuff's pretty toxic. Maybe you shouldn't take so much.' He immediately regretted it. Under no circumstances did he want her looking elsewhere for her medicine. He'd discovered that her sexual desire intensified as soon as her migraine disappeared, and he wasn't about to share this with anyone else.

But whether it was toxic or not was of no concern to Pola. She climbed off the bed and sat down at her dressing table. As she hurriedly retouched her eyes and mouth, she said to the mirror: 'Mauritz is working on a new film. It's a wonderful script about a beautiful woman who falls in love with handsome composer, but she goes blind after an eye operation. I know for sure he's going to give me the part, I can just feel it from the way he looks at me.'

Lucien studied her naked buttocks on the taboret, and his eyes traced the length of her back up to her dark hair. 'Of course he'll give you the part. You're a born talent, head and shoulders above...' No, don't say that name out loud – an attack of post-migraine aggression can come on so suddenly.

'Exactly. Far better than that horrid woman...' she sighed, 'although playing a blind person will be awfully demanding.'

Relieved at having warded off a tantrum, he said: 'My darling, this will be your big break, I can feel it in my bones.' She turned and faced him. Her big sad eyes told him that the mere thought of her despised rival was bringing on a new migraine. He didn't want to disappoint her, but they'd need to hurry if he wasn't to collapse in a heap before the next round.

He told her about the Harley-Davidson while she let the second packet of powder take effect. Again she reached for him longingly and mumbled, as her lips glided over his jaw: 'So where do you go on this motorbike of yours? Tell me all about your journeys to exotic places.'

He slid his hands over her buttocks and thighs, bent over her and pulled her knees up in the air. 'I've been in Flanders, near the front.'

'Oh Lucien, how exciting... do tell! I'm sure you saw the most horrid things.' She pushed his hand between her legs. Suddenly he was back in the middle of that claustrophobic throng in front of the Thielt railway station. No matter how much he resisted, he kept coming back to the wounded soldier with no face. He shook his head violently to try and banish the screaming. 'Horrid things...' he repeated. 'We got caught in crossfire, had to run for our lives,' he continued, doing his best to satisfy her expectations. Don't think about the German officer dangling from the ceiling. For God's sake, just don't think about it. 'Grenades flew past my head, the machine guns...' Pola groaned loudly. He suddenly wondered how many chairs were in that hotel room. Two, no, just one... He was sure of it. That's the chair the German must have climbed on. He'd made a noose out of his belt, or a piece of rope. Then he slipped it over his head and kicked the chair out from under him… Lucien flopped to one side and clutched at his throat. He was short of breath and lay there gasping. Pola stared at him, motionless. 'He stood on that chair,' he stammered, 'the same chair I sat on all night…'

12

A serious problem

Lucien was of two minds. He couldn't decide whether the blue worsted suit in combination with the cream-coloured cravat and a light waistcoat better suited his mood than the brown blazer and plain beige trousers he'd just taken out of the cupboard. The floor was strewn with shoes – five new pairs, he couldn't make up his mind about those either – and the bed was a jumbled mass of shirts. He studied himself in the oval mirror on the wardrobe and ran his fingers through his thick, dark hair. It was time he got a haircut. Or should he let it grow, wear it a bit longer like the Parisian bohemians, men who were indifferent to prevailing fashion – wasn't he also averse to stodgy conventions of any kind? In any event, he badly needed to go for a shave.

Whistling to himself, he ambled over to the window and looked outside. It was partly clouded over and, judging from the swaying treetops along the water, there was a stiff breeze blowing. He'd wear his Burberry overcoat into town when he went to book their trip. Come to think of it, the garage next to the Raambrug was on the way; perhaps it'd be a good idea to drop by there first. He'd finally made the decision that morning: with autumn approaching he wanted to have a motorcar in addition to the Harley, and he'd set his sights on a Mercedes Tourer, the type he'd seen crossing the square in front of Café-Restaurant Brinkman. Lucien smiled contentedly. He'd woken from a long, deep sleep feeling himself again, full of energy and resolve. The ghosts he'd brought back with him from Thielt weren't plaguing him any longer. They had vanished out of his life as suddenly as they'd burst in on it. But whether they were gone for good, he couldn't say for sure. That's why he needed to take action, to have something to look forward to. So he hatched a plan that would create a real buzz back at home: he'd surprise Swanny and Tosca by organizing a trip to London at Christmas. The English really knew how to celebrate the holidays; the streets were gaily lit and extravagantly decorated. They could stay in a posh hotel, shop at Harrods and Savory & Moore, eat out at the best restaurants and call on Brian Kirkpatrick. Swanny would be delighted to put their English lessons into practice and at the same time visit her favourite Englishman. He'd ring Kirkpatrick that afternoon; besides, he was anxious to know when he could expect the telegram about the next shipment. But first he'd have to call on the freight company that generally handled the firm's shipments to England. He wanted decent passenger accommodation and not, like Kirkpatrick, to be crammed between crates of fish in the hold.

He heard footsteps hurrying up the stairs. When the skipping gait reached the squeaky floorboards of the landing, he instantly recognized it. Panting, Swanny threw open his bedroom door. She had been outdoors, and the wind had blown her hat askew so that it looked like a capsized sailboat. But before she could say anything, Lucien took her by the shoulders and said: 'Swan, I've got a terrific idea!' He was too excited to conceal his surprise any longer. 'You, Tosca and I are going to celebrate Christmas in London!' he exclaimed. 'It's always so festive there this time of year. We can go to museums and art exhibitions or to the theatre, whatever you two want!'

Swanny stared at him, bemused, and wrinkled her nose. 'Honestly, Lucien! England's in the middle of a war. Tens of thousands of English boys are dying, and you want to go and celebrate Christmas in London among all those wretched people? Celebrate, indeed!' She shook her head. 'And after all that you've seen in Flanders!'

He took a quick breath and choked a little, as though there was something caught in his throat.

'Are you all right?' she asked.

'Yes, of course, I'm fine. I just wanted to please you, but perhaps you're right.' He wondered why she'd come home. 'Why aren't you at the food distribution centre?' he asked.

'I'm in a terrible bind. Have you got a moment?' Lucien nodded. 'Well, that old banger we've been using has given up the ghost and we've got to take round the food parcels. Old people and families with children are really desperate. I don't know how we're going to get it all delivered. I was wondering if you'd got the company car.'

'No, I'm using the Harley.'

'Oh… yes, of course.' She gave him a imploring look. 'Have you bought that sidecar yet? Then you still might be able to help us.'

He could see she was anxious and remembered there was a second-hand sidecar at Drummer's garage, not really a model he'd be interested in buying, but surely they'd be able to borrow or hire it for a couple of hours. 'I think I can get hold of one.'

Swanny heaved a sigh of relief. 'Lucien, you're a darling!'

They went downstairs together. 'Do you dare sit in it?' he asked, still reeling slightly from her outright rejection of his travel plans.

Before she could answer him, Pleun appeared at the foot of the stairs with a bucket in one hand and a mop in the other. 'The telephone rang several times,' she said.

'Why didn't you call me?' asked Lucien.

'I wasn't to disturb you, because you needed a good night's sleep. You said so yesterday.'

'Well, who was it?' She shrugged her shoulders. Of course, Pleun only touched the telephone if it needed dusting, and had no further truck with newfangled devices. He put his hand around Swanny's waist and they walked towards the door. But the phone rang again before they could leave. He hesitated. Swanny looked at him anxiously. 'I'd better answer it.' He went back to what used to be his father's office, picked up the receiver and listened. All he said in response was: 'Tell them I'm on my way.'

Swanny was waiting impatiently out on the doorstep. 'That was Mr. Cremers' secretary. I've got to get to the office of the Koloniale Bank on the double. They're expecting me in an hour… I'm awfully sorry. I'll try to be back within a couple of hours.' He shrugged his shoulders in a gesture of helplessness.

Swanny fixed her hat and kicked away a fallen branch. 'Didn't you tell them…'

'Of course I told them, but something really urgent has come up. Swanny, please try to understand.'

'I can ask our Theo,' said Pleun, who had appeared in the doorway. She was already undoing her apron. 'Maybe he can borrow the greengrocer's delivery bike.'

'Grand! Thank you, Pleun!' said Lucien as he buttoned up

his jacket. 'Tell your son I'll reimburse all his expenses.' He gave Swanny a kiss and hurried to the shed, where the Harley was stowed. He wondered what in God's name could be so urgent that he was being summoned to the Herengracht.

Cremers received him in the richly appointed regents' room, with its ornamental ceiling, massive mantelpiece and Dutch Masters adorning the walls. Lucien had been in the canal house only once before, when H.W.J. Peereboom, Esq., president of the Koloniale Bank and director of the Netherlands Cocaine Factory, officially offered him a position with the company. Just like then, Lucien felt oppressed by all this conspicuous opulence from a bygone era.

Peereboom, seated at the head of the conference table, nodded curtly. Cremers introduced the two other gentlemen present: Mr. Van Bosse Loman, chairman of the board of commissioners, and – to his surprise – Marnix Christiaans. He hadn't recognized him from behind when he entered the room. Marnix got up and shook his hand, but unlike at Swanny's soirée, now he was distant and businesslike. Cremers explained that Mr. Christiaans represented the Ministry of Foreign Affairs in his capacity as the government's advisor on opium affairs. 'But I understand you're already acquainted,' he added. Lucien wondered what Marnix had told him. This wouldn't have something to do with that business on Java, would it, which he had of course neglected to mention on his original application?

They offered him a seat and shifted their chairs in order to face him directly. Peereboom began: 'Do you have any idea why we've called you here at such short notice?'

Lucien was taken aback. It felt like the start of an

interrogation. They knew something he didn't know, but ought to. Better to keep things vague. Smiling, he raised his eyebrows. 'No, gentlemen, but I certainly did wonder as much on the way here.'

Peereboom glanced briefly at Cremers.

'Two days ago you went to Thielt in Flanders to deliver an order. Can you describe the trip, the delivery of goods and any-thing unusual you may have noticed?' Lucien stared blankly at him for a few moments. 'Go ahead,' Peereboom prodded.

Lucien took a deep breath and gave, to the best of his ability, a detailed account of the journey. He mentioned the incident outside the customs office, which hadn't really disrupted the smooth handling of the formalities, described the remainder of the trip to Thielt – uneventful, with the exception of the many time-consuming checkpoints – and their search for the build-ing behind the monastery, relying on Biedermann's instruc-tions; he went on to relate how they had handed the goods over to the staff officer of the medicine reserve depot, P. Wammeier, and finally, how they had spent the night at the Grand Hôtel de la Gare, across from the railway station in Thielt. When he'd finished he quickly retraced his thoughts, to make sure he hadn't forgotten anything. He saw no point in mention-ing having slept through the entire outward journey because of a hangover, or bribing the German guards with a bottle of jenever. And although it was the first thing that entered his mind, the hotelier's request to smuggle his son out of the country was hardly relevant; the screaming mass of wounded soldiers at the station and the German officer's suicide, too, were completely beside the point.

As Lucien was speaking, Cremers' attention was focused on a piece of paper in front of him. Once in a while he checked something off with his fountain pen. Lucien imagined that his story was being corroborated with Albert Ketting's; they'd probably questioned the driver first. Would he have mentioned the hotelier, the wounded soldiers or the German officer? No, of course not; refusing an illegal proposal would only meet with their approval, and what did they care about the German wounded and a dead officer? So what was this interview all about then? 'May I ask what the problem is?' he ventured.

Peereboom raised his hand, signalling that he was the one asking the questions here. 'You offered, without it being asked of you, to accompany this shipment. You don't normally do so; why now?'

Lucien's eyes were drawn to the threatening skies above a cow pasture. A landscape by the same painter his father admired, no doubt about it. Peereboom had to repeat the question. 'Because…' Lucien was thinking fast. 'As Flanders is a war zone, I thought it was better for me to join the driver in case of unforeseen problems at the border.'

'Why would there be any problems? The export papers were in order.'

'Well, Mr. Cremers gave me the impression that the delivery might be problematic, and that he was uncomfortable with a shipment so close to the front.' He purposely avoided making eye contact with Cremers, but he felt the full force of the boss's glare. Would this comment get him into hot water, or let him off the hook? What else could he say? 'To be honest, I also wanted to rectify an error,' he added quickly. 'I should have consulted Mr. Cremers before agreeing to Biedermann's terms.'

Cremers coughed and screwed the cap back on his pen. 'Quite right. I'm not in favour of personnel taking this kind of decision without clearing it with me first.'

Lucien held his breath. He'd deftly wriggled out of a precarious situation by acknowledging the technical director's authority.

Silence. A Frisian grandfather clock ticked loudly, the mechanism winding up to chime the half-hour. All eyes were focused on Peereboom. He fiddled with a loose hair on his moustache for a moment. 'All right. The reason for this investigation is this: we received word from the German ministry of war this morning that the shipment delivered to Thielt was 100 kilos short of the amount on the invoice.'

Lucien was dumbstruck. 'That can't be!' he blurted out. 'That's impossible! I was with it from beginning to end.' He racked his brains. 'The lorry was never left unattended, Ketting and I were with it the entire time. And the number of crates tallied at every single checkpoint in Flanders…' Their eyes continued to bore into him. Storm clouds gathered in his head. 'I'm telling you, it's impossible!' he shouted. 'The Germans are lying!'

'Calm down, Hirschland, there's no reason to raise your voice,' Peereboom said coolly.

No reason to raise his voice! He was being addressed accusingly, treated like an embezzler, a common thief, or at least an accomplice! He went over the delivery in his head, step by step… They had opened just one vial; he had given Wammeier a sample of cocaine to test, it was approved and then… well, then they left. 'Wammeier didn't count the crates, at least not while I was there. I couldn't say why,' he thought out loud.

'Did you speak to anyone about this transaction?' asked Van Bosse Loman, from the board of commissioners.

Nonplussed, Lucien furrowed his brow. 'Of course not, sir, I never discuss matters concerning the business. And certainly not concerning deliveries. No, I can assure you that no one knew about this trip.' He recalled Swanny boasting, with Christiaans in the room, that he had just returned from Flanders. His hands trembled ever so slightly. But Marnix just stared at the ceiling. Desperation was beginning to mount. What could have happened? Biedermann! That conniving German dog! Wasn't he in Thielt just before they arrived? Could he be behind these allegations? To get back at the Dutch for claiming damages for the torpedoed cargo ship? He almost mentioned it, but thought better of it – let them come to that conclusion themselves. 'As far as I'm concerned,' he said assertively, 'it's the Germans' problem!'

'At the moment, Hirschland, it's our problem,' said Cremers. 'The Germans are refusing to pay for the hundred kilos they say they didn't receive. Without any evidence, we can hardly accuse them of stealing it. It certainly wouldn't do our trade relations any good.' He glanced at Peereboom. 'Seeing as the German army is an important client,' the bank president chipped in, 'we've decided to send them those hundred kilos free of charge. It means a double loss. You'll understand that your commission will be adjusted accordingly. We won't hold you responsible, since we have to presume neither you nor Ketting had anything to do with the disappearance of the cocaine.'

Now Lucien was angry. 'Of course I've nothing to do with it. You don't think I'd jeopardize my job? And what would I do with all that cocaine? Go and peddle it to pharmacists in my spare time?'

Peereboom struck the table with both hands. 'Mr. Hirschland, you surprise me! Are you really so naïve? Or do you think we were born yesterday? You know as well as I do that a hundred kilos of cocaine is worth a fortune on the black market!'

Then Marnix Christiaans joined the discussion: 'I think we can assume that Mr. Hirschland acted in good faith. In order to sell such a large quantity illegally, you'd need certain contacts that, according to our information, Mr. Hirschland does not have.'

Lucien glowered at the wall. Confound it, what did a Foreign Office civil servant have to do with a transaction between a manufacturer and customer? And what was 'according to our information' supposed to mean?

Peereboom made a questioning gesture toward Cremers and Van Bosse Loman, concluded that the interview was finished and said to Lucien: 'We'll be investigating this business thoroughly and I'm counting on your full co-operation.'

Cremers nodded at Lucien as a sign he could go. Lucien got up and wished the gentlemen a good day. Marnix walked him to the door. But instead of closing it behind him, he accompanied him out into the marble hallway. Lucien could no longer contain himself. 'Marnix, what's this all about? What are you doing here?'

Marnix put his arms pensively behind his back and slowed his pace. 'Like Peereboom said: I'm the government's advisor on opium affairs; that means all narcotics, including cocaine. My minister appreciates being kept informed of any difficulties with foreign trade partners.'

'Even a bit of missing cocaine?' asked Lucien incredulously.

'One hundred kilos, Lucien, that's more than a "bit". The point is, we're concerned about the illicit trade. There's already enough smuggling going on in this country. The production of cocaine is of economic importance to the state, so The Hague and your firm – in this case the Koloniale Bank – have a mutual interest.'

'I've never heard anything about a black market,' said Lucien sulkily.

'That's an inherent risk with this kind of product. That's why I'm personally in favour of a state monopoly on both the harvest of coca leaves and the production of cocaine, like we do with opium. There's no better way to keep smuggling and illegal trafficking under control. I've advocated this position a number of times at the international opium conferences in The Hague. But the Americans are against it; they cling to their free-market principles and accuse us of using the cocaine trade to top up the state's coffers. They're not entirely wrong there – a good deal of our colonial profits come from the government's opium factory in the East Indies, and the same would go for profits from state-run cocaine production. What's wrong with that?'

'I understand that in England and Germany they've brought cocaine supplies more or less under government control,' said Lucien.

'Exactly. It confirms how afraid they are of illegal trafficking. The Germans in particular are incredibly jittery about cocaine hitting the streets. There's enough public discontent there already. They know full well there's a black market, and it's not out of the question that their own military is doing the supplying. But since they can't be sure, they're happy to blame us for the time being – and they get 100 free kilos to boot.'

'So why grill me like I'm a suspect?'

'We have to be sure that none of our cocaine is disappearing into the black market via a Dutch smuggling network. We simply can't afford that kind of suspicion. Our business dealings have to be completely above board, otherwise there'll be hell to pay with the Americans and the English – they're all scared to death of street drugs. Peereboom wants to find out if you have any contact with obscure dealers. As a commercial traveller you're bound to get some pretty attractive offers…' He smiled reassuringly. 'But I know that's not the case, so you needn't worry.'

Lucien stared at the ground and considered how best to voice his own suspicions. 'Listen, just between us: Franz Biedermann, the buyer from Merck… I do business with him. I think he made off with that hundred kilos.'

'Franz Biedermann… No, no, he has nothing to gain from it. He's trying to work the war to his advantage from an entirely different angle.'

'Good God, Marnix, what the hell is it with Biedermann? Who is he?'

Christiaans looked at his watch. 'Another time… I've got to get back to the meeting now, we've got other business to discuss.' He held the street door open for Lucien and hesitated. 'I'm assuming, like you have, that a few officers in Thielt have set up a profitable little trade.' He offered Lucien his hand. 'Do give my regards to Swanny,' he said amicably. 'We'll have dinner soon, the three of us, like I promised. I'm looking forward to it.'

Lucien yanked the Harley off its kickstand. Marnix's comment about a bunch of German officers operating a profitable little trade surprised him. He hadn't said anything of the kind… Marnix had a crafty way of putting words into your mouth. He kick-started the bike, threw it into gear and drove along the canal. At any rate, he'd come out of it unscathed. But he resolved never again to interfere with the transportation and delivery of an order. He'd stick to his job: sales, drawing up contracts and seeing to the proper signatures. Where the cocaine went, who used it, and whether smugglers or drug traffickers were involved, was none of his business.

13

The fishing otter

The black clouds of the battlefield slowly dissipated. The mud, blood and filth faded to a colourless haze in his memory. Each new hospital where Robin was taken, ever further from the front, was brighter and more immaculate than the one before it. Each nurse, each doctor that bent over him was more spotlessly dressed than the previous one. He had already dreamt that they were cherubs accompanying him to Paradise. Someone up there must have decided to let the grimness he had seen dissolve into a dazzling light.

But the hospital where he now found himself topped them all: the flood of natural light that streamed in made the pristine white walls and ceiling positively luminous. The bed sheets crackled with freshness, as did his pyjamas and even Robin himself: never before had he been so thoroughly scrubbed.

Even his thoughts began to clear. They'd discontinued the morphine once he stopped complaining about the pain. But even though he'd jumped off the narcotic carousel, the sudden withdrawal made him prone to phantoms that preyed on his sanity. They had to be conquered, and he expended all his energy and willpower on the struggle. He knew he was on the mend; he started to recognize himself, as though he was being reunited with the old Robin. He spent sleepless nights testing and mastering his mental faculties, trying to put the chaotic scenes at the front into some kind of order. Regaining his life was like painstakingly rebuilding a collapsed structure, brick by brick. Every hour he began anew, adding another bittter memory, another nightmarish recollection.

But once immersed in sleep he lost his grip on his thoughts, and the one thing that really mattered drove out all the others, the question he'd asked himself at the very last moment, when the shrapnel hit him: what had happened to his face? He hadn't asked, and no one offered an explanation – until the crossing from Calais to Dover, when the pitching made him so seasick that he vomited into the dressing. The contents of his stomach sloshed under the bandage. He felt the damp gauze against his skin, but there was no trace of the penetrating smell of sick. How was that possible? The bandage was soaked through, so why couldn't he smell anything? Was there something wrong with his nose? He lay on his back, the blanket tucked snugly around him, right up to his chin. He didn't dare wriggle his arms loose to grope over the bandage. '*Grand dieu*, they've made a mess of this,' the voice was saying.

He suddenly remembered having seen, before they embarked, a small card attached to his buttonhole with his medical particulars. Probably name, address, destination and who knows what else… Maybe something about the nature of his wound. He had to find out what was on that card. But the medics and nurses tending to the patients bustled about so briskly amongst the rows of stretchers that he couldn't seem to attract their attention. Only a wounded soldier on crutches, leaning up against the wall, responded to Robin's groans. His mouth was dry and it was difficult to speak clearly through the bandage, but he managed to ask him to read what was on the card. The soldier sank down on one knee – his other leg was reduced to a stump – found the card and read out loud: 'Shrapnel wound – Face – Serious.'

'What does that mean?' asked Robin.

'Your head's half blown off, I expect,' answered the soldier. He pulled himself upright and hobbled back to his spot against the wall. 'Says your destination is Queen Mary's Hospital.'

Serious. What on earth would constitute 'serious' in this God-awful war? Did 'serious mean' the same thing as 'a goner'? Was he going to that hospital to wait for the end?

Once he'd got used to the dazzling light of Queen Mary's Hospital, and the morphine had worked itself out of his system, he realized that this was a special institution for 'Shrapnel wound – Face – Serious' cases. In the bed next to him lay a man with only half a face; on the other side a boy, no older than eighteen, whose whole jaw had been ripped away. He had to be fed through a tube attached to a funnel, with a small bowl held where his chin used to be. Robin knew that there were at least ten more men on the ward, but he didn't dare look at them and kept his one eye closed as much as he could, so he could concentrate on what was going on inside his head. The outside world was just too much for him.

But this morning, his third day at the hospital, he couldn't bear it any more and summoned the courage to speak to Nurse Jenkins, who had already changed his dressings twice – which meant she'd seen his face. When she had finished attending to him and was getting ready to leave, he asked: 'Nurse… do I still have a nose?'

She nodded sympathetically, as though she'd been expecting the question, pulled a chair over to his bedside and sat down in it like she had all the time in the world. 'Your face has been badly wounded, Robin,' she answered calmly. 'You've been brought here so something can be done about it. It's not for me to go into details, but Dr. Gillies will explain everything. He should be doing his rounds any moment. So we'll just have to sit tight.' She'd called him by his first name and spoken to him in a normal tone of voice. It was the first time in weeks he'd been treated to anything other than curt instructions and anonymous jabber.

She seemed to want to pass the time until the doctor came, and asked if he knew where Queen Mary's Hospital was. 'Have you ever heard of Sidcup?' He couldn't remember, maybe he'd heard of it once, or should have. But, lest she doubt his mental faculties or imagine the explosion had somehow damaged his brain, he didn't answer. 'Sidcup's in Kent, southwest of London,' she explained, 'and Queen Mary's Hospital…' she gestured at the stark white walls, 'has only been open a few weeks. Even the paint's still fresh.' So it smelled of paint… if he still had a nose he'd have smelt it. As though aware of her slip of the tongue, she smoothed out the edge of the sheet while she carried on chatting. 'We've been so lucky. Dr. Gillies supervised the purchase of this estate, and brand-new wards were built in record time, so we've now got six hundred beds! We're also fortunate to have such delightful surroundings. Once you're feeling better you should go for walks in the park; I find it so restful.' She glanced out the window, her head tilted slightly, and then turned back to him. 'Shall I swing your bed around so you can look outside?' He shook his head. 'Well, perhaps later…' She glanced at the wall clock and continued: 'We've got the best surgeons, internists, radiologists, jaw specialists and anaesthetists, and of course –' she smiled mischievously

'– lots of nurses. We're all here to help you.' Although she was clearly doing her best to put him at ease, he was still on edge. She'd refused to say anything about his nose.

Nurse Jenkins got up and pushed the chair back up alongside the head of his bed. A tall, gaunt man in a doctor's coat appeared in the doorway. His wiry legs, long neck and jutting head gave him the appearance of a crane. Without looking up from his notebook, he walked straight towards Robin. When he reached the bed he slid the notebook into his pocket and looked at him intently. 'I'm Dr. Harold Gillies,' he began, 'and you are Robin Ryder.' The seriousness vanished as soon as he started to talk; his tone was more confidential than friendly. 'You're here thanks to my good friend Auguste Valadier. He thinks I can do something with your face.' Valadier – he pronounced it with a French accent. That voice: another piece of the puzzle between the devastating explosion and this hospital bed.

'I understand from your papers that you come from Great Yarmouth and you're a schoolteacher,' said Gillies. 'Have you contacted your parents yet?' Robin did not know how to answer; he just shuddered. He hadn't dared give Mum and Dad more than a fleeting thought. Gillies looked at him steadily. 'You're their only son, they'll be worried sick. Would you like to let them know you're here, and that we'll notify them when you're ready for them to visit?'

Robin nodded.

'And do you have a fiancée or a sweetheart you'd like us to contact?'

The panic returned. Just the words 'fiancée' and 'sweetheart' made him think of Mary, and the vague recollection of having done something awful to her, something violent... probably in a morphine-induced stupor, but still he was overcome by shame just at the thought of it.

Gillies didn't pursue the subject. He put on his half-glasses. 'Let's have a look, shall we.' The nurse had positioned herself on the opposite side of the bed and deftly unwound the bandages. Gillies studied his face thoroughly, but his eyes didn't betray anything 'serious'. He carefully ran his long fingers over the place where Robin experienced a strange pain, as though the skin wanted to tear open. Gillies pulled the chair over and sat down. 'Here's how things stand. A large part of your left cheek is gone, and the upper part of your nose as well. You already know you've lost your left eye. It's a pity the surgeon did such a sloppy job, very sloppy indeed... Working under enormous pressure, I'm sure, but still... a great pity.' Gillies wrinkled his brow just a bit, out of irritation or maybe even anger. 'We're going to do our best to put it right.'

Robin listened silently and attentively. He wasn't sure if he'd understood everything.

'Have you seen yourself without the bandage yet?' Gillies asked. Robin just stared back at him. 'It'd be wise do so as soon as possible.' Nurse Jenkins helped Robin prop himself up against the pillows, went off and came back with a mirror. She waited for a sign from the doctor. Gillies was glancing through his notes, probably to give Robin a few moments to prepare himself. He nodded and Jenkins raised the mirror, not abruptly, but gradually.

All the same, it was as though disaster came rushing head-long at him. He snapped his eye shut. He desperately tried to think of something else... What would be on the menu this afternoon? Hopefully a piece of meat, once in a while they got a piece of meat.... He heard the doctor clear his throat. He knew he had to look. There was no point in avoiding it. He opened his eye and focused on the reflection in the mirror, but what he saw was entirely unrecognizable. 'That's not me…' he whispered, relieved, and averted his glance.

'It *is* you, Robin. You've no other choice than to accept it, no matter how difficult that is,' said Gillies. He gave him a full minute. 'Robin! Try it again,' he urged. 'I want you to look. What you see is not the end; try to see it as a beginning.'

Robin looked back at that unfamiliar person in the mirror. The left cheek was pretty much gone. The skin over the cheek-bone was crudely stitched to the skin of the jaw, pulling the right cheek taut, contorting the entire face, especially the mouth. Where the missing eye had once been was now a swollen, red scar. There was a hole at the top of the nose. That was the strangest part: a dark hole in the middle of the face, as though the cranium was open for public inspection.

The nurse lowered the mirror. Robin could breathe easy again. It was as though that spotlessly white hospital ward had a hatch that opened up onto a chamber of horrors. Now everything was back to normal. That horrendous, disfigured head no longer existed. But Dr. Gillies saw through his evasiveness, and went on: 'We're going to do our best to reconstruct your appearance. For starters we'll need a photograph of you from before you were injured. Have you got one, or shall I ask your parents to send one?'

Oh no, there he was bringing up Mum and Dad again. The hatch to the torture chamber opened again for an instant. He realized he'd better accept it: he had seen himself. And what he saw approached the unfathomable. He'd lost more than just his nose, his entire face was irreparably maimed. How could he ever ask his parents to come and see a monster, a deformed clown?

Gillies continued: 'You do want me to make you look like your old self, don't you… and not someone else?' He smiled at him, perhaps checking whether Robin was ready for a little joke. Robin gestured in the direction of the nightstand containing his personal belongings. The nurse fished around in the drawer and pulled out his wallet. She knew, of course, where soldiers usually kept their photos.

He took the wallet from her. The leather was still spattered with blood and mud… when had he last held it in his hands? He pulled a snapshot from one of the pockets, of him and his mother. His uncle had taken the photo just before he got on the train. Mum wasn't looking her best – she glowered, still angry that he'd volunteered. She'd given him the photograph anyway, maybe in the hope that it would offer some sort of protection, or just because that's what one did. But he'd never looked at it or shown it to anyone else. He folded the photo in half, with Mum to the back, and handed it to Dr. Gillies. 'Ah, a handsome young man… Now, we'll make a ladykiller out of you yet.' The nurse laughed like it wasn't the first time she'd heard this line. Robin appreciated that the doctor took the trouble to get to know his patients, and to joke with them to try and coax a smile out of those broken faces. That was important; it was part of the acceptance process. Gillies knew, of course, that his patients also suffered from invisible wounds, wounds no surgical knife could ever reach. Robin didn't want to disappoint him and produced a crooked, painful grimace – but it was his first attempt at a smile since he'd been hit. Satisfied, Dr. Gillies nodded and said jauntily to Nurse Jenkins: 'I can see that soldier Robin Ryder is going to be an excellent and co-operative patient.'

They left him alone without re-wrapping his face in gauze

bandages. Only the hole above his nose was taped shut. From now on he was on show for the whole world. Not that it mattered in this ward full of cripples, and the doctors and nurses were used to it by now. But what did matter was that Gillies' visit had, in one fell swoop, robbed this radiantly fresh hospital ward of its illusion as a safe haven. One glance in the mirror was enough to remind him of the outside world. One day in the not-so-distant future he'd have to go out there with this face of his. Dr. Gillies didn't fool him: he was mangled, and there wasn't much to be done about it. Suddenly he saw that horribly disfigured face right down to the smallest detail. Ashamed and disgusted, he buried his arms deep between his legs, afraid his fingers would accidentally touch his face, reminding him that it really did belong to him. He hated that head – it wasn't his at all. He'd ignore it, shun it. It was the enemy that had stayed with him, and he'd fight it by never, ever looking at it again… But even if he managed that, there'd always be the stares. The dread and pity in other peoples' eyes would always, forever and ever, remind him of that hellish sight – that damned eye of his would see to that. He wished to God he was blind. No, no, no… no one from his former life would ever lay eyes on him. Not Mum and Dad, not family or friends, not the children in his class – they wouldn't even recognize him, or worse yet, they'd be terrified of him. Oh God, the school… the most wrenching pain rushed to the fore. Mary, Mary… Now he no longer had a cheek, how could he ever rest it lovingly against hers? How could he ever kiss her, now that instead of a mouth there was only a revolting cavern? How could he ever smell her delicious scent, now that he had no sense of smell? And worst of all: how could she ever bear to be in his presence without seeing him as a patient and taking on the role of nurse? He turned on his side and dug himself deep under the blankets. He sobbed, the anguished tears painfully pressing out of that one eye.

He felt a hand glide over the blanket, caressing his back. 'Please, Robin, come out,' Nurse Jenkins said softly. 'There's no point in hiding.' She drew back the blanket and gently pulled him up until he was lying normally again. Then she took his head in her hands and kissed him on his disfigured cheek.

Dr. Gillies' treatment programme began the next morning. Nurse Jenkins helped Robin into his dressing gown and led him, gently but with a professional distance, to a room not far from the ward. They were eagerly welcomed by a small, pudding-faced man fiddling with a camera on a tripod. He appeared pleased to meet his new client. 'Come in, welcome! We're going to make some fine portraits of you!' The walls of the studio were covered with photographic prints, all the same format. As Robin walked past the collection he was reminded of an exhibition he'd once seen. An explorer had photographed exotic peoples from all corners of the world. They showed a fascinating array of deliberate body modifications: the lower lip stretched out with large disks; pointy, unnaturally trussed-up heads; stretched-out necks held up with a stack of metal rings; pierced noses and terrifyingly tattooed faces… The public had been shocked. It struck him that the photos on this wall could be turned into an exhibition that would make viewers reel back in horror, for these were no foreign barbarians but their own fathers, brothers and sons.

The photographer sat Robin on a bench and shifted a few lamps into place. He suddenly found himself bathed in a harsh light. 'Wonderful! Wonderful!', the photographer cried. He positioned himself behind the camera, looked through the lens and instructed Robin to sit perfectly still. The soft click of the shutter told Robin his mangled face was being captured for eternity. He was photographed from three sides. Soon he would take his place in the freak show on the wall.

That afternoon Dr. Gillies fetched him from the ward in person, and together they walked through the long corridors of the hospital. Robin had not yet ventured so far from his bed. He lowered his head timidly when they passed hospital staff. Dr. Gillies paid it no heed and gave an animated account of the artist whose studio they were about to visit. Henry Tonks, a friend of Gillies, was a former surgeon who'd fallen in love with painting. His passion now served him well. 'Henry's going to paint you,' Gillies explained, 'his colour portrait, and the photos, will tell us more about your wounds and give me a better idea of how to restore your face.' He added, with a laugh: 'Be grateful he's doing the painting, because otherwise, heaven forbid, I'd have done it myself.' He looked askance at Robin. 'I even took a painting class, you know, but portraits weren't exactly my forte… I couldn't even produce a reasonable sketch.'

He opened the studio door and introduced him to Tonks as though Robin was a new addition to their circle of friends. As Gillies walked from one easel to the next, inspecting the half-finished portraits, he picked up brushes and fingered tubes of paint. Tonks winked at Robin and told Gillies to keep his mitts off the tools. 'Professional jealousy,' Tonks said.

'I can't bear it that you're good at something I'm not!' exclaimed Gillies.

'Rubbish! You can do what no one else can.' Tonks pulled on a paint-smeared smock. Robin eyed them both and wondered what drove these two extraordinary men. Was it really about helping the patients as best they could, or did all these mutilated creatures simply give them the chance to show off their special talents? Gillies excused himself and Tonks invited Robin to take a seat on a high stool so he could study his face. He came so close that Robin could feel his breath on his skin.

At first Robin felt ill at ease, but in the days that followed, during the many hours he spent in the studio, he became accustomed to, and even familiar with, Henry Tonks' unwavering gaze. He even summoned up the courage to make the daily trip to the studio on his own, and did his best to greet the nurses on the way. He also started to take an interest in Tonks' work, following the process of mixing just the right tint of watercolour. Tonks encouraged him to give his opinion at the end of each session; at first he didn't want to look but after a few days he couldn't resist, and the ideas gushed out. Tonks listened attentively and praised Robin's artistic insight, even encouraged him to try his hand at painting himself. If he wanted, he could start right now, in a corner of the studio. 'Plenty of materials, as you can see. We've got generous sponsors!'

Gillies came to inspect the final result. His hands behind his back, he studied the painting and nodded his approval and admiration. Oddly, Robin felt as though he'd a hand in Tonks' success. Who cared if it was the portrait of a cripple: it was an accurate rendition, with well-chosen colours and precise details, and Robin was convinced his input had contributed to the end result. 'Robin's got talent,' said Tonks. 'I think he should have a go at it himself one of these days.' Gillies agreed, but for now appeared to have other plans and motioned to Robin to follow him.

He led him to his office, three doors further on. Large sheets of paper with Robin's portraits pasted to them were spread out on a table. Pen marks dotted the photographs, with scribbled comments fanning out onto the paper. This, thought Robin, was where Gillies' special expertise came in. The doctor bent his lanky frame over the table and pointed to one of the photographs. The hole in the nose was circled, with a capital A in it. A square had been lightly sketched into the forehead, also marked with an A. The two A's were connected by an arrow. 'Now, here's how we're going to close up your nose. I'm going to cut away a piece of cell tissue from your forehead, just under the hairline, leaving it connected on one side. I'll stitch the opposite side to your nose just under the hole. That flap of tissue will be temporarily sewn shut, to ensure proper circulation and prevent the tissue from dying off.' He peered over his glasses to gauge Robin's reaction. He just gaped at the photos. 'It'll look like you've got a living tube going from your forehead to your nose,' continued Gillies. 'Once it's properly attached I'll separate the tissue from your forehead and use it to seal off your nose. What do you think?' he asked, clearly pleased with his impressive plan.

'Incredible…' was all that Robin could think of.

'And now your cheek.' Gillies took another white sheet of paper with a print of the same photograph. A loose sketch of a neck and torso more than confirmed the doctor's inability to draw. Gillies explained that he'd proceed in the same manner here: another, wider flap of skin tissue would be sliced from his chest, which would be attached to his cheekbone, forming a larger tube than the previous one. It would provide enough new tissue for the reconstruction of his cheek. Now Robin understood why some of the other patients seemed to have weird tubes growing out of their arms, forehead or chest and leading to their face. What he had taken for bizarre wounds were in fact the creations of Dr. Harold Gillies. 'So what do you think?' he asked again.

'Incredible,' Robin repeated, for he genuinely found it all hard to believe.

'We're going to patch you up using your body's own tissue, isn't that wonderful?'

'It's terrific, Dr. Gillies,' Robin said, genuinely awestruck. 'Is this your own discovery?'

'It certainly is, and I'm very proud of it, although there's still plenty of room for improvement.'

Robin stared at him. 'Have you ever thought of becoming a plumber?'

Gillies roared with laughter and slapped Robin on the shoulder.

Five months and three operations later, in January 1918, Robin's eye socket was neatly sewn shut, and the hole in his nose had also been repaired with tissue taken from his forehead. But Gillies wasn't satisfied with the result. The bridge of his nose was too broad and rough, and would have to be redone. But first he had to construct the tube from his chest that would be used to close off his cheek. That was planned for the following week, but first Gillies wanted Robin to go to the dentist. The impact had knocked some of Robin's teeth out of kilter, and they'd have to be pulled. His twisted bite and inflamed gums caused Robin a great deal of pain, but he never mentioned it. First because he didn't want any more morphine, and second because he knew exactly where these complaints would lead. The mere thought of a dentist was enough to conjure up the bitter childhood memory of the dentist's assistant holding him tightly in the chair while an ingrowing wisdom tooth was pulled.

Even though a visit to the dentist was inevitable, and a trifle compared to the surgery he'd undergone, he still couldn't sleep the night before. Thrashing around, he searched feverishly for anything that might distract his thoughts. At the first glow of daylight he caught sight of the clock: 4 a.m. Another five hours to go. He buried himself under the blankets, hoping to surrender to sleep. 'You needn't pretend,' a voice whispered in his ear. 'I know you're awake.' It was Gillies. 'Come with me.'

Relieved, Robin got out of bed, put on his dressing gown and followed Gillies to the room where the nurses took their daytime tea breaks. The doctor sat down at the table, stretched his legs out over a chair and lit a cigarette. With his index finger he flicked the pack in Robin's direction. Robin shook his head; he hadn't smoked in ages, and besides, it didn't much appeal to him, what with his mouth being all misshapen and inflamed. Gillies closed his eyes for a moment. Robin could see that he was pallid from fatigue. Who knows how long he'd been hunched over an operating table? After a few minutes Gillies opened his eyes and sat up straight. 'I know you're worried about the dentist,' he said in a calm voice. 'It seems absurd, seeing as you've weathered everything else so bravely. But our course is a long one, and something as trivial as a visit to the dentist can suddenly look daunting. Perhaps when you're sitting in that chair later this morning it might help to relax by concentrating on something pleasant.' He took a drag on his cigarette, studied the long ash and, not finding an ashtray within reach, let it flutter to the floor. 'A few weeks ago I was so tired,' he continued, 'that I went fishing for an hour or so. Nothing relaxes me more. Usually I just nod off, but this time I caught sight of something fascinating among the reeds a little way further upstream. I saw an otter fishing… a beautiful, glistening otter with a long, sleek body. I watched him for a long time, how elegantly he dived and resurfaced… it brought tears to my eyes.' He leant back, like he could see the animal in front of him once more. 'Since then, whenever I'm facing a challenge, I think of that otter. My brain associates it with a pleasant sensation. Try that, try to remember something, some happy moment or event, and concentrate on it while you're sitting in that dentist's chair.'

That won't be hard, thought Robin. The doctor's story had triggered an old memory of his own. He saw himself sitting with Dad on the quayside of the Great Yarmouth fishing harbour, their rods close together above the water. At the end of the day he ran into the kitchen to show off his catch to Mum.

For months now, he'd managed to fend off a visit from his parents, no matter how much they pleaded in their letters. Dad had written that it didn't make a damn bit of difference that his face had been injured, and Mum had scribbled underneath that no matter what he looked like, he was still her boy, her only child, her son… But confronting them was too much for him. Suddenly Robin felt tears well up in his eye, tears not of grief but of anger. Not because Gillies had tweaked his guilty conscience about Dad and Mum, but because he'd told him about going fishing. This threw a spanner into everything they'd so carefully built up. He couldn't bear the thought that the doctor had a life outside the hospital. Gillies was suddenly a killjoy, or worse still, a traitor… he'd breached the protective confines of the hospital. Just like with the mirror, another hole had been smashed in the wall, and he was forced to look outside. There was no avoiding it now – the day would come when he had to leave the hospital, when he'd stand there with his suitcase on the platform of Sidcup railway station, waiting for a train to take him home.

'What are you crying about, Robin?' asked Gillies in a tired voice.

'About the otter,' he answered truthfully.

Gillies gave a weak laugh. 'Try to get some sleep, lad.'

A dental assistant ushered him in at nine o'clock sharp. A jaw surgeon and dental technician were also there as observers. Fortunately they were deep in conversation, allowing him to settle into the chair and close his eye. After his chat with Gillies he didn't sleep a wink, and now he was so exhausted that the dentist had to shake him out of his slumber a few minutes later. He obediently opened his mouth as wide as possible, and the assistant handed the dentist a pair of surgical forceps to pull open the corner of his mouth. The others looked on intently.

Suddenly the fear came back in full spate. Robin began shaking violently and the assistant rushed to the chair and grasped his shoulders. The dentist tried to reassure him. 'Don't worry, I won't pull everything at once, and I'll give you a local anaesthetic.' He chatted as a distraction while he smeared some stuff on Robin's gums. 'Once your cheek has been patched up we'll give you some new teeth. It'll fill your face up properly. Wait till you see how much better you look.' He removed his finger and fumbled around the tray of instruments. Robin lay back and the feeling drained away from the left side of his mouth. Before his tongue also went numb, he ran it quickly over his gums. He recognized the bitter taste at the back of his throat, a taste that brought back pleasant memories.

When the dentist bent back over him, Robin closed his eye and smiled blissfully. Charlie was back, finally… They sat together on the quayside. Their fishing rods hung alongside each other above the water, and further up, in the reeds, a glistening otter fished.

14

Armistice

Lucien and Biedermann shuffled along the row in search of decent seats. Lucien kept his coat on: it was nearly as cold inside the theatre as outdoors. It was a chilly, overcast afternoon in November. Biedermann, his woollen scarf wound double and pulled up to just under his moustache, followed close behind. Behind them other cinemagoers shushed impatiently – the shorts had finished and the feature film was about to start. They quickly took their seats. Lucien glanced furtively at Biedermann, who sat huddled, hands tucked into his armpits, snugly in his fur coat. He looked a bit like a marmot.

A half-empty, ice-cold cinema, thought Lucien irritably, was not the ideal place to warm Biedermann up to Pola's acting talent. Still, unforeseen circumstances had given them this unique opportunity: Biedermann had telephoned unexpectedly a few days earlier with the news that he'd be in Amsterdam for business and wanted to get together. They hadn't seen one another since the incident of the missing cocaine, more than a year ago. It hadn't been necessary; negotiations concerning amounts, prices and discounts could all be conducted by telegraph and the occasional brief, businesslike telephone call. The Koloniale Bank had arranged for the Germans to set up their own depot on Dutch soil, where they could collect and check their orders themselves, so ruling out any suspicion of Dutch complicity in black-market trading. Lucien suspected that Marnix Christiaans was behind this clever move, but never asked him.

And then, out of the blue, Biedermann rang him up, not at the factory but at home on the Oranjekade. Adopting a chummy tone, Franz asked after him and his sister, and inquired whether that *wunderschöne* Pola Pauwlova was still enjoying a successful film career. He didn't give any reason for wanting to meet, but it must be something important, that much was clear. Lucien bet that German drug companies must be facing hard times now that Germany had pretty much lost the war. Perhaps Biedermann was looking to secure his future by returning to the film industry. He'll have remembered Pola and – clever old fox – planned to make his comeback as a producer using her as his trump card. A year ago Lucien might have stymied it, but now he was willing to take the risk. Pola had been in a funk for months, ever since Mauritz Binger had once again given a leading role that Pola had set her heart on to Annie Bos. So Franz's call came like manna from heaven.

But to his astonishment, straight after they'd drunk a quick cup of coffee on his arrival at the Central Station, without more ado Biedermann came right out and asked if he could arrange a meeting with Thomas Olyrook, preferably that same day. 'You'll find out why soon enough,' he added, as if some treat was in store. But Lucien's disappointment at this strange request evaporated when Biedermann readily accepted his offer to go and see Pola's latest film. As it was still a couple of hours until their appointment with Olyrook, the cinema excursion slotted neatly into their schedule.

The lights dimmed, and the film's title appeared on the screen. Lucien leant over, translated it for his companion as *When the Lights Went Out* and added: 'Appropriate, isn't it?' Biedermann chuckled. Lucien was relieved: Franz was clearly in a good mood and was absorbed by the action on screen. Annie and Pola played two sisters vying for the affections of a handsome composer. Lucien was also seeing the film for the first time; he'd been incredibly busy in recent months, and these past few weeks in particular he'd secured a lot of orders. He had to concentrate on the plot, because Biedermann would surely want to talk about it after. The composer clearly preferred Annie, which condemned Pola to the role of the jealous sister; adding insult to injury, Annie then married the composer. Thank God, within minutes tragedy struck: Annie came down with an eye disease and went blind. Now Lucien understood why Pola had wanted Annie's role so badly: a character with a physical handicap gave an actress a golden opportunity to pull out all the stops. Poor Pola. All that was left for her was to play housekeeper to the blind Annie. This kind of humiliation could not go unpunished. She retaliated in spades – you could count on Pola for that – seducing the composer and deviously snatching him from under Annie's nose. It was a role that did full justice to her talent.

The dramatic climax of the story, no doubt culminating in a happy ending for Annie and disgrace for Pola, had to wait until the operator had changed film reels. In this break, Lucien turned to Biedermann in the hope of sounding out his initial reaction, but was interrupted by a man who climbed on stage in front of the screen and introduced himself as the house manager. He apologized for the disruption but had an important announcement to make. 'I have just learned that the armistice took effect today, 11 November, at 11 o'clock in the morning!' he exclaimed. 'Soldiers have laid down their weapons, and the guns are silent. We are at peace, ladies and gentlemen! I just wanted to share this excellent news with you.' The manager was evidently a devout Christian, for he ended his little speech by folding his hands together piously and closing his eyes for a moment. A mild hubbub arose; here and there seats banged shut as people got up and hurriedly left the theatre.

Lucien remained seated with his hands in his lap. It was embarrassing to hear this news in the company of someone from the losing side. Biedermann coughed and turned to him. 'Pola Pauwlova is an excellent actress,' he whispered, 'and she is indeed a ravishing woman.' Lucien nodded awkwardly and momentarily considered raising the subject of a German film role, but thought it more seemly to express his concern first. 'Franz… Germany has lost – what'll it mean for you?' Biedermann nudged the scarf down with his chin. 'That's why I'm here,' he answered, smiling. The film resumed. Lucien was left to ponder on what Biedermann's reply, not to mention his roguish smile, might have meant. Was his hunch correct that Franz's visit had to do with a new career at Universum Film? But then why would he want to speak to Thomas? No, it must have something to do with Merck and the factory. Maybe Biedermann had decided not to put all his eggs in one basket.

On screen, Annie Bos had got wind of the adulterous affair between her husband and her sister, and decided to hurl herself into the sea. Behind them, someone sighed indignantly. Lucien began to realize why Pola was so down about this role: the real drama was that she was plainly not the heroine and had no chance of winning the audience's hearts. She was no more than a cheap hussy who had stolen her sister's husband. Film audiences didn't forgive that kind of thing so easily, and winning back their favour was going to be no simple task. Once a tart, always a tart – she could forget any leading roles as kindly, caring women for the time being. Besides, they usually asked blonde actresses to play those roles; brunettes were always the sultry seductresses, which of course suited Pola down to the ground.

Once the lights came back up they stood up to leave. The few remaining patrons left with their shoulders hunched, bracing themselves for the cold outside. Biedermann smoothed down his overcoat and looked at his watch. 'Is that coffee-house far from here?'

'No, no, we've plenty of time,' Lucien assured him as they walked up the aisle, and asked what he'd thought of the film. 'Excellent,' Franz instantly responded. 'Pola Pauwlova is headed for great things.' Well, that sounded encouraging. First the meeting with Olyrook, and then he'd bring it up again.

They only needed to cross three narrow side streets to reach the coffee-house Olyrook had suggested. Lucien went in first, holding the leather curtain aside. The blast of damp heat gave him a momentary shock. He blinked into the dense pall of smoke and looked around the café, spotting Thomas Olyrook at a table in the corner next to a large potbelly stove. He was surprised to see Jan Palacky with him. He waved and pressed his way through the noisy throng of people, with Franz hard on his heels. Reaching the table, Franz took off his hat and unwrapped his enormous scarf. Lucien introduced everybody, and they took the two empty seats with their backs to the crowded café. This seemed not to suit Biedermann, though, as he turned his chair around to face the room. It brought him closer to the roaring stove, where a pair of young men with steaming jackets and holding beer mugs were having an heated argument. Lucien hoped it wasn't about the armistice, peppered with the usual derogatory comments about Germans.

'How was the film?' asked Olyrook.

'Excellent,' Biedermann repeated, and Jan Palacky, who it turned out spoke fluent German, jumped headlong into the conversation. He'd seen the film as well and proceeded to give a blow-by-blow account of the plot, with plenty of personal commentary. Lucien noticed that the years had not been particularly kind to Palacky; the first cracks were starting to show in his youthful good looks. Biedermann shifted impatiently in his chair, loosened his tie, undid his jacket and removed his collar. Perspiration glistened on his forehead. As Jan began to wax lyrical about the American film idol John Barrymore, Biedermann broke in, asking Olyrook if they couldn't perhaps find a quieter location. Palacky, put out at having been so rudely interrupted, took an irritated slurp of his coffee. Thomas looked coolly at Biedermann through his thick spectacles. 'Whatever you have to discuss with me can be discussed here.'

If Biedermann was at all annoyed by his bluntness, he didn't show it, simply nodding his assent. 'I want to talk to you about the future.' He leant over the table, as if to underscore the confidential nature of the discussion. 'Now that the war has turned out so badly for Germany, I'm forced to rethink my position there.' He paused, thoughtfully twirling the ends of his moustache. 'It's a well-known fact that you're an outstanding chemist.'

'As are you,' Olyrook answered with chilly politeness. 'I'm aware of your reputation.'

Lucien looked from one to the other, somewhat taken aback

that Thomas too was aware of Biedermann's reputation as a chemist. Damn it all, it seemed to be some sort of open secret, and he – the one who'd done business with the German for years – was the only one who wasn't in on it.

'As you know, I am employed by Merck & Co.'

'Not for the ministry of war anymore, then?' asked Olyrook. 'If that even exists still.' Biedermann smiled good-naturedly, as though indulging a naughty boy his waspish wisecrack. 'The American branch of the firm has invited me to go and work there,' he continued calmly. 'It's a very attractive offer. The Americans are extremely interested in chemists with, as you call it, a reputation…'

It began to dawn on Lucien that Biedermann had come to extend the same attractive offer to Olyrook. Blood rushed to his head in indignation. Did Biedermann really have the gall to try to lure Thomas Olyrook, a key employee at the factory, to America with promises of a comfortable salary and a huge bonus for himself? This was a brazen attempt at bribery. Olyrook's eyes caught Lucien's for an instant, as if trying to reassure him. Of course, Thomas, who had such a long history with the firm, would never desert it.

'Thomas, you won't go to America, will you?' chimed in Jan Palacky.

Biedermann raised his hand defensively. 'That wasn't my question,' he quickly interposed. 'To be honest, I'm not even considering it myself. I only wanted to emphasize that skilled professionals like us have countless opportunities in such a rapidly-changing world.' He got up, took off his jacket, draped it over the back of the chair and sat down again. The others waited in silent expectation. 'My plan is to start a pharmaceutical business in Berlin, and I'm looking for a number of highly qualified colleagues, perhaps business partners too.' He beckoned over a waiter and ordered a round of coffee, giving them time for the full implication of his words to sink in. Lucien wondered whether he should signal his displeasure at Biedermann's tack straight away; after all, it was only thanks to his mediation that the German was here at all. He glanced at Olyrook, who had taken off his spectacles and was slowly polishing the lenses with his handkerchief. Lucien made desperate eye contact with Jan Palacky.

'And we're not going to Berlin either!' the Czech exclaimed.

'Berlin's a lot closer to Prague than Amsterdam,' Biedermann countered. 'So much easier for you to visit your family.'

'What makes you think I'd even consider it?' Olyrook asked, putting his spectacles back on.

Biedermann looked hard at him. 'Because you and I have the same thing in mind.' Lucien had no idea what he was driving it, but Olyrook apparently did, because he spat back: 'Perhaps I do, but not necessarily with you.'

'If you just think about it, and recall the events of the past year…' – Biedermann scanned the crowd for the waiter – 'then the only possible conclusion you can come to is that you really do want to work with me.'

'Bloody hell!' Jan Palacky was indignant. 'I don't know what this is all about, but it sounds like plain old blackmail to me!'

Olyrook patted him on the arm. 'Not to worry, my dear Jan, it's nothing more than a business proposal.' He cupped his chin in his hand and looked lost in thought. They waited in silence while the waiter set a tray of coffee on the table. 'I suppose I shall need some time to think about it,' said Olyrook finally in a resigned tone. Biedermann nodded, leant back in his chair and turned to Lucien. 'I want to make you the same offer. An outstanding salesman like you who knows the product inside-out would be invaluable to us. I guarantee you that within no time you'll be earning twice what you do now.'

Lucien quickly put his coffee cup back down. He hadn't counted on this. He'd assumed that this attempted bribery – or should he call it the 'interesting offer'? – only applied to Olyrook. On the other hand, though, a new company would clearly need an experienced salesman. And Biedermann was right: Lucien was an outstanding salesman and intimately familiar with the product. His present income was reasonable enough, but no more than that. Just imagine, earning twice what he earned now, and working with Biedermann and Olyrook in Berlin! He knew nothing of Berlin except the film studios there… and in an instant it dawned on him that here was a golden opportunity to kill two birds with one stone. 'I might consider the offer,' he replied, 'on condition that Pola be guaranteed work at UFA.' He reckoned he'd played a strong hand. 'Now that you're here I can arrange a meeting this evening. We can discuss when you'll introduce her to your ex-colleague – the film director, remember? The one who had a role for her a couple of years ago. What do you say, Franz?'

Now it was Biedermann's turn to be surprised. Lucien congratulated himself at having chosen precisely the right moment to corner him. But Franz just burst out laughing. 'Good God, Hirschland, film director? Ex-colleague? What on Earth are you talking about?'

Lucien flushed. He looked down at his shoes and dropped the subject. How could he have been so naïve? This damned German had been pulling the wool over his eyes for years. He saw through the rest of his spiel, but had fallen for this line. All that talk about connections in the film industry was baloney.

Maybe Biedermann had never even been a producer.

But Jan Palacky wasn't quite so quick on the uptake. 'Oh good, then we'll all go to Berlin!' he exclaimed, his smile revealing a gold tooth. 'Pola will become an international film diva and I…,' he said, glowering at Biedermann, 'I also demand to be introduced to that film director. I've always wanted to act! So, *Herr* Biedermann… film roles for Pola and me in return for Thomas and Lucien.' Satisfied with himself, he ran his many-ringed fingers through his hair. 'I also know a thing or two about blackmail!'

Olyrook smiled. 'I second the motion. If you can manage to swing film roles for Pola and Jan, then I promise I'll consider your offer.'

Thomas knew full well that Biedermann had nothing to do with the German film industry, but at the same time he seemed to know where Biedermann's interests lay. And he wanted no truck with the whole business.

'Lucien, have you heard? Armistice!' Swanny was ecstatic. Even before he'd had a chance to take off his coat she burst into the hallway and flung her arms around his neck. Over her shoulder, he saw Tosca Tilanus leaning around the salon doorway, triumphantly clutching a bottle of wine. He took Swanny by the shoulders and held her at arm's length. Her eyes glistened with emotion. No one in the world was as sincere and innocent as his sister. 'I've just heard,' he said warmly, 'and my first reaction was: get home! An historic day like this should be celebrated together!' He beckoned to Tosca to share in the moment. The three of them stood there for a moment in an embrace until Tosca, who was quite sober, decided it was time to open the bottle.

He was relieved to be home again. He'd made swift work of seeing Biedermann off at the train station, to prevent Franz from pressing him to accept the offer, make a new appointment or remind him of the nonexistent film director. Franz, though, didn't refer to the matter any further. He gave the impression of being quite content, although what he had to be satisfied about escaped Lucien. It hadn't exactly been what you'd call a successful mission. Lucien was just pleased that he'd managed to wriggle out of this tight spot and sidestep the row between Olyrook and Jan Palacky. Just before the leaving the coffee-house he'd overheard Thomas desperately trying to convince Jan that Franz had nothing to do with films.

On his perch in the salon, Karel seemed just as delighted with news of the truce as the people; he chirped and screeched while Swanny scratched the back of his neck. Tosca filled three glasses from a bottle of fine red wine, doubtless pilfered from her father's cellar. Handing each of them a glass, she gave a rousing toast: 'To peace!' Swanny choked back her emotions. 'To peace!' Lucien echoed, and at once a marvellous brainwave struck him. 'You know what? We'll celebrate the armistice with the English! Let's all go to London this Christmas. We can stay over New Year's Eve – after four years of war, the British'll want to celebrate their first year of peace in style.' Swanny let out a cheer and looked expectantly at Tosca. 'What a splendid idea! Christmas in England!' she cried, wiggling her hips. She could already picture herself shimmying through the streets of London. Then the doorbell rang.

Christiaans, thought Lucien. Tosca went out into the hall and returned with Marnix, hidden behind an enormous bouquet. Roses in November! They'd have cost him a pretty penny. 'Wonderful news, wonderful news,' he kept repeating. Swanny hugged him and ran to the kitchen with her roses; maybe she was afraid they'd wither before she got them to a vase.

'You're just in time, old man,' Lucien announced cheerfully, 'we've just opened an exceptional bottle of wine.' Even though Marnix was a regular visitor by now, he never quite knew how to act around him. He was obviously here for his sister, though he'd still not made any direct advances. Swanny had told Lucien as much when he last asked. And to his question of whether she felt anything for Marnix, she answered hesitantly: 'I really don't know…' Only after some prodding did she confess that Tosca didn't care for him because he was terribly conservative. Lucien had to realize that Tosca's opinions mattered very much to her; not only was Tosca her best friend, but she was also a really shrewd judge of character. Lucien suspected there was more to it than that. After all, who really cared if someone was conservative? And what did that mean, anyway? 'On the other hand,' Swanny added, 'I don't want you to have to take care of me forever.'

Swanny brought the roses, artfully arranged in a vase, into the salon. Lucien refilled their glasses and was about to propose a toast to Tosca's fine choice of pilfered wine, but she beat him to it: 'To all the refugees who can finally return home!' Marnix's presence seemed to act like a red rag to Tosca, goading her into airing her provocative political views. 'Revolution has broken out all over Europe: soldiers, seamen and labourers are taking control! Down with repression! Down with the ruling class! Long live the revolution!' she cried, as if she was no longer standing in a chic Bloemendaal villa but behind a barricade in some urban slum. Only Swanny joined in, timidly: 'Long live the revolution…' Lucien and Marnix raised their glass out of politeness.

'Fusty old monarchies are being thrown out left and right.' Tosca turned to Marnix. 'And here, the Dutch royal family welcomes the German Kaiser with open arms! What's that all about? The man's a war criminal!'

'Not my department, Tosca,' said Marnix, making an attempt at a smile.

'But you do have an opinion, don't you?' she prodded.

'I'm a civil servant. We're not supposed to have opinions about those sorts of issues.'

'Oh, please, let's not squabble about politics,' Swanny begged, 'not on a day like today!'

There was an uncomfortable silence. Lucien looked at Karel. A bit of his screeching would be a welcome distraction, but the stupid bird was too busy picking at peanuts from his food dish. It surprised him that Swanny hadn't taken advantage of their planned trip to London, which just a few minutes ago caused such a hullabaloo, to divert the conversation. Perhaps she didn't want to have to invite Marnix along. In any case, Tosca decided to postpone any further hostilities and to amuse herself with Swanny. She pulled her over to a stack of gramophone records she'd brought with her. 'I'm going to teach you a few ragtime dances for you-know-where,' she giggled. 'You choose: the foxtrot, the kangaroo hop, the duck waddle or the turkey trot!'

Marnix sat down on the sofa and watched in amusement as the two women made their first attempts at the new dance steps. Lucien, meanwhile, had found a second bottle from the famous Tilanus wine cellar, and as he uncorked it he wondered whether he ought to tell Marnix about Biedermann's offer. It might be a way of getting to the bottom of Biedermann's plans; as a government advisor, Marnix would no doubt have some inside information on the German pharmaceutical industry. Lucien sat down next to Mamix, refilled his glass and offered him a cigar. For a moment they sat in silence, watching Tosca's dance lesson. 'Sidestep, back back, sidestep, smooth and sweep through…' Swanny was doing her best to master the basic steps of the foxtrot.

'I had a strange encounter today,' Lucien began. He chose his words carefully, but knew that if he wanted information from Marnix he'd have to be pretty frank himself.

Marnix listened without taking his eyes off the women. Occasionally he chuckled at Swanny's clumsy attempts to get the hang of the dance steps. Even after Lucien had finished he remained silent. Lucien then asked him outright for his opinion. Marnix pursed his lips and shrugged his shoulders. 'It doesn't really surprise me. Merck's position is uncertain at best. The future of German industry will depend a great deal on what's decided at the peace negotiations. Biedermann seems to prefer to play it safe and start up his own business. But why in Berlin? That part I don't understand. Of course, the Americans will want to get their hands on him.'

It irritated Lucien that Marnix showed no surprise at what he'd told him, but what vexed him the most was his apparent indifference. 'In any event,' he said nonchalantly, 'I'm taking the offer very seriously. I quite fancy the idea of moving to Berlin with Swanny.' Marnix shot him a probing look. 'But first I want to know what Franz Biedermann's game is.'

'I can tell you that,' Marnix said, turning towards Lucien. 'Biedermann's quite some fellow. He's got a colourful past. He started out at the end of the last century as an assistant to Theodor Aschenbrandt, a German army surgeon. At that time Aschenbrandt was experimenting extensively with cocaine, but

Biedermann quickly outstripped him as a scientist. In the end they quarrelled over who had the rights to the research data. Biedermann's always been arrogant and ambitious – probably with good reason – and he's a brilliant chemist with quite a few patents to his name. I imagine he's bitter, because during the war he had to stand by and watch the British flout his patent rights and manufacture products he'd devised.'

'He never let on that he was anything more than an ordinary buyer for Merck.'

'Ah, but the real clincher is that he's also a high-ranking German officer, don't forget. Maybe he was using you to find out who was buying cocaine, and how much.'

Lucien thought about it. He couldn't recall Biedermann ever prying for information. 'I do know that Kirkpatrick wanted to know the same thing.'

'Naturally. The same goes for the English. Every nation at war wants to sound out the enemy's battle readiness.'

'Battle readiness?'

Marnix laid his cigar in the ashtray and took a gulp of wine. 'The availability of certain drugs can be a key factor in wartime.'

Lucien let this sink in. '…meaning a diminished demand for these products in peacetime. This could have serious repercussions for our sales now the war is over.'

Tosca was busy demonstrating another dance, by the looks of it the kangaroo hop. Marnix looked on, smiling. Swanny squealed with delight as she twisted herself into all sorts of contortions.

'So why would Biedermann ask me?' Lucien wondered out loud.

'No idea. You're obviously a good salesman, but there are plenty of those in Germany. Maybe he thinks he can only hook

Olyrook by taking you as part of the bargain. I don't know how close you are to Olyrook.'

'So I'd be better off staying with the firm?'

'I think so. I'd strongly advise against going to Berlin. It's a hornet's nest.'

Lucien looked up, startled. It was the second time he heard something bang against the window, even over the noise of the music. He got up and pulled the curtain aside. Pola was standing on the doorstep, her hair dishevelled and a large stone in her hand. He stormed into the hall and opened the front door. 'Pola!' he shouted as the stone whizzed past his head. Inside, the music stopped abruptly with a grating scratch, and instantly Swanny and Tosca appeared behind him. 'Nothing to worry about!' said Lucien, but Pola was already inside the hallway, screaming: 'Bastard! You bastard! You left me in the lurch again!' Swanny and Tosca rushed to his side. He tried in vain to push them away.

As soon as she caught sight of the two women, Pola began to wail pitifully. Tosca reached her first and tried to find out, through the blubbering, what was wrong. It took Pola just half a minute to blurt out what she'd always thought of Lucien: unreliable, completely untrustworthy, a selfish good-for-nothing... 'He promised to bring me medicine for my migraine,' she sobbed.

The women led Pola inside, and tried to calm her down with a glass of wine. Swanny glared at Lucien, who cast around for excuses that would satisfy both her and Pola. The only thing he could come up with was the armistice: he'd been so absorbed with the plight of the refugees and war casualties that her migraine had completely slipped his mind.

'Can't you see how much pain she's in?' snapped Tosca,

laying a damp cloth over Pola's forehead. Lucien glanced over his shoulder at Marnix, who had lit a fresh cigar and was leaning back comfortably, legs crossed, on the sofa. He just grinned and shook his head.

'Where's her medicine?' demanded Swanny.

'I haven't got any…' was Lucien's lame reply.

'Then you just get yourself down to the pharmacy this instant for some aspirin!' said Swanny in a tone of voice that told him she was not to be crossed.

15

The mask

Snippets of patriotic songs came wafting up the drive. The sound of boisterous shouting drifted across the lawn, echoing through the corridors. Nearer and nearer came the noise until, finally, the doors to the ward were flung open to reveal Corporal Jonas, who roared: 'The bloody war's over!' The other revellers, patients from the hospital who'd been fit enough to travel up to London, tripped over him as they spilled into the ward, yelling: 'We've won! The fighting's over! They've closed the abattoir! No more bloody mess!' Their hospital uniforms were soaked, their wet hair clung to their misshapen heads and raindrops beaded their scars.

'It was bloody terrific!' Jonas strolled among the beds, his arms spread wide like a preacher's. 'The city was chock-a-block! Everyone was outside, no hats, no jackets… Massive crowds, all shouting and singing, it was completely mad!' he shouted, his voice hoarse. Robin eyed him over the top of his book. Jonas approached his bed, bringing a wave of outdoor dampness with him.

'You really missed something, we were almost buried in streamers! And everybody tooting on little bugles and waving flags, thousands of flags… and of course the Union Jack, Jesus

Christ, man, the Union Jack flying everywhere. I was nearly in tears.' His voice became choked with emotion. Willie, a thick-set Welsh miner whose half a tongue made him almost impossible to understand, picked up the baton. 'And all those uniforms! It was a rainbow of khaki and pilots in light blue and officers with gold collars and colonels and majors all riding in Red Tab motorcars!'

Robin sank deeper behind his book, but Jonas yanked it out of his hands and gazed at him with tears in his eyes. 'Whole families hanging out the window, Pa, Ma, the kiddies, granny, all of 'em shouting: "Thanks, boys! Thanks! You won the war!" Waving, hats in the air, thumbs up, kisses – all for us!' He stank of cigarettes, drink and fresh air. His hair was a tangle of confetti and leaves. Behind him, a boy from Glasgow tugged nervously at his cap; he stared intensely at Jonas's lips. He had no ears. 'You know,' Jonas continued, a tear rolling down his disfigured cheek, 'even Crimean War veterans were there, wheeled out of Chelsea Hospital in their red uniforms!' He covered his face with his hands. The others went from bed to bed, giving their own noisy account of the armistice party to the patients.

'And whole battalions of ambulance nurses were dancing through the streets, arm in arm with farm volunteers!' Jonas licked his lips. 'You could take your pick of lovely girls!' The others chimed in, crowding around Robin's bed. 'You should've seen 'im!' exclaimed Willie, gesturing at Jonas. 'A firecracker went off and 'e jumped ten foot in the air and burst out cryin'!'

'Shut up, you pillock!' bellowed Jonas, flailing wildly at Willie. 'I'd just got meself a Red Cross nurse, if you please, her tits heaving with medals, and me asking 'er: "Mind if I take a closer look?"' They all roared with laughter.

'That's right, today this bleeding hospital uniform was just the ticket! Today, for once, you were somebody, not just a pathetic crip!' Willie straightened his red tie, the war wounded's special insignia.

'Long live the crips! Long live the war wounded! Long live us, the heroes!' shouted Jonas.

Nurse Jenkins came in, a strand of streamers dangling off her cap. 'Calm down, gentlemen, I think that's enough for now, let's take the party back into the corridor! Think of the boys in bed.' Laughing, she fended off Willie, who seemed determined to hug her. The group shuffled submissively out into the passage. Jonas turned and shouted back at Robin: 'Come on, mate, you can come and sit with us, can't ya?'

'Maybe later,' he replied. He put his book down on the nightstand and turned his back to the door, pulling the sheet up over his head. Armistice. Big party, lots of booze. He could see it already: flags waving, the streets littered with confetti, and everywhere widows and orphans, heroes and martyrs, black-market traders and war profiteers, all dancing and singing, arm in arm: the country's been saved, the war's been won, the Hun crushed. Would the streets of Great Yarmouth be full of revellers as well? Of course, why not? Dad and Mum would be looking at all the commotion from their porch; it wouldn't do to join the raucous party on the street while their son was lying injured in hospital. But they could raise a toast to peace with the neighbours. 'Pity your Robin isn't home yet,' the man next door would say. Mum just dabbed her eyes with a handkerchief and sighed. Dad went on and on about how lucky they were he was still alive. 'Surely he's been given a medal for heroism,' the neighbour's wife wanted to know. 'On a day like today,' answered Dad, 'our thoughts are with those parents who've lost a child.' It was all he could say, of course… there'd been no word of any medals.

Out in the corridor, Jonas and the rest kept telling their boisterous tales of willing girls. Nurse Jenkins's voice began to take on an impatient tone.

Did the parents of the children in his class let them stay up late and join the festivities? Would someone have told them their teacher had been wounded? Of course. The headmaster had gone to his class and told them Mr. Ryder was a war hero, a courageous soldier who'd risked his life for God, King, and Country – and most of all, don't forget, for freedom, *their* freedom. They must never forget that. But naturally they'd already forgotten it – children at that age forget quickly, and they'd already got used to their new teacher. Perhaps they'd gone to Mary's class. Mary. Would the sight of a wounded soldier in a wheelchair today remind her of him, or was she blissfully promenading on the arm of some handsome pilot in one of those dazzling light-blue uniforms? She'd come round to ask after him a few times, so he'd heard from Dad and Mum. Dad had told that charming lass from the school the hard truth. 'What else could we do, son?' he'd said, when they'd visited him last week. 'She'd find out sooner or later.' Dr. Gillies had finally convinced him to let them come and visit; in his experience, parents were the first to accept their son's injuries. It might help him.

He'd had six operations in the past year. Gillies had reconstructed the bridge of his nose with some success, though it felt permanently blocked. Once, he really did think he smelt something when Nurse Jenkins came close: a whiff of lavender… He didn't dare ask her, to spare himself the disappointment of having imagined it. But his cheek was a problem, and Gillies was far from satisfied. The transplant from his chest went well; there was enough tissue to close the gaping hole, but there was unsightly swelling around the sutures, especially on his jaw. Gillies wanted to operate again.

Robin had been dreading Mum and Dad's visit. Three times he nearly asked Nurse Jenkins to cancel, but Gillies would get wind of it and he didn't feel like another lecture. And anyway, there was no dodging it, he couldn't hide here forever. He just had to grin and bear it, in an hour it'd be over. But the day before they were due to arrive he was suddenly seized by a claustrophobic dread, followed by blind panic. He simply couldn't face seeing his parents again. He knew exactly how it would go: Mum would burst into tears and blame him for having enlisted in the first place, she was against it then, and now look what had happened! And then Dad... white as a sheet, the colour drained from his lips, speechless because it was so much worse than he'd imagined, even in his worst nightmares. And who could blame them: what sane person would guess that valiantly defending your country could lead to this? Who could have ever imagined that the price of freedom would be sacrificing your face?

There was a way out. They still had to pull one more tooth, and the dental technician wanted to fit his new prosthesis one last time. He managed to shift the appointment to the morning of their visit, two hours before he had to confront his parents.

Robin's fear of the dentist had long since vanished – he even looked forward to sinking into the chair and enjoying a couple of hours in that blissful state. The dentist was an older, good-natured man who showed compassion for his patients. He believed that the boys in this hospital had suffered enough, and didn't want to add to their pain. So when Robin complained nervously that the anaesthetic wasn't working, and that he still had feeling in his jaw, the dentist smeared another dose – a generous one this time – of that delectable stuff over his gums, which Robin greedily scooped up with his tongue. The taste of ether burned the back of his throat. Charlie was back. He could have whooped for joy… Half an hour later, the hole in his jaw oozing blood, he returned to the ward, all the while hatching fabulous plans for the future with Charlie. Now he felt invincible and well primed for the reunion with his parents.

An hour later, his senses were tingling, but somehow he felt strangely indifferent as he watched them walk through the door. They strode straight up to his bed with forced smiles; Gillies must have given them a pep talk. No trace of surprise or dismay. Christ, they were looking at him like there was nothing at all the matter, as if it was the same son they had waved off at Great Yarmouth station. His mother stood next to his bed, a slight twitch in her eye and a homemade apple pie in a cardboard box in her hand.

'I'm so pleased to see you again, son,' she said stiffly. 'Can I give you a kiss, or is the wound still too sore?'

Oh-oh, she'd forgotten to ask that. Tell me, doctor, will he fall to bits if I give him a kiss? He pulled his arm defensively over his face; he wasn't ready for any intimacy with his mother. She sank bank mechanically into a chair. Her thumbs pressed tiny dents into the box. Dad shook his hand and said that it wasn't so bad after all. Typical Dad, like a bull in a china shop: "Don't mention his face straight off the bat, Mr. Ryder". Jesus, what a blunder… Just look at him biting his lip. And well he might! Not so bad after all, Christ! Just look at your son, your brave bloody son, who's got a train wreck for a face, more sloppily patched up than a five-year-old would do with a rag doll.

'We've brought some clothes for you. They were hanging in

your cupboard anyway and we didn't dare buy new ones; we weren't sure if your size... you know what I...' Dad said nervously as he slid a case full of Robin's old clothes against the foot of the bed. An awkward silence followed. He'd no intention of helping them out. Let them sweat and suffer.

'We're really proud of you,' Dad began afresh. 'The whole family's awfully proud of you, especially your aunt and uncle...' he paused for a moment, '... and the neighbours, even Waters, the greengrocer on the corner, and Brian Temple, you remember him, from the draper's next door to the shoemaker, they all wanted me to tell you how proud they are... in fact, that goes for the whole street...'

Proud of what? That he'd got himself blown sky-high? That this 'war hero' hadn't fired a single shot? Morons! The whole street should be buried under half-decomposed bodies so they couldn't even get out of their front doors!

'We took an early train this morning. It was a terribly long trip, you know.' Here we go, Mum and her usual moaning. 'But at least it's a glorious day, an autumn like we haven't had in years, and you've got that fine park outside. What a lovely view! We saw some boys walking in the park; that's one advantage over a city hospital. I'm sure you go outdoors often.'

Outdoors? Outdoors!? As if he had any intention of going outdoors. One little sliver of metal, Mum, one sliver of red-hot metal was enough to make me never want to go outdoors again.

'Dr. Gillies says you're healing well,' Dad said. Robin's silence seemed to give them the impression they had carte blanche to talk openly about his condition. 'The doctor expects you'll be completely mended after a couple more operations... You'll be the old Robin again, sweetheart, just you wait,' Mum chirruped on, 'I've heard they perform miracles here. You just have to be patient, really patient, they say that's very important.' Suddenly she stuck out her neck like a tortoise, her head sliding forward out of her collar. 'Just look at where your left eye used to be, why it's healed marvellously! And thank God you've still got your other eye.'

Amazing! Lucky blighter, one eye left! Tell me, Mum, have you ever seen what happens to a bloke's eyes when you stick a bayonet into his gut? Poof! The lights go out, just like that, you stupid woman. That's right, your fine son, your war hero murdered a boy, he was probably British too, one of us you might say, with a father and mother and a whole street that's awfully proud of him because he's bought it!

'I'm sure you'll be decorated.' Dad again. 'Soldiers who were wounded and went beyond the call of duty get a distinction. That's what I've heard, at least.'

Ha, ha, long live the war wounded! Bring out the medals! You hear them, all those fellows with a belly full of shrapnel? What d'you think they're groaning and screaming about? They want their medals!

Mum got up from her chair. It seemed she'd made up her mind. Her hat was balanced awkwardly on her head. She put the box with that vile apple pie on his nightstand and leaned over him. 'I do so want to give you a kiss, dear...' she said. What a nerve! He saw her looming over him, eyes wide open and a demonic expression on her face, like a vulture about to devour its own young. A wave of rage came over him, and with all the force he could muster he spat a great wad of blood in her face.

Mum's screams brought Nurse Jenkins running. Robin closed his eye and wondered where Charlie had got to... but there he was again, a little way off, a bit hazy in a misty landscape. Come on, Charlie! Come on! You know I need you at times like this… His parents were led away, thank Christ, he couldn't bear their presence for another moment.

He heard Dr. Gillies' voice next to his bed. Jenkins, of course, had called for him. 'I'm so sorry, I should have stayed with you,' he was saying. 'He's just not ready. Don't forget how much he's been through…' Well, you could say that again – but whose fault was that? Who'd made him undergo all those operations? Who'd put him under with that horrible ether that always made him so sick? Who was to blame for all this pain? That damned Harold Gillies, that's who! Oh yes, Robin Ryder had been a wonderful guinea pig for the famous doctor. What a stroke of luck the war had been for the great Dr. Gillies, providing him with masses of human material to carry out his mad experiments on. The war had made his name!

'Robin! Robin, please talk to me,' he was pleading. But Robin refused to exchange even a word with that quack.

Only some hours later, when he was back to his miserable, depressed and guilt-ridden self, was Robin prepared to listen. Gillies took plenty of time; he appeared concerned, but said nothing of the incident with his parents. Robin wasn't even sure if it really happened, or was just a figment of his over-wrought imagination. 'What do you think,' asked Gillies, 'are you up to another operation?' Robin hardly dared look him in the eye, not until he was sure he hadn't delivered his diatribe against the doctor out loud.

'We could take a break, so that you only have the next opera-tion in six months' or a year's time. You need time to find your feet again.' Relieved, Robin concluded Gillies hadn't heard his hateful rant, otherwise he wouldn't be so understanding now. 'I've spoken to your parents about it. If you want to postpone things, they think it'd be better if you stayed with your uncle for a while instead of going straight home. They said you get along well with him. Give it some thought.'

Oh God, this was his punishment for what he'd done. Gillies wanted rid of him... He had to 'find his feet' and that wasn't something he could do here. He was being kicked out.

He made his decision the morning after the armistice. When Gillies came past on his rounds, Robin told him he wasn't ready for another operation yet. 'I just can't face it,' he said. 'I'll go to my uncle and come back in six months.' The doctor nodded thoughtfully. 'Wise choice. But promise me you'll come back once you can stomach it again. I'm convinced we can go a long way in restoring your face.' Robin gave him his hand. Gillies took it, satisfied, and laid his free hand on top. 'In the meantime we'll make you a mask. It'll make things easier for you in public.' Robin was relieved that he hadn't had to broach the subject himself. Of course, he knew all about what the men in the ward called the 'tin noses shop'. There they made small masks that covered the worst-affected areas of the face, and that's exactly what he was after. Gillies was wasting no time. Maybe he needed Robin's bed; he'd heard the nurses discussing the impending arrival of a set of new patients from France. That very afternoon he could go and see Francis Derwent Wood, a sculptor whom Gillies had brought in specially to make the masks.

The long table in the sculptor's studio was full of strange materials; the only thing Robin could positively identify was a sprinkling of leftover plaster of Paris. The shelves were full of plaster casts, three-dimensional replicas of the photographic portraits hanging behind them. Derwent Wood walked him along this impressive display, explaining everything with the same zeal that seemed to possess all of Gillies' colleagues. But Robin's curiosity was particularly drawn to a shelf full of fragile metal segments of the human face. There was a row of noses, a nicely shaped ear, a single eyebrow and entire jaws, some fitted with a moustache or even a beard. 'They're not made of tin, actually,' explained Derwent Wood. 'We use a thinner, more lightweight metal that's easier to wear.' Robin studied the photos of patients with their masks on. It might simply have been the light, or their distance from the camera, but it was almost impossible to see just where the mask ended and the face began.

Derwent Wood offered Robin a chair. An assistant tipped him back like he was about to give him a shave, but instead smeared his face with oil and his eyebrows with Vaseline. 'That way we don't have to chisel the plaster cast off,' explained Derwent Wood while mixing a batch of plaster. Robin closed his eye and felt the warm plaster being brushed onto his face, layer by layer. It dried fast, making his skin tighten. While waiting for the cast to set, he imagined himself strolling down the street with his new mask. He greeted acquaintances, old friends, new friends. No one was any the wiser. Maybe only a chosen few would know this wasn't his real face... or maybe no one at all.

When the cast was peeled off, he saw the negative image of his face, swellings and all. Derwent Wood told him that a positive would be made from clay, and then from it another negative. 'We'll use these to mould a plasticine replica, which will form the basis for a mask that will cover your left cheek and eye socket. That'll leave as much as possible of your own face visible. That's important, otherwise no one will recognize you.'

On subsequent visits he watched it progress from plasticine death mask to thin metal plate with an open eye drawn on it. Day after day the plate was fitted and adjusted. Once Derwent Wood was satisfied that it sat perfectly, the mask was covered in a thin layer of silver, the undercoat for the oil paint. This final stage was a demanding process, as the colours had to match his skin tone precisely. Derwent Wood spent a great deal of time on the eye, to ensure the colours of the pupil and white wouldn't clash with his real eye. Finally, eyelashes were attached, and to hold the mask in place he attached a pair of spectacles fitted with plain glass, for his good eye was still as sharp as ever.

When it was finally ready, Dr. Gillies went with Lucien to pick up the mask. He could hardly contain his excitement: 'I'm always curious to see what Francis has concocted.'

The mask was fitted one last time, and Derwent Wood showed him how to attach it to his skin with gum Arabic; the spectacles were mainly to keep it from sliding off. Robin turned toward Gillies, who stood at a slight distance, walked towards him, squinted a bit and clapped his hands together. 'Now that's craftsmanship! This will give you the confidence to face the world.' Robin shook his head back and forth to make sure the mask didn't shift or fall off, and walked over to the window while checking himself from various angles in a hand mirror. Gillies and Derwent Wood watched him, smiling. 'Watch out you don't fall in love with yourself!' joked Gillies.

Standing at the window, Robin suddenly lowered the mirror. The daylight was unsparing in its harshness: no matter how skilfully it was painted, it was no more than a dead, gawping eye, and the edges of the mask became apparent as soon as he changed expression. Even a smile would be out of the question. This was no more than a failed attempt at cosmetic camouflage.

'Have you arranged things with your uncle?' asked Gillies as he inspected a new pair of ears.

'Yes, yes…' Robin answered.

'Nurse Jenkins will take you to Sidcup station tomorrow afternoon. After that you're on your own. Do you think you can handle it, or shall I send someone with you to London?'

'No, that won't be necessary. I'll be fine.'

Gillies placed his hands on Robin's shoulders. 'I can see your disappointment, Robin. Just remember, it'll take some getting used to, and in your case it's only a stop-gap. A year from now we'll do everything we can to get you walking down the street without a mask. Have a little faith, promise me that?'

Robin nodded.

'Excellent. Come and see me tomorrow morning for one last check-up before you leave.'

Robin lay on his bed with his mask on. Nurse Jenkins dropped by, despite the imminent influx of new patients. She was delighted with the result. Jonas and Willie too had sworn they'd never seen such a good one, even close up you could hardly tell. Bunch of filthy liars, he thought, from close up you could see perfectly well that one eye was lifeless and half his cheek was a piece of painted metal. How was he supposed to go outside like this? He could already see passers-by nudging one another, pointing, smirking: there goes some weird bloke wearing a mask… the children in his class gawping at him and then bursting out laughing. They were no longer afraid of him; now he was afraid of them. Mary, of course, would swear on her life that he looked exactly the same, just as Nurse Jenkins had done. But he'd never dare let her get close. He was determined to keep her at a distance of at least three yards.

He needed some time to figure out how to proceed. It wouldn't be easy, but it was certainly possible… He decided not to sleep that night, not even for an hour. Too risky. He kept his eye on the clock. It seemed to take an age, but finally, at ten past two, he heard the rumble of trucks and ambulances coming up the drive. Hurried footsteps in the corridors. Nurse Jenkins appeared in the doorway and motioned to a nurse keeping watch over a fellow who was restless after his operation. Robin heard her whisper that new patients were arriving and needed to be brought in quickly. It was all hands on deck. There were more than a hundred of them… Wounded just before the armistice, Robin reckoned. For a few minutes he listened to the snores from the next bed, then slipped out of his own bed and pulled out the case. Crouched alongside his bed, he changed out of his pyjamas and into the clothes Mum and Dad had brought. He crept out of the ward, and as expected, the corridor was deserted. He heard voices in the distance, orders being shouted and stretchers being brought in. The squeak of the gurney wheels rasped through the silent corridors.

He made his way to the dentist's office unnoticed. He forced the lock using a chisel he'd stolen from Derwent Wood's studio the day before. He groped his way to the medicine cabinet, smashed the glass with the handle of the chisel and removed the bottle of cocaine. Even though he was trembling from nerves and haste, the temptation was too great. He opened the bottle, tipped a bit of powder into his hand and licked it up. Just a bit more… he'd be needing an extra boost for the journey. He shut his eye for a few seconds… ahh… His heartbeat jumped to a higher gear, his muscles tensed with activity and a wave of invincibility washed over him. He quickly wrapped the bottle in a shirt and thrust it into the suitcase. He wondered if there was time to look for more – surely the dentist would have a supply somewhere. No, no, no time!, shouted Charlie, hurry up, you idiot! Get the hell out of there before they catch you!

Pursued by a rush of footsteps that seemed to bear down on him from all sides, he found the rear exit and raced across the lawn. There was a bite in the night air that energized him, spurred him on, made him feel exhilarated. Once he'd made it to the trees he stopped to catch his breath, and in his euphoria he suddenly saw himself, the new Robin... He laughed out loud. Here he was, back from the dead! Look, look! Watch him go! The courageous soldier Robin Ryder! And on he ran, bursting with energy, towards a brilliant future.

16

An unavoidable collision

It was pleasantly cool in Technical Director W.H.J. Cremers's office. A light spring breeze wafted through the half-open window, carrying with it familiar sounds from the factory. Lucien Hirschland lit a cigarette and rested his forearms languidly on the arms of the wing armchair. He was thoroughly satisfied with their discussion of the annual report. His own contribution had been crisp and to the point: the numbers spoke for themselves. But Cremers was still at his desk, tracing the revenue and expenditure columns with his fountain pen for one last time, as though some devious figure might be lurking in the ledger sheets that would cast an entirely different light on the bottom line.

At length, Cremers laid down his pen and took off his reading glasses. 'OK – it tallies alright…' he concluded. '1919 has been a good year – an excellent one, I must say – with impressive financial results. We sold a total of 13,941 kilos of cocaine.' It was April, and as usual Cremers was preparing himself thoroughly for the annual meeting of the Board of Directors at the Koloniale Bank. 'The anticipated setback in sales hasn't materialized, and we can look forward to 1920 with guarded optimism.' His pursed lips, however, suggested he wasn't entirely convinced of even this sober prognosis.

Lucien decided to lend him a helping hand. 'Why so tentative?' he asked. 'We still have a clear lead on the competition, and our share of the world market keeps growing. Based on the first-quarter results, we can be sure of doing a booming trade this year. We might even double our returns.'

'Yes, well, but… ahem, how shall I put it…?'

'What more do you want? It's a perfectly respectable annual report. The Koloniale Bank will be happy, their board of directors even more so, and the shareholders delighted. I'm sure they'll be heaping praise on you tomorrow.'

'Me? No, no, my good man, not only me. A lot of our success is down to your tireless perseverance and outstanding commercial instinct.'

Lucien waved away the compliment. Though Cremers was right, of course. Since the end of the war, he'd poured his energy into keeping the firm's sales on track – and very successfully at that. No one could doubt his extraordinary talents as a salesman.

Cremers scratched his ear thoughtfully. 'By the way, Hirschland, we can count on you next week, can't we? It's an important concert. As you know, my wife, and Mrs. Peereboom in particular, are awfully fond of youthful companionship. So it'd be nice if you could bring your fiancée along too. The ladies recently saw a film with Miss Pauwlova in the lead role and were most impressed with her acting.' He even cracked a smile at this point. 'You understand, of course, how thrilled they'd be to be seen in the company of a famous film star.'

Lucien picked up his hat. 'Oh, Pola will be delighted. She adores classical music, and is enthralled by Dopper's cantatas.' He could imagine Pola pulling a face. Yawn, a concert! Convincing her to go would be no easy matter. Perhaps if he dropped a hint that the Amsterdam Concertgebouw was a regular haunt of film producers these days...

'I assume we'll dine together beforehand?' asked Cremers.

'Naturally.' Lucien tipped the brim of his hat and decided to check the factory's supply of coca leaves before going home. Rush orders had come in from France and Switzerland. Now that German submarines no longer prowled the seas, unheard-of quantities of leaves were being shipped in from the East Indies, more than 800,000 kilos in the last few months. They even needed to acquire more warehouse space at Het Veem, and hire extra personnel. All the same, he'd already noticed that the flow of leaves from the warehouse had ground to a halt.

The problem was probably the new bookkeeper, whose job it was to keep track of stocks. The insufferable but highly capable Jannes Jongejan had died suddenly three months earlier. One morning a secretary found him slumped over his desk. A doctor was hastily summoned, and concluded that he must have inhaled a lethal dose of chemical vapours from the factory. The doctor warned them of the acute danger to the other personnel, but Cremers calculated that the cost of safety measures far outweighed a few floral arrangements for the widows and newspaper ads for job vacancies. But the techni-cal director did take the danger of explosion seriously enough to build an underground bunker at a safe distance from the ammonia, sulphuric ether and hydrochloric acid storage – no doubt just large enough for him alone.

So Jongejan was buried under an impressive funeral wreath, compliments of the Dutch Cocaine Factory Ltd., the company he'd served for many years so diligently and punctiliously. After the service Albert Ketting commented that the chances of reaching a ripe old age at the firm were pretty slim. 'The only ones who don't seem to have any problem with all that disgusting chemical muck are the works inspectors – Mr. Cremers's boxes of cigars have seen to that.' Don't let management hear you say that, Lucien laughed to himself. Ketting was a bit of a Bolshie and Cremers wasn't particularly fond of socialists. He much preferred Catholic workers, who were so submissive that they didn't even dare cough in his presence.

Lucien was relieved to find the storerooms filled to the rafters. He was about to inquire after the production, but checked himself. He avoided the lab if at all possible. The beakers, funnels and scales made him nostalgic and evoked too many memories. Pleasant memories, he finally dared to admit. But the sudden departure of Thomas Olyrook a year ago had been a real slap in the face. He'd heard it from Cremers, but the boss was so furious he'd kept his account to a bare minimum. Why hadn't Thomas informed him himself? Why had he chosen to vanish like a thief in the night? Hadn't they been on friendly terms? He couldn't help but see it as a personal affront, and as a stab in the back to the firm. The loss of such a key employee, and one with such vast experience, was a serious setback for the company, though Cremers had managed to lure another reputable chemist away from the pharmaceutical firm of Brocades & Stheeman, guaranteeing the quality and level of production.

So now he had to deal with this new laboratory chief. A really nasty bit of work; within three weeks someone had been fired on the spot on suspicion of leaking company secrets to a family member. Lucien laughed it off, but he realized soon enough that there were consequences for him as well. The new lab chief made no bones about his determination to run a tight ship when it came to their valuable product. He made careful note of how much Lucien was given for customer samples, carefully weighing what he brought back. Why all the suspicion? Had he gone through his predecessor's books and discovered how lax Olyrook had been with his admin? Or was he just making clear who was boss here? In any event, Lucien was no longer able to supply his – that is, Pola's – needs, which in the past year had certainly not dwindled in the slightest.

This put him in a nasty fix. Within a few weeks of Olyrook's departure he was so strapped for cocaine for Pola that he swallowed his pride and rang Olyrook at home. Thomas acted like nothing had ever happened, and invited him to come have a look at his new premises in nearby Weesp, where they'd nearly finished refurbishing an existing factory. Necessity and curiosity promptly brought Lucien to the gates of this small building, where he was surprised to be greeted by Jan Palacky. Jan oozed friendliness and apologized for Thomas's absence. He let him no further than an almost-empty office space, gave him his packet and nattered on about the weather and unreliable builders. As Lucien was leaving, he was overcome by a sense of duplicity, as though he was in league with the enemy. He hoped to God that no one he knew had seen him. Cremers mustn't find out.

Since then he limited his visits to Thomas's new business to the bare minimum dictated by Pola's demands. He never once spoke to Thomas, or even saw him from a distance. Palacky fobbed him off with a different excuse every time: a meeting, busy schedule, even illness. Perhaps Thomas wanted to avoid a painful reunion. Lucien thought it best not to quiz Palacky about the details of Thomas's departure. They might end up arguing, and he didn't want to jeopardize his supply.

Seated behind the wheel of his Mercedes 37 Tourer, which he'd finally been able to buy after the war, he drove through the city centre, turning onto the Haarlemerweg and heading for home. He was delighted with the car, but since Deumer, his mechanic, had shown him a picture of the new Silver Ghost a few weeks ago, a bit of shine had gone off the Mercedes. The new Rolls-Royce was a fast, sporty coupé roadster. He had to check his finances to see whether he could afford an expensive Rolls. This past year he had raked in quite a handsome income on commissions. But it wasn't just the money: it had been a vintage year in all respects. His stock within the firm and at the Koloniale Bank had risen considerably, and best of all he felt alive again.

Things hadn't looked so rosy at the outset. The end of the war meant to the loss of some of their most lucrative clients: sales plummeted and orders dwindled. But peace also had its upside. In search of new clients, Lucien was free to travel throughout Europe, with Albert Ketting as his chauffeur. At first he sat up front, but Albert had never been one for small-talk, so he moved to the back seat, where he could work in peace. Even so, a certain rapport had grown up between them on their long trips. He liked Albert, especially for his discretion. He'd never heard Ketting gossip to colleagues about his boss's excursions to big-city casinos and nightclubs, or the frequent late-night female visitors to his hotel room, forcing him to catch up on lost sleep on the back seat. He was sure that even Mrs. Ketting knew nothing.

Lucien hummed to himself, drummed on the steering wheel and congratulated himself on the gift he'd picked up for Swanny's birthday. In the past year he'd showered his sister with souvenirs from his travels: crystal glassware from Switzerland, elegant woodcarvings from Germany, French porcelain, an Austrian cuckoo clock and an enormous number of scarves, hats and pieces of jewellery. Most of the stuff had already mysteriously disappeared. She'd most likely given it away or sold it to donate to poor relief, but had kept mum about it to spare his feelings. But he was sure she'd be thrilled with this handy folding Kodak Autographic Brownie camera.

It was a splendid afternoon. The trees lining the canals were sprouting young leaves, and the Haarlemmers had begun to go out without their heavy winter coats. He swung into the Oranjekade and slowed down for a couple of neighbourhood boys playing football in the road, the sons of a lawyer who lived a few doors down. The older one waited, his foot resting on the ball, until Lucien drew level and then deftly lobbed it over the car. Lucien smiled; he liked to think of spring as the time of year when, like an uncaged animal, he could get outdoors to play as well. Also, he always associated it with Swanny's birthday. He could never wait until the day itself to give her her present. His mother always had to hold the gift in safekeeping until the morning of the big day. Amused, he wondered if he'd be able to contain his enthusiasm this time and wait till tomorrow mor— … He slammed on the brakes.

A dark object had suddenly shot in front of his car from behind a parked barrow. Damn! How could he have not seen it? What was it? A dog? A big black dog? His heart beat wildly. Swanny would never forgive him if he ran over a dog. He threw open the door and raced round to the front of the car. Someone was lying on the ground, it looked like a man… He lay crumpled, his knees pulled up, a greyish coat twisted around his body. He wasn't moving.

Lucien panicked. He had to do something. Just as he was

bending forward, the figure began to stir. The man tried to haul himself upright. Lucien extended his hand to help him, but the man recoiled, grabbed his cap from between the front wheels and pulled it over his head. Unaided, he got up into a kneeling position and turned up the collar of his jacket.

'I'm so sorry,' said Lucien. 'I honestly didn't see you.' The man stood up, his shoulders hunched and head bent. His coat was covered with dirt. All Lucien could think of doing was to repeat his apology. The man lifted his head and turned to look at him. Luckily, his spectacles weren't broken. 'Are you injured?' asked Lucien. There was something strange about that face; most of the left side was expressionless. It almost looked unreal.

'I'm very sorry,' the man said hoarsely, in English. 'It was entirely my fault…'

Lucien repeated his question in English. He noticed, behind the glasses, a metal plate with an artificial eye. The man clutched at his own shoulder, as though in considerable pain. He must have taken quite a whack from the bumper, or even the wheels, and hit the pavement with some force.

'It's all right,' gasped the Englishman. 'My fault, my own fault, I should have been looking where I was going.'

Suddenly Lucien realized that the fake eye was in fact painted on the mask. 'Are you English?'

The man nodded and tried to catch his breath. His whole bearing was craven and downtrodden. 'I hope your car isn't damaged.'

Lucien made a dismissive gesture. 'Can I run you anywhere? Where are you staying?' He suddenly realized that the over-sized coat was military issue, and noticed several frayed patches where epaulettes and military insignia had been torn off.

The man shook his head. 'I don't have a place to stay yet. Most of the boarding houses are full. I'm trying to find something here in the neighbourhood.'

'Oh, there's nothing here. But I'd be happy to help you find a place.'

The man thrust his hands deep into his coat pockets. 'No, thank you, I don't want to be any trouble.' He made a move to leave.

Lucien hesitated. He couldn't just let the fellow go. 'Won't you come inside? You can catch your breath; maybe you've hurt more than just your shoulder. I live right here…' He pointed to the large windows of his house, at the same time checking to see if Swanny had come running at the sound of the squealing brakes and the collision. She'd be home now from her work at the library. But he couldn't see her. 'You really must let me offer you something,' he persisted. The man's body language showed he was wavering. 'I insist you come in with me, even if it's just for a moment. My sister will never forgive me if I just let you go.' The Englishman capitulated.

'I'll just move the car off the road.' A dairy farmer with his cart was waiting patiently. Lucien ignored the broken headlamp and pulled the Mercedes half onto the pavement. In the rear-view mirror he saw the man stoop over, with difficulty, to pick up a battered suitcase. Lucien got out quickly and fetched it for him. Then he opened the front door and asked the man to be patient for a moment while he summoned his sister.

But Swanny had already heard the door open and emerged from the kitchen. Lucien intercepted her, giving his account of what had happened: just outside the house he had – through no fault of his own – run into an Englishman, and felt it was his duty to bring him inside to recover. Swanny barely let him finish, yanking off her apron as she hurried towards the front hall. She helped the man take off his coat. Without his cap he looked much younger. His tattered clothes hung on him like rags, and he was as thin as a rail. But this is no tramp, thought Lucien, his manners and language were far too polished.

In the salon, Karel danced back and forth along his perch, letting out a few screeches, but once Swanny scolded him he settled back into his plumage. She offered the stranger the most comfortable armchair and asked if she should send for the doctor to make sure he hadn't broken anything. He refused. 'No, thank you. My shoulder hurts a bit, but it's really nothing…' Swanny sighed and paused, lost in thought. Lucien was surprised: it seemed like she was completely oblivious to his bizarre appearance. 'What happened, then?' She glared at Lucien. Her voice contained a hint of reproach. 'Were you dozing at the wheel?'

'Of course not! It happened so fast, suddenly I saw something appear in front of the car, and thought…' Better not mention the dog.

'Miss, it was entirely my fault. I was lost in thought and crossed the street without thinking. I should be the one apologizing.'

'Nonsense,' said Swanny. 'Can I offer you some hot chocolate, or would you prefer tea?' The man looked her up and down with his one eye. 'Hot chocolate please, Miss.' Swanny turned and marched off to the kitchen. Lucien deduced from the fact that he wasn't offered anything that she saw him as the guilty party. A huge motorcar versus an innocent pedestrian – the cards were stacked against him. The fellow sat dejectedly. Lucien sized him up. How old was he? Late twenties, possibly, about the same age as him. It struck him that his guest could probably use something a bit stronger than hot chocolate. 'Wouldn't you prefer a glass of whisky?' The portion of the face not covered by the mask broke into a crooked smile. Lucien was relieved to have finally come up with a proposal someone approved of.

Swanny laughed when she returned from the kitchen. 'Of course, whisky – far more practical!' She was about to turn back with the serving tray, but the man set his glass down and reached for the cup of hot chocolate and the slice of cake, which he gobbled down in a single bite. Lucien wondered if he was perhaps on the doss after all. 'Mustn't drink alcohol on an empty stomach,' the man said as he carefully wiped the corners of his mouth with a filthy handkerchief.

'When did you last eat?' asked Swanny with her usual directness.

'Two days ago, I think.'

She shook her head. 'I'll go and fix something warm for you.' The man protested, but Swanny persisted until he agreed to eat a small bite. This fellow could just as easily be a fraudster, Lucien thought, who wheedles his way into your home and can only be fobbed off with a wad of money. Swanny was a sucker for that kind of riff-raff.

Suddenly the man stood up and stuck out his hand. 'My name is Robin Ryder. I'm from London.' He bowed slightly to Swanny and added: 'I'm a war veteran.'

'On my goodness, you were in the trenches, then? Were you wounded?' Realizing the stupidity of her question, she blushed deeply.

'I was hit by a German grenade near Ypres, in Flanders, in 1917. My face was half blown away and I've had lots of operations.' He tapped on the mask. 'They gave me this in hospital.'

'How awful, I'm so sorry for you,' said Swanny. 'Here in Holland we're really quite unaware of the terrible consequences of the war.'

'Well, I've come out of it relatively unscathed,' he said quietly. 'Some of them are much worse off. I've still got my arms and legs. I can get around on my own, that's something, at least.'

'Is there a special reason you've come to Holland, Mr. Ryder?' asked Lucien. He noticed Swanny fidgeting with her dress, her classic sign of distress.

'Please call me Robin. I want to try to find a job here. It's hard times in England, what with so many war veterans looking for work.' He took a sip of whisky. 'And it's especially difficult for me.' He fell silent.

'Did you have a job before the war?' Lucien was determined to keep up a normal conversation before his sister's emotions got the upper hand.

'I was a schoolteacher in my home town, Great Yarmouth.'

'Oh, you're a teacher!' Swanny exclaimed, as though that made things even worse. 'Can't you go back to your old school?'

Robin hesitated and asked permission to smoke. Taking a crumpled pack of cigarettes from his pocket, he lit one. 'Um, no…that didn't work out… The children in my class were rather afraid of me.'

Swanny put her hand over her mouth. 'How dreadful! The war has cost you dear.'

'Indeed it has. I've had a rough time of it, so I figured I'd go abroad and try to make a fresh start.'

Lucien looked Ryder over again. Not only was he dressed in rags, but his bare feet were stuck in trench boots with tattered soles. He was wearing neither a ring nor a wristwatch, and there wouldn't be much of value in that battered old suitcase of his. How did a schoolteacher, even if he was maimed, manage to sink so low? 'What kind of work are you looking for?' he asked.

'It doesn't matter, as long as I can save enough for a new operation to make my face more presentable.'

'You're saving up for a new face!...' Swanny gasped.

'I'm setting aside every cent I have for the operation. That's why I look rather like a tramp. I'm sorry.'

Lucien got up and refilled his glass. The whisky was doing Ryder good: the colour was returning to the right side of his face, and his body appeared to relax a little. 'When did you arrive?' Lucien asked.

'Yesterday morning.'

'Of course, you're looking for a boarding house,' Lucien recalled. 'So where did you sleep last night?'

Robin lowered his head, embarrassed.

'You don't mean to say you slept rough?' Swanny had shifted to the edge of her chair.

'I do apologize. That's why I'm so filthy. I hadn't any choice. I couldn't get a lift with anyone. Once in a while a car or a farm wagon stopped, but as soon as they saw my face they drove on. So I slept at the side of the road.'

'You're not serious!' she exclaimed.

Lucien got up and went to the door. 'I'll ring Hotel Brinkman. They know me there, I often reserve rooms for foreign visitors.'

Swanny grabbed his wrist as he passed her. 'Not a bit of it! Robin's staying right here.' She opened her eyes wide. In other words, it was a done deal.

'Of course... Of course he can stay here.'

'No, no, no...' Robin protested, already half out of his chair. 'I mustn't take advantage of your hospitality. I should be going.'

But Swanny was already at his side. She crouched down next to him and put her hand on his arm. 'You must give us the chance to prove that there are some decent people in this country.' Her gaze rested for moment on the carpet. Lucien knew she was going through the house in her mind's eye, from room to room. The large room alongside Lucien's, the only one fit to be called a guest room, was crammed full of old furniture. A few months ago Lucien had had the salon, the hall and the dining room completely redone in Art Deco style. He had, as usual, set to work enthusiastically with the idea of surprising Swanny, but neglected to make arrangements for the removal of the old furniture that Swan wanted to give to charity. There was simply nowhere else to stow it. He'd just have to call Hotel Brinkman after all.

'You know what, Robin can use your old bedroom upstairs,' Swanny suddenly piped up.

'But that's full as well.'

'Well, just move the crates up to the attic. If you go and see to the room, I'll start dinner,' she said. Her tone was clearly meant to remind him who had run into this poor war veteran. She invited Robin to join her in the kitchen so that he needn't wait alone in the salon. Lucien picked up the whisky bottle, but a glance from her dissuaded him from refilling their glasses. A fine homecoming! Rather than stretching out on the sofa, he'd have to go and drag heavy crates up to the attic.

He went upstairs, crossed the landing and opened the door to a narrow staircase leading to his old bedroom, the former servant's quarters. He hadn't been up there in some time, and a musty but not unfamiliar smell greeted him. Pleun probably aired it now and again, but apparently not very often. He leant against the doorpost. What a fuss he'd had to kick up to get this room! His father had agreed right away, because it meant he'd get a quiet study where he could read his manuscripts in peace. But his mother thought that the mysterious little room at the back of the house was too cramped and too far away. But once she'd twigged that that was the whole point, she not only went along with it but visited Lucien regularly with arm-loads of wonderful books about exotic locales, illustrated by Gustav Doré. She also introduced him to Jules Verne, and his fantastic tales of travel and adventure. His favourite gift from her had been a large atlas. He'd inherited her wanderlust. After her death the room became a sort of hideaway, where he holed up until his departure for Java. But when he returned from the Indies, he realized he'd outgrown his old room, not to mention all the furniture he'd brought back with him. And so he moved to the master bedroom on the first floor, and Swanny stayed in her room downstairs, next to the study. And his boyhood lair had lain empty and unused – until today.

Now he was going to have to drag the crates up to the attic by himself. All that for just one night. They still contained some of his Javanese souvenirs. Out of curiosity, he opened one of them, and buried in the straw he found some old tins of Turkish coffee, but also *krisses*, ceremonial swords and pottery. They were so much more attractive then he remembered, and he resolved to find a suitable place for them in his room.

After he'd moved some of the crates to his own room and the others up to the attic, he checked to see if everything was in order for their lodger. The oak desk, where he'd so often sat daydreaming, was in its same old position. The atlas still lay there, and the heavy bronze lion with one raised paw, which had always played a role in his adventures, was still in its old place. He was surprised at how small the room really was. Even with the chair pushed right under the writing table, you could only just squeeze between it and the single bed. That snugness had always been this room's great asset. He remembered how, at the age of seven or eight, he would slip down into that space with only his pillow and blanket, and hey presto! – he was on board a three-master, sailing across the seas in search of uncharted islands inhabited by wild savages. He was always relieved when he didn't actually come face to face with hostile natives, because in truth he wasn't terribly brave. He smiled to himself and felt the uncontrollable urge to slip into his hut one last time. But when he heard Swanny call from downstairs, he quickly stood up and, slightly embarrassed, put the pillow and blanket back on the bed.

17

Swanny's birthday

Lucien bowed gallantly, kissed her on both cheeks and, with a theatrical flourish, whipped her festively wrapped gift out from behind his back. Swanny beamed with delight. 'Oh Lucien, how sweet of you.' She let the long satin ribbons glide through her fingers, shook the box gently next to her ear and then put it, still wrapped, in the kitchen cabinet. 'I'll wait until tonight to open it, when all the guests are here. That's much more fun.'

'Are you sure?' he prodded. 'It's something really special…' But she'd already turned her attention back to the chafing dish; the little candle was refusing to light. Robin Ryder stood next to the table. He was scrubbed clean and gave off a slight scent of floral soap. His dark hair, and even his damaged skin, glistened. No wonder, thought Lucien, he'd spent at least half an hour in the bathroom. Ryder took the breakfast plates from Swanny, arranged them meticulously on the table and placed the cutlery alongside them. He picked up a knife, held it close to his eye, and deeming it smudged, polished its blade with a tea towel before replacing it. He was wearing a fresh set of clothes that struck Lucien as vaguely familiar.

Pleun came into the kitchen and greeted him with a wider-than-usual smile. He'd heard her up in his old room, probably already stripping the bed. She examined the breakfast table, fists resting on her hips, and clicked her tongue approvingly. She went to the cabinet and handed Ryder a stack of serviettes, which he accepted with a polite 'dank u'. Surprised, Pleun clasped her hands together. 'Well, well, well, just one day in Haarlem and he can already say "dank u".'

'Quite astonishing, isn't it…' Lucien mumbled as he reached for the newspaper.

'You can tell he's a teacher,' said Swanny from the cooker. She repeated it in English, and Ryder smiled at her wryly. He folded the serviettes into tidy triangles and laid them next to the plates. Lucien half expected him to ruffle them into little swans. What was going on here? Did English manners oblige one to lend a hand with domestic chores in exchange for hospitality? The strange part was that the women tolerated his helpfulness; whenever Lucien so much as raised a finger, they always shooed him away. 'How's your shoulder?' he asked as he scanned the morning paper.

'Still a bit sore,' answered Robin, 'but I'm already feeling much better.'

Now Lucien recognized the tailored sports jacket as part of his summer ensemble from last year. Swan had given it to Ryder without asking his permission. Well, at least it looked good on him, even made him presentable, come to that. As long as he stood with his back to you, anyway. That maimed face wasn't just ugly, it was unsettling; there was something about it that bothered him, although he couldn't put his finger on it. He had already decided to call Hotel Brinkman after breakfast to reserve a room; he would pay for a week up front. That should give Ryder enough time to find work and arrange his own accommodation. He'd drive him there himself. Lucien reckoned Swanny would appreciate his generosity. But the atmosphere in the kitchen, he suspected, did not augur a speedy departure – on the contrary, Robin appeared to have already become a household fixture.

Swanny invited Robin to take a seat. Pleun poured a cup of coffee for Lucien, while the others, to his astonishment, drank tea. They never drank tea at breakfast. Swanny stood next to him with a frying pan and dished up. '*Fried eggs*,' she said in English, winking at Ryder. 'Robin taught me – *absolutely delicious!*' Pleun wiggled her palm alongside her cheek, a local gesture signifying that she'd never in her life tasted such a delicacy. Ryder shot Lucien a timid glance. In that one eye he read insecurity – fear, almost – as though Robin had signed a pact with the women without asking Lucien's permission.

As soon as they were finished, Robin got up to help clear the table, but Swanny placed her hand firmly on his shoulder. Her gesture said it all: he had proved himself admirably, and from now on Swan and Pleun would care for and spoil him. The crippled veteran had sparked their maternal instinct, and if no one intervened they'd never give up their prey.

'I'd better ring Hotel Brinkman now,' said Lucien, laying down his serviette, 'before all their rooms are taken.'

As if stung by a wasp, Swanny swung round from the counter. She pulled Lucien aside and whispered: 'Why? He can stay here a bit longer. Your room's empty anyway.' He was right, she wasn't about to let Robin go anytime soon.

Lucien pulled an apprehensive face that he let dissolve into an indulgent look. 'Well, all right, seeing as it's your birthday.' There was no point at all in resisting; at this stage the wounded war veteran would win hands down. He'd give Ryder two days, but then he really had to go. He didn't like having strangers under his roof, it disrupted things, made him feel uneasy... Why exactly, he couldn't say. Maybe it was that dreadful face.

'We're going to do the shopping together for this evening,' Swanny said in English as she filled the washing-up tub with water. 'I can show Robin the city and the shops, he'll see where you can buy things and have his first Dutch lesson at the same time.' She translated everything for Pleun, who nodded energetically. 'Dank u wel,' said Ryder. By golly, he'd learned another word already! The women laughed affectionately. Lucien sighed in resignation. Well, at least it saved him a trip to Brinkman's. He was in a hurry; the Koloniale Bank's board of directors was meeting in a couple of hours. He wished Ryder a pleasant day, said goodbye to Pleun and promised Swanny he would be back by late afternoon for her birthday party. 'We're keeping it small,' she said, just in case he'd expected a big gathering. 'Just Tosca, Robin, Pleun and maybe Casper. And of course you can bring somebody. Why don't you ask Pola, if she's not working?'

The city's steadily growing number of bicycles, lorries and cars made it impossible to park in front of the bank's headquarters at Herengracht 553. So a courtyard further up, which had once been used for coaches and horses, was now doing duty as a car park for the management of the Koloniale Bank and its visitors. The serried ranks of Cadillacs, Stanley Steamers, Daimlers and Chevrolets left no doubt that the bank, and by extension the firm, was doing very well indeed.

As Lucien pulled into the courtyard, President-Director Peereboom's chauffeur stepped forward from a group of liveried men and offered to park the Mercedes. Lucien got out and reached for his attaché case. The chauffeur examined the front of the car with his hands folded behind his back. 'Have a little accident, Mr. Hirschland?' he asked. 'Something like that,' Lucien replied. Before leaving home he'd noticed, to his chagrin, that his collision with Ryder had not only damaged the headlamp but the left wing as well. It wasn't much more than a dimple, but it did rather put a dent in the car's status. He'd ring Ketting to come and fetch him this afternoon. They could drive back to Haarlem together, and Albert could take the car round to Deumers to be repaired.

He checked his watch and hurried to the massive front door, which a clerk opened before he'd had a chance to ring the bell. He hurried through the marble passage to the regents' room. No doubt he'd be the last to arrive.

'Aha... what did I tell you?' someone exclaimed, laughing. 'Hirschland's bringing up the rear as usual!' So now they were even taking bets on his lateness. 'Been out on the town last night?' asked Van Bosse Loman, chairman of the board of commissioners, in his high-pitched voice.

'Me? Out on the town? Gentlemen, surely you know me better than that. "Early to bed, early to rise..."' He pulled out a chair, took his regular place at the conference table and started removing his papers.

'Ah, but the question is, with whom?' said Peereboom, running his hand over his close-cropped hair. The atmosphere during meetings this past year had become much more informal, and the director of the Koloniale Bank, who was in his early sixties, did his best to present himself as a modern man on the same wavelength as the younger generation. The wife's influence, Cremers had cynically remarked.

'For me to know and for you to find out.' Lucien shot Peereboom an ambiguous glance and placed the annual report on top of his stack of papers. This kind of entrance would have been unthinkable two years ago. But now he was one of the boys, and seeing as his future plans were aimed at a decent position with the Koloniale Bank, he contributed wholeheartedly to their jovial banter. They were like a pack of dogs who met once a week in the park and never got enough of sniffing one another's backsides.

'When can we expect Christiaans back from Versailles?' asked Cremers, who set great store by maintaining decorum at the AGM.

'Soon. I expect he'll be wanting to sign a little treaty with a Parisian dance-hall girl first,' laughed Peereboom, and when Cremers did not react, he continued in more serious vein: 'It's taking longer than expected to round things off. As soon as he's back we'll be clear about the ramifications of the new treaty.'

'Did you hear that Christiaans had orders from the Queen to get the peace conference held in The Hague?' Van Bosse Loman leant across the table conspiratorially, like he was sharing the latest gossip. 'She thought the Netherlands was the obvious choice as mediator. Even offered her own residence for the talks.' He grimaced. 'But Christiaans was told that our services wouldn't be necessary. Their view – though they didn't shout it from the rooftops – was that the Netherlands had profited shamelessly from the conflict and had turned a blind eye to people's suffering during the war.'

'The English were behind it,' said Cremers, who seemed nervous.

'Could be,' Van Bosse Loman said. 'Still,' he winced, 'I'd hate to have to be the one to inform Her Majesty… my God, I pitied him.'

Peereboom, who was not only modern but a royalist too,

reacted coolly: 'Christiaans can handle it. He's an outstanding diplomat. The German defeat has made Her Majesty realize that our relationship with the former Allies could use some improvement. That's where our interests lie at the moment.' He pulled out his pocketwatch and checked the time. 'Let's start. First of all, I'd like to know if there's any information yet about the new Opium Law.'

'I can tell you about that,' said Cremers. Peereboom's sharp tone of voice obviously did not do Cremers any good. 'The law, once it goes into effect, will prohibit private individuals from producing, selling or trading in cocaine. The health department of the Ministry of Labour will only issue licenses to major pharmaceutical companies. That shouldn't be any problem for us.' A bronze female statuette on the mantelpiece caught Lucien's eye. His thoughts drifted to the lion with the raised paw in his old room. He hoped Ryder would have the decency to keep his own paws off Lucien's things. Just in time, he heard Cremers launch into a rambling explanation of last year's revenue and expenditure results, in a tone suggesting it was not quite up to scratch. Since Peereboom and Van Bosse Loman didn't immediately contradict him, as Lucien had anticipated, he chipped in encouragingly: 'We can safely conclude that 1919 was an excellent year, with impressive profits. Financially speaking, the firm is very healthy indeed.' The others pulled sour faces at this. It was, of course, completely out of line for a salesman to draw these conclusions, but he wasn't about to let Cremers's gloom pour cold water on their outstanding results. It could jeopardize his future prospects.

'So, what's the prognosis for the rest of this year?' asked Peereboom.

'That remains to be seen...' Cremers began, clearing his

throat. 'At the moment we don't have much competition from abroad. England, France and Belgium have been economically drained by the war, and we have nothing to fear from Germany for the time being. But I'm still concerned. We still have to prepare ourselves for shrinking markets and a slump in income...'

Damn it all, thought Lucien, that was no way to present the prospects for the coming year. 'Naturally, Mr. Cremers is correct in his cautious assessment,' Lucien interjected again, 'but this year's first-quarter figures confirm our position as the world's leading producer. Even though our deliveries to military medical services have declined, a considerable portion – may I say the lion's share – of our sales is still directly related to the war. What I mean is that the orders placed by companies in England, Belgium, France, Austria and Germany are now supplying the hospitals treating the war wounded.'

'And there, indeed, lies the problem.' Cremers wasn't to be budged from his pessimism. 'We can expect the demand from hospitals to ebb drastically as the wounded recuperate. It's exactly that shrinking market that worries me. Because once the pharmaceutical industries in competing countries have recovered and resumed production, we're looking at overproduction and falling prices.'

Jesus... shrinking market, overproduction, falling prices – could that fool be any more downbeat about it? Now he'd got Peereboom alarmed, of course. 'That's a good point,' the President-Director said pensively, 'plus, now the restrictions have been lifted, Javanese coca can be traded freely. Every Tom, Dick and Harry can start importing leaves and producing high-grade cocaine.' Cremers fidgeted nervously with his fountain pen.

'I don't think it will come to that,' Lucien attempted anew. 'For the time being there isn't a single company that can guarantee our level of quality, thanks to Mr. Cremers, who managed to recruit a new laboratory chief in no time.' More sour faces; no one had forgotten Olyrook's sneaky departure. Lucien moved quickly to gloss over his gaffe. 'I'm convinced we can not only maintain our current market position, but even improve it significantly. In particular I'd like to concentrate on exploiting new markets. Not only in Europe but also in the United States, where it seems there's huge demand for our product.'

'Excellent, excellent,' mumbled Peereboom.

'What about the Dutch market?' asked Van Bosse Loman.

Honestly, where was the man's sense? 'It's still negligible,' answered Lucien, 'and the chance of creating a demand is, in my opinion, minimal.'

'Speaking of the Dutch market...' Peereboom rested his elbows on the table and sat with his fingertips pressed together. 'Any idea what Olyrook's up to with that little enterprise of his? What's he playing at? He wouldn't get it into his head to start dabbling in cocaine, would he?'

Well, well, thought Lucien, the man who not so long ago was an esteemed chemist was now being painted as some common quack. All faces turned to him. He felt put on the spot. Better not admit to his regular visits to Weesp. On the other hand, they must be looking at him for a reason... maybe it's leaked out already. He sighed heavily. He had to play up his distaste for this unsavoury character. 'True... we mustn't underestimate Olyrook. I wondered as much myself, so I launched my own modest investigation. While I get the impression he intends to enter the cocaine market, I wonder if he's capable of producing it in significant quantities. But if he does have ambitious plans, he'll have to find himself a market.' Thinking quickly on his feet, he found himself an alibi. 'I can make contact with him on a personal basis. He has an interesting collection of antiques, it's a shared hobby of ours. I could make some informal inquiries.'

'Excellent, excellent,' Peereboom repeated.

'How does he manage to finance this scheme of his? As far as I know, not a single bank will give him a loan,' said Van Bosse Loman, implying that Olyrook was now a potential crook as well. 'Try to get to the bottom of that too, Hirschland. If there's anything untoward about it, we can see to it that he doesn't get a license.' My God, they must really loathe Olyrook.

'I agree entirely,' said Peereboom. 'Check it out. But be careful, he mustn't get wind that we're the least bit interested in him.'

Lucien nodded, relieved that now he had a legitimate reason to go see Thomas.

'I suggest that Lucien concentrates for now on establishing new markets,' said Cremers, steering the conversation back to the financial report.

'Of course,' Peereboom replied. 'Perhaps you should go to New York soon. Take that charming fiancée of yours with you – the Americans love European film stars.' He rubbed his stomach, signalling that it was time for lunch. 'In short, I trust that you'll keep the order books full, as you've done so superbly this past year… yes, excellent indeed. We can look forward to a lucrative year ahead.'

As they drove back to Haarlem, Lucien stretched out on the back seat of the Mercedes, replete from the copious meal at

Hotel L'Europe. He didn't hold back with the wine either, knowing that Ketting would deliver him safely back home. Albert shook his head as he pointed to the dent in the wing and the broken headlamp, which Lucien had patched up with some tape. Ketting was in love with the Mercedes, although he'd never admit it. He spent hours looking after it; never a spot or smudge, you could see your face in the gleaming bodywork. He'd even seen the missus cleaning the tyres with a scrubbing brush. If it had been a racehorse, those two wouldn't have taken better care of it.

He slid the cushion Mrs. Ketting had made specially for him behind his head, closed his eyes and thought back on the meeting. It had been a success, truly 'excellent'. He wondered when they'd offer him a place on the board of commissioners. Then his rise at the Bank would be unstoppable. His future had never been rosier. And he could swan off on another tour of Europe, with first-class hotels, casinos, nightclubs and female companionship – and thanks to Peereboom he'd even be going to New York. His only concern was that Cremers was, of course, completely right. It'd be an uphill struggle finding new markets now that the fighting was over, and Europe so war-weary. First things first: he had to find out how much Thomas Olyrook was manufacturing. His turnover couldn't be that big; his name had never come up in foreign deals. Still, he must have his outlets. You can't live on thin air. How and where had he managed to build up a clientele? It was important to find that out, for Olyrook couldn't be allowed to become a competitor. That was a very real prospect, certainly once the factory in Weesp was up and running. But even that was unclear. Palacky still wouldn't let him inside; they were obviously shielding the place from prying eyes. In any case,

Thomas's cocaine was first-rate, otherwise Pola would have complained. He smiled… 'and take that charming fiancée of yours with you'. He wondered what kind of erotic fantasies Peereboom entertained about her.

He suddenly remembered that he'd promised Swanny to invite Pola to her birthday party. Too late: Ketting was already turning into the Oranjekade. He didn't feel like battling his way through the busy city centre again. But he couldn't disappoint Swanny, so he leant forward and said to Ketting: 'Say, Albert, it's my sister's birthday and we're going to drink a toast to her health. I know she'd be delighted if you stopped in to wish her all the best.'

Ketting spoke over his shoulder, all the while keeping his eyes on the road. 'But I still have to go round to Deumers, and I promised my wife I'd be home in time for supper.'

'Nonsense, man, Deumers is open late and I'll ring the factory straightaway so your wife knows you're delayed. She'll appreciate how much it means to my sister.'

Albert grunted. Lucien knew from experience that meant yes.

There was no one in the salon. The only sign of any festivities was an enormous bunch of roses next to the fireplace. Lucien didn't need to look at the card to know they were from Marnix. Marnix had kept his recent engagement warm all the way from Paris with the occasional letter and a steady stream of flowers. The guests must be out back, then. He and Albert walked through the dining room to the French doors leading to the garden, toward the sound of voices, laughter and music. Tosca had taken the gramophone outside, naturally. The garden was decorated with colourful lanterns hung on branches; later, as always, they'd put candles in them.

Their entrance was greeted with a cheer whose gusto could only be explained by the number of empty wine bottles on the table. Swanny rushed over to them, her cheeks flushed. She was so delighted to see Ketting that she gave him a spontaneous kiss. He lowered his eyes in embarrassment. 'Many happy returns, Miss,' he said. 'I didn't know, otherwise my wife would have got you a present.'

'Don't be silly, that's entirely unnecessary!' cried Swanny and dragged him off to be introduced to the other guests. He'd already met Tosca before. She was wearing a skimpy dress that tapered asymmetrically and was covered with glittering sequins. The low-cut neckline, the sheer stockings: they were all deliciously shocking. Even her bobbed hair, and the headband with a feather sticking out of it, were utterly brazen. Tosca never let you down. Ketting's mouth fell open. She laughed loudly and did a little pirouette for him. 'So, Mr. Ketting, what do you think? Wouldn't this be something for your wife?' Albert shook his head. 'No, Miss, that wouldn't suit her, I'm sure.'

'You just wait,' teased Swanny, who was wearing a much less provocative dress. What a shame it would be, Lucien thought, if Tosca were to talk her into cutting her beautiful long hair. Albert was then introduced to Casper Bartholomeus, draped decadently over a garden chair. According to Swanny, he wasn't just the next-door neighbour but one of Haarlem's very best portrait painters. Oh dear, just one glass of wine and his sister had lost all sense of proportion. Lucien was relieved that Casper was the only one of Swanny's soirée chums at the party. There was no way Casper couldn't be invited, anyway: he'd have bounded over the hedge at the first sound of a popping cork. Finally, it was Robin Ryder's turn. He stood, head bowed, next to Karel, who was skipping back and forth on his perch.

So that damned bird was here too: even a cockatoo can feel left out, he could just hear Swanny saying.

Tosca turned down the music, like a literary host preparing to announce a guest speaker. 'This is Robin Ryder,' said Swanny, 'a war veteran from England who is lodging with us while he looks for work.' Ketting gave him a firm handshake and mumbled something, knowing that the Englishman wouldn't understand him. 'Mr. Ketting says it's an honour to meet you because you fought on the side of freedom,' Swanny translated. Tosca joined them and threw her arm around Robin's shoulder. So now even Tosca had become a fan.

Meanwhile, Casper had managed to extricate himself from the garden chair and was busy opening another bottle of wine. A Château Dauzac Margaux: the Tilanus wine cellar had been raided again. Lucien wondered if the old man had any idea his daughter was plundering his valuable collection. 'Tosca,' he cried, 'we've got decent wine of our own, you don't have to pinch your father's!'

'Go on, you don't know the first thing about wine,' she laughed. 'You're just an accomplished drinker. And anyway, I'm looking forward to the old boy finding out.'

Ketting sat down next to Pleun, with whom he obviously felt most comfortable. Birds of a feather... that's just how it is. Now that the company was complete, it was time to open the gifts. Tosca passed them to Swanny one at a time. Casper had come up with the original idea of giving her one of his own paintings, a female nude. A small one, and not half bad at that, thankfully, because of course it would have to go up in the salon. Pleun's husband had knocked together a jewellery box, covered in an overlay that Pleun had embroidered herself. Swan smothered her in a warm embrace. Tosca, of course, had really gone to town: a stack of gramophone records, a sequined dress, two necklaces and a gilded powder compact. The charming thing about Tosca was that she wasn't trying to outdo the others, that wasn't her style, she was simply mad about her best friend. Swanny protested that it was too, too much! But she held the dress up against herself and promised to try it on presently. Suddenly Karel let out a shriek. All eyes turned to him. Robin scratched the bird's head and said timidly that he regretted he didn't have a gift for her. 'Don't be ridiculous!' Swanny exclaimed. 'The fact that you're here is the best gift of all.'

Lucien saw the eye behind the spectacles gaze back at her. Funny how difficult it was to guess what emotions were concealed behind that mask.

Then Tosca handed Swanny Lucien's gift. She sat down, placed it on her lap, carefully undid the wrapping and opened the box. Beaming, she held the camera up. Tosca bent over and together they examined it. 'Is it ready to use?' Swanny asked.

'Sure is,' answered Lucien. 'Why don't I take a group photo as a souvenir of this evening?' Everyone gathered around. Casper, despite having a bad case of the wobbles, decided that he, being the artist with an infallible feeling for ambience, should organize the shot and positioned himself in front of the French windows. With a little jerk of the head Pleun signalled to Albert Ketting to join them. He clearly felt he had no business being in the photo, but he was used to taking orders from women like Pleun, and followed obediently. Tosca placed the birthday girl in the middle. 'Robin and Karel too!' Swanny cried. Lucien noticed that Robin had remained aside from the group, next to the cockatoo. Swanny insisted that the entire party rearrange itself around Karel's perch.

Lucien snapped open the camera, slid out the bellows and

reached for the focus lever. He gestured for them to move closer together. A shuffling of feet, even a bit of jostling; Lucien saw Robin cautiously work his way backwards. 'Come on, Robin, get back in the picture!' he called as he looked through the viewfinder again to make sure everyone was in shot. Swanny turned and walked over to Robin, who had ambled off into the garden. She put her arm round his shoulder and whispered something in his ear. Lucien lowered the camera. Ketting said, just loud enough to hear, 'Of course he doesn't want to be in the photo, it must be awful for him… with that face.'

'All right, then, a photo without Robin,' said Lucien. But no one resumed their place, and Swanny shouted from the back of the garden: 'Never mind the photograph! We'll do it another time.' The guests returned hesitantly to their chairs. Lucien went off to find Swanny and Robin, who had disappeared behind some bushes. As he approached, Swanny waved him away. Lucien saw Robin's shoulders heaving. He was crying.

Back with the others, he said that Swanny was right, they'd do it another time. Ketting put down his glass and announced he'd be getting along, as he still had to get to the garage. He pulled his cap down over his eyes and asked if they'd give Miss Swanny his compliments. Casper, bored, hung around the gramophone and swung the needle back over the record. Tosca strode over to him, knocked his hand aside and snapped: 'We don't feel like any music right now!' Casper retreated sulkily to the fence, snatching up a Château Dauzac on the way.

As dusk fell over the garden, Pleun set an oil lamp on the table. Swanny was still at the back of the garden with Robin. 'I must say, Lucien…' Tosca began, 'I think it's wonderful of you to let

Robin stay here while he's looking for work. I didn't expect it of you.'

'Well, I can't just put the fellow out on the street, can I?' he answered without flinching.

'There are plenty of people who would,' said Pleun.

Lucien smiled indulgently and refilled his glass. What a terrific bloke he was! Some brainless veteran bangs up his car and he doesn't think twice about taking the poor fellow under his wing. Of course they appreciate that. Heart-warming, it was. Women... If he'd brought back a three-legged dog they'd have gushed just as much.

Swanny finally returned, with Robin, his head lowered, at her side. He fidgeted with his mask and disappeared into the house. 'Robin's going to freshen up a bit,' she said. Lucien could see that her eyes were red and swollen. 'He doesn't want to be photographed. I told him we all understand perfectly.'

'I can well imagine,' said Pleun. 'Just think how it must feel...' To hide her emotions she went off to light the lanterns hanging in the trees.

Robin returned a quarter of an hour later. He'd washed his face; his collar had wet spots and his bangs clung damply to his forehead. You could tell from his gait that he felt better. He apologized for disrupting the party and attempted a modest smile, which gave his face a remorseful look. So he was capable of showing his emotions! Then he asked if they could put on a record. While Tosca shuffled through the stack for something suitable, he suddenly drew himself up to his full height and announced: 'I was always a good dancer, and I still am.' Tosca cranked up the gramophone and put the needle on the record. Robin went up to Swanny and bowed. Smiling, she placed her fingers in his outstretched hand. Elegantly, his elbow bent slightly, he led her to the closely cropped bit of lawn beside the flowerbeds and the hedge. Under the light of the lanterns, he placed his hand lightly on her waist and they danced. From the gramophone horn came a crackly voice: *I'm Always Chasing Rainbows...*

18

Compassion

Well, that was no easy ride. It had taken him nearly three quarters of an hour. With the Mercedes still in the garage while waiting for a replacement part for the headlamp, a spin on the Harley seemed like a nice diversion. At last, the chance to speed off to Amsterdam again, taking the country roads at full throttle, the moonless night adding to the excitement. But the Harley's gearbox was acting up; there seemed to be something wrong with the clutch. Maybe the bike had been sitting in the shed for too long, or perhaps it was just time to trade it in for a new one, like the latest ultra-fast Harley-Davidson Sport Twin.

Weaving between cars and squealing trams, he rode along the Stadhouderskade to the Weteringschans, passed the Paleis voor Volksvlijt, crossed the bridge over the Amstel and turned left, cutting across tram line 10, onto the Weesperzijde. He shifted to the lowest gear and admired the scene. The towering elms along the Amstel river were shedding their seeds, which fluttered like confetti through the air. The wind swept a carpet of tiny white leaves over the road surface, depositing them in large piles along the gutters. He followed the scattering leaves in the gaslight as they stuck in the graceful Renaissance stonework adorning the façades. These 19th-century townhouses were among Amsterdam's grandest, and this stretch of the Weesperzijde, built for the prosperous élite, had stolen his heart. He wondered who had the status and capital to buy such houses these days: bank directors, major stockholders, commissioners? He'd have to look into what a house like this cost, although moving to Amsterdam was out of the question for the time being. Swanny would never agree to leave Haarlem, and he couldn't very well leave her on her own on the Oranjekade. It would be an entirely different story, of course, if she decided to marry Marnix.

Just before reaching Café De IJsbreker he cut the engine, dismounted and pushed the Harley onto the pavement. Since the AGM he'd been pondering how best to sound out Olyrook without arousing suspicion. In any event, calling on him here, in the relaxed atmosphere of his own home, would be preferable to a visit to Weesp. Jan Palacky had recently excused Olyrook's absence under the pretext of illness – so why not play the compassionate card and come calling to ask after his health? To avoid the risk of being fobbed off by telephone, he took the old-fashioned route, announcing himself by letter, hand-delivered by Ketting. Since there had been no reply to the contrary, he assumed he was welcome. He'd considered taking a fruit basket but in the end opted for a bottle of cognac, which was always appropriate, whatever the occasion.

He was surprised at his uneasiness. He had no idea how to proceed and would have to rely on his instinct. One thing was certain: he mustn't broach the thorny subject of Thomas's unexpected departure. That could spoil the atmosphere completely. Hopefully the affable and talkative Jan Palacky would be there; he'd surely keep the mood from turning sour.

He parked the Harley outside Olyrook's house so he could

keep an eye on it from the living room. He'd heard that in Amsterdam bicycles and even motorbikes were stolen all the time. But the curtains behind the two large ground-floor windows were drawn. He rang the bell and almost immediately heard the metallic sliding of bolts. An unfamiliar young man opened the door. He smiled pleasantly, invited him inside and courteously helped him off with his jacket. The man then threw open the door to the living room, the way a butler would, and modestly backed away. The air in the room was musty and stale – they obviously never opened the windows. A single floor lamp with a parchment shade cast outsized shadows on the walls. The dark antique furniture that still filled the room contributed to the gloomy atmosphere. Thomas sat, wreathed in a cloud of cigar smoke, in the same leather armchair from which he'd given Lucien his first sales lesson all those years ago. Only when the smoke wafted up to the ceiling could Lucien make out the thick lenses of his spectacles.

'So, my boy, finally paying your old friend a visit?' said Olyrook.

'About time, isn't it?' Lucien sank into the chair across from him. The young man had entered quietly and replaced the full ashtray on Olyrook's side table with a clean one. 'Anton…' said Thomas, 'do pour us drink, won't you?' Anton heaved a sigh and asked Lucien what he would prefer. 'Coffee?'

'Give him a cognac,' Thomas instructed.

Lucien had intended not to drink, so as to keep a clear head, but the poorly lit room and Palacky's absence threw him off guard, and he nodded in assent. They waited in silence as Anton handed him a glass, dribbled a minuscule refill into Thomas's and demonstratively returned the bottle to the cabinet before withdrawing with exaggerated servility.

'New lodger?' asked Lucien.

'There was an empty room. Pity to let it go to waste.'

Lucien watched Olyrook drain his glass behind a new cloud of smoke. He wondered if Palacky had been evicted, or if he was just elsewhere, perhaps in Weesp. Although something told him Jan would have been here if he'd known Lucien were coming. Better not to ask.

'So how are you?' asked Lucien in an attempt to get the ball rolling.

Thomas didn't beat around the bush. 'I suffer from rheumatism,' he answered. 'It's tolerable at times, excruciating at others.' Only now did Lucien notice how gnarled his hands were. 'It's chronic. Sitting here in my chair is painful, but getting up is worse.' He paused. 'But you probably reckon it serves me right.'

'Don't be stupid, of course not,' replied Lucien, taken aback.

'Come now, do you really think I don't see how angry you are at me? You've been oozing resentment since the moment you walked in. Mind you, I understand completely. You feel betrayed. I'd feel the same way.'

'Certainly not, what makes you think that? You've every right to make your own choices.'

'Of course I do. But you'd have preferred me to have discussed it with you first, at the very least.'

'Maybe.' There was no avoiding the subject now. He had to clear the air as quickly as possible. 'Since you didn't say anything, it was like we were suddenly in opposing camps. Competitors. Quite unpleasant, really.'

'Understandable. Well, there's none of that. It was just too painful, you staying with the firm and all. I'd had my fill of Cremers and Peereboom, not to mention our friend Jongejan, although now he's free to cock things up elsewhere. But the main thing was the urge for freedom. Surely you can understand that. It's always surprised me that you continue to toe the line. Although by now you'll have got yourself a decent position.'

'I can't complain. Business has been pretty good this past year.' He realized he'd been too quick in referring to the firm's sales; he mustn't show his hand so soon. Then again, it was just innocent small talk. So he forged ahead: 'And you?'

'No complaints here either. Starting a new business is always tricky, but I've got a good reputation for delivering quality.' He stared into his empty glass and gestured to the cupboard where Anton had put the bottle. Even lifting his arm appeared painful.

Lucien fetched the bottle of cognac and refilled their glasses, Thomas's more than half-full. He stood with the bottle in his hand and raised his eyebrows questioningly.

'Put it back. That snot-nosed puppy thinks I should drink less. When you're gone he'll check to see how much we've drunk, and then I'm in for it.' He gave a tired laugh. 'Nice, eh? Harrassing a sick old man.'

Strange – he talked about freedom, but allowed himself to be bullied by his young lodger. So what was up with Jan? But he didn't want to lose the thread. 'When Cremers told me you quit, I really thought for a moment that you'd taken Biedermann up on his offer.' He flicked his wrist as though to whisk away so rash a thought.

'I've no desire whatsoever to work in Germany,' replied Thomas. 'I prefer to stay here, especially now my health is so poor. Much better to be your own boss.'

Naturally. The question remained, though, how much this

'own boss' could produce. And how he managed to finance the laboratory, extraction and processing apparatus, the equipment and chemicals. And none of Peereboom's contacts in the banking world had been able to discover where he'd secured a loan from. Was he independently wealthy, or had a rich aunt left him an inheritance? Lucien glanced round the room. Aside from the elegant cabinets and Empire armchairs, there were three antique clocks on the mantelpiece, an Amsterdam grandfather clock against the wall and, displayed on a chiffonnière, a clock in the form of a cathedral. 'Beautiful pieces,' he said, impressed. 'So you're still collecting?'

'I certainly am, especially clocks… one of my few remaining pleasures. I can enjoy them from my chair.' His face turned wistful. 'When I close my eyes I hear time tick agreeably by.'

Lucien suddenly felt sorry for him. It was sad to see Thomas reduced to this. He truly didn't deserve it.

Olyrook abruptly changed the subject. 'How are things with your girlfriend, our glamorous film star?'

'Fine – she's got a shot at a new role, not easy nowadays with all those young actresses.'

'That won't be doing her migraine any good,' Thomas said with a grin. Physically he might be a wreck, but inside he was still the same old Thomas.

'Where's Jan, by the way?' The question no longer seemed inappropriate.

Thomas stiffened. The grin dissolved under the sharp lines along his nose. 'Jan is visiting his family in Czechoslovakia. He should be back one of these days.'

'I thought maybe you'd kicked him out and given his room to the new lodger.' Lucien regretted his rudeness at once. And he was genuinely relieved that Jan was not gone for good.

'Not at all, why should I? Jan is a fine fellow – at least he doesn't harangue me about drinking like that snotnose does. We've only taken Anton in because Jan doesn't have time for the household chores anymore, and could use the help.'

'He must have his hands full down in Weesp.'

Thomas struck a match with difficulty and lit a fresh cigar. Then he reached for a silver table-bell next to the ashtray and rang it vigorously, his thick spectacles glued to the door. He hadn't done that on Lucien's previous visit: back then, he'd the strength to call for Jan. Anton appeared in the doorway; his eyes shooting to the glasses and then to Thomas. He raised his chin in a questioning gesture. 'Bring the packet for Mr. Hirschland.' Anton left the room and was back in a trice, as though it been lying ready just around the corner. Of course, Thomas took it for granted that this was why he was here. Lucien removed the cocaine, wrapped per gram in individual white paper packets, from a rolled-up sheet of newspaper. Not to check it, but to give Anton time to clear off. As he took out his wallet he wondered if it was still worth fishing for information about Thomas's sales.

'Just give me half what you usually do,' Thomas said as he disappeared behind a cloud of smoke. 'Consider it a peace offering, amends for making you feel like I've betrayed you.'

Lucien was surprised by his generosity; until now, the price had gone up at regular intervals. An uneasy feeling crept over him. Thomas was behaving like someone who hadn't much time to live, with this gesture as a kind of farewell. Alarmed by the thought, he wanted to protest. But when the smoke cleared he could see that Thomas had closed his eyes. Lucien got up and placed the money next to the ashtray. He pulled the bottle of cognac he'd brought out of his bag and put it behind the chair. 'Keep it out of the brat's sight,' he whispered and laid his hand on Thomas's bony shoulder. His cheek rested for a moment against Lucien's fingers. It was all better, all better now, which made Lucien genuinely happy. 'Thomas, I can see you're tired. I'll be going now. Take care of yourself. I'll come back again soon to see how you're doing. Give my regards to Jan.'

Thomas nodded, his eyes still closed.

He was still slightly shaken by the visit as he drew up in front of Pola's house. He no longer cared that he hadn't got any information out of him. And besides, it felt wrong to take advantage of Olyrook's ill health. He'd tell Cremers his inquiry had turned up nothing of interest; that would sound plausible, at least. In any case, he had more than enough cocaine for the time being – twenty grams, he reckoned – and buoyed by his reconciliation with Thomas, he decided to spoil Pola a bit. Within reason, of course. Pola's wild fits of euphoria could make her volatile sometimes.

She'd recently taken to searching through his clothes, so he put three packets in his inside pocket and hid the rest under the saddle of the motorbike. Out of the corner of his eye he saw that the shopkeeper below Pola's flat was, even at this late hour, still stocking her shelves, so he asked her to keep an eye on the Harley. He opened the door himself; he'd had his own key for a month now, a symbolic gesture letting him know he was the man of the house. He appreciated the implicit message: come and go as you please, you won't find another man in my bed.

He'd barely reached the top of the stairs when a plate whizzed past him, narrowly missing his ear. The Wedgwood porcelain shattered against the stairway wall behind him. Lucien stormed inside. 'Hey ho! What's going on here,' he laughed as he grabbed Pola, 'are you training for the discus?' Furious – of course she was furious, he was late as usual. Standard procedure. He'd give her a couple of hours to reach boiling point, then she'd lash out theatrically at him, get her fix of rage, and then her pent-up fury would transform into the sexual voracity he came for. He released his grip and pulled a packet out of his pocket, waved it at her tauntingly, and, like baiting a kitten with a piece of string, he lured her into the bedroom. He backed into the edge of the bed. She leapt upon him and he relinquished her prey. While she indulged herself with the white powder he poured himself a glass of whisky and sank into a chair. It always took a couple of minutes for her to get wound up. As Pola sat hunched over the saucer and little silver spoon, he was reminded how thin she'd become over these last six months. The voluptuous curves had been replaced by an angular figure. He knew thin was fashionable, but still… What he regretted most was that she had cut her long, thick hair and wore it slicked back. But she was still a beautiful, desirable woman. Every time he saw her he fell in love all over again. Oh yes, mustn't forget to invite her to that concert.

She gazed at him from under her long lashes with sparkling eyes, and smiled sweetly. 'I'd appreciate it if you didn't pelt me with plates when I'm a bit late,' he said as he took off his shoes. 'It's not only expensive stuff, but one of these days you'll hit me, and then who'd make you happy?'

She pouted. 'You disappoint me so,' she slurred, 'and not just by being late.'

Lucien got up and sank to the bed with Pola in his arms. He undid the front of her dress, exposing her breasts. 'We've been together for so long now,' she whispered into his neck. He propped himself up on one elbow and unbuttoned his trousers. 'And you still treat me like your courtesan, your mistress, your whore...'

He pulled her leg up alongside his hip. The word 'whore' only aroused him even more.

'I'm getting older too, and want to settle down. Plenty of men around, you know.'

He restrained himself for a moment. What was she on about?

'Maybe I'd like to have children,' she snivelled.

He shut his eyes. God damn it, why couldn't she keep her trap shut? Children? What now? She relaxed her grip on him, and he felt himself go limp. He rolled over to one side. 'What do you mean, children?' he asked, slightly irritated.

'I have normal needs, Lucien. Just like any other woman I'd like a husband, a nice house and a child, maybe even two.'

He stared at her, astonished. He'd never once associated her with a loving mother. Here they were, supposed to be making passionate love, and visions of his own mother suddenly appeared before his eyes. The combination extinguished every shred of lust.

'You don't understand me,' she whined.

'I do understand you.' He braced himself. 'But Pola, darling... you simply aren't the mothering type, you're an actress.' He simply couldn't imagine her in the kitchen; he'd never seen her cook anything before. This was a woman you took out to a fancy restaurant, whom you showed off, not a housewife who slaved over a hot stove.

Now Pola was weeping pitifully. One false eyelash had come undone. He tried to stroke her cheek, but she pushed his hand away and said: 'Have you never pictured us as a married couple?'

No, he hadn't. The whole subject of marriage, with anyone, was something he preferred to put off, because it meant constant nagging about being home on time, about... damn it, about everything. It meant just one thing: an end to his freedom.

'You're almost thirty,' she continued, nattering away as usual after a fix, 'and so am I, we belong together, we can't live without each other, we'd make such a divine couple.'

Good God, that would mean being with Pola every single day. The eroticism would dwindle and worse, much worse... she wouldn't tolerate him having his own life. What's more, she was fickle: one minute ebullient and outgoing, the next minute aggressive and obnoxious. That made for an exciting sexual relationship, but in a marriage... Thick tears left greasy trails of makeup on her cheeks. This was the first time he'd seen her so upset. It was almost believable. 'You know I only want to make you happy,' he said with the air of an unfairly badgered lover. 'Look, I've got a bit more, take it, you'll feel better soon.'

Her eyes shot open. He hurried from the bed before she could burst into tears again. She dried her cheeks with the back of her hand, wiped away the smeared makeup with a damp fingertip, replaced the eyelash and sat on the edge of the bed, spoon in hand.

He pulled off his trousers and shirt while she snorted it up, and installed himself on the satin sheets, leaning back on the pillow with his arms behind his head. His desire was quick in returning. She was still seated, hunched forward with her back to him, and suddenly jerked herself upright. But instead of taking off her dress, she agitatedly buttoned it shut, stepped into her shoes and picked up her bag. He couldn't believe his eyes. 'What are you doing?' he asked.

The wild look in her eyes heralded a new tantrum. 'I have another date!' she screamed. 'With a film producer. He's going to give me the best role I've ever been offered!'

'You're lying!'

'Am I?'

Was she really planning to leave him? This was no less than an act of vengeance. All that blubbering about marriage and children was for real. Damn it, if he'd only taken the trouble to be a bit more understanding, she'd be lying here with him in bed.

Look at her standing there, his beautiful Fury. What a turn-on.

'Please, Pola, don't be silly. Let's talk about it,' he begged, patting his hand on the bed next to him.

'Talk, talk, talk!' she shouted, her hand on the doorknob. 'What's there to talk about with a stupid actress? With a woman you can't imagine as a mother!'

'Wait, don't go! I didn't mean it!' He leapt up, and realizing he was naked reached for his clothes. But she'd already slammed the door behind her.

At home, in his own room, Lucien put on his blue kimono, flopped back on the four-poster bed and stared up at the knotted *klamboe*. What a fool he'd been not to see the row with Pola coming. It was to be expected, of course, that after all this time she'd be hoping for a commitment. He just had to try to picture her in another role: that of a wife, a mother. Why not? Perhaps the lack of stability of married life was the cause of her capriciousness. It was true, he did treat her like his mistress. But under all that makeup she was just plain old Carla Pauw from Alkmaar, who had given herself a Russian-sounding stage name. A perfectly ordinary woman with perfectly ordinary desires. He was the immature one, who lived for his own hedonistic pleasures, who was convinced that being unattached was the same as being happy, and who showed no willingness whatsoever to take responsibility for a family. He was, in fact, a first-class prick.

Sounds of a disturbance outside jolted him out of his reverie. He got up and looked out the window. A group of young men, students apparently, lurched along the canal, singing and whooping. They jostled one another towards the water. One of them, wearing a bowler hat, teetered on the edge of the canal wall, almost lost his balance, and at the last moment was rescued by his comrades from an involuntary plunge. Their voices faded as they staggered off. Lucien glanced at the clock on his nightstand: 1 a.m. He suddenly became aware of the silence. He couldn't remember having noticed the night-time quiet in the house before. Whenever he came home late, Swanny was already asleep in her room, downstairs at the end of the passage. He wondered if he'd hear her if she called for help. Weren't their bedrooms a bit too far apart? On an impulse he left his room, walked to the end of the hall and listened at the top of the stairs. Everything was quiet. Instead of returning to his bedroom, he walked further back along the passage and opened the door that led to his old room. Careful not to make a sound, he climbed the narrow stairs, skipping the two squeaky ones; even in the dark they were imprinted in his memory.

Halfway up he heard sounds coming from the room. Regular footsteps, like marching, and a voice, talking in a monotone to someone. Could Swanny be in there? He listened intently, holding his breath, but couldn't hear her voice. Only one person was speaking, a man. Robin. Why would he make so much racket in the middle of the night? Didn't he realize that Swanny's room was almost directly under his, and that all his muttering and thumping around could wake her?

He took the rest of the stairs in three strides and knocked at the door. The droning voice stopped. Lucien waited a few seconds and opened the door. Robin stood in the narrow space between the bed and the desk, his face turned away as he fumbled to put on the mask. Lucien was embarrassed at having almost caught Robin with his face uncovered. His hair was dishevelled and he was wearing only long underwear. His tannish torso was covered in scars; some appeared to have only recently healed. His whole body was tense, his neck muscles were visibly taut. Robin quickly felt behind his ears for the curled ends of the eyeglasses and looked at Lucien helplessly.

'Are you feeling all right?' he asked.

'Yes, yes, fine.' Robin sat down on the bed, as though he needed to make space. Lucien hesitated. 'Sorry, I just wanted to see if there was anything wrong,' he said. 'I heard you walking about and talking. Maybe you could keep it down a bit. Swanny's asleep, you might wake her.'

Robin started. 'Oh, I didn't realize… I'll be extra quiet.'

'Having trouble sleeping?'

'I hardly dare to sleep. So I pace up and down and talk to myself. I'm sorry.' He seemed agitated.

'Why can't you sleep?'

Robin hesitated before replying. 'I have nightmares. As soon as I close my eyes I'm back at the front. I think it's the darkness: you see, we always went over the top just before daybreak, at the whistle signal… I still hear that whistle. Then it started. You had to leave the trench. That's why I stay on my feet. As long as I'm walking I feel like I'm still safely in the trench, don't have to go over the top yet…' He shook his head vehemently. 'And I talk and talk just to keep my head above the din… the roar of the cannon, I can still hear it, and the screaming, the wailing of soldiers whose arms and legs have been ripped off and are waiting to die…'

Lucien could see that even the effort of groping for the words to describe those horrific memories made Robin shudder. The poor bastard, no wonder he didn't dare sleep – and then he had to spend the night cooped up in this stuffy little room. 'It must be awfully cramped in here if you can't sleep,' he said.

'Oh no, in fact I like it here, it makes me feel safe.'

'You know what, I'll go and get you something to help you sleep. I use it myself now and again.' He hesitated with his hand on the doorpost, and said in a confidential tone: 'Don't mention it to Swanny, though. She doesn't hold with medicines.' He wanted to tell him what had happened to his mother, but checked himself.

He went to his room and returned with the sleeping powders he'd confiscated from Pola one day, when he'd suddenly had enough of all the medicine she was using. Robin was still sitting tensely on the bed. Lucien filled a glass from the carafe and offered him the box. While Robin slid some powder onto his tongue and washed it down with water, Lucien noticed his suitcase next to the desk. On top there were a few personal items: soap and a shaving-brush, a notebook and some loose change. Next to the desk lamp was a small bottle whose label seemed vaguely familiar. The edge of the neck was chipped, and the glass was dull with scratches – obviously a much-used old bottle. He picked it up and held it under the light. He could just make out the words *Tabloid* and *Forced March* on the filthy label. It came back to him at once, and he smiled as he recalled the stench of fish. 'I know this stuff,' he said. 'Someone showed it to me once.' He pulled out the half-crumbled cork and looked inside: two pills left.

'My pain medication,' said Robin as he took hold of the bottle, politely but resolutely, as though Lucien might take it from him.

Snippets of the conversation with Brian Kirkpatrick drifted back. 'Did you buy it at Harrods?' asked Lucien, recalling that the famous department store sold the product.

Robin looked at him, perplexed. 'No, no, not at Harrods. I got these on prescription from my doctor.'

'Looks like that was some time ago, judging from the bottle.'

'That's right, I keep getting it refilled…'

What had Brian had said about those tablets? He could only remember that Kirkpatrick was irritated; he objected to the combination of caffeine and cocaine… or was it something else? 'Anyway, these won't help you sleep, they'll just keep you awake,' he explained.

'Really? I didn't know that.'

Lucien leaned against the desk. 'It's a relaxant but it can also work as a stimulant. If you use it for too long you eventually become dependent, which you don't want, because you have to keep going back to the doctor.'

Robin turned the bottle over in his hands. 'Then I'd better be careful with it.'

'You'll have to be, there's only a couple of pills left. Maybe you should stop once these are finished; your insomnia should go away by itself. Tomorrow I'll give you some aspirin for the pain and some more sleeping powder to get you through the first few nights.' Lucien was pleased to be able to put his professional expertise to personal use.

'Thanks. I'll use those aspirins instead, then.'

'That would be wise.' He could see Robin looking him up and down. He'd probably never seen a Chinese kimono before. 'Brought it back from Java,' he explained, running his hands over the blue silk. He turned to show off the dragon embroidered on the back. 'Why don't you lie down,' he suggested, 'and I'll keep you company for a while.' He leaned back against the desk as Robin settled down on his side. Maybe he should talk to him, to block out the whistles and cannon and screams. He'd have to relax if he was going to get some sleep. 'Have you been to look for work yet?' he asked.

The panic returned at once. 'Sorry, I haven't, I helped Swanny and Pleun clear up the garden, trimmed the hedge and mowed the grass. So there's wasn't any time left for job-hunting. I'll start tomorrow.'

'Take your time. Just get back on your feet first, you've had a hard time of it lately.'

Robin didn't answer. His eyelid drooped. He clearly wasn't used to sedatives. Perhaps it was better to leave him alone. 'Sleep well,' he whispered. Robin's eye was completely shut now. Lucien bent over him and considered removing the mask, but thought better of it. He pulled the sheet and blanket from under him and turned him carefully so his head lay on the pillow. He straightened his legs and laid the covers over him. And as an afterthought he tucked the bedclothes under the mattress, just like his mother had done for him hundreds of times.

19

War veteran seeks employment

The next morning, Robin awoke refreshed and full of resolve. Today he would convince them of his sincere intentions. He wanted to prove himself to Lucien, and show Swanny that he wasn't a crippled loser, a pathetic sod, but a man in the prime of his life, physically and emotionally capable of building an independent, respectable existence... He glanced at the clock, dressed quickly and hurried downstairs. He mustn't miss her.

She already had her hat and coat on, ready to leave for the library. He had overslept, apologies, but where might he find this week's newspapers? He wanted to look for suitable job openings. 'You needn't do that yet,' Swanny protested. 'What's the hurry?' He was determined. It was high time he found work. He felt strong enough. 'But you can't even read the advertisements!' she said, 'and Pleun won't be able to help you.' But he'd thought of everything: reaching into the kitchen cabinet, he pulled out a Dutch-English dictionary and held it to his chest like a preacher would a bible. That brought a broad smile to her face. He promised, cross his heart, not to set out until she was back from work. Wouldn't she be impressed at how much he'd accomplished by the time she got home!

Excited at the thought of getting his life back on track, he retired to his room and, seated at the desk, began thumbing through the newspapers with the open dictionary at his side. He translated, word for word, anything that looked to him like a job advert. But he was always just off the mark: accountants offering their services, someone after a parcel of land, or three young ladies who were looking for pleasant accommodation. For two hours he slogged through a morass of black newsprint, notating page after page of translated words with no coherent connection whatever. Finally he shoved the notebook aside; his hands were clammy and the scars constricted painfully. And those sounds coming from behind the wallpaper: how was he to concentrate with that relentless distraction? But he was pushed for time and opened another page of classifieds. Within half an hour he'd managed to decipher two adverts for a manservant. He was disappointed, and felt humiliated by a newspaper that could help situate unemployed servants but was no good to him. He angrily threw it aside and lay down on his bed.

Now he heard it again, quite clearly. Something was scratching quietly behind the wallpaper beside his bed. A mouse… No, that was no innocent little mouse scavenging for food, those were much bigger teeth gnawing through the paper. It had to be a rat… he knew it, a dirty, stinking, sticky-whiskered rat, maybe even a whole pack of them. They were looking for him, they'd followed his smell, the stench of the trenches that every veteran carried with him forever. He had to get the hell out of this room before they gnawed their way through the lath and plaster and the wallpaper. But he didn't dare put his feet on the ground, the trench was no longer safe, they'd look for him there first… He needed help, he couldn't tackle those filthy beasts on his own. Leaning across the desk, he grasped the edge and reached for the bottle. He hesitated... just one pill, or both? This was an emergency. Why save one for this afternoon? Better take both at once, how else was he going to get rid of that cold tingling under his fingernails? It wasn't long before the rats had retreated, but there was no guarantee they weren't lying in wait to ambush him. He grabbed his old army coat, bounded to the door and crept outside to avoid bumping into Pleun.

It must have been around noon. Throngs of people were pressing through the city on their way to lunch. Cars and bicycles vied for space in the narrow streets. Horses pulled wagons, boys pushed handcarts and everywhere there were basket-carrying market women, scurrying children and barking dogs. It was an unbelievable hubbub. He drifted along the shopfronts and houses, his head down, doing his best to avoid the bustling masses of pedestrians on the pavement. He saw only the confident gait of shoes and boots. They were going somewhere, they had a clear purpose. He too had somewhere to go, he too had a clear purpose, only he didn't know the way. At first he recognized the shops Swanny had pointed out to him: a greengrocer, a baker, but soon he lost his way in the labyrinth of lanes and alleys. He should never have left London – he was totally alone here, and didn't have his friend Harry to show him the way. They'd made a good team. Damn it, they'd been invincible!

They'd met in a pub. Harry was a veteran too. He was missing his right leg – he'd left it behind in the mud somewhere near Ypres on 31 July 1917... the same day a grenade had ripped off half of Robin's face – so they had something in common straight away. Not that they ever talked about it; they had other concerns on their minds. The other thing they had in common was that neither of them had two pennies to rub together. After the armistice, Harry had been involved in a fight somewhere in the East End; something awful must have happened, Robin wasn't sure what, but it was serious enough for them to terminate Harry's war pension. Robin himself didn't have a pension, of course, not after doing a bunk from Sidcup. Both of them flat broke: that was more than having something in common, it made them allies, because without money you're lost. Harry was an experienced panhandler. 'But damn it all, just one leg gone, that ain't worth beans,' said Harry. There were already plenty of beggars who'd lost both legs, and maybe even an arm too. If people had to choose, they gave to the ones with the fewest limbs. That's just how it went. And that's why Harry latched onto Robin: a mutilated face, now there's an injury for you! A fellow could miss a leg or two, but such a horrific mug... even the most hurried passer-by couldn't miss that.

So they bagged a secure begging spot near King's Cross Station. Harry played passable banjo, but the competition was tough: a little way further on, there were crippled professional musicians playing violins or flutes. People even clapped those bastards. On the third day, with not a single coin tossed into the cup all morning, Harry suddenly shouted: 'Let 'em see your mug!' But Robin refused. 'Take off the fucking mask, arsehole!' Robin could see it would boost their chances, but he found it hard to summon up the courage. Once he managed to overcome the shame, Harry had to continually nag him not to let his chin droop. 'What good is that face of yours if no one can see it!'

At first they each had a sign reading 'WAR VETERAN SEEKS EMPLOYMENT', but after some Good Samaritan offered Harry an odd job, they changed their signs to 'DISABLED WAR

VETERAN'. All they wanted was money, and fast. Robin shed his shame and brazenly stared passers-by in the face; they were, after all, paying for it. His self-loathing grew along with their takings. But Harry just laughed. 'Jesus, man, didn't I tell you? That ugly phiz of yours is a goldmine!'

In the evening they headed off to the East End with a full tin cup. That's where the pubs were, places where other veterans, whores, pimps and all kinds of lowlife came in search of cocaine. That's where you found them, the small-time criminals lurking in dark corners, asking exorbitant sums for some adulterated rubbish. Still, they'd kill for a hit of dope, even the cut stuff. Because, oh my God, with some coke in your nose things felt so much better; for the time being at least, no hunger, no fatigue, you could handle the world and the world could handle you. They talked, talked, talked, not with each other but with provincials out on the town in the East End, who lapped up their stories of the front, bloody stories, because the bloodier they were, the more lucrative – money in return for sensation, blood-drenched sensation! They rabbited on and on, vying to outdo each other. Not about what really happened, that was too banal for words – just a loud bang, and off with your leg, off with half your face! – no, they invented lurid tales off the cuff. They were unstoppable, and bloody easy it was too… But sometimes, in the middle of that endless prattle, fiction and reality would start to merge, and then came the tears – which only helped them rake in even more money. They trawled the sewer of their memories until they were so emotionally drained that the only thing that helped was yet more cocaine.

Sometimes, when they'd stocked up on the powder or robbed some poor armless and defenceless veteran of his, things got completely out of hand. Then they'd end up back on the streets, lower lips hanging flabbily, tongues dangling, their bodies twitching spastically. Harry couldn't be bothered to play the banjo anymore, he'd just stand there swearing and screaming. 'Bastards! Filthy scum! Here we are, your heroes!!!' he roared at shocked Londoners. 'Look, just look! Bunch of motherfuckers!' screamed Robin. 'Have a look at my mug! Blown to smithereens for king and country!' Aghast, passers-by gave them a wide berth and hurried on, some fumbling in their pockets for small change. 'Many thanks, you sons of bitches! You call this thanks for defending the fatherland?' An old man made a comment. The wrong comment. Harry whacked him with his crutch. They doubled up with laughter. 'Give! Give! Give! We'll have his mangled head cast in bronze and put up in Trafalgar Square,' yelled Harry, 'with a plaque underneath: "War hero who defended civilization"!' They nearly fell off their stools with hilarity. But by nightfall they were penniless again. They couldn't afford the shelter, so they slept in a park or on a bench beside the Thames with the other homeless, huddled close together in the icy cold that seeped through the cracked leather of their boots. They dreamt of their next hit, and waited for the footsteps of the policeman who'd come and chase them away. Early in the morning Robin would glower malevolently at the passing trams full of well-fed Londoners who didn't even deign to give him a second glance as he stood, stripped to the waist, with numbed fingers, washing himself in a horse trough.

Their resolution to buy only *Forced March* tablets and to take them only in each other's company, no more than two a day, lasted less than a week. Throbbing headaches, dizziness, anxiety and depression: they didn't even have the energy to go out to beg, until the hunger left them no other choice. This time Harry wanted to try a more effective tack. He decided that being pathetic was no longer enough; they had to add an element of respectability – the combination would tweak people's consciences. Harry still had his uniform, but Robin had to pinch an army coat and cap. They robbed a blind veteran of his medals, because being undecorated was a genuine handicap. Robin pinned on the medals and kept his mask on. The tributes to his heroism on his chest and the decently-covered facial wounds would be enough. They kept their vulgar mouths shut and made a show of humility. 'God bless you, God bless you and your loved ones…' they murmured as the coins jingled into the cup. It worked a treat. But soon they were back to square one: the East End pub landlords were sick to death of the hundreds of addicted veterans, the war still in their system, who brawled with one another at the drop of a hat. He and Harry scuffled too, and were thrown out of the pubs. They weren't welcome anywhere, and in the end all they did was wander the streets, crying and screaming. Until one day, when they themselves came to blows.

So here Robin was roaming the streets again, this time in a foreign city, surrounded by people he found strange and malicious. He was irritated and his anger swelled. His bottle was empty. He knew what was coming, how he'd soon be driven half-mad by the dreadful panic of being out of pills. Why had that bastard fobbed him off with some useless sleeping powders, damn it… He felt in his pocket: a few coins and a crumpled bill. Would it be enough? And where in this fucking city were you supposed by buy cocaine? All those respectable coffeehouses, all those fancy restaurants, all those bloody upright citizens! Surely this place had cafés or pubs where the whores, pimps, drunks and addicts hung out? What kind of a place was this? How could he have made such a stupid mistake? He should have stayed in London, where he at least knew his way around.

Passing a pharmacy, he stopped at the window. No, forget it, robbing a chemist's was something he could only manage with Harry, and forging a prescription was out of the question. Across the way, a hunched, bedraggled man with a swollen-up face staggered along the pavement, obviously half-cut. Robin crossed the street and asked him if he knew of a café where they sold medicine. The fellow looked at him, perplexed. 'Drugs, man, drugs!' The man held up his hand, as though Robin was asking for money. Robin gave him a swift kick and ran off. He soon gave up; he was hopelessly lost. Dizzy and gasping for air, he approached a well-dressed lady wearing a fox stole around her neck. She stopped and looked at him inquisitively. In response to his query about where to buy medicine, she answered in English and pointed to the chemist's. Suddenly his legs gave out and he had to grab a lamppost for support. Concerned, she inquired if he was ill. He shook his head and asked the way to the Oranjekade. Without hesitating, she offered to escort him there; it was on her way. As they walked off together, he eyed her fox stole, that fancy hat, an expensive leather handbag... No, leave it, not today, he was simply too tired.

To his surprise, Swanny was standing in the doorway. She must have been on the lookout for him. 'Where have you been?' she asked. 'We were worried sick!' The lady with the expensive handbag told her what had happened, and Swanny gasped in alarm. 'Thank you, thank you ever so much,' she said. The woman straightened her fox stole and left with a friendly goodbye. Now Pleun appeared in the door as well. She grasped Robin under his armpit and led him to the kitchen table like he was some bloody invalid. Flushed, Swanny stammered that Pleun had discovered he'd vanished, just gone off without eating... The housekeeper nodded vigorously. As if that was the worst thing a body could do: go off without eating! 'She came straight to the library to tell me,' Swanny continued, 'and I rang Lucien immediately. He said you'd come back, but I wasn't sure, you don't know your way around the city and I was afraid...' She fell silent for a moment. 'I was afraid that maybe you didn't feel welcome, that you felt out of place here. Especially after you started looking through the adverts this morning.' Tenderly, intimately, she rested her hand on his arm. 'Really, you can stay here as long as you want.'

Robin sighed. He forced himself to sit stock still, not wanting her to release her hand, whose warmth he could feel even through his sleeve.

'What happened?' she asked.

'My face was hurting so much I went out to see if I could get some medicine.'

'Oh, you poor thing. You should have asked Pleun...'

'I didn't want to be a bother.'

'I'll hear nothing of the sort.' Gone was the hand. Gone was the comforting hand. Gone was the warmth. Swanny got into an unintelligible discussion with Pleun. 'Pleun knows just the thing,' she said to him, 'she'll make a compress of...' her eyes darted in search of the Dutch-English dictionary... 'no, wait, I know, a cabbage leaf compress for your face. Far better than medicine.'

Robin looked at her and turned slowly to Pleun. That horrid old witch with her medieval sorcery gawped at him, patting

her own cheek encouragingly. 'How kind of her,' Robin said
appreciatively, 'but I've tried that already. I can't bear it, especially if I'm in pain.'

·'Did you at least find the chemist? There's one very close by.'

Robin fiddled nervously with the earpieces of his spectacles.'
I don't want to lie to you,' he whispered, so softly that she was
forced to lean close to him. He caught a whiff of violet. 'I did
find the chemist, but I didn't dare go in.'

'Why not? Surely he speaks English.'

'That's not it...' He hesitated, and then opened his mouth,
but no sound came out.

'Ohhhh...' She leapt up. 'Of course you didn't dare go in!
Well, never you mind. If you need anything, just ask.'

'No, really, I have to try, otherwise I'll never find work.'

'You can't go looking for work with your face in pain!'
Swanny turned to the cooker, taking the delicious violet scent
with her. 'Pleun will go and fetch some aspirin for you. In the
meantime I'll make you something to eat, you're shaking with
hunger. It's important that you eat well!'

That evening, after picking up the Mercedes from Deumers,
Lucien found Swanny on her knees in the salon, sweeping up
crumbs from under Karel's perch. The cockatoo cracked and
peeled the seeds in his feed trough and spewed the shells every
which way. 'Why are you so late?' she asked without looking
up. 'Have you eaten?'

'Yes, with a client.'

'Do you know that poor Robin spent the entire afternoon
wandering round the city because his face was in pain?'

He'd entirely forgotten. 'How vexing for him. Where is he
now?'

'In his room. He's had something to eat and went to have a rest. But when I went to check on him a little while ago, I heard him pacing about and talking to himself. I'm so worried; he's really not well. And he wants to go and look for work in that condition! But he really needs to get better first, don't you think?'

Lucien didn't answer. He wished he felt better himself. Somehow or other, an order from Germany had been snatched from under his nose, clearly someone was undercutting them. And to cap it all, he'd had to dine with a Swiss client who bored him to tears with interminable stories in all but incomprehensible German. Swanny looked at him, waiting for a response. 'Yes, you're right,' he replied. 'Maybe he should see Dr. Van Rhijn, he'll know more about it…'

'Of course. I'll take Robin to see him first thing.'

An envelope with a French postmark lay unopened on the mantelpiece behind the Yué vase. Swanny hadn't even bothered to find out what her fiancé had to report from Paris. 'Let me do it. He might be embarrassed to go to the doctor with a woman.'

'I hadn't thought of that,' said Swanny. 'That's sweet of you. I'm so glad you've taken an interest in Robin.'

'That's me, always concerned with my fellow man. Just a Good Samaritan at heart.' She returned his grin with a disapproving scowl. True enough, he could be an appalling hypocrite at times. 'I'll go up and see him,' he said guiltily.

He could hear shuffling and muttering from the bedroom. Something fell with a heavy thud. There was no response to his urgent knocking, so he opened the door. Robin was standing with the bronze lion in his hand. They stared at each other. This was the first time Lucien saw him without his mask, and was shocked at what he saw. Where the dead eye had once been, there was now just a hollow, covered with a flap of smooth skin, and the cheek looked like a patchwork quilt. Robin quickly put down the lion and reached for the mask. 'I'm terribly sorry...' was all that Lucien could blurt out. This was more painful than seeing him naked. His disfigurement was his most intimate secret, his own business and nobody else's. Robin stood thererigidly, his arms tight against his side like he was standing at attention – or maybe there was just no room to move in the cramped space. 'I'd like to talk to you,' said Lucien amicably. 'Let's go to my room, we can sit in comfort there.'

Robin followed meekly. Lucien offered him the chaise longue and Robin sat uneasily on the edge. 'Why did you take off like that today?' asked Lucien bluntly. Robin bit his lip and rubbed his temples. 'I was looking for a pharmacy.'

'Were you after painkillers?'

'Yes... The pain was unbearable this morning, so I took both tablets. My bottle's empty now. I didn't tell Swanny. That's what you said, right? You both think aspirin's enough, but that just won't cut it. Not for now, at least...'

'Mmm... Why didn't you bring more tablets with you from England?'

'My doctor tried everywhere. But they're becoming more and more difficult to get hold of. Beats me, maybe they're being taken off the market for some reason.' He looked imploringly at Lucien. 'I really need them, I can't do without them. I'm at the end of my tether.'

Lucien was in two minds. Pure cocaine would bring him relief, probably better than *Forced March*, but he didn't feel like becoming Robin's dealer. 'Tell you what, I can give you something that will certainly help, but only if you agree to let me take you to our family doctor tomorrow. He'll be able to write you out a prescription.'

'Thank you, of course I'd be happy to see a doctor.' Robin clasped his hands together thankfully and his desperation ebbed away. Lucien opened the top drawer of the dresser and took out the last packet. 'It's not a tablet,' he warned. 'You'll have to sniff it, can you manage that?'

Robin nodded and his breathing increased noticeably. He took the paper packet, knelt at the low table, unfolded it and, using the long fingernail of his little finger, divided the white powder in half. He sniffed half in one nostril and the rest in the other. Then he meticulously licked the paper clean and settled back onto the chaise longue.

Lucien smiled. The contented curl of Robin's mouth reminded him of Pola. That morning, in a repentant mood, he'd had a bouquet of spring flowers delivered to her. In it he'd hidden a silver powder compact, the contents replaced with her beloved powder. She'd appreciate his ingenuity. He looked at Robin. His one eye was closed, but the other one, painted on the mask, stared into space. When he opened his real eye, his face was suddenly out of balance: the living pupil was much larger than the painted one.

Robin whistled softly through his teeth. 'Jesus, what great stuff... haven't had it in such a long time, well never, actually.'

'Doesn't surprise me, we produce top quality stuff here.' As he set a bottle of whisky on the table, Lucien wondered if Robin had any inkling of his line of work. Probably not, he never asked questions, too well-mannered for that. 'I work for a pharmaceutical company, you see. Is it helping?'

'It's helping, all right! I'm feeling no pain,' he laughed loudly. 'My head doesn't even exist!'

'What do you expect? This is pure cocaine,' said Lucien, not without pride.

Robin drained his glass in a single gulp. 'It's not only that the pain is gone, you know... at last I can think of something else, of the future, all the things I could be doing.'

Lucien was pleased to be able to extend a helping hand again. Just imagine being in his shoes... my God, it didn't bear thinking about. He'd lose everything, everything: his work, his contacts... his whole world would collapse, everyone would shun him, Pola, other women... everyone. Everyone except Swanny, that is.

Suddenly, Robin leapt up and looked around the room in amazement. 'What a place, I've never seen anything like it,' he exclaimed. He walked between the tall palm trees directly toward the sabres and *krisses* on the wall.

'I used to live on Java, that's where most of this stuff comes from.'

'And you've recreated your own tropical paradise here,' Robin replied. He pulled a sabre out of its sheath, struck a warrior-like pose, leapt about and took a few swipes at an imaginary enemy.

'Hey, watch out, you!' laughed Lucien.

Robin replaced the sabre. Stroking the satin sheets, he remarked: 'I'll bet you enjoyed it there.'

'It was fantastic; I think back on it often: evenings on the veranda, hanging about with friends, the beautiful country-side, and of course the hunting parties...' Lucien dished up his favourite hunting story while refilling their glasses.

Robin paced restlessly and ran his fingers along the palm leaves. He didn't seem too interested in the tiger. He opened the wardrobe uninvited and pulled out the blue kimono. He tore off his shirt, put on the silk robe, turned his back to the mirror and gazed over his shoulder at the dragon. His soon lost interest and meandered around the tables and cabinets. He picked up the oldest and most valuable Chinese plate from its wooden stand and turned it in his hands.

'Careful, don't drop it!' said Lucien, alarmed. 'That thing cost me a fortune!' Robin put it back and laughed out loud. Lucien noticed, behind the twisted lips, a fine set of straight white teeth. 'My God, man, wouldn't that be something,' Robin sighed. 'Spending time in the tropics, away from grey old bloody Europe, away from bloody England, away from bloody Holland, off to Jamaica, the West Indies...' He clenched his fists and stubbed the toe of his shoe impatiently into the carpet. 'I'd love to get away and see the most exotic places in the world.'

'Have you ever travelled?' Lucien gestured for him to sit down, hoping to forestall another assault on his expensive Persian rug.

Robin flopped back down on the chaise longue and let his legs dangle. 'Yes, I have! I took fantastic trip once. Me and a bunch of other happy-go-lucky fellows took a boat to France. We stayed in tents and then travelled by train – first class, of course – to beautiful Flanders, across wide expanses of open land. They put us up in unique outdoor accommodation that stretched for hundreds of kilometres. Every couple of days we took an excursion. It was all so fascinating, so exciting... We hiked through a deserted landscape dotted with little lakes and streams. Sometimes the quiet was so intense you could hear the worms nibbling at the earth under your feet, then, all at once, the most spectacular fireworks display you've ever seen exploded above your head. It was a landscape like you've never seen before, full of surprises: here and there a blown-off leg, a hand, a torso, a fellow trying to push his brains back into his skull... What we didn't know, silly saps that we were, was that this was one big hunting party. Oh, all the things that we hunted, that fucking tiger of yours was nothing by comparison: sixteen-, seventeen-year-old lads, newly married men, bakers with a son at home, teachers who thought they were fighting for a just cause... I have to say, it was an unforgettable experience for a fellow who'd never been out of England.'

Lucien just stared at him.

'Sorry, don't be alarmed,' said Robin, grinning. 'The war had its good sides, too. Camaraderie, genuine friendship, though usually short-lived, 'cause you could have a friend one day, and the next day he was a mass of blood and guts, no matter, plenty of friends around, thousands, tens of thousands... God knows how many. Decent, brave men, all of them, just like you! On the other side too, mind you, regular old German fathers, bakers, teachers. Hilarious, it was! Millions of decent fellows trying to blow each other's brains out or stick a bayonet in somebody's gut or burn each other alive... The more you slaughtered, the better! When we went home we weren't murderers, no sir! We were heroes! Long live the boys! And d'you know what the best part is? I'll bet you all those stupid fuckers, even though they've only got one leg, one arm and one eye, will be the first to line up for the next war!' He slapped his thighs and roared with laughter.

Then he started to cry. His whole body shook. He pulled his knees up and curled into a ball. Confused, Lucien went over and hunched next to him, stroking his back until he gradually regained his composure. 'Do you like motorbikes?' he asked.

Robin eyed him suspiciously.

'I've got a Harley-Davidson. Shall we take a spin on it sometime?'

Robin sat up. 'Really? Amazing. I've always wanted to! I saw Harleys at the front, but those officers... they wouldn't dream of offering a lift to a common soldier, sharing the feeling of a fresh breeze on your face.'

'Okay, you know what, soon you'll get to enjoy that feeling. It'll do you good.'

Robin leant back with his hands behind his head, his face the picture of bliss. 'Yeah, a little trip on the motorbike. That's just the ticket.'

20

The man from Paris

'Hullo, Jan!' exclaimed Lucien. 'Good to see you again.' He shook Palacky's hand warmly. 'What a shame, I'm expected in the Concertgebouw and as usual I'm...' He tapped on his wristwatch.

'Oh, come in for just a second.' Jan pulled him into the hallway, and inspected him at arm's length. 'My, don't you look dapper in evening dress!' With nimble fingers he straightened Lucien's bow tie and wing collar. 'Wait a minute, something's missing, something vital...' He fumbled in the drawer of a small chest, pulled out a tiepin with a gleaming gemstone at the end, and fastened it on Lucien's tie. He squinted at him for a moment and nodded, satisfied. 'There,' he pronounced. 'Now you're perfect.'

'Thanks, Jan, but I really must get moving. Have you got it?'

'Of course.' Palacky reached back into the drawer. The packet was larger than usual.

'Good Lord, how much is in there?' asked Lucien.

Jan smiled. 'Thomas was so pleased you came to see him that he wants you to have this for nothing, on the house.'

It certainly must have done Thomas good, thought Lucien, for this was the second time he'd splashed out so generously. 'How is he?'

'Hopefully a little better, now that I'm back,' said Jan. He was hardly in tip-top shape himself. His face was showing signs of fatigue, and his eyelids were heavy from lack of sleep.

'Did you have a good trip?' Lucien asked as he weighed the packet in his hand. He didn't dare leave this much unattended in the car.

Realizing Lucien's predicament, Jan took back the packet and divided the contents into separate little piles. As he did so, he muttered: 'I did, but Berlin's absolutely exhausting.' He patted the front panels of Lucien's tailcoat and stuck the wrappers in batches of three into the inside pockets, splitting the rest between the trouser pockets and one last one in the waistcoat pocket. He tugged the coat back into shape and ran his hands lightly over Lucien's body to see if the close-fitting suit revealed its secret stash. 'Nobody will see it,' he concluded.

Lucien grimaced apologetically. 'Higher forces control my fate, you understand.'

'Off you go then,' said Jan as he pushed him toward the door.

As he entered the Concertgebouw, Lucien scanned the crowded foyer for Cremers and his wife. He spotted them quickly amidst the throng of invited guests. They'd positioned themselves strategically. He approached them with upturned palms – his standard gesture of contrition – and apologized for his lateness, and for missing dinner. 'I had to hang on until just an hour ago for that telephone call,' he said to Cremers, loud enough for his wife to hear. He glanced around with demonstrative irritation. 'I didn't want to take any chances, you understand.'

Cremers nodded. 'And? Did it pan out?'

The Peerebooms joined them before he could answer. Grateful for the distraction, he gallantly kissed Mrs. Peereboom's hand. No, the telephone call from Germany had not resolved matters; he still had no idea why that large order had been cancelled. Mrs. Peereboom ignored the rest of the party and pulled him aside. He leant attentively toward her, in the process getting a close look at the expensive necklace draped over her huge bosom. You could have bought the latest Bentley with that thing and still have some spare change. 'Lucien! Why didn't you bring your fiancée with you?' she asked with feigned disappointment.

'She's working, sadly,' he sighed, rolling his eyes. 'Film stars… hopelessly unreliable…' – he produced his most charming smile – '… but the advantage is that I now have more time for you…'

Mrs. Peereboom appeared quite taken with that prospect and gave Lucien such an intense gaze that he took a furtive step backwards.

Only now did it strike him how full the foyer was. Despite the subdued tone of the individual conversations, the cumulative effect was a deafening buzz, as though a colossal swarm of bees had been let loose in the Concertgebouw. The place was crawling with VIPs, gentlemen in full evening dress decorated with sashes, decorations, and all manner of ribbons and medals; their wives in rustling taffeta, glittering with jewellery, and their hair, in keeping with the latest fashion, adorned with huge feathers that bobbed every which way, giving the foyer the appearance of a poultry farm. A few young women, he noticed, followed him with their eyes. Hardly surprising, really – the bigwigs, with their potbellies and double chins, were not what you would call appetizing. He was one of the few

attractive young men, if not the only one, present. But before
he could subject the young ladies to closer inspection to assess
his chances at a pleasurable night, they were joined by Van
Bosse Loman. On his own, for he'd recently been widowed.

'Well?' Cremers persisted. 'Any news on that order?'

'Nothing definite yet. It's just a matter of time. But Switzerland looks very promising indeed. I suspect I'll be having
to travel to Bern shortly.' The gong sounded before Van Bosse
Loman had the chance to say anything. The horde started
shifting at once.

The concert hall was festooned with flowers and garlands.
This wasn't just any concert, but the twenty-fifth anniversary
of Willem Mengelberg as conductor of the Concertgebouw
Orchestra. Not an enticing prospect: not only music that didn't
interest him in the slightest, but interminable and tedious
speeches to boot. And all this with Mrs. Peereboom next to
him. As he settled into his seat he felt the stiff paper wrappers jab into his legs. He'd be wise to keep his jacket buttoned
at all times. A sneaky feeling crept over him; he felt like he
was a dealer in illegal substances. He wondered what Cremers,
Peereboom and Van Bosse Loman would think if they knew
what his pockets were full of. Cocaine, and procured from the
enemy at that.

Mrs. Peereboom spread herself out generously and inquired
if he knew who the people sitting in front of them, evidently
the most important guests, were. 'No ma'am, perhaps you
can enlighten me.' She fluttered her eyelids and Lucien was
shocked to see that she was wearing false eyelashes. 'Call me
Bep, will you, I simply can't bear all that "ma'am" stuff.' Apparently her explanation required a certain discretion, for she
heaved her enormous body, wrapped in scarlet satin, in his

direction. Working row by row, she pointed out the various ambassadors whom she'd apparently met before, because she had some observations, mainly uncharitable, to make about their wives. The mayor of Amsterdam was present, as were a number of government ministers, including the Minister of Foreign Affairs, Fock.

What an unfortunate name, thought Lucien, for a government official who regularly had to receive foreign guests. 'Pleased to meet you, Fock's the name…' he whispered to Bep, mimicking an English pronunciation. She let out a little scream of delight, which was fortunately drowned out by a sudden shuffling. The entire audience stood up. 'Prince Hendrik,' she whispered, as Lucien helped her rise from her chair.

The prince was hidden behind rows of tuxedoed shoulders, and Lucien settled back into the rustling breakers. The first speaker had already appeared at the lectern: The Minister of Education, Bep confided, and went on to list the other speakers from the programme book. As the minister's words drifted through the hall, Lucien's thoughts strayed to Jan Palacky. What could he have been doing in Berlin? Could Olyrook have something to do with that cancelled order? He couldn't imagine Thomas being able to produce that much. No, it was just a coincidence; Jan had probably just stopped off in Berlin on his way back from Prague. The German capital had a reputation for its nightlife, especially the cabarets and nightclubs. That's why he looked such a wreck. He could well imagine Jan letting his hair down; after all, tending to his sick friend wasn't the be-all and end-all of his life. Lost in thought, Lucien jumped at the sudden thunder of applause and politely clapped along.

'One down, five to go,' said Bep without bothering to lower her voice.

'Have you ever been to Berlin?' he asked offhandedly.

Straight away a mischievous gleam appeared in her eyes. 'Unfortunately I haven't. They say it's a wonderfully depraved place. If it were up to me…'

He didn't get to hear the rest, as a snarl from her husband silenced her.

As another speaker left the stage amidst a round of applause and Lucien fought off boredom by imagining Pola's legs, Bep said: 'Thank heavens, it's the interval.' The audience filed out into the foyer, with Cremers, Peereboom and Van Bosse Loman leading the way. Now Bep could fill him in on 'if it were up to her'. She dragged Mrs. Cremers into her lamentation about Amsterdam's dreary social life and her desire to really paint the town red for once, in somewhere like Berlin. Judging from her prudish pout, Lucien doubted if Mrs. Cremers shared Bep's cravings.

Out of the corner of his eye he noticed Cremers, Peereboom and Van Bosse Loman in conversation with a bald man with a pince-nez. He interrupted Bep and nodded in the direction of their husbands. 'Who's that?'

'Oh him, that's the new German envoy,' she answered absentmindedly, eager to go into her debauched plans in more detail.

'My dear ladies, will you excuse me?' Lucien treated them to another of his charming smiles. 'I'd better join the gentlemen. Business, you understand…'

Bep sighed, disillusioned. 'And I'd so hoped you were different.'

Lucien brought his lips close to her ear and whispered: 'Oh, but I am.' He pressed his way with restrained haste towards the group, which just then broke into loud laughter. A waiter held a tray of glasses in front of his nose; he took one, but by the time he reached the men, the German envoy had wandered off. Lucien looked at Cremers and raised his eyebrows.

'Nothing important, just a quick chinwag, you never know when we might be needing him,' explained Cremers. 'Everything's topsy-turvy in Germany these days.'

Lucien looked around and realized how tactically they had positioned themselves. The most influential guests had gathered in this part of the foyer, making use of the cover of small talk to do business. It was a sort of round dance where no one had to move too far from his spot, yet with no more than a nod or slight gesture could glide effortlessly from one tête-a-tête to the other. The French ambassador executed a waltz-like spin and greeted Peereboom. They exchanged a few words about coffee and tobacco while Cremers conversed with someone else of undoubted usefulness to the firm.

A waiter appeared with a tray of refreshments, allowing them to follow Peereboom's lead in shifting a few steps, landing, as if by coincidence, face to face with a man the bank president had obviously already had his eye on. Handshakes all round. The men were already acquainted, for only Lucien needed to be introduced to the British ambassador, as 'Mr. Hirschland, an invaluable employee of the Nederlandsche Cocaïne Fabriek', no less. 'A young man with a promising future,' Peereboom added. Lucien could feel a commissionership heading his way at full steam. The evening had suddenly taken quite a pleasant turn. So that's why they invited him: this was his definitive introduction to the top echelons of the business world. Success, promotion, fat bonuses, a whopping salary – it was all within his grasp. Suppressing his excitement, he concentrated on the conversation with the British ambassador, which was none too jovial.

'... so there was a damned good reason for that confrontation

between your Foreign Ministry and our government delegation,' the ambassador said irritably. Lucien cottoned on at
once that he was referring to the unfortunate incident between
a Dutch and an English delegation he'd heard about from
Marnix Christiaans some time ago. The English had accused
Dutch firms of supplying the German army during the war, in
effect labelling them 'agents of a hostile state'. 'In Allied circles
your consignments were regarded, to put it mildly, as abetting
the enemy,' continued the ambassador. The subject apparently
bothered him enough to shed his diplomatic decorum. Both
Cremers and Peereboom were taken aback, and Van Bosse
Loman clearly had no idea what it was all about.

This was just the moment to intervene. 'I should like to
remind the gentleman that Mr. Christiaans from the Foreign
Ministry explicitly pointed out to his delegation that our
actions were entirely permissible under international law,' said
Lucien. 'These were not consignments that could be directly
used for military purposes, like weaponry, horses or war mate-
riel.' The ambassador raised his chin ever so slightly. Lucien
straightened his back. 'No one in his right mind would put
our product in that category. Besides, there's no denying that
our cocaine, an anaesthetic of the highest quality, contributed
significantly to your victory, which is our victory as well. We
came to the aid of countless English soldiers. Plus,' – Lucien
suddenly remembered Marnix having told him of a deft legal
move by the Dutch government – 'his Excellency is surely
aware that the English government agreed not to oppose the
sale of certain colonial goods to Germany… provided these
products were also delivered to the British.'

'Your product can hardly be considered colonial goods.' The
British ambassador was not going to give up that easily.

'Oh, but it can. Coca leaves are a medicinal plant grown in the Dutch East Indies, from which our cocaine is extracted and which, by the way, your own pharmaceutical company Burroughs Wellcome and other English firms in turn produce in tablet form.' Lucien's heart was beating wildly. It was risky to take this kind of tone, but it was a chance to prove his mettle, that he was one of them – better still, that he was someone who dared to tell the British ambassador some home truths.

The ambassador got the picture. He grinned at Cremers and Peereboom. 'My compliments, gentlemen, you've got yourselves quite a competent employee here.' He stuck a cigar between his lips and patted his pockets.

Lucien reached into his breast pocket, pulled out a box of matches and lit one. While the ambassador pulled on the flame, Lucien spotted a small white paper wrapper that had fallen out of his pocket and showed up glaringly against the dark carpeting. He quickly slid his shoe over it, nearly burning his fingers in the process.

Peereboom, meanwhile, had managed to steer the conversation to the new English *Dangerous Drugs Act* and its similarities with the Dutch Opium Law, eliciting a condescending comment from the ambassador about the Dutch even managing to frame their laws to accommodate their trading interests. Lucien sniffed another chance, but he was preoccupied by how to get that wrapper from under his shoe without anyone noticing.

The gong went again. The British ambassador retired with a curt nod and the whole group moved off. Peereboom shot Lucien a glance over his shoulder, expecting him to follow. Naturally, the president wanted to comment on the conversation with the ambassador. Lucien was anxious to join him, but how on Earth could he move his foot?

He felt a tap on his shoulder, and heard Bep say under her breath: 'Lucien, you've dropped something, pick it up before anyone notices.' He looked at her in desperation. 'No one will think anything of it,' she said mischievously, 'at most, they'll think you're throwing yourself at my feet!'

Back in his seat Lucien felt miserable. Thank God the cantata by Dopper was a monumental creation for chorus and orchestra. You could simply close your eyes, like you were lost in reverie. Lucien wondered if Bep had any idea what had fallen out of his pocket. Probably not. She'd hinted at something secretive, and judging from her ambiguous chuckle he'd bet she assumed it had something to do with sex, a condom perhaps. Bep and sex, Christ almighty… He preferred to find out what her husband had to say to him.

The next morning his head felt like it was slowly being squeezed in a vice. They'd made a late night of it at the Peerebooms' villa in Amsterdam-Zuid. The nightcap was Bep's idea – after the incident in the foyer she monopolized him unashamedly – although Peereboom managed to squeeze in a compliment on his truly excellent riposte to the unwarranted attack by the British ambassador.

So now here he was, at an impossibly early hour, sitting in the doctor's waiting room. Luckily the surgery was close by, because he was pressed for time. He was just about to ask Robin if he'd brought the bottle when the nurse called them in.

Dr. Van Rhijn, the Hirschland family GP since his childhood, stood up, shook his hand, asked after his health and cast an inquisitive glance at Robin. Lucien hadn't seen the doctor since coming home from Java. He'd aged quite a bit, thought Lucien; he was probably his father's age. 'I'm fine, thanks. I'm here for my friend,' he began, 'who as you see was severely injured during the war. He's in a lot of pain.' Van Rhijn came around his desk, asked Robin to remove the mask and studied the scars. The doctor nodded thoughtfully and asked Robin where the operation had taken place. Lucien interjected that Mr. Ryder only spoke English.

'My English isn't so good,' said Van Rhijn. 'Translate for me, will you?'

Lucien seemed to remember he'd been operated on in France.

Van Rhijn raised his eyebrows. 'I'm surprised. I've read that this kind of experimental operation was only carried out in England. A Dr. Gillies at Queen Mary's Hospital in Sidcup, if I remember correctly…'

'In any event,' said Lucien, 'as I said, he's in a lot of pain, but he's run out of the medicine his doctor in London prescribed. I was wondering if he could get a prescription for something similar.' He motioned to Robin to show the doctor his *Forced March* bottle.

Van Rhijn put on his spectacles, studied the label and, somewhat taken aback, remarked: 'This isn't medicine, it's a stimulant. Completely useless as a painkiller. There are far better medicines available.'

'But it's what he's used to.' Lucien refrained from translating this exchange, smiling reassuringly at Robin from time to time.

'I don't doubt it, but it's time the gentleman gave it up. Its use is highly ill-advised; there's hardly a doctor around these days who sees any benefit in it. It's believed to be quite toxic. I haven't prescribed opiates or cocaine myself since 1910. Cocaine isn't the wonder drug it's made out to be. I consider it a purely recreational substance, and a very dangerous one at that.'

If that's how Dutch doctors felt about it, thought Lucien, it was no surprise that it was impossible to generate a market here. 'During the war it was widely prescribed as a painkiller,' he said.

'Very unwise indeed,' Van Rhijn responded coolly. 'It's not only quite ineffective as a painkiller, but it's one of the most addictive substances we know of, and dangerous too. Cocaine constricts the blood vessels and increases the blood pressure. In other words: the heart races like mad, because the blood wants to get through but can't. In fact, every dose produces a near-stroke. It's the most violent thing you can do to your body. It's been proven by tests on rats.'

'That doesn't mean a thing,' said Lucien with growing irritation. 'We're humans, not rats. I work for a pharmaceutical company and cocaine is legally marketed as a medicinal substance.'

'I'm well aware of that. I also think the pharmaceutical industry is playing with fire. They're only creating addicts, perhaps intentionally in order to keep selling this infernal stuff. Do you know that the chances of kicking a cocaine addiction are less than with a morphine addiction?'

'If it's so dangerous, why hasn't the government put any restrictions on it?' demanded Lucien.

'You could say the Dutch government is also behaving irresponsibly,' responded Van Rhijn, sniffing disdainfully.

'What do you suggest he use then?'

'I'd advise him to take normal painkillers, and to stay off this stuff,' the doctor replied. 'Cocaine use is nothing more than an escape. It only offers an imaginary solution to the problems your friend obviously faces. He's got to either resolve or accept them. Continuing down this path shows weakness of character. There are plenty of war wounded who manage without cocaine.' He reached for his pen. 'I'll give you a prescription for aspirin.'

'I've plenty of aspirin myself; you can buy that over the counter at the pharmacy.'

The doctor gave Robin back the bottle and laid his hands on the table. 'As you wish. But under no circumstances will I write a prescription for cocaine.'

Lucien nodded at Robin, and they stood up together.

'I wish your friend all the best.' Van Rhijn shot Robin a worried look. 'It won't be easy, but the radical approach is the only way. Good day.'

Once outside, Robin asked nervously: 'What did he say?'

'He refused to give you a new prescription. That stick-in-the-mud's probably getting commission from Bayer in Germany for prescribing aspirin!'

Robin stuck his hands deep in his coat pockets and shivered. 'What now?'

'There's not much point in going to another doctor. We'll sort this out ourselves. We don't need that old fossil!'

Lucien was so angry that he kept silent the entire way home. When he saw the Mercedes parked outside, he remembered his appointment and fished around for his keys. 'I have to go to the factory now, someone's waiting for me there. But as soon as I'm home I'll give you some.' Robin turned away from him and hunched his shoulders. Lucien could well imagine he felt abandoned. How could a doctor refuse to assist a patient in need? Disgraceful. 'You know what,' he said as he opened the car door, 'tomorrow morning I can manage a couple of hours off, and we'll take a spin on the Harley, all right?'

It was already after five. The sun, low on the horizon, cast a dusty beam through the window. An explosive silence hung in the salon. But not for long. Tosca crossed her arms and demanded, for the third time: 'What was that all about?' Robin sat dejectedly on the sofa, his head buried in his hands. He dared not answer, nor look up, certainly not at Swanny. How could he ever explain how desperate he'd felt when Lucien drove off? How lost, when he came inside and found no one at home? How tormented by the disapproving, almost demeaning look in the doctor's eyes? There was only one way out. After all, Lucien promised they'd sort this out themselves. He'd understand if he helped himself in the meantime. In the cupboard drawer, where his salvation had come from the last time, he discovered a veritable treasure trove; he'd never seen so much before in one place. He'd deftly scooped a bit out of each wrapper into his empty bottle and dashed up to his room. He'd take just a little bit extra, it was the least he deserved after the visit to that horrible doctor. He could only make out a few snippets of the conversation between Lucien and Dr. Van Rhijn: Queen Mary's Hospital, Sidcup, Gillies… Those words pierced his guilty conscience like daggers.

Once he felt a bit better he reflected with remorse on Dr. Gillies and his uncle. It was high time he sent word home. Sitting at the desk, he quickly dashed off five pages describing his heart-warming experiences of the last few weeks. Even after posting the letter he was brimming with willpower and drive. Why had he procrastinated for so long? He had to buy a gift for Swanny at once. And not just any gift… something wonderful, something splendid, something that showed his deep feelings for her. Maybe the bracelet he'd seen in the jeweller's window. But the expensive postage stamps had used up the last of his coins. There was only one solution.

He found himself a busy street corner, took his cap in his hand and removed his mask. '*Veteraan oorlog! Veteraan oorlog!*' he cried out. He congratulated himself on his admirable Dutch. See? He was perfectly capable of surviving here after all: one passer-by after another reached for his wallet. My God, it was so much easier than in London. The locals here weren't so weary of war misery. If only Harry, that son of a bitch, could see him now! An old man even gave him a bank note. *Dank u, meneer, dank u...* He kept counting his takings. His coat pocket jingled with coins, but it still wasn't enough. Who knows how long he'd stood there shouting before Tosca suddenly appeared in front of him. Astonished, she stared at him and barked something he didn't understand. She shook him by the shoulders, as if trying to wake him from a deep sleep.

And now he was sitting there on the sofa like a criminal who'd been caught red-handed. He'd been begging. Oh God, begging! You couldn't sink lower than that. 'How'd you get it into your stupid head to go out scrounging on the street!?' Tosca screamed. 'Haarlem is a small place! You know how quickly people will find out where you live? Do you want them to think Swanny and Lucien are starving you?'

Swanny sat down next to him and asked why he'd done it – in a warm voice, of course, the tone you'd use when trying to extract a confession from a child. She laid her hand on his arm again; the warmth shot through his sleeve and deep into his skin. 'If you need money, you know you only have to ask.'

'I didn't want to ask...' he stammered.

'Can't you tell me what you needed money for? You've got board and lodging here, after all.' Her voice still had a tone of concern, not of irritation or disapproval.

He had no other choice but to explain. 'I sent a letter to

my parents telling them how kind you've been, and that I was going to look for work. I spent all my money on postage, but I still wanted to buy you a gift, for your birthday.' He mustn't give up now. He had to win her respect again. 'Without thinking, I slipped back into old habits. Habits I picked up when I couldn't go back to teaching and had to find some other employment. But work was so scarce, and if they could choose between a healthy man and a cripple, well, you can guess who they chose… And then there was competition with women. During the war they had to take over our jobs, and the last thing I wanted to do was bump a woman from her workplace. The only thing left was to beg. I was just one of thousands. It's humiliating to rely on charity, but with an empty stomach you lose your shame pretty fast. You just have to put a distance between yourself and the rest, reduce yourself to a nobody, till you're nothing but a victim, a misshapen face…'

Tosca listened intently. To his relief he saw her anger dissipate. A tear ran down Swanny's cheek. She shifted closer to him and put her arm around his shoulders. 'Oh, dear Robin,' she whispered, 'promise me you'll never, ever go begging again. From now on, anything you need, you'll get from us. Agreed?'

Tosca wagged her finger angrily. 'No, Swan! We mustn't make him dependent on charity all over again. He'll only be able to regain his confidence and self-esteem by earning money of his own. We've got to help him find a job…' She thought for a moment. 'Work that doesn't require face-to-face contact with others and…' She was interrupted by the doorbell. Swanny wiped her cheek dry, got up with an irritated sigh and walked to the front hall. There was surprised cry, and a few minutes later she reappeared in the company of a tall, well-dressed man. Swanny introduced him as Marnix Christiaans, her fiancé.

Fiancé? Where had he come from, all of a sudden? Why hadn't he heard anything about a fiancé before? Swanny explained to him that Marnix had been in Paris over the past few months at the peace negotiations. 'But now he's back, thankfully,' she said slightly nervously and explained to Christiaans how Robin came to be lodging with them. She explained that a string of unfortunate coincidences had led to something positive. She hadn't written him about it because she thought it would be so much better to tell it all in person, with Robin present. Christiaans absorbed it all with interest: that Robin was a schoolteacher from Great Yarmouth, had been wounded at Ypres and was staying here until he could find work... She said nothing about the begging. Robin glanced at Tosca, who, to his surprise, winked back. He heard Swanny say how pleased she was that he and Lucien were planning to go out tomorrow. This showed how confident he was feeling, that after all the wretchedness he'd been through, he was looking forward to getting out into the open air... Tosca handed Christiaans a glass of wine and together they toasted his kind-hearted fiancée. He then reached into his breast pocket and pulled out a small, exquisitely-wrapped box. A gift, no doubt, from Paris.

Swanny seemed to stiffen. She thanked him politely and sank into a chair, sitting there, eyes downcast, with the unopened present in her lap. Christiaans asked something unintelligible. Robin saw her hesitate, and then undo the ribbon and wrapping paper, revealing a small black case. She opened it, glanced inside and shut it again. She got up quickly, thanked Christiaans, laid the box and wrapping on the mantelpiece and sat back down with her hands in her lap.

Robin couldn't bear one more second in the company of

this stranger. He excused himself under the pretext of a headache. Swanny nodded and said she understood.

Back in his room, he stood in front of the wardrobe, tried to get his breathing back under control and summoned up all his courage. He had to do it, he had to... He removed the mask. Then he yanked away the scarf covering the mirror. In the reflection he saw the man he'd been running away from ever since Sidcup. He had to face it: this is how the world saw him, and this was how he had to accept himself. Just as he was forced to accept that no woman would ever want him now, not even kind-hearted Swanny... certainly not as her fiancé, as her husband.

Just as Mary hadn't wanted him. Oh, she'd thought it was a good idea to meet, but preferably not at home, no, no, in a tea room on the other side of town, far away from school and their neighbourhood. She shook his hand, no kiss, just a handshake, and while they drank their tea she looked everywhere except at him, first out of the window, then into her teacup; not at his face, not into his one good eye. It was as though she was afraid of him. She wept a bit into her hankie out of politeness, and then came to the point: it would be better if he didn't return to school. Perfectly understandable, he said, it would frighten the children. No, no, that wasn't it, Mary conceded hesitantly, they think you're dead. It was like this: James Foyler's son kept asking when Mister Ryder would be coming back, because his own father hadn't returned. He hoped that his teacher would know what happened to Dad, because they'd fought together at Ypres. The boy pestered them incessantly, so the headmaster, at the end of his tether, told the lad that Mister Ryder had also been killed. Robin had to try to understand. It made it easier on the boy, on everyone actually. She hadn't expected him to return either, because his mother had told her he'd lost his mind, that he'd spat blood at her. He'd probably go straight from the hospital to an asylum or some kind of institution. Only then did it dawn on him that Mary was truly afraid of him. He wasn't only monstrously deformed, but insane as well... He needn't even ask how she was; she came right out and told him she was to be married shortly, to an officer. She hoped he'd understand.

He sat down on the bed. How was he going to get through the night? Don't reach for the bottle, just leave it in the cupboard. He'd be needing it tomorrow morning. Tomorrow was important, he still had a chance, perhaps not to win her affection, but at least her respect. He had to prove to Swanny that he wasn't a pathetic beggar, a sponger, a washout, but a man bursting with energy and lust for life, a man who knew how to enjoy being out in the open air...

21

A motorbike accident

Of course it was awfully inconvenient. That's with the thing about impulsive promises. Cremers had requested a word with Lucien prior to the meeting. Robin would surely understand; they could just as well go the following day. But when he saw Swanny bustling through the house with his old motorcycle coat over her arm, he realized there was no getting out of it. He phoned Trudie at the company office. Family circumstances meant that he'd only be able to make it in for the afternoon. No, no one had died. He promised to be on time for the meeting with Christiaans. Then he pulled the Harley out of the shed, checked the petrol and oil and wondered if the pillion would actually hold a passenger. No one had ridden on the back since Biedermann in Arnhem. Pity he'd never got round to buying that sidecar.

Looking up at the sky, he tossed his scarf around his neck. A few threatening clouds passed over, but it looked like the weather would clear up. Swanny and Robin were already waiting on the front step. She carefully pulled the goggles over his mask and eyeglasses, and tugged the brim of the cap firmly over his forehead. Robin put up with it all like an impatient schoolboy. He could hardly stand still. Swanny laughed. 'Hold on tight,' she warned, 'Lucien takes the curves far too fast.' Robin bounded over to the motorbike and climbed on. 'Can't be fast enough for me!' he exclaimed boldly.

You asked for it, thought Lucien, as he kick-started the motor, stuck up his hand to Swanny and drove off. Robin waved without turning around. 'I'm free as a bird!' he shouted, his arms outstretched and head thrown back. Lucien grinned and without warning accelerated to a higher gear. Robin's body was thrust backward and he shouted with delight. Before they reached the corner he had to grab onto him: free as a bird now, but a dead duck soon if he didn't hang on.

Lucien reckoned there was just enough time to get to IJmuiden, where they could have a look at the fleet of fishing trawlers and pick up some fresh cod at the fish market. They sped out of Haarlem towards Overveen, and Lucien decided to take the scenic route around Bloemendaal, where overhanging branches formed a leafy tunnel. On the winding lane around the town of Santpoort he could push the Harley to its limits, taking the curves at full throttle. To show that this model could handle rough terrain, he turned into a sandy hill track, climbed a steep dune and thundered down the other side, the motorbike skidding in the sand. Behind him, Robin shouted wildly and egged him on to go faster and faster. He'd been chattering ever since they left home, doing his best to shout above the roar of the engine. He didn't know to lean with the motorbike in the curves, and a few times Lucien had to reach back and grab him by his coat to keep him from falling off.

They entered IJmuiden and drove along the Havenkade, where he was forced to slow down, and eventually stop completely, for a passing funeral procession. He turned to Robin and told him to pipe down. Not wanting to drive along the harbour front with his boisterous passenger, he proceeded at a snail's pace via a narrow path leading to the fisherman's wharf. They got off at the fish market, and although Lucien was only planning to stay for a short while, he pulled the motorbike up onto its stand. He needed to stretch his legs and relax his back.

Sloops, cutters and luggers were moored close to one another, and fishermen, heavy baskets on their shoulders, pushed their way through other sailors and stacks of crates along the quay. Robin stood in his ankle-length motorcycle coat, took off the goggles and let them dangle under his chin. He seemed intrigued by the activity and walked toward a couple of boatman who were busy dragging a trawler cable along the quayside.

Lucien loosened his scarf and looked up at the clear sky as one last cloud drifted off. A group of young fishermen stood some way off, cigarettes dangling from their lips, eyeing his motorcycle with interest. They shuffled nonchalantly in his direction, but stopped some distance from him, legs spread and arms folded. They exchanged a few words among themselves; Lucien couldn't hear what they were saying, but they were clearly fascinated by his Harley.

A burly fisherman with a dashing haircut and cap pushed back on his head broke loose from the little group had sauntered over to him. He looked at Lucien, raised his chin questioningly and held both hands out toward the handlebars. Lucien shrugged and nodded: why not, go ahead and touch it. The fellow grasped the handgrips and stood next to the motorbike, leaning forward and looking off into the distance, as though he imagined himself bucketing along the quayside at full speed. The others came closer and formed a circle around the Harley. The young man glanced over his shoulder again at Lucien and raised his leg, like a dog would at a tree. Lucien smiled; they communicated like deaf-mutes, did they maybe think he was a foreigner? Judging from the fellow's girth, Lucien figured it was better to take the bike down off its stand.

But before he could reach the bike, Robin shot out of nowhere. He shoved the group of young men brusquely aside and leapt onto the back of the one about to mount the motorbike. 'Fuck off!' he screamed. For a brief, shocked moment the fellow stood motionless, bent over under Robin's weight. The surprise in his eyes turned to anger. He effortlessly shook Robin loose and stood up straight. Robin had landed on his knees but got back up at once and swung at him, hitting the young fisherman squarely on the nose. He staggered at this unexpected attack and fell to the ground. The others, who had watched with mouths agape, now sprang into action. It took a fraction of a second for Lucien to realize what was going on. They were gearing up to lay into Robin, who, meanwhile, had thrown off his heavy leather coat and was looking wildly from side to side for an advantageous position from which to fight them off. While the fishermen inched forward, gauging how best to subdue him, Robin again surprised them with his astonishing speed. He floored the nearest one and quickly dealt another one a hefty blow in the stomach. Robin's fury made the fisherman wary, but the fellow who had been hit first, and was bleeding heavily from his nose, lost all inhibition and waded blindly into Robin. Robin took up a boxer's stance and hit the man full on the nose again, who backed off, roaring in pain. His nose was surely broken. Lucien panicked, shouting: 'Stop! Stop!' But he knew there was no point in trying to reason with Robin. 'I'll kill them! I'll kill them! Fucking bastards!' he screamed hysterically, knocking yet another one to the ground.

The group closed in on him. 'Grab him!' they yelled. Robin took a sharp kick to the legs, but although he wobbled, it only fuelled his crazed rage. Despite being laid into from all sides, he was fearless and managed to deliver some telling blows. He struck out like a maniac prepared to fight to the death. A boy who lay near his feet got a merciless kick in the face.

Then a large fellow hit him squarely on the head with his fist, knocking the mask and spectacles to the ground. Lucien watched them fly through the air and in a reflex reaction dived to the ground to rescue the pieces from the stomping feet. He quickly stuck them in his pocket. Robin, meanwhile, had been cornered and forced back against a wall. He was yelling furiously. There was a gash on his forehead. His bloody, maimed face gave him a terrifying appearance. The group backed off. Someone in the circle of bystanders started to laugh. 'Hey, look! It's a monster!' Slowly, as it dawned on them that the ferocious warrior was nothing more than a miserable cripple, the jeering swelled. A crowd of dockworkers and fisherman, who had watched the brawl with relish, began to ridicule him.

Robin crumpled. All the fight had gone out of him. He seemed to shrink in the face of the taunting – Lucien realized that no physical blow could hurt him more than this. Still, he knew this was the only way to put an end to his outburst. Once they were done laughing, they'd realize how easy it was to bring down this loser, and then Robin was done for.

'Stop it! That's enough!' he shouted at the fishermen. 'Can't you see he's a wounded war veteran! He can't do anything about it.' He knew this was hardly a compelling argument, but it was enough to bring a brief lull in the jeering. 'Don't you get it? The war made him go off his head!' The mob fell silent. They stared at Robin, who was leaning weakly against the wall like a pathetic stray dog. It looked like their anger had abated, for the time being at least.

Lucien went over and grabbed Robin by the armpits. His body was limp. He helped him over to the motorbike, left him there leaning on it and strode over to the fishermen who'd been involved in the fracas. 'This whole thing was my friend's fault,' he said, pulling out his wallet. 'I'll make it up to you. Get yourselves a drink on me.' He handed a few banknotes to the nearest fellow, who took them in silence. Lucien returned to the motorbike, started it up, and with a stern glance motioned to Robin to climb on behind him. He sped away from the harbour, along the same road they'd come in on. On the way back he turned onto a side path leading into the dunes. Robin slumped against his back like a sack of salt.

Lucien stopped and dismounted. He needed some time to calm down. His legs were trembling. Robin slid off the pillion and sat down beside the path, surrounded by dune grasses. The leather coat was still back at the wharf, the cap and goggles were gone, his shirt was covered with blood. He clasped his hands behind his neck, bent his head forward and rocked back and forth. Lucien stood next to him, dispirited and helpless. He wasn't sure what he felt more: anger or compassion.

'My face…' Robin groaned. Lucien knelt down in front of him and gently dabbed the wound with his handkerchief. It seemed to be no more than a cut under a scar on his forehead, just below the hairline. He gave Robin the handkerchief and told him to keep pressure on the wound. 'My mask, where's my mask?' Robin whispered.

'Relax, I have it,' said Lucien. 'It's here…' As he felt in his coat pocket, he remembered that it was broken; he gingerly brought out the pieces. The eyeglasses, even the lenses, were undamaged, but the metal plate had come loose and was broken in half. Tears welled up in Robin's eye as he inspected the damage. 'I'll get it fixed for you,' Lucien said quickly, for he could see that Robin's world was fast collapsing around him

'I can't go on like this…' Robin moaned. 'I'm a wreck, I don't recognize myself anymore.'

'I'm sure it's all down to the war.' Lucien sat down next to him. 'But listen, you're no longer a soldier. You have to learn to control yourself, otherwise you'll get yourself into a lot of trouble.'

'I'm already in a lot of trouble.' Robin laid his head on his raised knees. 'It's no use…'

'Nonsense. We'll get the mask repaired and forget the brawl back there. Those guys are no strangers to that kind of thing.'

'Have you got some with you?' Robin asked, raising his head.

'Some what?'

'You know, the stuff… mine's run out.'

Lucien looked at him in surprise. 'Jesus, man, you don't really think that's going to help?'

'It's the *only* thing that'll help.'

'If I'd known, I'd have brought some with me.'

Robin heaved a sigh.

'You've got to stop using it. Pretty soon you won't be able to go anywhere without it.'

'I do want to stop. As soon as I've got work, but not now. I need it, otherwise I'll fall apart… I don't want Swanny to see me in this state.'

Lucien looked out across the dunes; screeching gulls flew overhead. Robin was right. She mustn't see him like this. His face might swell up and then he'd have to own up to the fight.

And who'd get the blame? Lucien, of course. He had to avoid that at all costs.

'Come on, we'll go home, Swanny's not there so she won't see you. We'll clean you up, put some ice on your forehead and I'll give you something to make you feel better, all right? If Swanny asks what happened, just say you slipped off the bike. For God's sake don't say anything about the punch-up.'

Robin stood up. 'But I don't want her to see me without the mask,' he said softly.

'She doesn't have to. We'll have it repaired as soon as we get back to Haarlem.'

On the way back Lucien tried to think who might be able to mend the mask on the spot. There was a jeweller near the Grote Markt, but Swanny occasionally took a clock there for repairs. The shopkeeper was a real talker and would probably spill the beans. And how would you fix it anyway? The metal was split in half; the two pieces would somehow have to be joined together again. Deumers, of course! They soldered metal at his garage. All right, they'd stop by Deumers' garage to see if he could do it right away.

Panting, he rushed into the director's office. More than an hour late. Cremers looked up annoyed from his papers, even Peereboom coolly studied his fingernails. Before anyone could comment, Lucien exclaimed: 'I'm terribly sorry, I was involved in a motorbike accident this morning. It's a miracle I came out of it unscathed.' He pulled up a chair, because it was clear that Marnix Christiaans not only couldn't care less about his well-being, but had already begun presenting his report. 'I've just given a detailed explanation of the coupling of the Opium Convention to the Treaty of Versailles.' Christiaans gestured in

the direction of the secretary. 'You can read it in the minutes…
Very briefly: after three failed conferences in The Hague over
the last few decades, the participating nations finally managed
to ratify the International Opium Convention, which also
covers cocaine. The signatories agree to the restrictions already
in place under our Opium Law. The defeated nations were
required to sign. We see it as a significant victory in breaking
the Germans' military and economic stranglehold. And we can
conclude that in doing so, the German pharmaceutical industry has been brought under control.'

'Well, that's a relief,' said Lucien in an attempt to show he
was on top of things. 'And the Americans, did they sign too?'
He shuffled hurriedly through his papers, as though searching
for exhaustive notes on his research into the American market.
In actual fact he hadn't done a thing yet.

'Of course they signed,' answered Marnix. 'They didn't have
much choice. The Americans, after all, have been pushing for
strict regulation of opiates and cocaine since the first conference.' He leant back and ran his hand over his meticulously-
styled hair. 'I've always thought it quite hypocritical of them.
Criticizing us for years with all that humanitarian humbug,
while using cocaine at home on a vast scale to increase produc-
tivity among Negro plantation labourers and factory workers.
They even added it to soft drinks, encouraging office personnel
to drink at least one glass of it during their afternoon break.'
Cremers nodded attentively.

Lucien noticed a smear of blood on his cuff and pulled it up
under his sleeve. 'Wouldn't that be something for the Dutch
market?' he asked quickly.

'Not a chance – after work people can't seem to keep off
it. That's why doctors and medical organizations have formed

a powerful lobby to warn of the hazardous side effects. The newspapers are full of hysterical articles, calling for a ban on soft drinks and even throat lozenges containing cocaine. The government was obliged to take measures, which they wanted to enforce internationally as well. Meanwhile the production and use of cocaine in the States has risen rather than declined.'

'So it's thanks to the Americans that we're stuck with the Opium Law?' asked Cremers.

'Indirectly, yes. I suspect they were using their weight at the negotiating table in Versailles to thwart the competition and protect their own pharmaceutical industry.'

'Where do they get their leaves from, incidentally?' asked Peereboom. 'Hardly any of it comes from Java.'

'I've only recently found that out. The problem the Americans face is that they have no colonies and can't grow the stuff themselves. That's why they set up new plantations in Peru during the war. I've no information about the extent of their operation, but they obviously have big plans. For starters, they're even trying to eradicate coca-chewing in Peru and the surrounding countries. The locals chew up a fortune in coca leaves every year, while the U.S. could be making cocaine from it. So the Peruvian coca leaf, although inferior in quality, could prove a serious competi–'

There was a knock at the door and Trudie stuck her head in. 'Excuse the interruption, but there's an urgent telephone call for you, Mr. Christiaans.' Marnix got up and excused himself.

Peereboom slid a few reports over to Cremers, and while they pored over them Lucien began to speculate on the American market: they obviously didn't want to become dependent on European suppliers. He wondered how they were going to break the Indians of their chewing habit, and his thoughts drifted to Robin. Deumers had looked at the damaged mask and remarked: 'More a job for a jeweller…' Only after Lucien insisted did he agree to solder it. But after re-attaching the two pieces and smoothing the seam with a file and sandpaper, Deumers was far from satisfied: 'This isn't my line of work, sir.' And indeed, although it was back in one piece, the mask did not look at all good. But Lucien was in a hurry; they'd have to see about touching it up later. Robin put it on without a word, and Lucien, feeling guilty about the poor result, gave him an extra two grams once they were back home.

Christiaans came back into the room with a sour face. Before he sat down, he shot Lucien a chilly glance. 'Now then… to get back to the new international regulations,' he continued. 'They also have their downside. Such strict control could well stimulate illegal trade, which is a growing concern in Europe. There's no hard information on the scope of the problem, but it certainly could pose a threat to a firm like yours. I believe we mustn't underestimate the black market. Apparently there are already criminal gangs dealing clandestinely in cocaine.'

'Criminals?' Lucien asked. 'How do they get their hands on it?'

Marnix shrugged his shoulders. 'We only know that they're able to get hold of it, which could affect the price in the long term.'

'What's the government going to do about it?' Cremers asked nervously.

'Well, the best way to cut off the criminals and curb the black market is to protect the legal trade as much as possible.'

The others nodded in agreement. 'So we needn't expect these new regulations to cause us headaches with export authorization?' inquired Peereboom.

'Absolutely not. The government sees no reason to limit production or exports. As I said: supporting our pharmaceutical companies is the best weapon against further expansion of the black market.' Christiaans closed his portfolio; as far as he was concerned the meeting could be adjourned. Peereboom thanked him for his contribution. Marnix got up and signalled to Lucien that he wanted a word. Outside the building he said Swanny had just phoned to cancel their dinner date for this evening. 'She sounded rather upset and said it was impossible for her to leave, due to your English houseguest. You apparently caused a motorbike accident.'

Lucien gnashed his teeth. 'That's rich! Caused an accident! He fell off on his own… Anyhow, nothing worse than a scratch on his forehead. You know how Swanny can dramatize things.'

'Who is this Englishman, anyway? Why did you take him in?'

Lucien couldn't come up with a ready answer. Having explained about the motorbike accident, he could hardly admit to having hit the Englishman with his car as well. 'Charity, Marnix, your fiancée's unadulterated charity…' he answered and walked over to the Mercedes. It was time he had a serious talk with the veteran.

Robin sat with the mask in his hand. The seam where it had been welded was rough and unsightly. Their attempt to smooth it out with sandpaper had disastrous results. The paint had been almost entirely scratched off; the painted eye was only vaguely visible, like an ancient fresco. He tried to retouch it himself with pencil and ink, which only made it worse. He put it on again and looked in the mirror. Now it was as though the mask had a scar too.

Swanny had come upstairs unexpectedly an hour ago. There'd been no time to wash the blood from his face and for moment it looked like she would faint from shock. The wound had stopped bleeding, but on his forehead was a nasty bluish lump with a red gash in it. She recovered quickly, ran downstairs and came back up with Pleun and a bottle of antiseptic. Only after she'd disinfected the wound did she ask what had happened.

'I lost my coat and cap and goggles,' he admitted first.

'Never mind that, how did you hurt yourself?'

After he'd related the entire incident, she exploded: 'So he let you fall off the bike! I told him to be careful. Just look at you! He's so reckless, just wait till I get my hands on him!'

'No, no…' At once he realized the trap he'd walked into, 'it was my own fault really. If I'd just held on properly I wouldn't have fallen and my mask wouldn't be busted now. And besides, Lucien had it mended right away at a garage.' Swanny brought her face close to his, studied the mask and snorted angrily. 'At a garage! Honestly! What on earth was he thinking!'

'Please don't say anything about it,' he begged. 'He was only trying to show me a good time.'

'You don't have to defend him, dear.' Swanny stood lost in thought.

'He might have a concussion,' said Pleun.

'That's just what I was thinking… shall I ring Dr. Van Rhijn?'

'No, that's totally unnecessary!' cried Robin. 'There's nothing wrong with my head, I'm sure of it.'

She suddenly remembered her date. 'Bother, and now I've got Marnix this evening…'

Robin lightly touched his forehead and winced with pain.

'I'm not leaving you alone tonight,' she announced. 'You

come first. Marnix will understand. You go and freshen up and come downstairs. It's such fine weather, we can sit in the garden.' She hesitated and turned to Pleun with a conspiratorial smile. 'Perhaps… No! I'm not saying anything yet! Let's wait until we're sure.'

Washed and in a clean set of clothes, Robin heard the garden doors being opened downstairs. From behind the lace curtain in his window he could peer into the garden. The setting sun cast an orange light over the lawn. Pleun appeared with a bucket and rag, and started wiping down the white outdoor furniture while Swanny followed her carrying a large tray, with a brightly-coloured tablecloth stuck under her arm. She spread the cloth and set out the tea service, plates of cookies and other sweets, and a little vase of flowers. Pleun reappeared with glasses and bottles. Finally Karel was brought out to his usual spot. One loud screech was enough to chase the birds out of the surrounding trees. Swanny stood inspecting the set-up, her hands on her hips and head tilted sideways. For some reason she shifted two chairs and examined it again. Satisfied, she disappeared into the house. When she came back out, not ten minutes later, she turned and looked up at his window, shading her eyes against the sun. He drew the curtain aside and saw her beckon to him cheerfully. He waved back.

He took the packets Lucien had given him, shook them out onto the desktop and sniffed up the powder. He wobbled briefly from the explosion in the back of his head. His blood began to churn and his heart beat wildly in his ribcage. He couldn't care less anymore about the ruined mask and the wound on his forehead. The only thing that counted was that Swanny had made the garden cheery and festive just for him. She smiled at him and waved! She had cancelled her date with

Christiaans for him! She wanted to be alone with him! He came first, she'd said. That could only mean one thing: that she was going to break off her engagement with Christiaans… for him!

He bounded down the stairs and froze in the doorway leading out to the garden. The disappointment hit him like a ton of bricks. Suddenly the garden was full of people. Not only Tosca, but the neighbour too, that tedious portraitist, who had installed himself prominently next to a woman with slicked-back hair and lots of make-up. They were engaged in an animated conversation. As soon as Swanny spotted him she hurried over to him. Her face radiated like never before. 'Come with me! We've got such good news for you!' she exclaimed, pulling him by the hand. She introduced him to the new woman: Pola Pauwlova, a film star who was also Lucien's fiancée. So Lucien was engaged too! While Swanny reeled off her latest films, Pola took him in with great interest. 'Lucien really is a bum, you know,' she said. 'Just look at the state you're in.' She patted the seat of the chair next to her. Her hand was covered in rings and the nails were painted green, and she wore a provocative red dress that exposed quite a lot of cleavage. Swanny nodded encouragingly. Grudgingly he sat down and Pola Pauwlova turned directly toward him with her back to the neighbour, who was clearly put out that he no longer had her full attention.

Tosca and Swanny positioned themselves in front of him, like they were about to recite a poem. They were obviously bursting to reveal some piece of news. Robin held his breath, this was the moment…

'The marvellous news is…' said Swanny, gritting her teeth in excitement, '…that Tosca and Pola have found a job for you.' Her face clouded over. 'Oh dear, I do hope you'll like it…'

Tosca jabbed her in the back. 'We know you prefer to avoid busy situations,' she continued, 'so we've found you work as a projectionist at a cinema not far from here – if you want to do it, that is. Pola knows the owner and they're desperate for somebody, especially for the evening performances. What do you think?' She anxiously waited for his response.

Robin looked from the one to the other. This was the last thing he'd expected. He swallowed his disappointment, took a deep breath and leapt out of his chair. 'Terrific! Fantastic!'

Swanny yelped, hugged him and planted a kiss on his exposed cheek. 'Projectionist, that's right up my street! Couldn't be better…' he whispered, hoping Swanny's embrace would last forever. But she let go of him to help Tosca uncork the wine. This kind of news deserved a toast, of course. '*Dank u, mevrouw,*' he said to the film star, 'I'm most grateful.'

The corners of her blood-red lips curled slightly. 'When I heard what had happened to your face, I thought, I've got to help him. We in the film business know how important one's appearance is.'

Robin tried to contain his chaotic feelings. He had to be patient, but this was a golden opportunity. He'd prove to Swanny he could easily hold down such a lousy little job, plus it would bring in some money so he could finally buy her a gift, something better than that bastard Christiaans had brought with him from Paris. He settled back blissfully into the chair. Then, suddenly, he felt Pola's hand on his arm.

'So tell me, where do you get your stuff?' she asked, leaning closer to him.

Alarm bells went off in his head. 'I don't know what you're talking about.' He wanted to get up, but she held him firmly in her grip.

'Come on, don't play the innocent with me, you know very well what I'm talking about. I see it in that one eye of yours. Lucien gives it to you, doesn't he?'

He broke into a cold sweat. The blood pounded in his neck. How did she know? Not from Lucien, otherwise she wouldn't need to ask. A little smile still played around her pouting lips, but there was now also something hard as nails in her gaze. He knew she wouldn't leave him in peace until she got a satisfactory answer. He nodded. She let go of his arm at once and turned the other way, mumbling something to the portrait painter. Maybe she was blabbing about it already. What business was it of that lush? Supposing he told Swanny... Think how disappointed she'd be, how deceived she'd feel. She might throw him out. He heard her voice. She was standing in front of him, asking something, there was no reproach in her voice, not yet... He had to tell her everything, everything, before she heard it from someone else.

Swanny was about to repeat her question when Lucien appeared in the doorway. She walked straight up to him. Robin sat frozen in his chair, trying to remember how he'd explained away his wound. A motorbike accident, that was it, a motorbike accident... He saw them engage in an intense discussion, but when she came back, Swanny still wore a cheerful expression. However angry she might be at Lucien, the good news about Robin's job still carried the day.

Lucien greeted the guests, gave Robin the once-over and poured himself half a glass of wine. 'I believe we owe you our thanks,' he said to Pola. She gave him a sugary smile, pulled herself up onto those elegant long legs of hers and sidled up to him. Robin heard her ask in a soft, girlish voice: 'Could we go up to your room for a moment? There's something I urgently need to talk to you about.' Lucien hesitated, but she was evidently practised in persistence. Robin's hands started to sweat again. She was going to blow the gaff, accuse Lucien of providing him with dope. Ever since their visit to the family doctor he sensed a conspiracy to cut off his supply of cocaine. How could he get that woman to keep quiet? Too late... they'd already disappeared.

Suddenly the neighbour swung a chair around and sat down next to him. Now what did he want from him?

'Let's have a look at that mask.' Casper placed his index finger under Robin's chin and turned his face toward him. 'It's been broken, hasn't it, and some fool has tried to weld it back together.' He whistled to himself. 'Really, it looks quite appalling... Listen, I'm an artist and have the proper materials. Shall I repair it for you properly and repaint it? What do you say?'

Robin was bowled over. So that's what the film actress had been whispering to him about. 'How much will it cost?' he asked.

'Don't be ridiculous! Nothing, of course, I'd be happy to do it for you.'

Robin picked up his glass. Just then he saw Swanny wink at him. Of course, he should have known. She'd asked Casper to do it.

22

In the national interest

They decided to take an after-dinner stroll. It was just a short distance and according to the thermometer it was still, even at this late hour, warm – 18 degrees. Nor was it a bad idea to stretch their legs after the lavish meal in the first-class restaurant on the Grote Markt. The crossed the square and headed toward the Koningstraat. Marnix's chauffeur followed in the Bentley at a respectful distance. Slightly ridiculous, thought Lucien. But the entire situation struck him as rather absurd. Here they were, two couples walking through the centre of Haarlem – at first glance ordinary, upper middle-class couples spending a pleasant Saturday evening in each other's company. Marnix Christiaans and Swanny walked ahead, arm in arm. What an incredibly tall fellow, Lucien thought, nearly two metres. Alongside Mamix, his sister looked more than ever a half-pint. He and Pola followed, likewise arm in arm – or, rather, with Pola hanging on his arm. She'd been in excellent humour the entire evening, but now she shambled along in peevish silence, dragging her pumps over the pavement like a grumpy teenager.

It had been Swanny's idea for them to eat out together. Christiaans would surely have envisaged an intimate dinner after his long absence, and Lucien wondered how grudgingly he went along with it. Pola hadn't been easy to convince, either. Only his offhand remark that he'd heard rumours of foreign film producers being spotted this particular restaurant brought her round. She fell for it every time. But when he went to fetch her earlier in the evening, she was still in her peignoir, without makeup, and only a sniff of powder had guaranteed she wouldn't turn the dinner into a complete fiasco – her specialty. She'd cheered up instantly, of course, but she could still fly off the handle at any moment. She was unpredictable and would think nothing of ruining the evening with catty comments about overpaid civil servants who did nothing but shuffle papers all day long and wine and dine their way to the top. And she wasn't beneath being quite vulgar on occasion.

But to his relief she'd been the very picture of cheerfulness over dinner. In fact, her presence salvaged an otherwise tedious evening. She regaled them with gossip about the film industry and fellow actors. Annie Bos took a thrashing, other members of acting profession fared little better, and Mauritz Binger received the full brunt of her scorn. She then proceeded to make mincemeat of the renowned Filmfabriek Hollandia. Marnix sat there with well-mannered disinterest, but Swanny listened amusedly, asking questions and lapping up all the behind-the-scenes gossip from the glamourous film world.

Rounding off the meal with coffee, cognac and petit-fours, Swanny suggested they swing by Robin on the way home. He'd been working at the cinema every evening for the past week, and she thought a show of support would boost his self-confidence. Perhaps they could surprise him once the performance was finished. From the way Marnix set down his coffee cup, it was clear he wasn't exactly thrilled with the plan, but Swanny was oblivious. She raved about how Robin had visibly perked up from the job. How – when he wasn't depressed – they had fascinating conversations about all sorts of things, and what an intelligent and well-read man he was. 'Funny how quickly you get used to a face,' she said. 'Sometimes I completely forget he's wearing a mask. Casper touched it up so brilliantly, and the eye has completely returned to life. It's like it's his real face!'

'Ah, but it isn't,' said Marnix. 'The point of a mask is usually to hide who you really are. Back in ancient Greece and Rome, actors used masks so that they could pretend to be someone else.'

'Tsk, tsk, that's so unkind,' Swanny said. 'Of course I know it's not his own face. But that's got its advantages too. You're not distracted by expressions; you can listen more intently and get a much better insight into someone's innermost thoughts...'

Marnix smiled apologetically. 'Sorry, I was only teasing you.' Pola had apparently been irritated by his remarks on the theatre, and she now began lobbying vociferously for Swanny's proposal. She'd ask the cinema manager personally if they could visit Robin in the projection room.

But since leaving the restaurant, Pola had suffered a relapse. She tugged on Lucien's arm and insisted that she wanted to go home; she was sick to death of all this joviality and had played the loving fiancée for long enough. 'Or should I say your mistress, your kept woman...' She grew more hostile by the minute, and Lucien knew it wouldn't be long before she started running shrieking through the streets that he used her as his whore. He had to stop her from having a tantrum in front of the others. He felt in his coat pocket and pulled out a wrapper. 'Only if you don't make a scene,' he whispered, but she grabbed hold of his wrist before he could put it back, and to avoid a wrestling match he let her have it.

Now she was in such a hurry that she dragged him past Marnix and Swanny and was the first to enter the cinema. She marched straight to the manager's office, returned with permission for them to go up to the projection room, and pointed to the stairs. At once her face contorted with the painful expression Lucien knew only too well. She turned to Swanny and Marnix and, placing the back of her hand against her forehead, announced that she had a frightful migraine.

Swanny's concern kicked in immediately. 'How awful, do you still suffer from them? Pola knew she could count on Swanny for sympathy. 'There's only one thing to be done,' she groaned, 'home, to bed, lights out and wait for it to blow over. Otherwise it can go on for days…' Her hand went back to the forehead, now with the eyelids shut, like she was in unbearable pain. Tonight wasn't her best performance, thought Lucien, she looked like that hammy tragedienne Sarah Bernhardt.

'Oh, how dreadful!', cried Swanny. 'You're absolutely right, you mustn't risk that. Lucien will take you home this instant.'

Pola raised her hand in protest. 'No, no, I don't want to spoil your evening too, I live close by and can be home in five minutes.' But Swanny persisted, adamant that she mustn't walk home alone in this condition. By the time Lucien decided to put an end to the discussion and take Pola home, she'd already turned abruptly, wished them good night and marched off on her own.

'You've got to take her to a doctor, Lucien!' Swanny insisted. 'Just look at the state she's in, it can't go on like this!'

'Swanny's right, she really must see a doctor,' Marnix chimed in. Swanny beamed at him, grateful that he shared her concern.

From behind the closed doors they could hear the swell of the theatre organ as the film came to its climax. 'Maybe we should wait till it's over,' suggested Lucien.

'Nonsense, it will be so nice to see him at work. If we slip in quietly, we won't disturb anyone.' Swan pulled herself along the banister in the dark and once at the top of the steep staircase, she opened a door. The cabin was cramped and sweltering from the heat of the projector.

Robin stood next to the projector with a film reel in his hands. He seemed to freeze in mid-action. His one eye shot at lightning speed along Swanny, his gaze fixing on a spot behind her: Marnix. Timid to the point of terror, Robin shuffled backwards, as though trying to hide himself from view.

Taken aback, Swanny drew a breath to speak, but the words stuck in her throat. Then she whispered over her shoulder: 'This was a mistake. Wait for me downstairs.'

Not five minutes later the doors to the theatre opened and the audience started to trickle out into the foyer, buttoning up their coats. Marnix and Lucien stepped aside to let them pass, standing in front of a glass display case of film posters. Lucien prayed that the bustle of the departing moviegoers would make a conversation impossible. But Marnix stood, hands clasped behind his back, inspecting an illustrated poster of *Een Carmen van het Noorden*, Pola's most recent film. Her character, the deceived girlfriend, had a prominent place in the tableau. 'What's wrong with Pola, anyway?' he asked.

Lucien shrugged his shoulders. 'Headache. She often gets them.'

Marnix cleared his throat. 'Seems to me it's more than just that.'

'She does lay it on a bit thick sometimes. Pure drama. Just ignore it.'

'That's not what I mean. She looks awful. Just look here...' He pointed to the poster. 'She's become a shadow of her old self.'

Lucien recoiled from this indelicate criticism. 'Oh, those film posters... nothing but propaganda,' he laughed. 'You should see those actresses in real life.'

'Yes, I know that. But all the same, she got a sickly look to her.'

'What're you going on about? She's lost weight, of course, but that's part of the image. All these film stars starve themselves.'

Marnix lowered his voice. 'Lucien, let's not beat around the bush. Those sunken cheeks, the dilated pupils and that jittery behaviour... everything about her tells me she's using certain substances. I've seen plenty of women like her in the cabarets and clubs in Paris. They take morphine and cocaine like it's candy. And it shows in their appearance. They turn into walking skeletons, with deep-set eyes and nervous tics. Maybe you haven't noticed it, but others do.'

The last visitors had disappeared though the outside doors. Lucien glanced at the stairs, hoping that Swanny would reappear. He didn't like this conversation one bit. But Marnix wasn't through yet. 'While we're on the subject, your English houseguest looks like he's addicted as well. You don't have to confess to me that you're supplying those two with cocaine, but I'd be careful if I were you. That stuff has side effects you might not be aware of. You can easily take too much. In Paris I heard of instances where a person died of an overdose. Look, I don't give a damn who you give the stuff to, but I object to Swanny unwittingly being in the company of an addict.'

Lucien held his breath. 'You're well wide of the mark,' he lied. 'Pola's had migraines for years and Robin's been traumatized by the war, as you're bound to have noticed. I appreciate that you know a lot about anaesthetics because of your work, but that doesn't make everyone with a weak constitution a drug addict.'

Marnix shot him a sceptical glance. 'Come on, Lucien, don't pretend to be so innocent. Besides, it's not just about Swanny. It won't do for you to hang around with addicts. It could be disastrous for the firm's reputation. You're their commercial traveller, their calling card. The new Opium Law's is quite explicit on this point: only doctors and pharmacists are allowed to prescribe cocaine. If you distribute it freely, you're no longer dealing in medical products but in stimulants, which makes you a drug pusher – not to mention the question of how you got it in the first place. As you know, in Paris one of the main topics was the growth in illegal trade. We have to steer well clear of that. In the Netherlands we can still boast that, despite being one of the world's leading cocaine producers, we don't have a problem with drug addicts. And why not? For the simple reason that there is no public outcry. And I'd like to keep it that way. In the national interest! As soon as it gets out that a famous actress like Pola Pauwlova is a cocaine addict, it'll be all over the newspapers, followed by the inevitable question of who's giving it to her… Be sensible, don't put your job at risk for some over-the-hill actress and a crippled ex-soldier who should be being taken care of by his own family and not by our bighearted Swanny.'

'Give me a break, man, I'm not mad, you know! You don't really think I'm supplying those two with cocaine? Where d'you suppose I'd get it? The new laboratory chief is incredibly strict, go ask him yourself if you don't believe me!' Even so, for all his indignation, Lucien decided not to antagonize Christiaans further; he genuinely was in a position to get Lucien into hot water at work. He ran his hand through his hair, like he was seriously mulling over the scenario Marnix had just outlined. 'Maybe you're right… Pola should be treated by a doctor. I'll get onto it. As far as Robin is concerned, the fellow's a war victim, and Swan sees it as her duty to help him, so there's nothing you, me or anyone else can do to dissuade her.' He thought quickly. 'But I've been giving it some thought myself. Ryder's saving up for a new op on his face. As soon as he's earned some money, I'll give him the rest so he can go back to England. Swanny's sure to go along with it.'

'Good, I'm counting on it.' Marnix turned to Swanny, who was just coming down the stairs. She was pale and upset. 'Robin thinks we were checking up on him,' she said. 'I'm so ashamed. How could I have made such an appalling mistake?'

'It's not your fault. You meant well,' said Marnix sympathetically. 'Come on, let's leave him in peace; it's probably wiser.' The Bentley was waiting outside; the chauffeur had already opened the back door. Lucien told Swanny he'd prefer to stop in on Pola, to see if she was OK. She nodded understandingly.

It started to rain, and he pulled up his collar. What a palaver! Marnix was really putting the heat on him. Of course he smelt a rat. And Pola had misbehaved terribly. Anyone with Marnix's practiced eye could see in a split second that she was craving her fix. And then Robin crawling away like a scared puppy – no clearer evidence that he had something to hide. Offering him a one-way ticket to England wasn't such a bad idea after all. Swanny would think it truly admirable of him to fork out for the operation. But the real problem, of course, was Marnix. Even though they were as good as family now, an uptight civil servant like him wouldn't hold his tongue if the unsullied reputation of the nation was at risk. And all those dark hints about his job. Visions of a disastrous future loomed: jeopardizing the position he'd worked so hard to achieve, letting a commissioner's post slip through his fingers – in the worst case even losing his job altogether because he'd broken the law. He could lose everything... Until now, cocaine had been a blessing, but now the stuff was starting to turn against him. And whose fault was that? Those two weaklings! Dr. Van Rhijn was right: other veterans managed without it. And what Marnix had said about Pola was right too: she looked like an old hag, she was destroying herself, her career and pretty soon his as well. It couldn't go on like this. They both had to quit at once. There must be some remedy to help them break their habit. But what? He'd never heard of or read anything about it. Then, in a flash of inspiration, he thought of something, or rather someone: Olyrook... If he knew how to produce cocaine, then he'd surely know how to get someone off it, as well.

Owing to the urgency of this business, he appeared at Thomas's door unannounced the following evening. The new lodger bowed, butler-style, let him in without a word and took his coat. He found Jan Palacky in the living room reading a magazine. He looked up, surprised, almost like he'd been caught in the act. 'Lucien! I didn't know...'

'I should have rung.'

'No matter, no matter!' he exclaimed, his Czech accent sounding heavier than usual. He picked up a stack of newspapers from the chair. 'Do sit down.'

It struck Lucien that something about the room was different. 'Is Thomas home?' he asked.

'He's in bed. Rheumatism's giving him trouble. I'll go get him.' But he made no move to go upstairs, only poured two glasses of cognac. Lucien looked at the empty armchair. The leather seat had a worn imprint of Thomas's body. The lodger stuck his head around corner but Jan waved him hastily away and sat down on the footstool next to the armchair.

'How's life?' asked Lucien, not wanting to barge right in with the delicate issue he had come for. Now he saw what was different about the room: the beautiful mahogany cabinet, Thomas's pride and joy, was gone. In its place was a nondescript little chest. An attempt had been made to mask the lighter spot on the wallpaper with two paintings. Not very good ones, not what you'd expect from Thomas…

'Oh, all right,' said Jan. Not only did the room have a dismantled look to it, but Palacky himself was dishevelled. He looked as though he had slept in his suit and hadn't washed his hair in weeks. Lucien wondered if he should bring up his predicament now or wait until Thomas had joined them. But Jan crossed his legs, which didn't look at all like he was about to go fetch him. He seemed distracted.

'Thomas isn't ailing, is he?' asked Lucien.

'No, no, although there's not much improvement.'

'You're probably wondering why I showed up here unannounced,' Lucien began. 'You see, I've got a problem.'

Jan's head jerked upright. 'Oh God, a problem…' he said, as though he had feared as much.

'I didn't want to trouble you, but my back's against the wall and I was hoping your expertise might help.'

Jan watched him intensely. Then the door opened and Thomas came in, leaning on a cane. The lodger must have alerted him, because he didn't appear the least surprised by the unexpected visit. 'So, my dear boy, dropping by again?' He doddered over to the armchair and, aided by Jan, sank into it. As soon as he was settled, Jan said: 'Lucien's got a problem and would like to make use of your expertise.'

'A problem…' he repeated, just like Jan, but more accepting than shocked.

Lucien summed up Pola's worsening condition, concluding that she was using more and more cocaine at the cost of her good looks. 'Yesterday someone said she looked like a walking skeleton.'

Palacky bolted upright. 'Oh no! Such a beautiful woman, we can't let that happen. Thomas!'

But Olyrook raised his hand and instructed Lucien to continue. Better not to gloss over the problem, that way Thomas might do his best for him. 'I know it's Pola's own fault, but she really has to quit now. The problem is that Marnix Christiaans, he's an important…'

Thomas nodded. 'I know who Christiaans is. Has he figured out she's using it?'

'Yes, he brought it up yesterday, in connection, blast it all, with my job and the reputation of the firm, even in the "national interest", whatever that means. It kept me up all night. After all, Pola is a well-known film actress and if word gets out that she's addicted, a journalist will soon find his way to her boyfriend.'

Jan looked shocked to the core. 'Poor Pola, one single newspaper article could ruin her.'

'Or me…'

'Moreover, they'll be wanting to know where Lucien gets his cocaine,' said Thomas. 'That would be most unwelcome.'

Jan sighed. 'No, we don't need that on top of everything else.'

'How many people are you supplying now?' asked Thomas, eyeing him inquisitively from behind his thick eyeglasses. Lucien decided to keep mum about Robin; that would only complicate matters. 'Just Pola… but who knows, maybe she's passing it around.'

'Can't she just quit?' Jan insisted.

Olyrook shook his head. 'Stopping abruptly isn't easy. The withdrawal symptoms are dreadful, you have no idea. No comparison to a hangover.'

'And aspirin?'

'That only helps the throbbing headaches, but does nothing for the craving… I'll have to think about it, but for the time being start with novocaine.'

Lucien slid forward in his chair. 'Have you got some?'

'I produce it on a small scale. Actually, I'd like to switch over to it entirely in the future; it's a good alternative to cocaine, less toxic and non-addictive.' He leaned back and shut his eyes. 'Start by cutting the cocaine with a small amount of novocaine, and if they're satisfied with that, gradually add more. Jan, go to my room, you know where to find it.'

'So this is the solution?'

'I don't know, it's worth a try…' Thomas picked up his diary from the side table and raised it close to his spectacles. He paged through it until he found what he was looking for. 'If you come back in four days, I might have a better solution for you.'

23

A turn for the better

Lucien leafed through the contracts drawn up in recent weeks, comparing them with earlier forecasts. He re-examined them a second, and then a third time. Impossible... Had he made a mistake somewhere? He took a long gulp of the strong coffee Trudie had brought him. The sun was shining directly through the window and his office was sweltering. He'd already taken off his jacket and now flung off his waistcoat. His eyes ran down the figures yet again. He had to face facts: lately there had been a gradual, almost imperceptible drop in orders. Was the demand for cocaine decreasing? Or had he, due to all that bother at home, let things slide a bit? Had Cremers or Peereboom noticed yet? He had to find out what was up before the bosses started grumbling.

The heat was killing him. He walked over to the window. A couple of mosquitoes sat patiently on the windowpane, waiting to be let inside. He paced around the room, fanning himself with the ledger sheets. Concentrate. But how could he concentrate with that voice, that affected voice, nagging away in his head: don't put your job at risk for an actress and a crippled soldier! Don't put your job at risk... My eye! Would they dare fire the best commercial traveller the firm had ever seen?

The promising employee who had raked in huge profits for the company these past few years? The man with a bright future, whom even the British ambassador had complimented? Could it be that hospitals were switching over to eucaine and novocaine? Or was the number of war wounded fast declining? The war had been a terrific boon, but sales had taken a nosedive since the armistice. Even so, the world still had its share of armed conflicts. Not that he knew exactly where, but he occasionally heard Swanny, who read the papers from cover to cover, comment disapprovingly. He went over to the administrative office and asked Trudie if she'd saved last week's newspapers.

Seated at his desk, he perused the stack and an hour later had drawn up a list of current military conflicts. The most conspicuous one was being played out in Russia: civil war between the Bolsheviks and the forces of the White generals. The interesting part was that the Whites were being aided by England, France and the United States. The English were mainly active in the Caucasus and the French in Odessa. There was also unrest in Jordan and Palestine: an English presence once more. Churchill was bombarding Iraq, even mustard gas was being used. That was bound to cause massive casualties, but being Iraqis they had no potential interest to him as customers. His instructions were clear: supply only the former Allies and not their current enemies; that wouldn't go down well in The Hague. There had been enough recriminations about supplying the Germans during the war. Well, with all these restrictions it was hardly surprising that orders had tailed off. Then there was some business in the northwest provinces of India and Afghanistan, again involving the British. And then there was the French: they were trying to keep Syria and Lebanon under control, and were caught up in a rebellion in the Rif Mountains in Morocco and Algeria; there, too, chemical weapons were being used. He should've paid more attention to Swanny: no shortage of wars in the world.

He wrote out a new list, minus Russia: the Whites would probably get their cocaine from the former Allies, and he'd better not get involved with the Reds – he wasn't sure if the Dutch government had taken a neutral position in that conflict. Not likely, as Holland's royals were related to the Czar, who'd been murdered by the Bolsheviks a few years ago. He ended up with two columns of armed conflicts, one involving the English and one the French. Quite a list for nations still reeling from the last war. In neither country was cocaine production up and running yet, though one could safely assume there'd be considerable demand. More than he could deliver.

The competition mustn't be allowed to get a foot in the door. He had to find out which firms and wholesalers were supplying the military authorities and their medical services... Maybe he should go to Paris as soon as possible; you always found out more first-hand. And the English? Would Burroughs Wellcome still have the monopoly for the British Army? Maybe Brian Kirkpatrick could help. He was no longer employed by the company, but he'd surely have some information... All right, then, he'd go to Paris and then on to London, or perhaps the other way round. He phoned Trudie and asked her to look up Kirkpatrick's home address in the old files.

He leant back in his chair, put his feet up on the desk and stared at the ceiling. This was the right way to go about it: tally up all the wars going on and make a rough estimate of the manpower involved. It could well aqdd up to quite a figure. He closed his eyes. The sweat dripping down his face suddenly made him feel homesick for Java: stretched out in a chaise longue on the veranda, enjoying the cool air being fanned over him by the houseboy… Yes, it was high time he travelled again.

But first there was that damned business to sort out. It was just a matter of time, though, because that very morning he'd started both Pola and Robin on novocaine. Ignoring Olyrook's advice, he cut the novocaine with a small bit of cocaine, hoping it would break their habit more quickly. He'd had about all he could take from those two. They couldn't go a day without dope anymore! He had to keep a close eye on Ryder to make sure he didn't cave in, regularly checking his room for loose wrappers before Pleun or Swanny twigged to what was going on. Ironically, the more he gave him, the more Swanny was convinced of Robin's progress. She noticed encouraging signs: enthusiasm for his job, his eager contribution to the housekeeping, riveting conversations until the small hours… *so* wonderful, *so* interesting. Interesting indeed, thanks to all that powder that disappeared up his nose. Not wanting to shatter her illusions, he kept giving him more. The same went for Pola; she got her portions just to ward off suspicion. And look at the result: his life was being totally dominated by their addiction! That novocaine had to put a swift end to it so he could travel abroad with peace of mind.

But that afternoon all hopes of a carefree trip went up in smoke. Curious to see how the novocaine was working, he went to see Ryder in his room. What he saw made his heart sink. Robin had shifted the furniture around and stretched the bedding between the desk and the bed to create a rough-and-ready sort of hideaway. He'd barricaded himself in with a chair. Lucien sank to his knees and saw him scurry for shelter, shuddering and in complete panic. He kept calling for someone named Charlie, who he said would be back soon. Charlie, his best friend, who'd never abandon him. Robin cut such a crazed figure that Lucien was actually afraid. He still hadn't forgotten the fracas in IJmuiden. Quickly, before the others became alarmed, he ran to his room, got some cocaine, and lured Robin out of his lair as one would a dog with a bone. That bloody novocaine hadn't done a damn bit of good!

If it hadn't any effect on Robin, then Pola wasn't likely to fare any better. So he took off immediately for Filmfabriek Hollandia, where she had a small part in a new film. At the studio he ran into the director, Mauritz Binger, and a cameraman. When he asked where Pola was, Binger turned on his heel and strode off without a word, but the cameraman was more forthcoming. 'She's in the dressing room. Gone totally off her rocker again,' he sighed. 'If this doesn't stop she'll be out on her ear. Binger's completely hacked off.' Lucien had heard enough.

He found Pola sitting puffy-eyed on a stool in front of her make-up mirror. She was hunched over, a pathetic bundle of misery, and was plucking peevishly at her underclothes. The unflattering lights revealed the devastation of her body far more plainly than in her bedroom. She was a bag of skin and bones. She shot him an irate glance from under her painted eyebrows. 'What kind of rubbish was that!' He tried to reassure her, lying that it was a new sort of cocaine and she had to be patient for it to take effect. But Pola flew off her stool and pawed at his pockets. 'I know you've got some with you,' she panted, 'give it to me, give it to me, I'm begging you, I'll do anything you want, anything…' Lucien could see she meant it. She really was capable of anything, she'd think nothing of bashing in his head just for a sniff of powder. He was suddenly revolted by her sickly, jaundiced complexion, the hysterical look in those sunken eyes and that emaciated body. He shook himself free of her. She began to cry, wailing that she wasn't able to work properly, that he'd deliberately given her cocaine just to satisfy his own lust, and that it was his fault she was hooked on it! My fault, bollocks!, he thought angrily. But to avoid a scene he brought out two grams he kept in his pocket for emergencies. She'd have to make do with that for now. He tossed the wrappers onto her make-up table; they fell amongst the jars and bottles. Pola pounced on them and Lucien slammed the door behind him.

On his way back through the studio he felt the eyes following him. Had the other people on the set heard her yelling? Of course they'd heard. They always used to greet him, but now they looked the other away. They all knew he was Pola's lover, and they all saw how she was going downhill. Sooner or later they'd make the connection, however unfairly, and all fingers would point at him. And these people couldn't keep their mouths shut; the film world was the bitchiest clique around. They liked nothing better than to gossip to journalists about a colleague. What a mess! As long as he kept supplying her with cocaine he was at risk, but if he stopped providing it, he'd be in even greater danger.

Olyrook had better not try to fob me off with more junk this time, Lucien thought as he tossed his coat to the lodger, whose sanctimonious diffidence only added to his irritation. Novocaine was nothing more than an anaesthetic; Thomas surely knew that. Who was the chemist around here anyway, damn it? Lucien entered the living room and in the shadowy light of the standing lamp saw Olyrook seated in his armchair, his walking stick leaning against the armrest. 'Afternoon, Thomas,' he said brusquely, and, getting straight down to the reason for his visit, asked: 'Got anything better for me this time? That novocaine's useless, but then you know that already.' Thomas wasn't looking at him, but at the armchair across from his own, whose back faced Lucien. Someone was sitting there, and it wasn't Jan. Just above the high back he could make out a close-shaven neck and above it, a tuft of crisply-parted hair. Lucien walked around the chair and stood face to face with an old acquaintance.

Franz Biedermann got up, grinning from behind his enormous moustache, and extended his hand. 'Long time no see, Hirschland. Glad to bump into you again.' He tilted his head to one side as though to size him up, and added: 'You're looking in the pink – a bit tired, but in the pink all the same.'

Lucien was dumbfounded. The only thought that crossed his mind was that Biedermann hadn't changed a bit since their last meeting in the coffee house: the same shabby suit, the same red-veined pug nose, that pouting lower lip and most of all that brazen, mocking look. As he searched around for a spare chair he wondered what on Earth Franz was doing here, and why Thomas had insisted he come by today. 'You'll be surprised to see Franz here, no doubt,' said Olyrook, safely hidden behind a cloud of smoke.

'Nothing surprises me anymore these days,' Lucien replied absently.

'Well, there's a simple explanation. We're in the same business, so from time to time we meet up to discuss new developments.'

'Really. Must be fascinating.' Lucien was hoping Biedermann would push off before long, but the servile lodger came in with a tray of coffee. Three cups: Biedermann wouldn't be leaving anytime soon. Out of politeness, he asked: 'So how are you, Franz?'

'Fine, can't complain. Perhaps Thomas has told you that I've recently set up a scientific institute. At last I can devote myself entirely to producing new and better drugs.'

'What kind of drugs?'

Biedermann laughed. 'I'm not at liberty to say. I keep my cards close to my chest, you know me well enough by now.'

'I'm not sure I do,' Lucien responded coolly. 'For instance, I never knew you were a chemist and an officer in the German Army. You always pretended to be an innocent buyer for Merck.'

'Quite right. Times were different then. It was my duty was to guarantee that you people delivered top quality, which you always did. I never had any complaints on that score, as you know. Now that the war's over I can finally concentrate on my own profession.'

Thomas coughed into a handkerchief, his face contorted with pain. Lucien waited politely until Thomas's hacking spasm had subsided, and noticed that the room was even emptier than before. Thomas regained his composure and said hoarsely: 'Lucien, I've been thinking about your little problem and seeing as Franz is in Amsterdam anyway, I asked him to drop by. I think he might be able to help you.'

Biedermann stirred his coffee and lifted the cup with his little finger extended. 'Cocaine is truly a marvellous product, but addiction is an unwelcome side effect.' He took a sip. 'But there's hope – the medication I'm working on to counteract the withdrawal symptoms should be ready soon.'

Lucien was not best pleased that Thomas had discussed his private affairs with Biedermann unbidden, but his curiosity got the better of him. 'What kind of medication would that be, then?' he asked.

'I'd rather not say.'

'Fair enough. But how soon is soon?'

'Not much longer now. I still have a few experiments to do. There's bound to be quite a demand, but I promise you'll be the first to get it – after all, we're old friends.' Biedermann gulped down the rest of his coffee and peered over the rim of the cup.

Old friends. Lucien looked at Thomas. His eyes were drooping, like he was slowly nodding off. Now Lucien realized what was missing: the harmonious tick-tock of the antique pendulum clocks had been reduced to a single tick. Two of the three clocks were gone. 'And it's effective, you say?' he asked Biedermann.

'Count on it. Don't worry, I'm going to help you.'

'Oh, of course, Franz, you help me and I help you, isn't that how it goes? What's in it for you?' He knew full well who he was dealing with.

Biedermann laughed loudly. 'Of course I shall ask you for a service in return, but it's one you're bound to find interesting. It's like this: the development of new pharmaceutical products is a costly business, you're well aware of that, and in Germany there's no money these days, certainly not for scientific research. So, to secure the necessary finances, I occasionally sell cocaine to trusted parties.'

'You produce it yourself?'

Franz shook his head. 'Too much effort. I need my time for other things.'

Lucien looked at the pendulum clock as the big hand ticked forward. He decided to chance it. 'I assume Thomas is your supplier?'

'Indeed.'

Lucien crossed his legs, nodding thoughtfully. What unexpectedly good news! He could finally tell Cremers and Peereboom whom Olyrook was supplying. 'But his production can't meet my potential demand…' Biedermann went on. Just then, the lodger entered without knocking and asked if anyone wanted more coffee. 'No, sod off,' Thomas grunted.

'Isn't Jan here?' Lucien enquired.

Olyrook hesitated. He grimaced faintly, as though he was put out that Jan's name had been mentioned. 'No, he isn't,' Biedermann chipped in, clearly irritated by the constant interruptions.

'But Franz, you can order as much from me as you like,' Lucien volunteered. 'Surely there's no problem in that?'

Biedermann ignored Lucien and continued. 'I presume you mainly sell to wholesalers who supply hospitals.' Lucien didn't respond, nor did Franz expect him to. 'That market is dwindling, as I'm sure you're well aware. There's no profit to be had there anymore; the future lies elsewhere. I've established quite an extensive clientele in Germany by now.'

'Who, then?' Lucien asked, recalling the German order that had fallen through.

'I'd rather not say.' Biedermann grinned. 'Neither would you… What counts is that I can pay you a very good price, higher than you can charge the wholesalers. We're talking about large orders.'

'But why pay me a higher price if you can order directly from the wholesalers?'

'I'll tell you why. The Allies slapped all kinds of conditions on Germany at Versailles. The Brits and the Americans are keeping a close eye on us – they have their reasons – so wholesalers, scientific institutes, hospitals, industry and organizations are all thoroughly monitored. It makes doing business quite difficult.'

Lucien began to cotton on. 'Ah, so you're not licensed to sell cocaine. But why not? A scientific institute should be able to swing that easily enough.'

'You'd be surprised. I don't want to bore you with the current political situation in Germany, but believe me, it's rife with corruption. Besides, this government isn't interested in developing new medicines, so I have to finance my operations myself until a change in the political climate presents more favourable opportunities. But Lucien, remember: I'm talking about large orders, on the scale of what you sold us during the war. I'll also be able to guarantee you an extra commission from my end this time.'

'Come on, Franz, what do you take me for? You know I can't sell to companies without a license. That's the law.' Suddenly he saw Biedermann's motives as clear as day: he was selling cocaine on the black market in order to finance his experiments. Now *that* was a really interesting bit of information for Cremers and Peereboom, not to mention Marnix. Odd that Biedermann should take him, of all people, into his confidence. 'What you're asking me to do is strictly illegal.'

'Not if we come up with the right construction.'

'You don't really think my directors will go along with that, do you?' He glanced at Thomas; after all, he also knew Cremers and Peereboom. But Thomas just sat hunched over, staring at his gnarled fingers. He evidently wanted to stay well out of it.

'Not to worry. I'll provide you with the name of a company where the invoices can be sent, one with a proper license. For Cremers it'll be just another transaction, just like with any other customer in Germany.'

'What kind of company?'

'An old contact.'

'But you can just do your business via that company. Why make things so complicated?'

'It's better to keep my name out of it. I want to get on with my work in peace.'

Lucien grew steadily more convinced that this was all about the black market. Unbelievable, this information just falling into his lap! 'I'll think about it,' he promised. That was always the easiest way out.

'Trust me, this is the only way to get anything done in Germany now.' Franz tugged at his necktie. Predictably, it was stained, as always. 'I wouldn't think about it for too long. I'd like to order five hundred kilos for starters.'

Lucien plucked a piece of lint from his sleeve. Now that was an interesting order.

Thomas rang his bell, and the lodger appeared instantly with a fresh pot of coffee. He refilled their cups and slunk backwards out of the room, like the slave of some Oriental potentate. 'To return to your problem,' said Franz abruptly, 'I understand that if word gets out that Pola Pauwlova is addicted, it could be very damaging to your position and reputation.'

Now Lucien was even more vexed that Biedermann was privy to his personal problems. It made him feel claustrophobic.

'Maybe it'd help if she were out of sight temporarily,' Franz suggested. 'I can arrange work for her at the Berlin film studios.'

'Oh, Franz, please! Not that again…' Lucien sighed, exasperated. 'We both know full well you don't have a single contact in the German film industry.'

'What makes you say that?' Olyrook interjected. 'Of course Franz has connections at the UFA. It sounds like an excellent idea. Pola will jump at it. Besides, then he can administer his new drug in person.'

Lucien gaped at him, clearly recalling Thomas's sceptical comments that time in the coffee house about Biedermann's supposed connections with a film producer. Perhaps he'd learned differently in the meantime. Why would Thomas lie?

'There are a lot of films being made at the moment. My friend, the director Lorenz Fuchs, is quite enthusiastic about the idea,' Biedermann continued. 'Pola Pauwlova is well known there, and he's bound to have a role for her.'

Why not, thought Lucien. 'When?'

'I understand you're in a hurry. You can put her on the train to Berlin any time you like. Just let me know what day she'll arrive... The same goes for you. It might be an idea for you to deliver the consignment personally, so we can discuss future transactions. Consider it a deal; you can draw up the contract as soon as I give you the name of the company.' Lucien eyed him warily. 'Come now, Lucien, we've been doing business together for long enough. We've always trusted one another, so why not now?'

Lucien looked at Thomas. He nodded reassuringly.

That night Lucien lay in bed staring up at the knotted *klamboe*. He was facing an impasse, a moral conflict or, more precisely, a business dilemma. He weighed up the pros and cons: Cremers and Peereboom would certainly appreciate being told about the illegal trade, but then he could forget Biedermann's order and Pola wouldn't get to go to Berlin after all. Marnix was sure to be pleased with the tip-off about the shady dealings and in return would keep his mouth shut about Pola and Robin. On the other hand there was that tantalizing double commission.

But what if it came out that he had knowingly engaged in illegal trading? He'd be sunk. Word would get around and he'd have a devil of a time finding another job. No, better not take the risk; his position at the firm was more important. And as far as his private woes were concerned, Thomas would have to come up with something better than novocaine in exchange for Lucien keeping mum about his involvement with Biedermann.

Two days later he was sitting at the conference table with Cremers and Peereboom. He'd decided to lay all his cards on the table, and told them that while visiting Olyrook – who by the way only produced novocaine and had no further part in the whole business – he'd bumped into Franz Biedermann. He recounted the German's proposal and suggested that the company Biedermann was trading through might be a front, and that after careful consideration he had come to the conclusion that this was a clear case of black marketeering.

They let it sink in. 'How much does he want?' asked Peereboom.

'Five hundred kilos.'

'Well, well… he must have quite some clientele,' said Cremers. 'Buyers who can't do business through the usual channels.'

Lucien nodded vigorously in agreement. 'Exactly. It's just the ticket for illegal traders like Biedermann.'

'Not necessarily,' Peereboom interjected. 'Germany's in total chaos. Biedermann's probably right when he says corruption is rife. The only way to get a license, of course, is through the back door, the old boy network.'

'Quite right,' agreed Cremers. 'I'd say this isn't so much a question of illicit trade, more a practical solution for difficult times.'

Lucien did his best to contain his astonishment. 'So you don't think this is all about the black market, then?'

'Not if it hasn't been proven,' said Peereboom. 'We've an excellent history of business dealings with Biedermann. He's always been a decent, reliable client. Never had any problems with him.'

And what about those hundred kilos in Thielt, Lucien thought to himself, I'd certainly call that a problem.

'As long as there is a bona fide company name behind it, I see no impediment.' Cremers exchanged a glance with Peereboom. Lucien wondered why they couldn't grasp that the company probably wasn't on the level. 'I agree,' said Peereboom. 'Good of you to be so alert, Hirschland, but in this case there's nothing to worry about. Well done, you've secured a large order with prospects of more to come.'

'And the black market angle? Should I follow up on that?' he asked hesitantly. 'Christiaans is quite keen to follow up on it.'

'Of course, of course, I'll keep him posted.' Cremers got up and clapped him on the shoulder. 'But first, off you go to Berlin… and arrange everything down to the last detail, you know how those Germans are.'

It took him exactly the distance between Cremers' office and his own desk to realize that things had taken a distinct turn for the better. Satisfied directors, a double commission for him, a film role for Pola… and the opportunity to travel. To Berlin, as well! Europe's number one hot spot, the city of cabaret, jazz and outstanding restaurants. He reached for the phone at once and rang Biedermann, who showed little surprise at the lack of complications. He gave Lucien the company name: W.A. Kalbfleisch & Sohn in Berlin. All that now remained was to let him know when he could expect Pola and the shipment. Lucien promised to ring him back as soon as it was all arranged. Then he went to find Albert Ketting and told him an order would need to be driven to Berlin in about ten days' time. Ketting nodded, pleased. It was just like him to look forward to such an absurdly long journey in the lorry. Lucien had decided to take the international train, much more comfortable than the company truck.

After all this organizing he decided to go directly to see Pola. He felt on top of the world and couldn't keep this wonderful news from her a moment longer. At the Filmfabriek they told him she'd called in sick, so he drove straight over to her house and took the stairs two at a time. Pola was in bed with the covers pulled up over her head. Laughing, he yanked off the blanket. She glowered angrily at him. He stood frozen at the side of the bed. She looked awful. What had become of his beautiful Pola, with her voluptuous body, inviting breasts, full head of hair and sparkling dark eyes? He regained his composure; this surprise was sure to cheer her up. 'Pola, I've arranged a film role for you at the UFA in Berlin! Franz Biedermann, a good friend of mine, is a producer and he's got you into a film directed by Lorenz Fuchs.' She pulled herself up, folded her legs under her body and stared at him blankly. 'Berlin, a film role!' he repeated.

'Have you got any stuff with you, you bastard? Have you got any!?'

Lucien's shoulders slumped. He sighed, pulled a wrapper out his pocket and watched as she snorted the powder straight from the paper. She settled back down on the bed and pulled the blanket over her head. Good thing she was going to be kicking the habit soon, because this behaviour was becoming intolerable. She threw the blanket off again. 'What did you say?' He repeated the news, this time with far less enthusiasm. She slowly brought her hands to her face and shouted with delight. Ecstatic, she leapt off the bed and danced around wildly. Her scrawny arms and legs shot out in all directions. Suddenly she stopped and looked at Lucien suspiciously. 'You mean it? Of course, you're lying again… you lousy bastard, you're lying, aren't you!'

He scowled at her. 'Jesus, why would I lie? I'm going to buy you a ticket so you can take the first train to Berlin.'

That seemed to convince her. 'Lucien, you've saved my life! You've saved my life!' Then the tears started flowing. 'That swine Binger chucked me out, the little shit… Berlin! That'll teach them, those sods. I'll show them – a role in a German film.' Her face darkened again. 'Oh, I get it… You're trying to get rid of me. But I can't live without you! I won't live without you!' More tears.

It's my powder you can't live without, thought Lucien. 'My German contact can help you break your addiction, too.' He gazed intently at her. 'Do you hear what I'm saying?!'

'Yes, of course, I want nothing more than to be rid of that junk. It's ruining me. I'll do anything, anything your friend wants… A film role in Germany!' She started to rummage frantically through her things. 'What should I take? Oh dear, what should I take? I need to pack! All my clothes have to go, all my shoes… Where's my suitcase?' She grabbed him by the lapels and shook him violently. 'When do I go? Tomorrow! Tomorrow! Tomorrow! I need to go as soon as possible, otherwise they'll give the role to someone else!'

He prised her hands loose and wondered how long it would take to get the old Pola back. 'Hopefully the day after tomorrow, there's a train to Berlin then.'

She wasn't listening. She'd flung open her wardrobe, setting off an avalanche of brightly-coloured clothing. 'When do I go, Lucien? When?'

'Why don't you just pack? I'll take care of the rest.' She charged back into the wardrobe. He'd put her on the train himself with enough money not to be entirely dependent on Biedermann. He wondered if six or eight wrappers would be enough for the journey and the first part of her stay.

A week later, the day before his departure, he only needed to swing by Tosca's house in Bloemendaal. His plan was to spend ten days in Berlin, if possible, but his problem was only half-solved. He couldn't leave Robin behind without his daily portion.

He found the Tilanus's villa with no difficulty. Tosca still lived at home. 'He'd been there once before, years earlier, when he'd taken her home, dead drunk. He parked behind the Peugeot Quadrilette, her two-seater sports car that she always drove far too fast. He'd phoned the day before concerning a delicate matter regarding his trip to Berlin. 'Robin,' she guessed instantly.

Although he wouldn't have been surprised to be received by a liveried butler, it was Tosca who opened the door and with an exaggerated sweep of the hand beckoned him in. 'Run out of lackeys, have we?' he asked. She stuck out her tongue and led him into a cavernous entrance hall with imposing portraits, no doubt family members: wealthy traders in colonial goods, if he remembered correctly. A tennis racket and hockey stick were propped in the corner. 'Yours?'

She laughed. 'Of course, I'm the only athletic one around here.' In the ultra-modern reception room, the evening light shone beautifully through the high windows that looked out onto the garden, actually less a garden and more a well-tended park. She poured them both a glass of whisky. He was struck by the utter emptiness of the house.

'Aren't your parents at home?' he asked.

'Of course not, they're never home. I'm usually here on my own.'

So when Tosca wasn't with Swanny she just rattled around this enormous mansion. How many rooms would this place have? 'I'll bet a house like this costs a packet,' he said casually.

'Why, are you planning to give up the Oranjekade?'

'I think about it sometimes.'

'And leave Swanny behind on her own? You heartless monster!'

'I'd wait until she married, naturally.'

Tosca frowned at him, but left it at that. She handed him his glass and sank into a designer armchair. 'So what's the story?' He didn't know where to begin. So she answered for him, this time without laughing: 'You're going to Berlin for ten days and need someone to give Robin his cocaine.'

He whistled to himself, taken aback by her directness. 'How did you know?'

'I'm not stupid.'

'Then I hope you understand I'm only giving it to him to alleviate the pain. It's a temporary measure. I'm working on a solution. I'm hoping to get my hands on some medicine in Berlin that'll get him off the stuff.'

'Good. It'd be nice if he could quit before Swanny finds out.' She thought for a moment. 'Have you sent Pola packing because she couldn't do without it either?'

'I didn't send her packing! What do you take me for? I'm

mad about her. She's got a major film role lined up for her there, plus she can be treated with the same drug.' He pictured Pola sitting in the train compartment, her euphoria replaced by anxiety. Suddenly she was no longer the scandalous movie diva but an emaciated, confused little girl, self-conscious and afraid. She'd cried, and repeated her accusation that he wanted to get rid of her, that she knew full well he had no plans to marry her. After all, who wanted to be married to a drug addict? He felt so bad for her that for a moment he considered taking her back off the train.

'OK, then... You want me to give Robin some every day until you get back, is that it?'

He nodded. Tosca crossed her legs. With her short-cropped, boyish haircut and regular features, she was actually an elegant, attractive woman. She fitted into the modern interior like they were made for each other. 'I'll help you out, on condition that I can try some myself. I smoked opium once but it made me sick as a dog.'

'Jesus, Tosca, are you mad?' he exclaimed, shocked. 'If you're serious, then we can forget the whole thing.'

She smiled mischievously. 'Just testing... I was curious to see whether you cared about having another addict on your hands.'

'You're acting like it's my fault. They're adults. It's their own responsibility. They started using the stuff all by themselves.'

'Did they?'

'Anyway, how was I to know it's so hard to give up?'

'That's strange, since you've been selling it for years.' She smiled at him. 'I'm just teasing you. Of course I'll help you with Robin. Only Swanny mustn't find out. She'll never forgive me, not after what happened to your mother.'

'You're right. And for God's sake don't mention it to Marnix.'

'Oh my, already keeping secrets from your future brother-in-law? But don't you worry, I scarcely talk to that prig.'

'Prig?' asked Lucien. 'Well, Swanny's rather fond of him. She can't stay unmarried forever, you know.'

'Rather fond of him… That's it exactly. Do you really think that's enough for a marriage? But I'm afraid it may actually happen one day. She started on about it again yesterday, maybe because Pola left so suddenly. Pola put the idea into her head that you don't want to marry her because you have to look after your little sister. Now Swanny feels like a third wheel. If she ties the knot with Marnix then you'll be free to marry Pola.'

'You do realize that Pola's talking rubbish?'

'That's what I told Swanny, but she doesn't believe it.'

'We're going to have to convince her otherwise.'

'Well, we're off the hook for the time being. As long as Robin's living in the house, nothing will come of it. When she brought it up yesterday, he nearly went off the deep end. He started crying and only calmed down when she promised she'd never abandon him…'

Lucien rubbed his forehead. God, now this too. When Marnix found out about Robin's addiction, he'd wanted him out of Swanny's sight, but if he found out the Englishman was getting in the way of his marriage as well, he'd really hit the roof. Ryder had to be packed off back to England as soon as possible. He'd take care of that straight away once he was back from Berlin. Then he'd only have to explain to Swanny that he couldn't take care of her forever and that he was thinking about moving. Then there'd be no more obstacles to her marrying Marnix, and his own future would be secure.

24

Brüder, zur Sonne! Zur Freiheit!

Lucien arrived at the Potsdamer Bahnhof, the terminus for all continental express trains coming from the West, around noon. He took his fedora down from the hat rack, putting it on tilted casually to one side; he clamped the blue-glass lorgnette to his nose, straightened his light summer suit and left the compartment. Pausing on the top step, he glanced around the enormous train station before stepping eagerly down into the crowd. Suitcase firmly in hand, he zigzagged his way towards the exit. At once he got a full blast of the cosmopolitan city: the smell of petrol combined with the stench of horse dung and the scent of hordes of pedestrians, with their mixture of sweat, cheap toilet water and expensive perfumes. It was glorious weather. Berlin blew him a sundrenched kiss. He immediately decided to extend his stay by few days.

He hailed an open taxi and instructed the driver to give him a tour of the main tourist attractions on the way to the Hotel Excelsior on the Königgrätzer Strasse, where Biedermann had reserved him a room. The chauffeur tipped his cap and, one hand firmly on the klaxon, swung out into traffic, manoeuvring deftly amongst the automobiles, hackney cabs, buses and other taxis. He managed to make himself heard above the din, calling out the names of the streets and boulevards they crossed: the Leipzigerstrasse, Wilhelmstrasse, Kurfürstendamm; he pointed out the Brandenburg Gate, government buildings, ministries and the Reich Chancellery. Imposing buildings, to be sure, but Lucien's eye was caught mainly by the department stores and the stream of well-dressed shoppers going in and out of them, laden with purchases. They drove through the Mitte district, past outdoor cafés and ice cream parlours. The chauffeur shouted the names of various museums he thought worth a visit. When he saw that Lucien, distracted by an attractive woman with a long-haired Afghan hound, did not answer, the driver turned to him and offered to take the gentleman *aus Holland* to the best cabarets and nightclubs at any time of the day or night.

They stopped in front of the Excelsior, one of Europe's most luxurious hotels. Lucien got out and gave the chauffeur a generous tip. A porter in a red uniform with gold braid hastened to assist him. As he was reaching for his suitcase, Lucien caught sight, out of the corner of his eye, of the firm's lorry parked a little way up the street beside the broad pavement. Albert Ketting was leaning against the bonnet, leisurely smoking a cigarette. He had left Amsterdam four days earlier, and calculated that they'd arrive at around the same time. Lucien had secretly hoped Ketting would be delayed so he could explore the city on his own. Now, alas, he'd have to get straight down to business. Ketting spotted him and flicked his cigarette into the gutter.

He'd arrived the previous evening. 'That was quick,' said Lucien. 'Did you find a hotel?'

'I slept in the lorry. This isn't the kind of city where you leave cargo like ours unattended overnight.'

Lucien nodded. 'I'll bring my bags inside and ring Bieder-mann from my room. Then we can get rid of those crates as soon as possible.'

The bellboy led him to a modern suite on the third floor, looking out onto the bustling Askanischer Platz. While taking in the view he noticed the roof of the lorry and remembered he had to contact Biedermann for instructions on where and when to meet.

He freshened up in the bathroom and a quarter of an hour later they were underway. Following Biedermann's instruc-tions, they left the broad boulevards and entered a maze of narrow streets, which made it difficult for Ketting to manoeu-vre. The road surface was full of potholes, and on either side, unpainted houses sagged wearily against one another. From his high vantage point in the cab, Lucien could see into dimly-lit basement shops with damp-stained walls. Here and there, a long queue of shabbily dressed people stood waiting. It struck him that Berlin's boulevards were like a warm smile that con-cealed a set of horribly decayed teeth.

As they ventured deeper into the web of streets and alleyways, they noticed that it wasn't just a working-class neighbourhood they were in but also, judging from the many neon signs, a nightlife district too, with bars and clubs of the roughest sort. Lucien wondered if he'd understood Biedermann's instructions properly, because they should be close to his scientific insti-tute, near the Alexanderplatz in the Mitte. That sounded like the city centre to him, where he'd definitely expected more grandeur.

Ketting nudged him and pointed to a signpost on the wall of a corner house. It was the street Biedermann had mentioned. So the institute was here, after all. Halfway along they located the house number whitewashed on a peeling door. Lucien checked his notes one more time and jumped down from the cab. As there was no bell he banged on the door with his fist. The lorry was blocking the street and behind them, waiting cars had already started blowing their horns. Biedermann, wearing a long overcoat with a fur collar, opened the door, greeted him unceremoniously, as though they saw each other daily, and directed Ketting to a set of double stable doors about fifteen metres further up. He produced a huge set of keys and unlocked the gates. Ketting had to muster all his driving skills to manoeuvre the lorry inside.

Once inside the dimly-lit storage area, which still smelt of horses, Ketting immediately climbed into the back and started unloading the crates. Without saying a word, Biedermann split open the first crate with a crowbar and removed one of the bottles. Leaving Ketting to his task, Lucien followed Biedermann through a side door into a room whose only daylight came through high skylights. The laboratory was spick-and-span and looked very professional. Silently, Biedermann made for the flasks and beakers to test the cocaine. This time there were none of the insinuations of poor quality and diddling that had characterized their former dealings. Finally he nodded, satisfied, and having thoroughly washed and replaced his utensils, he asked: 'Is the hotel to your liking?' Without waiting for an answer, he added: 'Where's your driver sleeping?'

'We'll go and find something for him now.'

'I've made arrangements at the *pension* next door, with Frau Kalthoff. Reliable woman, I know her well.' Biedermann went back to Ketting and instructed him to call on Frau Kalthoff, who was expecting him, and to leave the lorry where it was. Lucien was taken aback by Biedermann's bossiness. So this was how he behaved on his own turf. 'I'll come round presently, Albert,' said Lucien. Ketting took his bag out of the cabin and Biedermann locked the door behind him. He then invited Lucien to accompany him to his apartment, next door to the laboratory, which could be reached from the inside. On the way upstairs, every door – there were at least five of them – was unlocked with the enormous bundle of keys and locked again behind them. Lucien wondered why Franz had given an address six doors away when he lived right here.

The living room was as clean and tidy as the lab, but austere, and far simpler than Lucien would have expected from someone with his own scientific institute. The small kitchen was equipped with no more than the bare necessities, and the double bed was covered with a rough spread. If Franz was mixed up in shady business, you wouldn't know it from the state of his flat.

'How's Pola?' asked Lucien.

'She's fine. But let's get down to business straight away.' They sat down at a plain wooden kitchen table and Biedermann took out a folder. Lucien opened his attaché case. The order form had been made out to Pharmazeutische Firma W.A. Kalbfleisch & Sohn, Budapesterstrasse 5, Berlin. 'Have you got the invoice?' Biedermann asked as he shuffled through his papers.

'No, our administration will send it by post, as usual,' replied Lucien.

'Come on, man, write one out yourself. It'll save time; the German postal system is terribly unreliable at the moment. Besides, I want to pay you in cash and I'll need a receipt.'

'Franz, this is highly irregular. Such large sums of money should be wired to our bank.'

Biedermann seemed irritated. 'Now listen, Kalbfleisch & Sohn doesn't wire money to banks. When will you get it through your head that this country's completely dysfunctional? We all have to make do. I went to a lot of trouble to scrape this much cash together.' He got up, bent over a large cardboard box that had once contained margarine, heaved it onto the table and opened it.

Astonished, Lucien stared at the contents. The box was stuffed with banknotes. He'd never seen so much cash before in his life. Normally all payments to his company were made by bank transfer, but this money – albeit crumpled and dirty – was suddenly tangible. He made an effort to count it, but soon gave up. Of course it was all there, Franz wouldn't be such a fool as to cheat him openly. He wrote out a receipt on the back of the order form and asked for a piece of string. As he was tying up the box, Franz slid a thick envelope across the table with his commission, went to the kitchen and came back with two shot glasses and an unlabelled bottle of schnapps. 'Good doing business with you again, Hirschland.' He raised his glass. 'To the future!'

Lucien swigged back the schnapps and shut his eyes tight. Undeniably homemade bootleg, distilled in the basement of some tenement. 'Now tell me how Pola is doing,' Lucien insisted.

'Fine, all things considered. She spent the first few days blubbering about one thing or another. But she's been in contact with the director. Now it's just a question of waiting; there's a new film in the works but the finance hasn't been finalized yet.'

'Where is she now?'

'As far as I know, in a photo studio. But she'll meet you presently in Club Medusa. Seems to be a favourite hangout of actresses and theatre people, not that I frequent that kind of joint myself. In any case, she goes there a lot.' Biedermann stroked his little tuft of hair with both hands, to stop even one strand from shifting out of place. 'I think she rather likes it here.'

'That's good to hear. How's it going with your new drug, are you making any progress?'

'What drug?' asked Franz as he made a move to refill their glasses. 'Oh, I know what you mean, forgive me, I'm working on so many different medicines. The preparation you're referring to should be ready in about a week. I still have to do a few tests and then I'll send you some as soon as possible.'

'Fine, as long as you give some to Pola straight away.'

'Of course.' Biedermann picked up the bottle. A sign on the opposite wall caught Lucien's eye: No Smoking. He got the sudden urge for a cigarette. Besides, the transaction has been completed and there was nothing further to discuss. He held his hand over his glass as a signal he was about to leave, and slid the chair back.

'Going so soon?'

'Yes, I want to look round Berlin.'

Biedermann's upper lip curled into a snarl. '*Mein Gott*, has the demise of a beautiful capital become a tourist attraction these days?'

'What do you mean, demise? Everyone raves about Berlin. It's a must-see city.'

'If you like sleaze, that is.'

'What do you mean?'

'Go see for yourself! Nothing but debauchery and decadence. Decent people can't survive here any more. The city's a magnet for scum: homosexuals, transvestites, whores, artists and all kinds of losers.' Lucien wondered what Franz suddenly had against debauchery and whores. But on the other hand, it was hard seeing your hometown fall on hard times. 'Though that lot's nothing compared to the communists and socialists!' continued Biedermann bitterly. 'They're trying to take over here. That rabble's responsible for Germany's defeat, damn them! Their antiwar propaganda undermined people's will on the home front and drove us to surrender.'

Lucien couldn't recall ever having heard Franz talk politics before.

'Enemies of the people! They stabbed the German army in the back. Look what the Treaty of Versailles has cost us. We've lost huge tracts of land, our colonies have been taken away, and worse still, Germany's become a vassal of the greedy Allies. But I'm not one of those who yearns for the old days of the Empire. Oh no, we need a strong figure, that's for sure, but not the Kaiser, you Dutch can keep him.' He refilled his glass. This was a side of Biedermann he'd never seen before, thought Lucien. 'You should have seen it last year… Endless demonstrations, revolutionary communists waving red flags, shouting for Bolshevism and singing: "*Brüder, zur Sonne! Zur Freiheit!*" Damn it, *zur* total barbarism would be more like it. Freedom, my arse! It would've degenerated into civil war if the authorities hadn't stepped in. The situation's got a bit more stable now. But it's still smouldering under the surface. It's not over yet…' Biedermann's puffy face had gone a deep puce colour. He looked at Lucien pityingly. 'And you, of course, still have no idea. You really should keep up with politics and read the right newspapers, Lucien.'

'Oh no, not me. I give politics a wide berth. I'm happy for people to leave me to get on with business.' He laughed uncomfortably.

'Nonsense. Everything's interconnected, especially now. Politicians, scientists, businessmen, we all need each other if we want a new world order.'

'God, Franz, big words!'

'Now's the time for big words and big ideas, you'll see. I want to do my bit. I see it as my solemn duty.'

The word 'duty' suddenly reminded Lucien of Ketting. 'I must be going now', he said. 'I have to speak to my driver and I want to call in on Pola.'

'Yes, of course. Well, I'm looking forward to continuing our association. It could be very significant.' Biedermann took out his bundle of keys and led him to the door. In passing he plucked the top copy from a pile of newspapers, all the same edition, and handed it to Lucien. 'Take it, it'll give you something to read on the way home.' They went downstairs and through the storage area. The lorry was still parked there, but to Lucien's surprise, the crates had already been cleared away.

Fortunately Ketting's guesthouse really was just two doors down the road, as lugging his hefty box of cash even twenty steps down the street made his heart race. Not that he was afraid of being robbed; instead, he felt like a criminal had thrust the contents of his safe into his arms just before a police raid. Frau Kalthoff showed him to 'Herr' Ketting's room.

Once inside, he slumped back, eyes closed, against the door. Then he set the margarine box down on the table and tossed the *Völkischer Beobachter* that Franz had given him into the waste basket. Ketting leant over the open box and scratched behind his ear. He too had never seen so much cash before.

'What d'you think, Albert? Shall we hightail it to a tropical island?' Lucien asked, grinning.

Ketting shook his head. 'Wouldn't work, my wife can find me anywhere.'

'Well, I still want to go to the club where Pola hangs out and I'd rather you came with me.' He couldn't face a showdown with a weepy Pola on his own.

'No, thanks, it's not my job to go on a bender in Berlin.'

'Do me a favour, will you, and come along. And anyway, we still have to eat.'

Ketting shook his head grumpily and cast a worried glance at the cardboard box. 'Can't. Somebody's got to stay here and look after that money.'

'Nah, we'll just stash it somewhere.' Lucien scanned the room, took the pillow from the bed, pulled off the pillowslip and started stuffing it with notes.

'I'm really not one for clubs,' Ketting protested. 'And I'm not dressed for it either.'

'Not to worry. Biedermann says it's nothing here but debauchery and decadence, nothing but homosexuals, transvestites, communists and other scum. So we'll hardly stick out.' But he knew the joke was wasted on Albert.

Lucien asked directions from a beggar, a soldier on crutches, in an alleyway. The man waited to see how much his information would earn him, before pointing to the flashing neon lights above his head: *Club Medusa*. As Lucien had been generous, he also pointed out a staircase that led down to a basement, from where the sounds of a swinging trombone wafted up. 'Doesn't sound bad, not bad at all…' Lucien mumbled, despite his sneaking suspicion that all he'd find was a seedy dive full of bawling actresses.

The basement was chock-a-block, with a suffocating fug

of sweat and perfume. Artistically-dressed bohemians, white-scarved dandies and women, lots of women, in provocative outfits and with eyes like tropical night animals, jostled in the red light. A small group of singers in tuxedos and silk hats stood close together in front of the jazz band, and men and women, hands on each other's hips, shuffled across the dance floor. The atmosphere seduced Lucien, prompting him to revise his opinion. He glanced over his shoulder at Ketting, who stared sullenly at the floor as he tagged along; he certainly wasn't about to revise his opinions.

Suddenly he found himself standing next to Pola. She sat in a niche at a small table, in the company of several extravagantly-dressed figures. She let out a scream, leapt up, threw her arms around him and exclaimed: '*Liebling, liebling…endlich!*' With a single flick of her green-nailed fingers she dismissed two girls and gestured to the vacant chairs. But rather than sit next to Lucien, she nestled into the semicircular divan across the table and cuddled up to the man next to her. 'This is Peter, my very, very best friend in Berlin…' Lucien recognized him at once. The strident laugh was also painfully familiar. Peter Wammeier, medical pharmacist and staff officer from the medicine reserve depot in Thielt.

'How's things?' Wammeier shouted, not at all surprised to see Lucien, and waved to a waitress to come and take their order. He ignored Ketting completely. The music was so loud that there was no point in trying to converse. Pola, her lips pursed, ostentatiously caressed Peter's cheek and demanded his attention. 'Not now, *Schätzchen*…' said Wammeier, who despite the sweltering heat was wearing a white polo-neck jersey and light blue flannel trousers. His hair glistened with brilliantine. Pola sat straight up, annoyed; all her theatrical effervescence vanished at once and her lacklustre gaze slid drowsily toward the dance floor. She had changed. The painted arches above her plucked eyebrows, the dark mascara around her eyes and the shocking red lips contrasted sharply with her face, which had been powdered white as a ghost. She looked like a doll, a sad little doll.

Lucien had to raise his voice to make himself heard above the music. 'Franz tells me you'll be getting a role soon.'

She let out a loud, unnatural laugh. 'Of course I'll be getting a role, I've nearly got a contract with the UFA!' She dug in her bag and pulled out a familiar-looking powder compact. 'Look around you, you fool!' she screamed. 'Every woman here's an actress, and they'll all be getting a role soon!' The girls at her table giggled sheepishly. They rubbed their nostrils nervously with the back of their hands and their mouths chewed constantly.

'But you have work already,' smiled Peter Wammeier, revealing a set of perfect white teeth. He was the only one in the entire company who looked at all wholesome.

'She's working as a photo model in an Oriental studio for now,' he explained. 'It pays well.'

'Nude photos always pay well!' snarled Pola.

Lucien dared not look at Ketting. 'Have you found a place to stay yet?' he asked, quickly changing the subject.

She dabbed at her cheeks with the powder puff. Her hands were trembling. 'I'm still living at Franz's place.'

Lucien was surprised. 'In that barren cell?'

She obviously didn't follow him. 'What do you mean, barren cell? Anyway, I'll be leaving soon,' she said, with a flirtatious glance sideways. 'I'm going to live with Peter.' He took a sip of beer and said, 'I've told you already, you're just fine staying with Franz.'

Pola ignored his comment and announced that she wanted

to dance. No one responded. As the waitress wriggled towards the table with a tray full of beer steins, Pola took the opportunity to lean behind her and ask Lucien in a low voice if he had anything for her. He kept his gaze on the waitress's back and shook his head. She gave him an angry slap on the shoulder and marched off to the dance floor, where she disappeared between the couples.

The band struck up a slow number, so they could converse again in normal voices. 'I don't like the look of her,' Lucien said to Wammeier. 'If you ask me, she's not well. Maybe it'd be better if I took her back home.'

Peter pensively took a yellow cigarette out of a silver holder. 'Why? She's in her element here.'

'Well, in any event, it'd better to wait until Biedermann has got that medicine for her, so she can go without that stuff and pull herself together.' Lucien suddenly bit his lip, thinking he'd betrayed an indiscretion to Ketting, before realizing with relief that he didn't understand German.

'What medicine?'

'Something to counteract her addiction. He should have it ready within a couple of weeks.'

Wammeier smirked mockingly. 'What have you let yourself be fooled into believing this time? A drug to counteract cocaine addiction! You really think Franz would be working on something like that? Wouldn't exactly be in his own interests, now would it?' He shoved aside a couple of glasses and leant halfway across the table. 'Listen, while we're on the subject... I know you're supplying Franz again.'

Lucien's head was spinning. So Biedermann had tricked him again. He'd fallen for it, hook, line and sinker, and this time he'd delivered Pola into the claws of that slippery bastard.

'Did you hear what I said?' Wammeier repeated.

'I heard, all right,' he snapped. 'What's it to you?'

'I sell the stuff for him.'

'And is this your clientele?' Lucien asked, jerking his head towards the dancing couples.

'Ach, they're just a bunch of failed artists, whores, gigolos…'

'Berlin's the tops, one big party…' slurred one of the girls. She didn't look a day older than sixteen and threatened to climb onto Peter's lap. He pushed her aside. 'Berlin's full of junkies,' he continued, 'you've no idea how many. It's a gold mine! Especially if we cut the stuff. Let's you and me set up a little business, leave Franz out of it, you can sell to me direct without him having to know.'

'I'd rather not supply private individuals.'

'Don't be stupid, who do you think Franz is supplying?… Like you don't already know.'

Lucien stared silently at the dance floor. By now the band had moved onto an upbeat number. Through the smoke, all he could see was emaciated, sweaty-headed and wide-eyed junkies making spastic movements. He thought he caught a glimpse of Pola. 'Look at that, will you. Doesn't it bother you?'

'Oh, and it bothers you, does it? They're nothing but the dregs of society.'

Lucien didn't know how to respond. A trumpet riff ripped through his eardrums. 'Please, let's go back to the *pension*,' said Ketting. Sweat dripped off his moustache and the hairs on his neck stood up from the dampness.

'Yes, of course, let's go…' Lucien got up but Wammeier grabbed him by his jacket. 'What about my proposal?'

'You mean get even more people addicted?'

'You don't have to be so smug about it,' Wammeier hissed.

'You didn't have much problem with it during the war, *Arschloch*!' Ketting went over and stood next to him with his arms crossed. Wammeier released his grip at once. Fresh air, thought Lucien, it's suffocating in here, fresh air, *now*. Ketting was already heading for the door, pushing his way through the crowd and warding off groping hands. Lucien followed him, but his eyes searched for Pola. He mustn't leave her behind, not now he knew Biedermann had lied about the medicine, about the film role, about everything... He'd take her back to Haarlem in the morning, even if she resisted. If need be, Ketting would have to lend a hand.

Suddenly she loomed up out of the crowd. She grabbed his hands and tried to get him to dance. 'Come home with me, Pola, please! Come home with me!' he begged. She threw her head back, laughing, and put her arms around his neck. 'Pola, I don't want you to ruin yourself here, please come home with me! I love you, I'll marry you, I'll do anything you want, as long as you come back with me!'

With her face close to his, she hissed: 'Give me some stuff... Give me some! Franz is so damned stingy with it!' Lucien stared at her bony white head and wrenched himself free. Her eyes suddenly fixed him with a sinister glare and she screamed: 'At least give me some money then! How do you expect me make it here without any money! You sent me here, remember, you prick? You bought me a train ticket to let me rot here!' Shocked, Lucien took out his wallet and pulled out 500 marks. She grabbed the bills out of his hand and, frightened that he'd try to take it off her, shot back to the dance floor. Ketting grabbed Lucien firmly by the jacket and dragged him towards the exit.

Lucien staggered up the stairs, gasping for breath, for

untainted, fresh air… Panting, he bent forward, his hands resting on his knees. It was all he could do not to burst into tears. The begging soldier hobbled over to him and shoved his cap under Lucien's nose. Doing his best to drown out the din from the basement, he broke into strident song: '*Brüder, zur Sonne! Zur Freiheit!*'

25

The favourite nephew

Three days after his return from Berlin, Lucien found himself hurrying through the main hall of Amsterdam's Central Station. He cast a worried glance at the timetables. Still ten minutes until the train was due to arrive. Reassured that they wouldn't miss one another, he proceeded to the platform indicated. He leant up against a placard advertising the station restaurant to catch his breath and allow the passengers and heavily-laden porters to pass unhindered. Taking out a cigarette, he held a match to it and mused on the curious conversation he'd just had with Cremers.

The director hadn't asked him a single thing. Not about his abrupt return from Berlin, not about Biedermann and not about the cardboard box filled with cash, which Lucien purposely didn't take to the bookkeeper, but gave to Cremers personally. After casting a cursory glance in the box, he laconically remarked that in some respects doing business in Germany nowadays had become a good deal easier, in any event less bureaucratic. Cremers did enquire when they might expect the next order from Berlin. That was exactly what Lucien wanted to discuss with him. Although he'd carefully worked out his argument in advance, he suddenly found it hard to put his experience into words. Should he begin by telling Cremers what he'd seen in that club: the wretched addicts, Wammeier and his proposal, or should he spill the beans about Biedermann and his shady dealings? He decided that the most urgent matter was the question of deliveries to Biedermann. It weighed heavily on his mind; after all, he was the one who'd got the firm into this fix in the first place. But he'd hardly started when Cremers interrupted him: 'Lucien, don't go chasing rainbows. The transaction's been conducted to everyone's satisfaction and the next order won't be long in coming, I trust.' And without pausing, he moved seamlessly on to talking about Mrs. Peereboom, who was driving him to distraction with her pleas to accompany Lucien to Berlin. 'She's very fond of you, you know.'

'Yes, quite,' he answered absent-mindedly. 'A most agreeable lady.' And suddenly, vexed over Cremers's lightheartedness, a mischievous thought occurred to him: 'Then she must come with me next time.'

'I'll tell her, she'll be delighted! Don't be surprised if she rings you herself. She's rather a forthright woman. She's in need of a little diversion, and to travel to Berlin in the company of a young man such as yourself... even if it's just to make her girlfriends jealous.' They both had a good laugh over it. Imbecile! It would serve them right: Mrs. Peereboom back from Berlin, hooked on cocaine. A new 'diversion' she could share with her friends, Mrs. Cremers, for instance...

And besides, it no longer mattered that he hadn't had a chance to air his suspicions. Quite by coincidence, that very morning, after his meeting with Cremers, he'd received a very welcome telephone call. Brian Kirkpatrick, who was in Rotterdam on business, wanted to meet up with him for a few hours in Amsterdam. Kirkpatrick was just the man to share his mis-givings with. Hadn't Brian vented his anger years ago about the ready availability of cocaine? What's more, he might be able to give him the lowdown on Burroughs Wellcome, in particular whether they were still supplying the British army. That was more important than ever now: securing a large order from Burroughs would allow him to ditch Biedermann without jeopardizing the company's profits.

The lanky Englishman stood out immediately among the dis-embarking passengers. Kirkpatrick had aged, Lucien thought, he was greyer at the temples, but still with that same upright posture and, as always, immaculately dressed. They initially made to shake one another's hands, but Lucien, in a surge of friendship, suddenly embraced Brian, who seemed moved by the reunion. As he hadn't any baggage, Lucien suggested they walk through the city centre and find a place for lunch along the way. He reckoned a stroll would make it easier to raise the subject of Biedermann and his illicit trade. As they passed the Victoria Hotel he inquired after Brian's family. It tuned out that in the past year two of his daughters had married respon-sible young men with good prospects, but sadly his wife was in poor health. When they reached the Dam, Lucien asked about the agricultural machinery Kirkpatrick was now selling, and as recompense for his feigned interest, particularly in the combines, Brian subjected him to an exhaustive description of all the technical details of the machinery.

Lucien was sure they'd find a restaurant behind the Royal Palace, along one of the canals. A meal and a decent bottle of wine would make it easier to talk. He wondered why he was so tentative in broaching the matter of Berlin. Perhaps because he didn't know why Kirkpatrick had left Burroughs Wellcome.

He couldn't rule out the possibility that Brian, like Dr. Van Rhijn, had become an outspoken opponent of cocaine. If so, the business with Biedermann would infuriate him, and he'd hardly be forthcoming with information about Burroughs Wellcome. Maybe it was better not to mention Berlin after all. On a bridge over the Herengracht they stepped aside for a woman pushing a pram and Brian asked, smiling: 'So... how are things with my nephew?'

Lucien raised his eyebrows. 'Forgive me, but I don't believe I know your nephew.'

Brian stopped dead in his tracks and looked at him, surprised. 'I'm talking about Robin... Robin Ryder?'

'Oh, of course I know Robin,' Lucien answered, confused, 'but I had no idea he was your nephew.'

'You had no idea...? That's odd, very odd indeed...'

'Robin's been staying at our house for some time now and – '

'I know that,' Brian interrupted. 'He didn't tell you he's the son of my eldest sister?'

'No.'

'So you didn't read the letter I'd sent with him?'

Lucien shook his head. They faced one another in silence.

'I explained in the letter that my nephew had become addicted to cocaine while serving on the front. It got him into a lot of trouble. I was at a loss what to do with him. There wasn't a doctor to be found who would help. He was determined to go abroad, so I gave him your address. I hoped that might know of a way for addicts to kick the habit.' He hesitated. 'I was at the end of my tether, you understand... I'm terribly sorry. Of course I should have called you first, but to be honest I hoped the letter would be enough. I assumed you'd turn him away if you weren't able to do anything for him. But I was relieved when he wrote back, telling me what a warm welcome you and Swanny had given him. He insisted I shouldn't contact him until he was completely cured.' He took an envelope out of his breast pocket, and held it in his hands for a few moments. 'But after this last letter I thought it was time we spoke in person.'

Lucien noticed the Dutch stamp, stuck on skewiff. 'Did Robin ask you to come?'

'He didn't, no... But it's a whole different situation now, what with the wedding and everything.'

'Wedding?'

Brian drew a sharp breath. 'He wrote that he was marrying your sister Swanny shortly.'

'Marrying Swanny...' Lucien repeated, vacantly.

Brian sighed. 'I take it that's not the case.'

'No, no... hardly. Swanny helped him get a job and looks on him as a friend, but marriage... no. Besides, she's engaged to someone else.'

Brian tucked the letter back into his pocket, stroked his chin nervously and asked, barely daring to look Lucien in the eye: 'Have you been giving him cocaine?'

'He promised to stop using it once he got a job, but he hasn't. I only give it to him because of Swanny. She hasn't the slightest inkling of his problem. Without his daily portion he becomes terribly depressed and I don't want her to worry.'

'So he's still addicted...' Kirkpatrick leant against the railing and closed his eyes briefly. 'Swanny must be a remarkably kind and caring woman. In his mixed-up state he's confused this with love, and sees marriage as a logical consequence. He's obviously latched onto this mad idea.' Brian shook his head.

'I've made a terrible mistake, I'm truly sorry. I don't know how to apologize. Thank God I didn't delay contacting you any longer.' He let go of the railing and watched pensively as a peat barge glided underneath them. 'It seems to me the best thing would be to take him back to London at once.'

Lucien laid his hand on Brian's shoulder. 'No need to take any rash decisions. Let's talk it over calmly.' He felt a sudden urge for a cup of coffee or, preferably, something stronger.

They found a window table in a café on the corner of the Herengracht. They stayed silent long after the waiter had brought them coffee and a cognac. Brian gazed out the window. He suddenly looked ten years older. It wasn't anger, Lucien thought, but shame, unfathomably deep shame. His nephew, his sister's son – a family member – had shamelessly abused the hospitality of an old business acquaintance and his big-hearted sister. Lucien recalled his first chance meeting with Robin. 'What beats me is why he didn't just ring the bell. The fool threw himself in front of my car! If I hadn't slammed on the brakes I could have killed him!'

Brian swallowed hard. 'It wouldn't be his first suicide attempt.'

Lucien was shocked. Imagine him trying it again once he realized this marriage notion was only a flight of fancy. Imagine him climbing up on a chair in his room and hanging himself from the lamp hook. Someone would find him... Imagine Swanny finding him dangling from the ceiling. It would be etched in her memory forever; she'd never get over a trauma like that. No, Robin had to be sent back to England as soon as possible.

'The tragic part, you know,' continued Brian, 'is that before the war he was such a fine chap. My favourite nephew. An excellent teacher, a true idealist bursting with plans to improve education and the lives of working-class children. I was so proud of him…'

Lucien suddenly remembered something, not long after Robin's arrival, that had reminded him of Brian. 'Do you remember showing me a bottle of *Forced March* once? Robin had that self same bottle with him when he first came here.'

'Doesn't surprise me. Those damned pills have only recently been taken off the market. They're the reason I had to leave Burroughs Wellcome. I was opposed to the over-the-counter sale of *Forced March*; it contains cocaine, after all. I felt it should only be made available to the army's medical services. They had experience with the stuff. It was thoroughly tested during the last Boer War; millions of tablets were sent to South Africa, so they knew how to dispense it. Up to the end of the war I convinced myself that the army was using it responsibly. But when I saw the state Robin came home in, I woke up to the harm it could do. He told me they were given it not just in tablets, but that it was probably also mixed with rum. The combination of alcohol and cocaine was extremely effective by all accounts. Those were his very words: extremely effective…'

'So you brought the matter up with Burroughs?'

'Yes, and they didn't take it kindly. It erupted into quite a row. *The Times* had already written that cocaine was as deadly for soldiers as bullets. I was so angry that I threatened to go to the press. That was madness, of course: you don't stand a chance against a pharmaceutical company and the Ministry of War. They were prepared to take me to court. They made no bones about it. How could I ever prove my case? That we supplied the army with cocaine was no secret, but the quantities and distribution were. They covered their tracks pretty thoroughly.

In official orders, the word "government" was replaced by a code, and the quantities and destinations were labelled "strictly confidential". So I resigned. For while I planned to take my story to a journalist. But in the end I let it go... I couldn't afford it; after all, I have a family to support. Imagine how despised I'd be if this all got out. In retrospect, it sheds a different light on the victory, on our soldiers and officers, and on the millions of deaths. No, I don't think the British public wants to know. People like you and me, those of us in the know, are better off keeping quiet, even if it does prick our conscience.'

'It's different for me, Brian,' said Lucien. 'I've got nothing to do with it. All I did was send medicine abroad; what they did with it there was their responsibility, not mine, and not the Nederlandsche Cocaïne Fabriek's. By the way, is Burroughs still supplying the British army?'

'No idea.' Brian fell silent and fiddled with his wedding ring. 'Where's Robin now?'

'At home. Or else he's just started his shift at the cinema.'

'I still want to take him home with me. Maybe we shouldn't wait. We'll still have to explain the situation to Swanny and give Robin time to pack his things. I'd like to catch the evening boat back if I can.'

Lucien nodded hesitantly. All of a sudden, he could feel himself getting cold feet. Send Robin back to England tonight? Explain the whole thing to Swanny? Tell her point-blank that Robin was a cocaine addict? Confess to giving him the stuff all along? She'd be livid. What was it that Tosca had said: *she'll never forgive you, not after what happened to your mother*. 'Look, Brian, now that I think about it, maybe it's not necessary to pack Robin off to London right away. My sister's so fond of him and I still very much want to help him...'

'Oh no, absolutely not,' Brian said adamantly. 'I saddled you two with a problem and I mean to solve it myself!'

'Listen, an acquaintance of mine, a respected chemist, is developing a drug to counteract the addiction. He still needs to do a few more experiments, but I'll be the first to get it.'

Kirkpatrick put down his coffee cup and buttoned up his jacket.

'Brian, trust me. I'll see to it that he gets off the stuff, no matter what it takes.'

The American film – he'd seen it umpteen times now – plodded towards its predictable ending, and as the leading man and his sweetheart walked off into the sunset the cinema began to empty. Robin turned off the projector and grabbed his coat. This evening there was no time to tidy up the cabin, as he was expected to do. He left the film reels and canisters scattered about, didn't bother to cover any of the equipment and even forgot to close the door behind him. He had to get home, for there was much to be done. Everything had to be ready before she got home, although he had no idea when that would be. He didn't even know where they'd gone: out to dinner, or a concert, or a lecture... When she'd returned home from the library that afternoon, she'd changed clothes and reappeared in the kitchen in her aqua dress, the one that looked so good on her and that she only wore for special occasions. Of course, she had a date with Marnix Christiaans. As a rule, she told him everything: where she was going, with whom, what time she'd be back... only not when Marnix took her out. She didn't want to talk about it. He spent many a sleepless night agonizing over why. Could Marnix be putting her under pressure? Making her keep to some commitment they'd made earlier? A commitment she now didn't know how to get out of it?

Arriving at the front door, Robin looked down the canal in both directions. Lucien's car wasn't parked anywhere, but that was to be expected, as he hardly ever came home before midnight. He carefully opened the door and heaved a sigh of relief: Swanny's coat wasn't there on the coat rack yet. The entire house lay waiting in silence. Quietly, so as not to disturb the calm, he took off his shoes and tiptoed through the hallway. He even managed to pass the salon without waking the cockatoo.

Up in his room, he went through his plan once again. Swanny mustn't suffer. Under no circumstances must she suffer. He'd anaesthetize her. He'd put her under temporarily, like for an operation. After all, it was no more than a minor surgical procedure. He took the sleeping powders he'd been saving up out of the desk drawer; that'd be more than enough. Just to make sure, he went to the wardrobe for the aspirins that Pleun had regularly bought for him. He shook the packets of powder onto the desktop and tipped the aspirin tablets out of their bottles. It dawned on him that she'd refuse to swallow a pill. Why hadn't he thought of that earlier? He'd never be able to force her to swallow them, no, he couldn't do that. The tablets would have to be ground up and mixed with the sleeping powders... When she got home he'd be waiting for her in the kitchen, and surprise her with a glass of wine. Now, he just needed something to grind up the tablets with, something heavy. He picked up the bronze lion and had just begun crushing the first tablet into a fine powder with it when he thought he heard the front door open. Impossible! Why would she come home so early, tonight of all nights? So much earlier than expected... He had to hurry up and then dash downstairs.

Lucien stood in the bedroom doorway, watching Robin hunched over the desk with the bronze lion in his hand. 'What are you doing?' he asked suspiciously.

Robin looked up, startled. 'Can't you knock first?' he growled. 'Leave me alone, will you?' And with that he brought the heavy base of the lion down onto a couple of pills.

But Lucien was already in the room. The floor was littered with empty aspirin bottles and sleeping powder packets. Most of the tablets had been pulverized; the rest lay beside them in a little pile on the desk. What on Earth was Robin up to? The answer dawned on Lucien slowly, and at the same time struck him like a bolt of lightning. The lunatic was going to take them all at once. 'Idiot!' he shouted, 'what's got into your head?'

Robin froze.

Lucien was at a loss what to do. Robin must have realized he was living in a fantasy world and decided to end it all. 'I know exactly what you're planning, you coward! How could you do this to Swanny?' He angrily swept the powder from the desk. 'I've just been talking to your uncle! I know every- thing. All your lies, all those stories of being off the cocaine and all the time coming to me for more. And I hope you realize that marrying Swanny is just another of your fantasies, you fool!' Before he'd finished his tirade, Robin slammed the lion down onto the desk, shoved him aside and stormed out of the room.

Lucien found him at the kitchen table with his head in his hands. 'I wanted to help you!' he shouted. He was still boiling with anger. 'But now it's clear you're nothing but a pathetic wretch who wants to take the coward's way out. You're going straight back to England. I've arranged it with your uncle Brian.' Robin looked at him with his one good eye. The pupil was dilated – how had he got his hands on the cocaine? Had he gone rifling through Lucien's drawers? He had difficulty controlling the urge to beat the living daylights out of Robin. 'I'm warning you, don't breathe a word of this crazy suicide attempt to Swanny. Selfish bastard! Do you really want to hurt her, after all she's done for you?'

Robin burst into tears and his head slumped forward onto his arms.

Lucien shook him violently. He wasn't going to let him off the hook so easily this time. He'd throw him out on his ear, no questions asked.

'What are you doing? Stop it!' shouted Swanny. She still had her coat on. 'Why's he crying? What have you done to upset him? Did you say something horrible?'

Before Lucien could explain, Robin sat up and spoke calmly to her, running his finger over the bridge his nose: 'It's all my fault… You mustn't blame Lucien. It's all my own doing.' Swanny came into the kitchen and stood across the table from him. 'I wanted to tell you earlier,' he continued, 'but I didn't dare, I was afraid you'd throw me out.' The tears started flowing again, but Swanny made no move to comfort him. She waited. The story came out in dribs and drabs: how they'd coerced him into taking cocaine in the trenches, to help overcome his mortal fear. How objecting almost landed him in front of the firing squad for insubordination and cowardice. That he was hooked, no matter how hard they'd tried to shake it, he and his pal Charlie, who'd also got addicted at the front. 'We tried and tried…' he sighed dejectedly.

'So how did the other soldiers manage?' snarled Lucien.

'Shut up, Lucien,' said Swanny. 'Let him finish.'

'It only got worse after I was wounded. Life was unbearable.

The depression was appalling. I know it's just weakness, Swanny, and believe me, I'm prepared to do anything and everything to stop, even if it means going through hell. Please understand, it's not my fault. How could I know it was such poison, and so horribly addictive too…'

Lucien listened in amazement. How had Robin managed to come up with such a convincing story so quickly?… Swanny slowly removed her coat and hung it over the armrest. 'Tell me honestly: where do you get your cocaine?' Robin let his head sink back down onto his outstretched arms. Swanny turned slowly towards Lucien. 'We hardly need to ask, do we? There's only one person here who has access to it.' There was a menacing, explosive edge to her voice, confirmed by the tears welling up in her eyes. Tears of bitter disappointment. 'And all this behind my back.'

'I was at my wit's end,' Robin mumbled, almost inaudibly. 'I was about to end it all…' Now *that* had its desired effect, thought Lucien. Swanny's hands went to her mouth. She walked around the table and caressed the back of Robin's head. 'See what happens with that filthy stuff!' she barked over her shoulder.

'Maybe he should try kicking the habit himself,' Lucien shot back. It only earned him a reproachful look.

She pensively stroked Robin's hair. 'We could ask Lisette for help; she works at a pharmacist's and might be able to suggest something.'

'That won't be necessary,' said Lucien quickly. 'A friend of mine in Berlin's working on a medicine to curb addiction. He's a recognized expert.' Robin raised his head and fumbled with his mask, which had shifted out of place.

'When can he get it?' asked Swanny.

'I'm not entirely sure, it won't be long, a matter of weeks…'

'Well, that's not much good to us now, is it? We'll have to come up with something ourselves in the meantime. I think the best thing is to lower his intake bit by bit, like with any addiction.' Robin gaped at her. She sat down next to him and took his hand in hers. 'We'll take it ever so slowly; I know something like this doesn't happen overnight.' Touched, Robin laid his hand on hers. 'We'll beat this together,' she said. After a brief thoughtful moment, she said in a commanding tone: 'Lucien, get the cocaine and give it to me. I'll see to it that Robin gets his daily portion.'

'You want me to…?' he asked incredulously.

'You're the one who deals in that rubbish. You're partly to blame for this mess and you'll help Robin solve his problem.' Her lips were drawn into an angry, thin line.

'Just go and get it from the doctor!'

'Oh no, there's no need for him to know anything about it. This is our business and nobody else's!'

'Besides,' protested Lucien, 'there's a new law making it illegal to supply private individuals.'

'You just explain to your director that it's for a war veteran who got addicted through no fault of his own. I'm sure he'll make an exception.'

'It's against the law, Swan…' Suddenly he became aware of another problem. 'If I do it, it's on condition that you swear not to say anything to Marnix. His job means he can't turn a blind eye to things like this.'

Swanny nodded impatiently. Her thoughts were already elsewhere, and she turned back to Robin. 'I'll ring your boss and tell him you're ill, that you'll need to rest over the coming week. I'll take some time off myself so that we can be together all day; that way at least I'll be around if you get into difficulties.' Robin sniffed.

Damn it all, thought Lucien, he's got it all mapped out pretty neatly. With his beloved Swanny all day, and her dispensing the cocaine to boot. And old muggins here just has to keep the supply coming! Swanny was busy making coffee, and although he'd have liked nothing more than to retreat to his room, he didn't want to leave without letting Robin know he was onto him. 'Did you know he's Brian Kirkpatrick's nephew?' he asked. 'Remember Kirkpatrick, from London?'

'Of course I remember. Really? Your uncle?' she exclaimed, turning to Robin. 'Why, what a coincidence… I thought your uncle was such an interesting and sympathetic man.'

Robin perked up. 'Uncle Brian is wonderful. I'm so grateful to him. He's always been so supportive.'

'Let's drop him a line right away to let him know you're finally going to try and kick your cocaine habit,' suggested Lucien.

'Don't be ridiculous!' Swanny exclaimed, giving him her menacing look once more. 'The dear man doesn't need to know a thing. We'll take care of this ourselves!'

26

Jan Palacky

In the days that followed, Swanny took charge of the situation, throwing herself body and soul into her duties as counsellor and nurse. Tosca and Pleun, her confidants and deputies, stood by her so that Robin was never without support or assistance for even a single moment. On Tosca's advice, he was allowed – under strict supervision – one gram every morning and evening, lowering the dosage by a small fraction each day. At first, Pleun scoffed at this course of action. 'Cut 'im off! Lock 'im up for a bit, that's what I'd do!' The women not only discussed Robin's condition at length but also consulted a stack of library books describing in great detail the effects of narcotics abuse. Cocaine, the books confirmed, was an extremely dangerous toxin; addiction could be countered by replacing it with alcohol, morphine or opium. Swanny objected vehemently, particularly to the opium. 'We'll stick to our original plan!' she declared. Which entailed a gradual reduction in Robin's dosage, healthy meals, afternoon naps on a chaise longue in the garden and, above all, providing the patient with affection and understanding.

Lucien observed the proceedings with resignation. His opinion was no longer asked for. He'd been reduced to the dispenser of a dangerous drug, a role that did not show him in his best light. Swanny treated him like a convicted criminal, whose only hope of redemption lay in his willingness to do as he was told, with no backchat. Every morning he produced two grams from his private stockpile and obediently handed the packets to Swanny. She took them without a word of thanks. Understandably, Robin gave him a wide berth, as Lucien was just itching to take him aside and tell him a few home truths. Even Pleun strode past him with scornful disdain. Only Tosca, who of course was not entirely without blame herself, tried to offset her companions' behaviour with the odd light-hearted remark. 'The only danger now is that we'll spoil him to death,' she once said with a laugh. Robin's room was spruced up, as well: too sombre, the women decided, so in came some cheerful floral curtains, a light blue bedspread and plenty of soft pillows. A week later even the wallpaper was changed. Robin improved visibly. He revelled in all this loving attention and appeared to submit to what Swanny called the 'detoxification programme'.

Still, Lucien remained suspicious. Once, he had the impression that his room had been searched. But Pleun exclaimed, insulted: 'You can excuse me forgetting something now and again, can't you, what with all the goings-on in this house!' Apparently she'd forgotten to close the top drawer of his commode after cleaning.

Ever since Swanny had informed the cinema manager not to expect him in the foreseeable future, Robin spent all his time at home. One evening Lucien overheard Swanny say to Tosca that an injured face didn't mean his brain had been damaged too. 'That job at the cinema was a silly mistake; anyone would be bored out of his mind changing film reels day-in, day-out.

He's a teacher, don't forget.' So they raided the library again, this time for books and essays on Dutch education. From then on, Robin and Swanny spent entire days poring over books, translating them word for word into English. They discussed the latest pedagogical theories, modern teaching methods and the best way to apply them to the English school system. They were constantly in conversation, in the salon, garden and kitchen.

Lucien sat with them now and then and tried to join in. But although Swanny was prepared to listen to his opinions, he still felt excluded. Especially in the evenings, when the furniture was pushed aside for King Oliver's Creole Jazz Band. This was one thing Robin hadn't lied or even bluffed about: he really was a first-rate dancer, and a fine teacher as well. He and Swanny made an impressive couple; no question, they'd walk away with first prize at any dance contest. Slumped on the sofa, Lucien watched with a pang of jealousy as they swung round the room with perfect timing. He didn't dare to ask her to dance himself.

His only consolation was that Marnix suffered the same fate. Marnix tried time and again to make dates with her, all in vain. Heeding Lucien's warning that his job would make him an awkward house guest, Swanny kept Marnix at arm's length. Tosca was the go-between. Her aversion could finally be put to good use. Lucien eavesdropped one time when she was putting a spoke in his wheel over the telephone. With a patronizing tone befitting a hospital matron, she inquired coolly if he still hadn't grasped that their English guest was suffering from a case of intoxication *intensivum* and required round-the-clock nursing, and that Swanny would ring him as soon as she was able. Too bad he couldn't hear Marnix's reply.

As if the physical exercise and discussions on educational reform weren't enough to promote the patient's emotional well-being, the women decided it was time Robin found an outlet for his creativity, as well. The best place for this was the salon, due to the excellent light. Out of solidarity – but mostly for the fun of it – Tosca and Swanny joined in this exercise in self-expression. A canvas sheet was laid on the floor, and three easels were purchased, as well as the requisite palettes, canvasses, brushes and boxes of paint. They spent whole days at their easels, painting still-lifes, floral arrangements, fruit bowls and the tree-lined canal. To Swanny's delight, Robin even began a portrait of Karel. Lucien regularly looked in on them them, muttering occasionally about his own artistic talents being stifled at school, but no one paid him any attention. Tosca did suggest that they were desperately in need of a nude model, but Swanny was too immersed in her work – a vase with three sagging roses – to laugh. Even as a target of mockery, he was redundant. After a week they decided to call in professional help, and the neighbour, Casper Bartholomeus, was summoned. In return for five bottles of Château Dauzac Margaux from old Tilanus's wine cellar, he offered to teach them the basics of painting.

Lucien had to admit that his mind wasn't entirely on his work. The upheaval at home and Swanny's chilly, reproachful behaviour so distracted him that he could hardly muster any interest in orders or deliveries, let alone in promoting the firm or scouting for new markets, although Cremers regularly badgered him for progress reports.

Whole days passed at his desk with barely a thought entering his head. Until one Saturday afternoon, at nearly five o'clock, Trudie came to tell him he was wanted on the telephone, a call from Berlin. His followed his gut instinct, instructing her to tell Biedermann he wasn't in. 'No, it's someone else,' she answered. He took the call and to his chagrin got Peter Wammeier on the line, who at once assumed a chummy attitude – hardly the same person who'd called him an asshole when they last met. After feigning interest in Lucien's health and the weather in Amsterdam, Wammeier got down to business, placing an order somewhat larger than his last one.

Lucien decided not to enquire why Biedermann hadn't rung himself. Wammeier, he could well imagine, was more than just a delivery boy who peddled cocaine in nightclubs; he must be Biedermann's right-hand man. Who knows since when. After exchanging all the relevant information, including repeat instructions to make the invoice out to W.A. Kalbfleisch & Sohn, Wammeier said he presumed Lucien would again accompany the delivery, so that payment could be made in the usual way. He urged Lucien to make haste.

Lucien promised to do everything he could, before asking after Pola. Wammeier replied that she was fine and no, there was no film role as yet, but she was thriving as a photo model. Lucien could tell he was lying through his teeth; Pola simply couldn't be thriving.

'Ask her to drop me a line, will you?' he asked.

'Drop you a line?'

'As in write a letter.'

'Of course, I'll tell her, but she doesn't strike me as the letter-writing type.'

Lucien rang off abruptly and stayed at his desk until all the office staff had gone home. Only the factory was still in operation. He wrote up the order and gave it to the first rinsing boy he came across, with the instructions to take it to the lab chief.

Then he drove straight to the Weesperzijde. His supply of cocaine for Swanny was running low, and he was determined to grill Thomas properly this time. They hadn't spoken since his return from Berlin; the lodger kept intercepting him, managing to fend Lucien off by handing over his packet at the door. Whenever he asked for Olyrook, the answer was invariably that Thomas was not in and Jan was abroad. He wouldn't let himself be fobbed off this time, if necessary he'd give the bloke a swift kick and force his way in. He had to know what Thomas was up to and especially why he was collaborating with that unscrupulous bastard in Berlin.

When Lucien arrived, Jan Palacky threw the door wide open for him. Lucien heaved a sigh of relief. 'Thank God you're back! Where have you been hiding out?'

'Oh, here and there…' Jan shrugged his shoulders and led him to the sitting room.

'Where's your lodger?'

'Threw him out. I can take care of the housework myself. By the way, Thomas is resting in bed and doesn't want to be disturbed.'

Lucien sank into a chair. The room looked desolate, not just because the closed curtains banished every molecule of sunlight, but it was becoming dreadfully bare, too. Jan sat down on the footstool next to the empty armchair. 'We have to keep selling things,' he said, gesturing around him. 'Acute financial difficulties, you see…'

'Damned unlucky,' said Lucien. 'Business slack?'

'What do you think? With declining production, and now that Biedermann prefers buying from you…'

'Surely you have other clients?'

'Hardly any, to be honest. He was our main customer.' Jan

had pulled his knees up and wrapped his arms around his legs as though he were cold. His slippered feet were perched on the edge of the footstool. 'I've done my best to scare up new customers, but I can't get a foot in the door. I don't have the connections and Thomas is far too ill. We've got some staff, but no chemist, and what do I know about the production process? I'm afraid we'll have to close down soon.'

'Close down? I don't get it. Why did Thomas let me take over Biedermann's orders? He even encouraged me!'

Palacky rested his chin on his knees and sighed. 'How can I possibly explain…'

'Just try. I've got a few things to tell you myself.'

Jan pointed to a bottle. 'Vodka, brought it with me from Prague. It's all I can offer you. Help yourself; I've had enough.'

Lucien got up and set the bottle and a glass down next to him.

'Well, all the trouble started during the war. Thomas longed to have his own laboratory. As a chemist he'd had enough of cocaine; he thought it was obsolete and worthless, and wanted to develop new medicines. But a lab and all the trappings, these things cost money…' He closed his eyes and ran his left hand over the fingers of his right. All his gold rings were gone too. 'Do you remember that big order you delivered to Thielt?'

'Absolutely, there was a real stink about it. The Germans claimed that a hundred kilos—' The blood pounded in his neck and he stared at Jan, immobilized.

'They were right. It was my idea to skim off those hundred kilos. A little bit out of each bottle, I thought no one would notice. How stupid of me! I so wanted Thomas to be able to begin on his own. But we reckoned without German military intelligence. They conducted a thorough investigation and put the finger on Thomas. How, I don't know, but Biedermann got wind of it. Contact with their spies, I suppose... He bided his time until he could use the information. His moment came at the end of the war. The day the armistice was signed he arranged a meeting with the three of us, remember? I didn't twig at the time, but it was clear to Thomas that we were finished. At first Biedermann wanted Thomas with him in Berlin, but when he refused, he came up with a new plan. We were to start a new factory here in Holland. He knew full well that the profits from those hundred kilos wouldn't be enough, so he financed most of it himself. That made him the major shareholder – the owner, in fact, although of course not on paper... in exchange he demanded all the cocaine.'

Lucien knocked back his vodka and refilled his glass. He vividly recalled the meeting in the coffee house that day. Biedermann, of course, must have planned to move in for the kill that afternoon. 'He also tried to drag you into his scheme, remember?' asked Jan. 'He wanted you as his salesman in Berlin. But he dropped the idea. The defection of two important employees from your firm might raise questions. The management could have started sniffing around.'

'So who did he get as a salesman?'

'Me.'

'You? Did you want that?'

'Of course not. But I was an easy target. Biedermann knew I'd deserted from the German army. He could still arrange for me to be put up in front of a firing squad, or so he said. He was bluffing, of course, but I wasn't about to take any chances.'

'I thought that Peter Wammeier...'

'Wammeier, that swine! You want to know how Biedermann got his hands on the money for our factory and his own laboratory? In the chaos after the war he and Wammeier stole the entire stock of cocaine left over in army depots. I only found this out recently, but I confronted them with it a few weeks ago, when I decided to quit. I couldn't take it anymore. Biedermann was forcing me to sell the stuff in clubs and bars in Berlin, Prague and other cities. It's a filthy world, full of violent criminal types, I'm just not cut out for it. The cocaine was adulterated with anything to hand: soda, kitchen salt and God knows what else... But those junkies aren't stupid; I was threatened and beat up. I had to stop, I just don't have the physique for that kind of work. Thomas was really scared. He was afraid Biedermann would harm me. He's lost so much because of that cocaine. He didn't want to lose me as well. We had a terrible row. I stormed out and when I came back he finally accepted it.'

Lucien felt dizzy and sick to his stomach. He picked up the vodka bottle and looked at the label. Good God, 105 degrees proof spirit, no wonder. Somewhere in his woozy brain a question hovered, something to do with what Jan had just told him.

'But what Thomas felt most guilty about was that we'd got you involved,' Jan said quietly. That was just what Lucien was wondering: why had Thomas handed over his business to him? 'Biedermann's demand kept growing,' Jan explained. 'Thomas's health worsened, the factory wasn't functioning properly, quality declined, we were up to our neck in problems and Biedermann got more and more aggressive. When we heard about your troubles with Pola, it looked like a way of appeasing him. We talked to Biedermann, and of course he came over at once. This was a golden opportunity for him: he could place large orders with a legal, reputable firm. Making the

Nederlandsche Cocaïne Fabriek an accomplice in his illegal trade only strengthened his position. He figured that with a film role and the fictitious new medicine for Pola as bait, you'd be bound to co-operate. And you did.'

Lucien's head was spinning. So they'd duped him. And what's more, he'd fallen for it! His boundless stupidity had led him to throw Pola to the sharks, rather than save her. 'I've got to go and get Pola back, she can't stay there any longer!'

'Get Pola back?'

'Yes, damn it! I handed her over to that bastard, that criminal…'

Jan rubbed his forehead. 'Let it go, Lucien. Pola's never going to recover from her addiction. Don't you understand? It's just a question of time before she takes an overdose.'

Lucien sat in his car, his forehead resting on the steering wheel. He reached for the bottle of vodka he'd swiped, in the face of Jan's loud protests, and swigged it dry. He'd been sitting in front of the Cremers' house for three-quarters of an hour, maybe more. The lights were on. Saturday evening – they had guests, and he knew full well who. His headlights were illuminating the rear bumper of Peereboom's Cadillac.

Then he made his move. The moment had arrived. He stubbed out his cigarette against the dashboard and fumbled for the door handle. The chilly night air hit him in the face, making him stagger. Lurching but determined, he made his way up the path. In his thoughts he was already in discussion with the directors. They had to understand that this was an extremely serious business that could well have repercussions for the future of the firm. Yes, well, so what if it was late! He didn't give a damn! Couldn't they see what was going on? That it was just a question of time before Pola… Yes, gentlemen, his Pola! A question of time, an overdose… He leant his full weight against the door, rang long and hard on the bell, and stumbled inside when it was opened. Mrs. Cremers, aided by Bep Peereboom, caught him as he reeled into the hall. 'I do beg your pardon…' he slurred, 'just lotht my balance a bit. A quethtion of…'

The women looked at him with delight. 'Oh Lucien,' Bep exclaimed, 'this can't possibly be a coincidence! It must be fate! We were just talking about you… Come in, come in!'

He tried to tear himself loose from his hazy stream of thoughts. Huh? Why were they just talking about him? Did they know about Biedermann? About Pola? Did they know everything already?

They dragged him in like a trophy animal. Cremers and Peereboom were sitting at the dining-room table, their waist-coats unbuttoned, chatting over after-dinner coffee and liqueur. Taken aback, they greeted him. 'Isn't this a marvellous coincidence!' blurted Bep. 'Speak of the devil… Do sit down, Lucien.' Before he could get a word in edgeways, he was forced to sit between the two women. 'I'm so looking forward to it,' Bep drawled, 'and Jannie's coming too.' Jannie, who in God's name is Jannie, Lucien wondered. 'We had to promise you'd take our wives with you to Berlin soon,' said Cremers with a grimace. 'A case of unadulterated blackmail,' said Peereboom, who appeared to be in somewhat better humour.

'That's what I mean by this crazy coincidence!' screeched Mrs. Peereboom. She was obviously tipsy herself. She reached for a bottle of red wine and poured Lucien a glass.

'I hear there are notorious cabarets and clubs where they play Negro music,' said Mrs. Cremers eagerly.

Lucien drained his glass and took a deep breath. 'Indeed, indeed, Mrs. Cremers,' he answered, trying desperately to remember exactly what he was doing here.

'When do we go?' Bep shouted in his ear. She came dangerously close. There was something green stuck between her teeth.

'Soon, I imagine,' said Cremers. 'I understand that another large order has come in.' Jesus, that lab chief had a big mouth. 'Excellent, excellent – I told you Biedermann was a good client.'

'I don't believe Biedermann is such a good client...' said Lucien, making a superhuman effort to keep his wits about him. It was now or never. 'I've come to warn you...it's urgent... I now know that he, Biedermann...'

'Not now, Hirschland,' said Peereboom. 'Have some more wine.'

'Oh, please, no business talk now!' Bep pulled her chair even closer. 'We want to know what women wear in those clubs.'

Peereboom continued to glower at him.

'Couldn't we go into the other room to talk?' Lucien implored.

'That won't be necessary,' said Peereboom. He nodded encouragingly at his wife.

'Exactly! I want to talk about Berlin. Is it really such an exhilarating city?' she asked breathlessly, already entirely in the mood.

'Bep, you have no idea,' answered Lucien. A tornado suddenly whirled through his head. What had that idiot said: 'Won't be necessary'... Pola's fate not an urgent matter? He leant over to Mrs. Peereboom and put on his most sultry voice. 'Y'know, Beppie, the clubs I'm going to take you to have the most terrific jazz bands, you can dance, drink and snort cocaine to your heart's content. Yes ma'am, cocaine, and as much as you want, too… black market cocaine, straight from the Nederlandsche Cocaïne Fabriek!'

A strange hush fell over the room. Lucien felt as though he were floating above the ground in a hot air balloon. Cremers and Peereboom looked like angry little men who had just received a bit of bad news. Suddenly he saw them both get up. Peereboom, the taller of the two, came up behind him and hissed in his ear to follow him at once. The ladies gaped at each other in shock.

'What are you going on about!' snarled Cremers once they had corralled him into the adjoining room. 'Talking such rubbish, and in front of our wives!'

Lucien felt himself come back to Earth. 'I beg your pardon, but I see it as my duty to report that the orders from Berlin are intended for the black market. The factory has unwittingly got involved in illegal transactions and I believe it must be stopped at once. Cocaine is ruining people's lives, not only actresses, but many others as well…'

'Oh, shut up, Hirschland!' Peereboom interrupted. 'You're drunk and blathering the most fantastic nonsense. There's nothing remotely illegal about our deliveries to Berlin. Kalb-fleisch & Sohn is a perfectly reputable firm.'

Lucien burst out laughing. 'It doesn't even exist!… it's a figment of Biedermann's imagination.'

'That's none of our business,' said Cremers. 'Herr Bieder-mann is forced to do business under extremely difficult cir-cumstances. This is clearly his way of dealing with it. I don't know if you've noticed, with your drinking problem, that sales have plummeted over the last few weeks, but I'll tell you right now we don't have the luxury of picking and choosing our clients.'

'All right, if you two won't listen, then I'll go to Marnix Christiaans! He knows exactly what I'm talking about!'

'That won't be necessary,' said Peereboom calmly. 'I'll inform Mr. Christiaans myself, and if anything looks suspicious, I'm sure he'll take appropriate measures.'

'Brilliant idea! And if he doesn't want to stir things up,' said Lucien conspiratorially, 'then we'll take care of it another way. There are plenty of journalists who'd be only too pleased to write a piece about black market cocaine!'

'Go and sleep it off, Hirschland. You're bound to see things differently tomorrow.' Cremers steered him into the hallway in the direction of the front door. Bep and Jannie stood there wide-eyed.

'My only concern is for the firm's good name!' he shouted over his shoulder in his defence.

'As it is ours!' said Cremers as he propelled him out of the door.

Lucien walked down the path in a daze and closed the gate behind him. As he attempted to drop the metal latch carefully onto the hook, he looked back toward the house. The lace curtains in the sitting room slid aside, almost imperceptibly.

27

Swanny's bridegroom

'I can't let Marnix down again,' said Swanny. 'He's been so patient already.' Robin understood. The opera tickets had been purchased a long time ago and Marnix had made it clear he wasn't going to be fobbed off again this time. 'And the rotten part is, I can't get out of my engagement either,' Tosca giggled. 'Without me, the whole evening will be a flop.' She had been rash enough to share her armchair expertise about addiction with a passing acquaintance, and now she'd been invited to give a lecture to the Temperance Association in Bloemendaal. And today of all days, Pleun had had to travel to Schagen for a niece's wedding. They were troubled by this unfortunate clash of commitments, as they didn't want to leave Robin alone. But he protested that they needn't worry, they mustn't be put out on his account, he'd have no problem surviving for an evening on his own. Still, Swanny had her doubts. 'You could come with us to the opera,' she suggested impulsively. No, no, Robin resolutely scotched that idea. He wasn't up to large crowds yet. Swanny was inclined to agree. But before she could suggest asking Lucien to keep him company, he came up with his own proposal: he could ask the neighbour if he'd spend the evening with him. After all, Casper had already invited him several times to come and see his studio and paint together. Of course the salon was a fine spot, but the studio of a professional painter, with all those wonderful portraits, that was something else entirely... Tosca clapped her hands together: brilliant idea! Problem solved! Swanny also agreed, relieved. Why hadn't she thought of it herself?

Marnix waited downstairs while Swanny dashed up to Robin's room to say goodbye. She confessed to being slightly jealous: Casper had never invited her to come over and paint with him. She wished him an inspiring evening.

As soon as the front door closed behind them, Robin went downstairs and grabbed his paintbox and palette. He sank onto his folding stool for a moment. He had to get his emotions under control before he went over to Casper's. The thought of Swanny spending another entire evening in Marnix's company was hard to take. But he had to accept it, there was no other choice: he had to give her the chance to finally break off the engagement. That kind of thing was always painful. Of course she'd have preferred him to be at her side for support. Now she'd have to break the news on her own. Still, it was better that way.

His heart was bursting with joy. The past few days had been perfect. Never before had he experienced such intense love, never had he had such intense conversations. It seemed his ideals chimed in completely with hers. They'd even made plans to write down their ideas; in the calm of her father's study he'd work on a book on new educational methods. Swanny had promised to find a publisher; her father, after all, had been an academic publisher. Oh, they'd made plans, plans for the future... and these had come from mutual respect, shared interests and a passion for the good, the positive in mankind...

Their feelings for each other had grown and deepened. The only reason they had not yet expressed their love outright was because she was still engaged to someone else.

He looked at the canvas in front of him: the beginnings of a portrait of Swanny. Even though it was still no more than a rough sketch, he could already make out her soft grey eyes. She looked at him, smiling, so full of faith in him, in their plans, in their future… He felt a sudden pang of shame, a feeling that had been nagging at him and that he could no longer suppress. He hadn't been entirely honest with her. He'd explain it to her in due course. My darling, please, I beg you, do try to understand: your 'detoxification programme' was too ambitious, these things take time, it can't go as quickly as you'd like. Certainly not now, with all the excitement of our love, our expectations, our goals and most of all the strain of you breaking off your engagement. Don't be disappointed. I need some extra help getting through this. But I can stop whenever I want, only not yet, just give me a little more time…

He was obliged to use subterfuge. He took a small amount from Lucien's room every day, taking the utmost care, for Lucien was sure to betray him if he found out. He was only too keen to prove to Swanny that her lover was a lost cause. So the bastard made it as tempting as possible, intentionally leaving the cocaine practically in the open, so he could easily find it. Only there wasn't as much as before, rarely more than just a few wrappers. Lucien was taunting him, punishing him – because there was no way these meagre pickings could satisfy his needs.

Casper took him straight through to the glass-enclosed veranda at the back of his house. It served as the studio where he painted the city's bigwigs – his main clientele. Five half-finished portraits sat perched on their easels.

Robin wasn't interested in them, though. He looked expectantly at Casper. 'And…?'

'Have you got money?' asked Casper. Robin pulled a couple of crumpled banknotes and some small change out of his pocket. He hadn't dared filch more from Tosca's handbag over the past few days. That, along with what he'd just managed to steal from the household change pot in the kitchen, would have to do. Casper counted it out cent for cent. 'It's really all I could get my hands on,' Robin said defensively. The money Swanny had given him now and again towards his operation had gone into previous transactions with Casper, during their lessons, while the women were engrossed in their still-lifes.

'I do have to buy it myself, you know,' Casper said grumpily. 'Don't think I get it for free.' Robin's mouth was getting dry; his tongue rasped along the roof of his mouth. Apparently satisfied with the amount, Casper pulled a vial from his pocket. Sprinkling some white powder on a marble slab, he handed Robin a small silver spoon. Robin knelt at the table, as though in prayer. Thank God, finally… His chest swelled as he sniffed it up. He leant back, his eye closed. A slight hiss preceded the impact. Projectiles shrieked and howled in all directions. The explosion hit him in the neck. Bull's-eye! He thrust himself upright, wobbled and regained his balance. The bitter tang burned the back of his throat. 'Brilliant stuff… Where'd you get it?'

'None of your damn business.' Casper rubbed the last bit of powder over his gums with his fingers.

Robin grinned. He knew Casper couldn't hold his tongue, and was bound to tell him.

Casper snorted noisily. 'Well, if you must know… as an artist I do more than paint portraits. I happen to be quite good at forging prescriptions.'

Robin recalled, laughing, how he and Harry and a few mates had sometimes broken into pharmacies.

But Casper wasn't listening. He'd leapt up. 'You know what? We're going to paint each other!' Saying this, he shoved two easels back to back, propped blank canvases on them and studied the arrangement, his eyes half-closed, as if he was preparing for a duel. He pulled over a small table with paint and brushes, and Robin opened his paintbox. Then Casper put a record on the gramophone and turned the horn towards them. '*Jazz! New Orleans! Let's go!*'

They took up their positions at the easels, palettes resting on their forearms and brushes in hand. Leaning out to one side from behind their canvases, they looked at each other briefly before disappearing back behind their respective easels. The first brushstrokes were slapped on with violent swipes. Aside from his sketches of Swanny, Robin had never attempted a portrait before. But how hard could it be? Piece of cake, really… Casper's gangly body danced behind the easel, his thin brush whooshing through the air like a conductor's baton. He dove at the canvas with a thick brush, the paint hitting it with a splat. 'Wow! This is the real thing!' He tossed the canvas aside and grabbed a fresh one. 'Let yourself go, let yourself totally go!' he shouted above a screeching trumpet. Robin attacked his canvas with broad, intense strokes. He'd plumped for dark colours: Casper had black hair, black eyes, he was dark, gloomy… He mixed brown with black on his palette and smeared the thick oil paint in circles onto the canvas. He couldn't quite produce a face… or could he? Suddenly Casper was standing next to him.

'Brilliant! You see? I told you you could do it! You're a natural!'
He tugged violently at Robin's sleeve. 'Come on, I've got some
more.' Robin dropped his brush and palette, and once more
they crouched over the marble slab. They knelt there in silence
until Robin let out a shout and keeled over in ecstacy onto
his side. What a fantastic evening! He could finally show the
world what he was capable of. At last he felt totally liberated.

They raced back to their easels and set to work. 'See the
blank canvas as a battleground,' bellowed Casper, 'the emptiness is your enemy, assault it, charge at it! The brush is
your machine gun, victory is in your hands!' Robin attacked
the canvas with furious, feverish gestures. He worked like a
madman, squeezing out random paint tubes onto his palette
or even directly onto the canvas. Meanwhile, Casper leapt
about, his sleek black hair flopping wildly over his crazed eyes,
with their dilated pupils. 'Enough of that kids' stuff! Long live
experimentation! Scandal is what we're after! Scandalous art!
An explosion, an eruption, burning colours, flames! Set the
canvas alight!' Robin was carried away by Casper's ecstatic outburst. He no longer needed to look at his subject; the features
were etched in his brain. He took a step back and looked at a
large dark splotch that could at any moment become Casper.

'Bugger, I should have had a model come and sit for us,'
Casper exclaimed. 'They'll spread their legs for an artist anytime!
Nothing like an eager little whore swooning at the feet of the
master!' He stole a glance at Robin's easel. 'And what about
you? Is that Tosca really a lesbian, or have you had her yet?'

Robin stared blankly at the black splotch. 'No, where did
you get that idea?…' He lowered his palette and brush. 'For
me there's only one woman: Swanny… there's no more beautiful, kinder, better person.'

'But she's engaged to that arsehole Marnix.'

'Not for long. She's breaking off the engagement this evening. Tomorrow I'll ask her to marry me.'

'Does she really want that?' Casper asked incredulously.

'In her heart, deep in her heart, she does…'

Casper started hooting derisively. 'You really are an idiot, aren't you! Do you really think that someone like Swanny Hirschland would want to marry you? Do you think she'll dump a catch like Marnix Christiaans? He's got a fantastic job, class, status, money… And a good looker as well, tall, well-built… an arrogant face, I'll grant you that, but a decent face at least!'

'Swanny's not interested in all that,' Robin stammered. 'She looks further, she looks deep into your soul…'

'Listen chum, let me tell you something about women: all they're after is money and looks. You don't seriously think she'll marry you with that mangled mug of yours?'

It was like he'd been hit by a sledgehammer. He'd forgotten about his face; in these last few blissful days he hadn't given it a second thought. For a while it had simply been erased from his consciousness… A mangled mug. She'd never want to marry a cripple with a hideous face…

Casper let out an exaggerated sigh: 'For Christ's sake, man, just look at yourself. A penniless junkie with a gruesome gob! A monster, a circus freak!' He grabbed his canvas from the easel and held it up triumphantly. 'Look! I've outdone myself this time! Your portrait!' Robin recognized himself at once in the horrendous orgy of purple, blood red and grey. An icy chill ran down his spine.

Casper roared with laughter. 'I'll call it "Swanny's bridegroom".'

The jagged, disordered sounds of the music, that vile jazz,

tore into his brain. Robin lunged forward, seized the canvas and put his foot through it. Casper blenched. Then the hideous monster clenched his fist and took an almighty swing. Casper went down like a sack of potatoes, falling onto the palettes and tubes of paint. Robin grabbed the easel and threw it on top of him. One swift kick put an end to the jazz.

He stormed out of the house and ran along the pavement until he reached the cellar door. Panting, he leant against the tiled wall. Here was where it had all started: he'd lain in wait for two full days, biding his time, until the afternoon he saw the Mercedes coming down the road. Without hesitating he threw himself in front of the car. If he survived, Hirschland would surely give him cocaine, purely out of a guilty conscience…

He shivered. The cold night air cut through his flimsy painter's smock. No matter, he had other things on his mind. Finally he saw Marnix's Bentley pull up in front of the house. Swanny got out and went inside alone. He waited. He'd wait as long as he needed to…

About an hour later he emerged from his hiding place, chilled to the bone, and taking out his latchkey softly opened the front door. The house was completely dark except for a small lamp in the hallway. Swanny's coat hung on the hook. She'd gone to bed; he mustn't wake her. The door to the salon was ajar. He reached out to close it, but just as his hand touched the handle the parrot started squawking loudly.

'Shut your trap! You'll wake her!' Robin hissed, approaching the bird's perch. 'I'll wring your neck, I'll bash your head in…' As if Karel realized the danger he was in, his whistling subsided into a gentle warble, then he went quiet altogether.

Back in the half-darkened hall, that dreadful explosion of purple, blood-red and grey surged up before his eyes once more. It was him, his image in the mirror. He needed more cocaine, if only to banish Casper's diabolical laughter. He crept up the stairs and listened. Cautiously he entered Lucien's room. The curtains were open and the streetlamps shone through the window onto the unslept-in bed. He hurried to the dresser and opened the drawer. He felt around but found nothing. With a jerk he pulled the drawer out, spilling its contents onto the floor. On his knees he fumbled through the objects, but there was nothing: no packets, no bottles, nothing… That bastard had hidden it, he'd found out and hidden it in order to torment him, to force him to search for it. I'll find it, just you wait. First the wardrobe. He yanked out the suits, the shirts, kimonos, shoes, nothing, nothing… He made his way through the room. A vase fell to the floor. Shards of glass on the rug. The Chinese platters hit the floor one by one. Where was it, damn it all, where was it? If only Charlie was here. Charlie would find it alright, Lucien couldn't pull the wool over Charlie's eyes! Nobody could fool Charlie… He uprooted the potted palms, knocked over tables and upset lamps, ripping off their shades. He was close, very close, he could almost smell the cocaine. The bed! He pushed off the mattress, jerked the mosquito net from its hooks and tipped over a nightstand, spilling a full ashtray onto the floor. The door of the nightstand fell open, and he spotted a wrapper. He could have shouted for joy. Shhh, quiet now, absolutely quiet… He unfolded the wrapper, but his hands were trembling so much that the contents spilled onto the floor. Before the powder could settle into the woollen hairs of the carpet, he bent over and licked it up. His tongue lapped furiously at the pile and when the impact hit he sagged back against the bed, his mouth full of dust. He lay there until his plan took full shape in his head. Getting it all in the right order, that was the key thing, the right order, without hesitating... Never hesitate, keep moving, don't stand still... Having regained control of his body, he went downstairs to the kitchen. Pleun's tidiness meant he didn't need to search. Everything was always in its place. The knife was precisely where he'd expected it to be.

As he walked along the passage he rehearsed his explanation to Swanny that it would be over quickly, that it was just a minor operation, that afterwards they'd be the same forever, true soulmates... But he reached her bedroom before he could finish. When saw her sleeping figure he was momentarily overcome with emotion. The way she lay there in her white night-dress, the covers tossed back to her hips, so sweet, so innocent, one arm outstretched, the other folded over her chest. He bent over her. Hurry up, get it over with quickly and then they could get on with their lives.

Suddenly she stirred, and looked at him with her beautiful grey eyes. He smiled. 'Don't be afraid,' he said, and a wave of warmth, of love, gushed through his veins. 'It won't take a moment...it'll bring us closer together.' A door closed some-where. He had to hurry. The enemy was in hot pursuit; he'd crept up on him unawares. He heard Swanny's voice. She was talking to him. Quiet, quiet... But he was distracted, there were sounds in the house, they were coming from upstairs. It was the enemy looking for cover. A counterattack was being planned. He had no time to lose. 'Robin, put that knife away,' said Swanny. Her voice was perfectly calm. Her voice, her sweet voice – he so wanted to listen to her. But not now. First the plan. 'Come on, Robin, let's have a calm chat. You've taken a lot of cocaine, I can see it on you.'

'Don't you see, we've got to be alike,' he pleaded, 'otherwise you won't want me.'

'Robin, that's not necessary, I love you just the way you are.'

He hesitated. What was that she'd just said? He wanted to say something too, he had to say something, but what? He heard a sound behind him; it didn't matter, nothing mattered anymore. He could have wept with delight – she loved him! There was a deafening yell and a heavy weight fell against his back. He pitched forward and landed on top of Swanny. Someone tugged him back up. Then he felt a terrific blow to his jaw. He spun around and sank to his knees.

Lucien roared with impotent fury. He kicked Robin in the ribs, and continued lashing out until he was certain he was unconscious. Then he quickly turned to Swanny and switched on the bedside lamp. He hardly dared look. Her face was covered in blood; it trickled down her cheek into her hair, leaving a dark stain on the pillow. She stared at him wide-eyed. The wind was knocked out of him and his body felt paralyzed.

'Send for the doctor,' she whispered.

He got up mechanically and ran to his father's study. He dialled the number and stammered into the receiver until he heard Van Rhijn say he was coming. Then he rang Tosca. 'Swanny's been hurt! Something terrible's happened!' He rushed back into the bedroom, terrified that Robin might have come to. But he was still rolled up in a ball on the floor. 'The doctor's on his way, and so is Tosca,' he whispered to Swanny. 'Don't move a muscle.' Behind him, Robin groaned. Once again Lucien saw red, and laid into Robin, battering him from head to toe. He only came to his senses when he heard Swanny's voice.

'Stop it! Stop it!' she screamed.

Of course he mustn't beat him senseless, not in front of her. He grabbed Robin by his soiled jacket, dragged him out of the room, opened the broom closet and shoved him inside. He slammed the door shut and locked it. Just in time. The doorbell rang and he let Van Rhijn in. 'Swanny…' He gasped, pointing. The doctor strode towards the bedroom, but Lucien couldn't bring himself to follow him. His mind went blank until he was roused by the sound of a racing car engine outside, which was abruptly cut off. Tosca shoved him aside and ran into Swanny's room. He stood in the doorway and watched as Tosca washed her hands in the washbasin before helping the doctor tend to the wound. Van Rhijn gave terse instructions and Tosca ran back and forth between the kitchen and bedroom. Lucien leant against the wall outside the door until his legs gave way and he slumped to the floor. Robin had tried to murder Swanny. Why? He was at a complete loss.

When Van Rhijn was finished and had buckled up his bag, he came into the hallway and stood over Lucien. 'What's up with you?' he asked coolly. 'Drunk as a lord, as usual, I see.' Lucien had no ready answer. 'Well, pull yourself together, your sister needs your help. She's got a deep wound in her cheek. I've stitched it. She'll need constant rest if it's going to heal properly.'

All he could think to ask was: 'Will there be a scar?'

'I don't know yet.' Van Rhijn hesitated. 'What happened?'

'She was attacked by a lunatic,' Lucien stammered. 'I've got him locked up in the cupboard, but I don't know what to do now.'

'That's none of my business,' replied the doctor. 'A matter for the police, I'd say.' He curtly wished Lucien a good night and took his leave.

Tosca sat on the edge of the bed. They were talking in subdued tones. As Lucien came towards them he noticed the mask and spectacles lying on the floor. Without hesitation he trod on them with his full weight, until he heard the glass splinter and the metal crunch under his shoe. He swept the shards together, went to the cupboard and opened the door. Robin was still curled in the same position, his one good eye staring blankly. Lucien threw the crumbled remnants of the mask in his face. He raised his fist, but before he could strike he felt a tug on his jacket.

'That's enough,' hissed Tosca. 'You'll kill him if you're not careful.'

'He's got it coming to him! I'm calling the police.'

Tosca blocked his path to the telephone. 'I wouldn't if I were you,' she said firmly. 'You still don't get it, do you?' She gave him a moment. But the vodka was still coursing too furiously through his veins for him to formulate a coherent answer. Tosca shook her head. 'Trust me, we'd best keep the police out of it. He's more coked up than Swanny's ever seen him. He must have snorted more than we give him, God knows where he got it. But I'll find out.' She grasped him by the shoulder. 'Go on, say something to her...'

He shuffled after her like a scolded child. Swanny's face had been bandaged and she lay on a fresh pillowcase. She looked at him gravely. He still couldn't utter a single word, it was as though his throat had been sewn shut. 'I'm very tired,' she said softly. 'You two see to Robin.' Tosca nodded and they left the room. Out in the hall they stood in front of the open cupboard. 'We'll let him sleep it off there,' said Tosca, tossing a blanket over him. She brought out a straight-backed chair from the study, left the cupboard door ajar and sat down in front of it, where she could also keep an eye on Swanny's bedroom. 'You can try and sleep off the booze,' she said, folding her arms, 'and I'll keep watch here.'

Lucien went upstairs. He switched on the light and his gaze fell once again on the ruins of his room: the toppled palms, the broken Chinese porcelain, the smashed lamps and teak cabinets; the mattress half on the floor and the mosquito net dangling from the ceiling like a dead butterfly. Everything that was dear to him had been reduced to rubble. He sat on the floor against the edge of the bed. He didn't care anymore, nothing mattered now… On the Persian rug, near his feet, lay an open paper wrapper, and next to it a smear of white powder.

28

Apologies

Racing through the barren landscape at top speed, he passed badly damaged farms, derelict pastures and columns of soldiers with deathly pale faces. He rode the Harley straight through barbed wire barricades, ignoring warning shots from military policemen. A low-flying Halberstadt whizzed overhead. He had only one fear: the ropes holding the medicine chest on the luggage rack mustn't work loose. He was in a terrible hurry. There wasn't a moment to lose. Out of the blue, a churning mass of soldiers appeared just in front of him. They were packed densely together, a wall of soldiers, but he wasn't to be deterred and rode straight into the crowd. Bodies flew left and right, sailing through the air and crumpling to the ground. Orders were shouted. Trains, with an interminable row of carriages, thundered close by; the approaching cannon roared in the distance. Above the din wafted the agonized screams of the wounded. A hellish cry for help. He stopped the motorcycle in front of an endless sea of stretchers. He grabbed the chest. The mummy lay inside. Just where the mouth should have been, the bandages slowly parted, releasing a piercing shriek. He started. He recognized the sound. He recognized the small mouth and the pink lips. Suddenly the orders and shouting ceased, the trains came to a halt, the crowd held its breath and even the artillery fell silent. A medic leant over the wounded mummy and called out to the crowd: 'Lucien Hirschland is too late! His sister is dead.'

Every morning he awoke with a start, the harsh accusation ringing in his head, and every time he wondered if the nightmare had been sparked by alarmed shouting in the house. He lay perfectly still and listened. But there was only silence, a profound silence, as though the house had been abandoned years ago and he alone remained. He looked at the clock: 5 a.m. But he got up anyway, put on his dressing gown and went downstairs. He lingered outside Swanny's bedroom, waiting at the doorway until he heard a sign of life: a yawn, or the rustling of the sheets as she turned over. Then he went back upstairs, passing his own room and proceeding to the attic. There, too, he stood listening. As long as no sound came from the room, he secretly hoped that Robin had died of internal bleeding. Then the punishment would be complete. But when he heard him walking about and sobbing, he was relieved all the same. Once he tried to enter, but Tosca and Pleun had locked Robin in. As far as he knew, he hadn't left the room in four days.

Then he went back to his room and stood behind the door, waiting. At eight o'clock he heard Pleun's heavy footsteps pass along the corridor and up to the attic, bringing Robin his food. Half an hour later she set a tray with Lucien's breakfast on the floor of the corridor. For he too kept his door locked, but from the inside. Around eleven, Tosca's pumps clicked over the floorboards, and sometimes it was an hour before he heard her pass by again. Once in a while, he felt the urge to fling open his door and confront her, but he never did. He couldn't say why, but he didn't dare start a conversation. The morning after the disaster, he saw Tosca bring in a suitcase from her car. She had installed herself in his father's room, apparently determined not to leave Swanny unattended. Judging from the hours she spent in Robin's room she was acting as a go-between. It alarmed him, but intrigued him as well. What could they possibly have to discuss?

He spent the rest of the day in bed. Pleun was barred from entering; it didn't need tidying. He'd attend to the devastation in his room alone, no-one else. He did his best to reattach the torn *klamboe* and sorted the shards of broken vases and plates, collecting them into small piles like archaeological artefacts. A fresh tube of glue lay next to them. He even tried repairing the broken lampshades with strung-together shoelaces and straightening the palms in their decorative pots. But the earth just crumbled in his hands and the damaged leaves sagged like they'd been ravaged by a tropical storm. No matter what he did to erase the evidence of what preceded the disaster, nothing helped. He gave up, slumped back against the pillows and stared into space. He was incapable of action. All he did was listen. There might be a knock at his door at any minute, or someone might call his name from the hallway. Surely they'd ask for his help. But the days passed, and his help was not asked for.

The doorbell rang often. Sometimes it was opened, sometimes not. And the phone rang constantly. He'd rung Trudie four days ago to say he was ill and didn't want to be disturbed. But that had cut no ice at the office, apparently, for it seemed every time the telephone rang, it was the factory; Cremers or Peereboom reminding him that there was an important meeting at the Koloniale Bank, or there were orders needing to be processed, and asking him when he planned to come in and apologise for his outburst? He had, after all, made a complete ass of himself. Flinging around all kinds of wild accusations in a drunken stupor, and in front of their wives to boot! What kind of accusations, God only knew, for his drunkenness and the awful events that followed had erased the details from his memory. But he knew that he'd behaved very badly indeed, and instead of offering his sincere apologies he called in sick. He couldn't act much guiltier than that.

On the morning of the fifth day he couldn't take it any longer. Just before eleven o'clock, after the phone rang for the third time, he decided to stop behaving like a coward and come out of hiding. He marched downstairs, but Tosca beat him to it. With her back to him she informed the caller that the patient still wasn't well, rang off and turned to go, but he grabbed her by the arm and demanded: 'Why don't you come and get me if I've got a telephone call?'

'It wasn't for you. That was Marnix. He rings all the time, and has come round three times already. I have to keep getting rid of him. He's got nothing to do with all this.'

'Hasn't he? He is Swanny's fiancé, after all.'

'Oh, so you think it's a good idea for him to visit, do you?' she asked sarcastically. 'What do you think he'll do then? He'll go straight to the police, that's what. Not to turn you in, oh no, not you with your respectable job. But Robin – he's just a junkie. That'd be something, wouldn't it, to see Robin marched off in handcuffs? That'll do wonders for Swanny's recovery!'

'Why in God's name would he want to turn me in?'

Tosca shut her eyes for a moment. 'You still don't get what happened, do you?' She sighed. 'The knife only went in when you jumped on Robin's back. Swanny nearly had him calmed down.'

*   *   *

His bedside visit to Swanny didn't last long. Lucien sat on a chair next to her and looked at her oval-shaped face, the grey eyes ringed with thick eyelashes, as dark as her beautiful hair, the elegant line of her chin and the small but remarkably sturdy nose, where all her willpower seemed to be stored. There lay his sweet, beautiful little sister. A long wound ran vertically down her left cheek. It was red and swollen, and was held together with stitches.

He stammered his apologies. It all sounded insipid and trivial, as though he was taking the blame for some reckless but insignificant act, for some unfortunate misunderstanding. He searched her eyes for forgiveness, but she avoided his gaze. She said quietly that she knew he was only trying to protect her. After a brief silence she asked him if he finally understood who was the victim and who the culprit… He nodded, hesitated, and then shook his head. 'Go up and talk to Robin,' she said, finally looking him in the eye. 'He's the one you need to apologise to, not me.'

29

A newspaper item

The newspaper lay unread next to his plate. Pleun reached over his shoulder, searching for a place on the overloaded breakfast table for the basket of toast, and poured tea while Robin served fried eggs with bacon, sausages and baked beans. 'A full English breakfast,' said Swanny cheerfully. This was their first meal together in a long time. The table, decked with the Christmas linen, was almost too small. Swanny, Robin, Tosca, Pleun and himself – sitting elbow to elbow, their knees and feet touching under the table. Mere words couldn't have forged a closer bond between them than this silent physical contact. Only Karel let out jealous screams from the salon. They laughed.

A quarter of an hour earlier, though, the mood had been much more sombre. Tosca had received a postcard from Casper, announcing his arrival in the Dordogne after an arduous train journey. The village was even sleepier than he'd expected, the locals were hostile to foreigners who did not speak their dialect and the wine was disappointing. But despite the drawbacks he would, as agreed – it was no secret that Tosca had paid him a visit with her hockey stick – devote himself for a year to the French landscape. They all nodded in agreement. Then Swanny, holding up a letter, asked for their attention. A few days earlier she had decided to write to Marnix with an honest explanation of the events of the last few months. She felt he deserved as much. His answer had arrived with the morning post.

She pulled the letter from the envelope. Marnix expressed great difficulty in accepting that she had kept so much from him. The only conclusion he could draw was that they had grown apart. Swanny hesitated, skipped a bit that she apparently considered too personal, and continued that he, to his great regret, saw no other choice than to break off the engagement. He signed the letter with 'respectfully yours'. She lay the letter on the sideboard and said that maybe it was all for the best. No one reacted. Tosca was the first to break the silence, with a chirpy: 'Well, no great loss, you two were a terrible match.'

Lucien agreed. Of course it suited him that from now on his relationship with Marnix would be purely professional. Certainly now that he was about to return to work this afternoon, after two weeks' sick leave. Trudie had informed him that there was to be an important meeting with Mr. Cremers and Mr. Peereboom. Mr. Christiaans would also be present. She hoped he had recuperated sufficiently, as it was an urgent matter. It must have something to do with Biedermann's illegitimate dealings, he thought. Peereboom had already briefed Marnix on the situation and it had been discussed with the minister. He presumed that Biedermann's most recent order would be cancelled, if it hadn't been already. He had pondered over the past few days how in future the factory might distance itself from illegal trade, and he planned to present his suggestions – he'd even jotted them down on a piece of paper – at the meeting. Most of all it would prove his continued devotion to the firm, but he also hoped that Cremers and Peereboom would by now have forgiven his outburst. In fact, he wasn't in any doubt on that score. No one had been particularly sober that evening. And while he really had chosen an inopportune moment, the urgency of his news more than justified it.

Robin helped Pleun clear the table. He'd been released from confinement the previous afternoon and gave the impression, even without his mask, of being completely at ease, as if a wave of calmness had washed over him. Swanny also made no effort to conceal the bright red scar on her cheek. She and Tosca were busy making plans, for there was much to do after breakfast. Kirkpatrick, now referred to as 'Uncle Brian', had written to say how delighted he was with his nephew's recovery, thanks to their joint efforts. He'd been in contact with Robin's parents and they too looked forward to finally welcoming their son home.

Lucien, for his part, had telephoned Dr. Harold Gillies at Queen Mary's Hospital several times. The practical and financial arrangements had been confirmed in writing. But the doctor insisted on hearing from Robin himself. So he composed a letter, beginning with his apologies for the theft and ending with an allusion to a fishing otter. According to Swanny, the letter read like a poem. The others attached a brief statement, signed by them all, affirming their faith in Robin and giving a guarantee that he was completely rehabilitated. Gillies responded straightaway that he looked forward to receiving Mr. Ryder in his surgery as soon as possible.

Robin was anxious to pack his things, but Lucien objected: wouldn't it be boring for him to travel on his own? If he remembered rightly, he still owed Swanny and Tosca a trip to London. Swanny shook her head and said she wouldn't go without him. Of course, Lucien would prefer to join them too. But he'd have to wait until after the meeting at the factory before he made a decision. If all went according to plan, he could combine business with pleasure, and visit a few new clients in London.

The table was cleared, and Lucien leaned back and loosened his belt: those English breakfasts were filling affairs. He opened the newspaper. He'd incorporated his earlier list of interesting armed conflicts into the proposal he'd present at the meeting. But since he hadn't followed the news these past few weeks, he wanted to check on any new developments. The front page offered nothing much of interest: a miners' strike in England, a bombing on Wall Street in New York and the execution of a young Irish student for political activities. On page 2 were reports of a ribbon-cutting ceremony by Her Majesty and the arrest of a notorious bank robber in Haarlem. Then his eyes lighted on a small news item at the bottom, reporting the death the previous day of a 28-year-old Czech man in an Amsterdam park, from an overdose of cocaine.

Lucien read the article three times over. Someone asked him something, but it didn't register. He got up and mumbled apologetically that he had an urgent appointment.

He waited on the front step, grasping the doorframe on either side. The curtains on the ground floor were drawn, as usual. Jan might appear at the door at any moment, he was sure of it. But nobody came. He crouched down and pressed open the flap of the letter slot with his thumbs, praying for a sign of life: a slamming door, footsteps, voices… He rang the bell a second time, and then a third. He hung his head dejectedly. He was just about to leave when the door suddenly opened. It was Thomas. Ashen and silent, he turned and shuffled back inside, leaning on his walking stick.

The sitting room was almost pitch-dark. Thomas sank into his armchair. Lucien switched on a lamp, pulled up a randomly placed chair and sat facing him. He didn't have to ask Thomas for confirmation of what he feared: misery and grief were written all over his face. 'What happened?' he asked.

Thomas looked at him. 'I just don't know.'

'Please, Thomas, surely you know something?'

'Jan left the house two days ago. He had an appointment. I didn't ask who with; he's been going his own way these past few weeks. Perhaps he wanted to spare me. But he didn't return, which was strange because he always came home to see to things. He'd cook and help me into bed. Usually he read aloud, Chekhov or Gogol.' There was a long silence; Thomas seemed overwhelmed by weariness. His head rested against the back of the chair. 'Yesterday morning two policemen came by. They'd found him dead in Sarphati Park. There were cocaine wrappers next to his body and he'd been injected.'

Lucien scowled. 'But Jan didn't use cocaine, did he?'

'No. I warned him against it from the start.'

'Why now, then?'

Thomas slowly shook his head. 'I asked the police if I could test the residue from the wrappers; maybe I can figure out where it came from and if it had been cut... They said they'd ask, but I haven't heard anything yet.'

'So you think someone may have forcibly injected him?'

'What does it matter?'

'Everything. It obviously has something to do with Berlin, with Biedermann. Who else would want to harm Jan?'

Thomas shifted, laying his gnarled hands lightly on his stomach. He shivered. 'Pass me that blanket, will you?' Lucien reached for a filthy blanket from a kitchen chair that stood haphazardly in the middle of the bare room, and spread it carefully over Thomas's legs.

'Shall I get a cushion for your head?' Lucien asked.

'No, sit down, there's something I have to tell you,' said Thomas, 'something about Franz Biedermann.' He closed his eyes, as though he required darkness to sift through his memory. 'You know, that man was once my hero, my role model. A leading chemist who'd been part of an important discovery. Back in the '80s – he'd have been in his early 20s – Biedermann started working as an assistant to Theodor Aschenbrandt, a German army surgeon who was experimenting with cocaine. Sigmund Freud had already discovered that the drug had remarkable therapeutic properties. But Aschenbrandt wanted to test it on Bavarian soldiers. They were given it surreptitiously, dissolved in water, just before long night marches. The effects proved interesting, you could even say extraordinary: cocaine suppressed the appetite, fatigue and tension, and most of all it made them feel invincible. In short, an ideal performance-boosting drug. It turned soldiers into fighting machines. That was a marvellous discovery, of course, when you consider how much is at stake in a war, and how much money's invested in new weaponry. But even the most modern weapons need soldiers to operate them, and exhausted or frightened soldiers are no good at all. I'd read about the experiments in a German pharmaceutical journal. As far as I know, Aschenbrandt only published one article about it, but I was fascinated. I was already employed at the firm and Cremers and I were keen to get our product to a wider market. Aschenbrandt and Biedermann had fallen out by that time, a row about patents I believe, and Biedermann had left to continue his research at the Merck laboratory. I made contact and paid him a visit. He was prepared to share the results of his experiments with me, because he only had Peruvian coca leaves at his disposal and was very interested in our product – Java coca, which he regarded as superior quality…'

'So you already knew Biedermann before the war?'

'Yes, I even introduced him to Cremers, who also appreciated the new opportunities it offered us. When the war broke out it was like a dream come true. Thanks to the Netherlands' neutrality we could supply all the warring parties, but preferably through established pharmaceutical companies. We had to be circumspect, of course: spies were everywhere and we didn't want trouble with anyone, least of all the Allies. That's why Biedermann had to be treated as a regular customer, especially after we found out he was actually a German officer. So we needed to find a sales rep who, being unaware of the background, could sell the product with no inhibitions. When I bumped into you, fresh back from the East Indies, I knew right away you were just our man.'

'And what made me "just your man"?'

'Well, my friend, if you don't mind my saying so, you're a good salesman and a hard worker, but you're naïve and you don't know a thing about politics. Your interests are motorcycles, fast cars and fancy women. Like I said: just our man.'

'Thanks a lot… So if I understand you correctly, you knew all along that cocaine was being used as more than just an anaesthetic?'

'To be honest, I couldn't care less what they used it for. I didn't even care who won the damned war. The factory was doing a roaring trade and I was excited that our product was mainly responsible.' His hand crept towards an empty glass on the table next to him.

Lucien got up and went over to the only cabinet that had survived the inventory sale. There was still a dribble of cognac left in one of the bottles. He poured and watched as Thomas sipped it.

'You know...' he went on, 'I only started questioning it all after the armistice. Maybe because Biedermann had me so completely under his thumb and was pressuring me to increase production. I couldn't understand why such huge quantities were needed after the war. For whom? Six months ago it finally dawned on me what Biedermann was up to. First Jan explained it – or should I say screamed it in my face – and later Biedermann confirmed it himself. The massive cocaine use in the trenches had created an entire army of addicts. Thousands, hundreds of thousands... If you think about how much our firm alone supplied, you can work it out. Everywhere – in England, France, Belgium, Austria, the United States, even in Australia and Canada – they're having huge problems with addicted veterans. And more often than not they're forced to turn to the black market. Biedermann, though, is mostly interested in German veterans. In Berlin alone, at least 20,000 have ended up in hospital already, though the actual number of addicts is of course much higher. He's got his eye on the former German and Austro-Hungarian territories, too, especially Czechoslovakia, which is why he needed Jan. Prague newspapers estimate there are some 10,000 severe cases there. Prague's one of Biedermann's main targets, being the doorway to Eastern Europe, an even larger market.'

'He'll have made a packet from it.' Lucien recalled the bare flat in Berlin and wondered where all the money had gone.

'It's not about the money. About six months ago, just before I got too ill to travel, he suddenly insisted I to come to Berlin.

I realized there it wasn't the profits, but the power cocaine gives him. German cities are overrun with addicted veterans, they're traumatized, jobless, on the scrapheap. He wants to gain control over these men. Don't forget, Biedermann was, and still is, a high-ranking German officer, one of the many who saw the Treaty of Versailles as a slap in the face. He's in contact with a wide range of influential figures – pillars of the German Empire, major landowners, powerful industrialists – who all despise the Weimar Republic and who long for the resurgence of a mighty Germany. They're organizing themselves into a radical nationalist party. He took me to a rally once where one of their leaders, some Austrian loudmouth, took the floor. Biedermann was keen to win me over to their cause, because he was still hoping to lure me to Berlin to work for him. He was quite open about recruiting the addicted veterans. He says they want to offer them a new future by forming a military wing of their party. He doesn't fool me. Offer them a future, my arse. They just want their own private thugs, and cocaine's just the job: nothing makes a man so dependent and compliant – and, of course, as aggressive as a pit bull.'

'So you think he's using the company's consignments for this kind of operation?' asked Lucien incredulously.

'Naturally, what else?' Thomas stared solemnly into his empty glass, but shook his head when Lucien made a move to get up. 'Can you imagine how sick it makes me that I got Jan mixed up in this filthy business? And you as well…'

'I've been meaning to ask you: why did you put me back in touch with Biedermann?'

'Out of fear. I was worried that Jan's big mouth would get him into trouble. So as not to dig ourselves in even deeper I suggested to Biedermann that he do business with you. I didn't think

Cremers would be so stupid as to go along with illegal dealings, not with that new law… This time your naïveté would be your saving grace; Biedermann couldn't accuse you of anything.'

'Well, apparently Cremers really is that stupid.' Lucien paused thoughtfully. 'There's a meeting at the factory in twenty minutes. The best thing I can do is present this new information to the directors – without mentioning your name, of course – so that steps can be taken.'

'Oh, my dear Lucien,' said Thomas despondently, 'please try to understand. They're not going to take any action. They knew full well what they were doing during the war. You really think Cremers or Peereboom give a damn what Biedermann's up to? They know cocaine is on its way out, that there are better alternatives on the market that the factory isn't producing yet. Their only priority is turning a profit.'

'Nonsense! And anyway, illegal trade is illegal trade. Marnix Christiaans will be there too. It's a personal crusade of his. He's already investigating Biedermann's activities and he'll be grateful for this extra information.'

'Marnix…' Thomas sighed. 'Have you ever wondered why, after all those conferences in The Hague going over and over the problems created by opium and cocaine – and there have been quite a few since 1901 – the Netherlands has never once ratified a treaty? Now that the war's over and they want to suck up to the Allies, they went along with all the other countries and signed at Versailles. Your friend Marnix was the Dutch delegate at the earlier conferences. He made all sorts of promises but never once put pen to paper. Our trading interests, be it opium or cocaine, had to be protected. And he saw to that. I believe he sabotaged every concrete measure against misuse.'

'Maybe, but things are different now the treaty's been signed.'

'We'll see.' Thomas hauled himself upright and reached for his cane. 'It's time for you to go, my boy. Mustn't be late for your meeting, we don't want it costing you your job… I'll see you out.'

Thomas kept him at the door. There was clearly something else he had to get off his chest. 'Because of this illness I've had a lot of time to think things over. Only now I see the role the pharmaceutical labs played in the war. Chemists and weapons dealers: strange bedfellows, eh? They need each other now. Right across the civilized world they're developing new drugs for new wars. How else will soldiers be able to face the horrors of modern weaponry? And I contributed to it…' He leant heavily on his cane and held up his gnarled right hand. 'Not only Jan's death is my punishment, but the rheumatism as well. I'll never work again with these hands.'

Lucien drove across the bridge to the south side of the Weespervaart. The Nederlandsche Cocaïne Fabriek lay before him in the peaceful afternoon sun. He took his foot off the accelerator and let the Mercedes coast, his arms draped over the steering wheel. He needed a moment to recover. How was it possible? Thomas had lost everything: his work, his health and especially Jan. He sounded so bitter and remorseful. And those accusations… could they really be true? Or was Thomas, at rock bottom and plagued by guilt, passing the buck to Marnix and the firm? Did he really believe that Cremers and Peereboom or a high-ranking civil servant like Marnix knew about the misuse of cocaine during the war? It was surely no more than wild speculation. In any case, he'd bring it up at the meeting, if only so that no one could accuse him of being naïve. If, as he expected, the allegations were unfounded, he could always shrug them off as a misunderstanding. As far as Biedermann was concerned, though, his illegal dealings had to be dealt with straightaway. The trade was not only against the law, but extremely dangerous as well; Jan's death proved that. He looked at his watch: the meeting started in three minutes.

He gunned the engine, drove into the courtyard and parked next to Marnix's Bentley. He grabbed his attaché case and slammed the door. Just then, Albert Ketting approached him from a side entrance leading to the storerooms, but stopped when Lucien urgently pointed to his watch. 'No time now, Albert,' he called out, 'but I'll speak to you after the meeting.' He strode quickly to Cremers' office.

When he entered, he saw Mamix leaning nonchalantly against the desk. 'Aren't Cremers and Peereboom here yet?' asked Lucien, relieved not to be the last.

'No, they've got obligations elsewhere. We can take care of this ourselves.'

'What, just the two of us?' Lucien asked, dumbfounded. 'But what I have to discuss concerns the factory and management.' Damn it, it had *everything* to do with management. But on the other hand, a one-on-one conversation with Marnix meant he could discuss the black market situation in detail. He pulled the newspaper out of his pocket. 'Did you know that the friend... er, a colleague of Thomas Olyrook has died of a cocaine overdose?'

'Yes, I read about that.'

'That's exactly what I want to talk to you about, regarding Biedermann's activities... You see, Jan Palacky worked for him.' Marnix nodded, but his face betrayed no emotion whatsoever, neither surprise nor consternation. 'It looks like Biedermann had something to do with his death, wouldn't you say?'

'Ach… I wouldn't go jumping to conclusions. Palacky was a small-time criminal who worked as a drug dealer. It's not the kind of crowd where you'd want to rub someone up the wrong way. He should've known better.'

'Damn it all, how dare you! Jan Palacky was no criminal.' Lucien took it as a personal affront; after all, he considered Jan a good friend. 'Palacky was forced into working for Biedermann.' He hoped Marnix wouldn't ask why. Jan's desertion, the missing hundred kilos, that would complicate things unnecessarily. 'There's plenty of evidence that Biedermann's involved in the black market.'

'Cremers told me about your misgivings,' said Marnix, 'and I've looked into it. According to our information, Biedermann works with the firm Kalbfleisch & Sohn. The invoices were made out to that firm's name on your request. I've checked them out: completely above board.'

'Above board! I've already told Cremers the firm doesn't exist. Biedermann invented it.'

'Strange that you recently wrote out an order in their name, then…'.

'That's beside the point,' snapped Lucien. 'The bottom line is that Biedermann is secretly supplying coke addicts. I saw it with my own eyes.'

'So I hear. Not very wise of you to visit a club in Berlin known as a hangout for riff-raff working the black market. I'm also quite shocked that you'd allow Pola Pauwlova to keep company with that sort. Though it's down to you that she's an addict in the first place.'

Lucien's head was spinning.

'You don't understand. Pola was offered a role by the UFA and that's a club where film people congregate.' He mustn't let himself get distracted by Marnix's sudden mention of Pola. 'What's more, it's not just about the black market anymore,' he added. 'Rumours are circulating that the factory's deliveries during the war were misused to enhance soldiers' performance on the battlefield. Cocaine wasn't just used as an anaesthetic, but as an instrument of war!'

Marnix shook his head wearily. 'Lucien, please... Nothing but rumours. You know as well as I do that the firm did not supply any goods that could be directly used to wage war. Mr. Peereboom recently reminded me how passionately you defended that point to the English ambassador.' Marnix pulled a cigar from his breast pocket and clipped off the tip. He pointed to a chair. 'I don't know who you've been talking to, but for God's sake just sit down and get a hold of yourself. You're starting to talk gibberish.'

'It's none of your damn business who I've been talking to,' Lucien snapped. 'I'm telling you Biedermann is supplying addicts, specifically many thousands of severely addicted veterans in Berlin.'

'We have no evidence of that whatsoever.'

'Jan Palacky did!'

'Jan Palacky is dead. But since you keep insisting: it appears that certain East-European underworld players are producing and selling adulterated cocaine in Berlin. Discussions are currently underway at a European level on how we can tackle these criminals.'

'Criminals! Don't make me laugh! You don't just whip up a batch of cocaine. Processing coca leaves requires expertise and expensive equipment. Don't you see? The black market cocaine was made in legal factories. The real criminals are the pharmaceutical companies, us, the Nederlandsche Cocaïne Fabriek.'

Marnix took a pull on his cigar. 'Lucien, what's come over you? Why are you turning on the firm like this? Is it because you supplied that English soldier with cocaine?'

'No! It's not that at all. Ryder got hooked in the trenches. Maybe I felt morally obliged to help him with a problem that was partly our doing.'

Marnix regarded him coolly. 'Don't think you can hide behind moral motivations. You know damn well that it's highly illegal to supply private individuals. I warned you about it once but you continued doing so.'

Lucien felt himself being slowly pushed into a corner. 'You haven't got a shred of evidence.'

'Haven't I? You and your sister provided cocaine to that Englishmen in your home without the consent of your family doctor, Van Rhijn. Dear openhearted and honest Swanny told me that herself in a letter. So it's all there, in black and white. We do wonder, of course, how you got that cocaine. We're not talking about trifling amounts, either. After all, not only the Englishman but Pola Pauwlova and in all likelihood your neighbour, Casper Bartholomeus, had to be supplied their daily ration. Did you steal it from the factory, or did you buy it somewhere illegally yourself? That would make you, not Biedermann, the black marketeer. Oh, and before I forget... We've had complaints from various chemists in Haarlem about forged prescriptions. I do hope you lot had nothing to do with that. It'd be a dreadful shame if the sales representative of the Nederlandsche Cocaïne Fabriek were mixed up in criminal activities, wouldn't you agree? Then we'd be forced to contact the appropriate authorities.'

Lucien gasped for breath. He knew he'd been checkmated. But even if he couldn't save himself, he had to protect Swanny. He stood up and took a step forward. 'I'd watch that threatening language of yours,' he hissed. 'I know exactly how you operate at those conferences in The Hague. How for years you sabotaged the international treaties. I think journalists might be rather interested in that story, don't you?'

Marnix slowly blew out a thin wisp of smoke. Lucien felt invigorated. He'd given that bastard a taste of his own medicine. But to avoid provoking him further, he haughtily wished Marnix a good day, picked up his case and slammed the door behind him. His heart pounded, and once outside he released a pent-up burst of scornful laughter.

Albert Ketting was still standing by his car; it seemed he hadn't budged the whole time. 'What is it, then?' Lucien asked him impatiently. He couldn't wait to get off the factory grounds.

'I just wanted to let you know I was fired today,' said Ketting.

30

Travel at last

He had just two weeks to get everything in order. There was much to be discussed, in Amsterdam as well as Haarlem, and within just a few days he'd chalked up more kilometres than in the entire preceding month. When he wasn't behind the wheel, with one eye on the long memo list on his lap, he was at the bank, transferring money to various accounts, both domestic and abroad. Until a helpful clerk brought it to his attention that, in view of the remaining balance, he might want to arrange a personal loan. He was surprised to find that even his handsome commissions in recent years apparently weren't enough to cover all his expenses. So he sold off what remained of his collection of valuable Chinese porcelain to an antique dealer, and finally the four-poster bed, the exotic furniture and his silk kimonos as well. The rest was flogged to a second-hand dealer. The proceeds were just enough to meet his remaining financial obligations. All his cherished personal belongings had now been sold, except the Harley-Davidson and the Mercedes.

No one at home showed much interest or made any comment when a pair of burly fellows carried off the furniture, chests and the dismantled bed. They were too busy readying themselves for their own journey. Only Swanny – once his things had been loaded into the lorry – looked around his empty room in surprise. 'Heavens above, was that really necessary?' she asked. 'It's just stuff,' he shrugged, 'worth only what a fool is willing to pay for it.' She nodded and hurried down to the kitchen for the daily household conference.

Every morning a new round of important decisions was taken: which clothes to take to London? How many overcoats, hats, dresses? What evening wear and, of course, which shoes? At least five pairs each, Tosca advised, for their programme included long walks, casual strolls, promenading and flirting. And when Robin was asked his opinion about a dress or a jacket – which he always was – he never failed to confirm that the article was essential for an expedition to London's uncharted interior. New luggage with protective wooden slats was crammed full, then unpacked again, and finally expertly repacked by Pleun.

Brian Kirkpatrick followed the preparations from what must have been an unbearable distance. He phoned every other day, either to report that Robin's parents had bought extra beds for the visit to Great Yarmouth, or to relay the message that the Ryders had accepted that the first visit would be a short one. Five days later he informed them that after exhaustive deliberations – he'd already shuttled between London to Great Yarmouth three times – it had been decided that Swanny and Tosca would lodge at his home for the duration of Robin's operation. His daughters were looking forward to showing them the city. Would they be so kind as to inform him of any special requests? Dr. Gillies, meanwhile, had set a date for Robin's stay at the hospital, and mindful of his convalescence period, Uncle Brian suggested they spend the time hiking in Scotland, where he had family. Tosca immediately kitted herself out with outdoor gear, but Swanny was dead set against the plan. She was determined to travel to Sidcup to visit Robin every day during his recuperation. The hiking trip to Scotland was duly postponed.

Lucien closed his old suitcase and scoured the room in case he'd forgotten anything. Swanny, Tosca and Robin had left early the previous morning. The neighbourhood boys interrupted their football to gawp as Albert Ketting lashed the huge assortment of suitcases to the roof of the Mercedes. Lucien waited for the travellers to finally make a move to depart, rocking impatiently on his heels. 'Come on, you lot!' he shouted down the hall at least three times. 'Any more dallying and you'll miss your boat!'

Tosca was the first to appear, decked out in a sensational travelling outfit. She twirled around a couple of times and asked if anything was missing. 'I'd say not,' answered Lucien. 'You're equipped for crossing the desert on a camel or going down the Amazon in a canoe.' She faced him for a moment, puffed up her cheeks, gave him a playful thump on the shoulder and climbed into the back of the car. Robin followed. He eyed Lucien calmly. He opened his mouth and then shut it again. Everything that needed to be said had been said already, and the rest could be left unspoken. They hugged, clapping each other awkwardly but firmly on the back.

Finally Swanny appeared in the doorway. Her eyes were tearful after saying goodbye to Pleun and Karel. She approached him, clearly meaning to keep a stiff upper lip, but he couldn't help noticing the corners of her mouth quiver. She threw her arms around his neck. 'Promise you'll write,' she whispered emotionally. 'Every week, d'you hear?' He released himself from her embrace and promised, Scout's honour, and plucked a white feather from her jacket. Go! Go now, for God's sake, he thought, let's get this painful farewell over with. He was anxious to retire to his room, his empty room. He and Pleun stood at the front door. Ketting tooted twice as they drove off, arms waving from the open windows.

Then it was his turn to prepare to leave. He spent his last night in his old room. To try and ward off nostalgia and melancholy, he ran through the list one more time, hoping to find some task that still needed doing. But nothing came to light. Besides, he was flat broke. Pleun had promised to look after Karel and the house until Swanny returned. He'd given his Harley-Davidson, after a thorough riding lesson, to her son Theo, who was thrilled to have it. Not so Albert Ketting. It took quite some convincing to get Albert to accept the Mercedes as a gift. Only after Lucien suggested he take Thomas Olyrook for an occasional spin in the motorcar did he give in. Ketting and his wife had moved to the top floor of Olyrook's house on the Weesperzijde a few weeks earlier. Along with his job, he'd lost the concierge cottage at the factory, and Thomas now needed round-the-clock nursing. Lucien had sold the factory in Weesp for him, giving him financial security for the time being. He'd also fixed Albert Ketting up with a job as a mechanic at a garage in Amsterdam run by Deumers' brother. He'd arranged what he could. But there was nothing he could do for Pola. The letter offering to pay for her ticket back to Haarlem, sent to Biedermann's address, remained unanswered.

With a heavy heart he sat in the back of a taxi to Amsterdam. They drove through the familiar polder landscape, the towering white clouds standing out against a wide blue sky. Only now did he notice the wildflowers lining the road. How many times had he driven this route by car or motorbike on the way to the factory without ever taking in the beauty of the countryside? Even that last time, when he'd been summoned to the offices of the Koloniale Bank, he just raced along the thoroughfare like he was wearing blinkers.

He realized full well he'd had only a Pyrrhic victory over Marnix. Ketting's dismissal, after refusing to divulge anything about their stay in Berlin, was the writing on the wall. But he was prepared to restate his case, this time with carefully chosen words and no emotion, although it seemed likely he too was going to be fired on the spot. Imagine being given the boot now, just when his expenses had gone through the roof! And where would he ever find work at such short notice after being sacked from a prominent chemical company? No, if necessary he'd swallow his pride and offer his apologies to Marnix.

Cremers, Peereboom and Marnix received him in the Regents' room. They were seated at their usual places around the conference table. They nodded at him formally, neutrally. He held his breath and sat down, waiting for the axe to fall. Cremers took the floor and with little preamble told Lucien he'd been invited here because a fortuitous situation had arisen. A 'fortuitous' situation? What on earth was fortuitous about it?

'Having reconsidered your performance over the last few years, we've concluded that you've done an excellent job: sales are exceptional, and your client list is impressive. Hats off to you, Hirschland. So it's high time you took the next step in your career.'

Excellent, exceptional, impressive... A commissionership floated momentarily before his eyes, only to vanish in a chill blast of realism: Why had no one mentioned the row with Marnix? His accusations? His threats? Or was that still to come?

'We'd like to offer you the opportunity to put your talents to good use elsewhere.'

Elsewhere! Put my talents to use elsewhere? He knew it… 'So I'm being fired?' he asked, hoping to put a swift end to the torment.

'I wouldn't put it like that,' Peereboom interjected. 'We just think you might expand your horizons abroad.'

'With excellent references from the firm as well as the Koloniale Bank, we've managed to secure you a top posting in Batavia,' continued Cremers, 'with a good salary and great prospects. Well deserved, Hirschland, well deserved indeed…' he exchanged glances with the others, '…though you do of course leave us with the problem of finding as capable a replacement.' He sighed as though the very prospect gave him a headache.

Peereboom chuckled at the technical director's theatrics.

So he was being kicked upstairs. Well, it wouldn't be the first time someone had been bundled off to the Indies after disgracing themselves. But then he suddenly thought of a way of throwing a spanner into the works. 'Gentlemen, with all due gratitude for your efforts, I can't possibly go back to Java. I left there under awkward circumstances, and although these were of a personal nature, I believe it'd be most unwise to return.'

'Don't worry, your problems out there have been resolved,' said Marnix, draping his arm over the back of the adjacent chair. 'The deputy governor and his wife Martha have recently returned to The Hague, and I expect you won't be hearing from the loan sharks again. Oh, and by the way, just to put your mind at ease: it's been decided not to take legal action against you and your sister for the time being.'

So there it was. He was not only being exiled, but all his escape routes had been blocked. He had no choice but to go along with it. 'And where will I be working?' he asked timidly.

Marnix smiled at him obligingly. 'At the Dutch state-owned opium factory.'

'The opium factory?'

'A chance of a lifetime, I'd say.'

'But Marnix! You know my mother died of laudanum poisoning!' he exclaimed indignantly. While she was holidaying in Switzerland some quack had given her an overdose of opium tincture.

'Yes, of course, a terrible tragedy,' said Marnix with compassion. 'And your sister will no doubt object to your working as the foreman of an opium factory, but you'll find a way to explain it to her.'

Peereboom appeared to sympathize with his painful situation. 'You can reassure your sister that the smoking opium manufactured there is sold mainly to the Chinese and natives through special state-run stores. I'm sure she'll be proud of you. It's not just a job! The state opium factory's a very successful enterprise. Last year they sold around two hundred thousand kilos. The profits, nearly 100 million guilders, are vital revenue for the nation.'

'What's more,' Cremers went on in the same upbeat tone, 'even though you'll be employed by the Dutch government, you won't lose contact with us, because we're planning to expand our range soon to include narcotics like papaverine and heroin. Given the problems with cocaine, which you're only too familiar with, we anticipate a big demand for these products prsently.'

He stared at them, each in turn, in shocked surprise.

'And as luck would have it, we'll still be working together as well,' added Marnix, 'because I'll be representing the government in an advisory commission on opium at the League of Nations, and in that role I'll certainly be involved with production and distribution at the Java factory. I'm looking forward to sharing a glass of whisky with you on the veranda of your house in Weltevreden.' Marnix offered him a cigar and Peereboom congratulated him on behalf of the others on his splendid promotion.

Lucien dreaded having to tell Swanny. Instead he took the cowardly way out and told her, with feigned enthusiasm, that he'd landed a plum job at a state-run factory for colonial products in the Dutch East Indies. It was only for a year.

For a moment she was downcast. 'Oh no, what a shame, now you can't come to London with us...' But her natural optimism soon resurfaced: 'Come to think of it, I'm ever so proud of you!' She gave him a kiss. 'You finally decided to put that awful cocaine business behind you.' Soon enough, she was in full flow: 'Oh, Lucien, how marvellous for you! I've always known your heart was in Indië. And it's only for a short while. So much has happened these last few months, perhaps it's a good thing for us to take a break in London, and you on Java. In a year we'll all be together again.'

The taxi drove onto the Amsterdam waterfront. He paid the driver, took his suitcase and got out. The mail packet to the Dutch East Indies was already under steam; passengers hung over the railings and crowded along the gangways, waving to family and friends seeing them off. The crew bustled back and forth along the quay, making their final preparations for departure. It seemed that all his fellow passengers were already on board. Once again, he'd contrived to be late. He hurried toward a steward, who checked off his name on the passenger list and wished him a safe journey. Lucien walked up the gangway. At the top, he turned and looked back. Only then did he catch sight of Albert Ketting standing on the quay. Next to him, Olyrook was leaning on his walking stick. Thomas was waving. Or was he beckoning him? Lucien wavered, but the gangway had already been hauled aboard.

Postscript

The Nederlandsche Cocaïne Fabriek

The Nederlandsche Cocaïne Fabriek Ltd. (NCF) was established on 12 March 1900 as a joint venture of the Koloniale Bank and a number of plantation owners in the Dutch East Indies. The factory produced cocaine from coca leaves grown in the colony. The *hortus botanicus* at Buitenzorg on Java had begun the experimental cultivation of coca plants imported from Peru as early as 1878. The crop thrived in the Javanese soil, and eventually 'Java coca' proved to be of higher quality than the Peruvian variety, which rarely exceeded 1.2% alkaloid content (the plant's active ingredient). The Java leaves, on the other hand, contained some 2% alkaloid, thus yielding almost twice as much cocaine. Before long, the Dutch East Indies surpassed Peru as the world's leading supplier of coca leaves. By the turn of the century Amsterdam had become the hub for the trade in Java coca.

The NCF had modest beginnings in a premises on the Schinkelkade in Amsterdam, where the laboratory was situated in a back room and a kitchen. The cocaine produced there was not only of outstanding quality, but the firm's profits were impressive: at the beginning of the 20th century, 100 kg of Java coca cost 50 guilders, while the cocaine extracted from it brought in 726 guilders. In order to expand production capacity, the factory moved in 1909 to a new facility on the south side of the Weespertrekvaart (later Duivendrechtsekade 67) on the outskirts of Amsterdam.

There were other cocaine producers in the Netherlands at the time as well, such as Cheiron and Brocades & Steehman, but the NCF could soon claim to be the largest single cocaine manufacturer in the world. In 1925, in marking the 25th anniversary of the NCF, the journal *Pharmaceutisch Weekblad* (*Pharmaceutical Weekly*) proudly reported: 'Without a doubt, this company belongs to the modern industries that will carry the fame of our nation abroad with resounding success.' *Het Handelsblad* was equally enthusiastic: 'The management (of the NCF) has always striven to ensure that its products are of the highest quality; they have long maintained a premier position in the world market.'

The NCF's production skyrocketed with the onset of World War I in 1914, necessitating two considerable expansions of the facilities during the war and as a result more than doubling the size of the factory complex. In 1939 the *Pharmaceutisch Weekblad* wrote: 'During the war years in particular, the Nederlandsche Cocaïne Fabriek underwent a large-scale expansion, as the demand for cocaine by the warring nations was great, and the Axis powers (Germany, Austria-Hungary) were cut off from the world's markets. In those days, moreover, cocaine was not yet produced in the British Empire or Japan, and these nations were major importers of this product. Their needs could be nearly entirely met by the Nederlandsche Cocaïne Fabriek.'

The Opium Law, published in the official government gazette *Staatsblad* in 1919, made it illegal to produce, process, sell, import or export opium, cocaine and other drugs without authorization. The introduction of the Opium Law, however, did not result in an immediate decrease in coca cultivation or cocaine production. On the contrary: in 1922 there were 72 coca plantations in the Dutch East Indies, a year later 88 and 1924 as many as 96. The NCF could still guarantee 20% of worldwide production. Nevertheless, these trade restrictions were probably the reason that in 1921 the NCF made moves to diversify its line with newer products such as novocaine. Ten years later they began processing raw opium into morphine and heroin.

In 1941 the NCF began producing amphetamine, a synthetic stimulant (nowadays also known as 'speed'). During World War II, amphetamine was widely used as a stimulant by both the German and the American armed forces. As the Netherlands was occupied by Germany, one may presume that the NCF did not supply the Americans. After the war the firm was still a 'perfectly healthy company', to quote a Koloniale Bank report dated 29 November 1945. Although shipments of coca continued to be imported from the Dutch East Indies (and later Indonesia) for processing, cocaine was no longer one of the NCF's priorities. In March 1965 the firm's name was changed to NCF Holding Ltd., a daughter company of the chemical concern AKZO.

The conferences

Contrary to the common assumption that at the beginning of the 20th century, the effects and dangers of cocaine were not known, warnings against its hazards had been issued since the end of the 19th century. The first International Opium Conference, convened in The Hague on 1 December 1911 and attended by 14 nations, discussed not only the problems pertaining to the opium trade but also that of morphine and cocaine. The Netherlands was not at all anxious to ratify the international treaties restricting the drug trade; its profits from cocaine and opium (produced in the state-owned factory in Batavia) were simply too lucrative. The conference resulted in the International Opium Convention, ratified on 23 January 1912. The convention sufficiently protected the economic interests of the participating nations, but could only be enforced once the remaining nations involved in the opium and cocaine trade (but not present at the conference) had signed it. The Netherlands had undertaken to approach these governments, but was not in much hurry to do so, and consequently new conferences were deemed necessary in 1913 in 1914.

Following World War I the Opium Convention was incorporated into the Treaty of Versailles, and its enforcement was turned over to the League of Nations. The *Staatsblad* published the Dutch Opium Law on 4 October 1919. The semi-legal and entirely illegal drug trade became a major problem after 1920, although its scale is difficult to reconstruct in retrospect. Police reports show that cocaine found in the smuggling circuit originated to a large extent at legitimate factories.

The research

Research for the historical and factual background of this novel took place at numerous archives and libraries. I would like to acknowledge the most prominent of these: the National Archive in The Hague, which, despite the loss of much material during World War II, still contains extensive documentation concerning coca cultivation, the international conferences and Dutch involvement in licit and illicit trade. The same holds true for the libraries/archives of the Vrije Universiteit Amsterdam, the

Royal Tropical Institute, the University of Wageningen, the International Institute of Social History, the Amsterdam Historical Museum, the Noord-Hollands Archief, the Stadsarchief Amsterdam, the Nederlands Economisch Historisch Archief Amsterdam and the Amsterdam Central Library.

I found a great deal of interesting material abroad as well, at institutions including the Wellcome Library, London; Merck Archiv Darmstadt Germany; the archive of In Flanders Fields Museum in Ypres, Belgium; the archive of the Heemkundige Kring de Roede van Thielt; the Memorial Museum Passchendaele; the Gillies Archives in Queen Mary's Hospital, Sidcup, UK; and the Powerhouse Museum in Sydney, Australia.

The most important sources I consulted include the *Pharmaceutisch Weekblad* 1914–1936, *The Lancet*, *The Times*, *Journal of the Royal Society of Medicine*, *Ons Amsterdam*, annual reports of the Coca Producers' Association, reports by the Dutch member of the Opium Advisory Commission of the League of Nations and correspondence between the Nederlandsche Cocaïne Fabriek and various government ministries.

Based on information gleaned from annual reports and other documents from the Koloniale Bank 1910–1922 and 1945, and annual reports of the Amsterdam Chamber of Commerce and Factories 1914–1925 (Nederlandsche Bank archives) and the Nederlandsche Handel-Maatschappij, I was able to make estimates as to the quantities of cocaine produced and exported during World War I.

Of the literature I consulted, I would like to name a few titles to which I am particularly indebted:

Aschenbrandt, Theodor, *Die psychologische Wirkung und Bedeutung des Cocain*, Deutsche Medicinische Wochenschrift, 1883

Berridge, Virginia, *War Conditions and Narcotics Control*, 1978

Church, Roy and Tansey, E.M., *Burroughs Wellcome & Co.: Knowledge, Trust, Profit and the Transformation of the British Pharmaceutical Industry, 1880–1940*, 2007

Freud, Sigmund, *Uber Coca*, 1884

Gootenberg, Paul, *Cocaine – Global Histories*, 1999

Hirschmüller, *E. Merck und das Kokain*, 1995

Jay, Mike, *Emperors of Dreams*, 2000

Jong, de, *Coca en de extractie der alkaloïden*, 1907

Korczak, Dieter, *Die betäubte Gesellschaft*, 1986

Kort, Marcel de, *Tussen patiënt en delinquent, geschiedenis van het Nederlands drugs beleid*, 1995

Macleod, Roy, *Frontline and Factory, Comparative Perspectives on the Chemical Industry at War 1914–1924*, 2007

Meister, W.B., *Cocainism in the Army*, The Military Surgeon, 1914

Musto, David F., *America's first cocaine epidemic*, 1989

Reems, Emma, *La coca de Java*, 1919

Vanvugt, Ewald, *Wettig Opium*, 1985

Winter, Denis, *Death's Men, Soldiers of the Great War*, 1978

Acknowledgements

My sincerest thanks to the many people who assisted me during my long and at times arduous research. Hoping not to give anyone less than his due, I would like to name in particular: Dr. Andrew Bamji, curator of the Gillies Archives, who afforded me free access to the archives of Dr. Harold Gillies and assisted me greatly with his impressive medical knowledge concerning World War I. Additionally, many thanks to Annick Vandenbilcke of the documentation centre In Flanders Fields for her enthusiasm and willingness to delve ever deeper into the archives. Dr. Dirk J. Korf of the Bonger Institute for Criminology and Dr. Marcel de Kort: their publications and assistance allowed me get my research off the ground. Mr. H. Kooger, who worked as a chemical analyst in the laboratory of the Nederlandsche Cocaïne Fabriek in the 1950s and was a great help in providing me with documents and sharing personal recollections. Paul van Soomeren, chairman of the board of directors at Het Veem, for bringing the photographs of coca warehouses to my attention. Aldo Hakman, who guided me through the at times hallucinogenic world of early 20th-century medicine. Hans and Marga Braam, with whom I took a fascinating journey through Flanders in search of cocaine bottles. Annemieke Schoen, director of the Velsen Library, who always knew, just at the right moment, which book I needed to consult and happened to have it on her shelves. Marloes van Gils, who collected countless vital facts. Annemarie de Wildt and Susan Legêne for their advice and assistance. Roel Huisman, whom I could endlessly consult with questions concerning the unfamiliar world of business. My daughter Tessel for her helping hand, emotional support and unconditional faith in her mother. And finally Vladimir Bakun, who kept me going with his unique *borscht*.

Conny Braam